THE BESTSELLING COZY MYSTERY SERIES

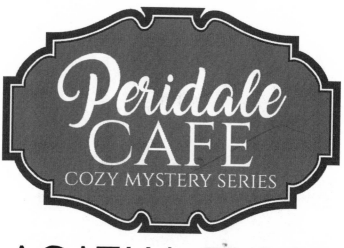

AGATHA FROST

Books in this box set:

Pancakes and Corpses
Lemonade and Lies
Doughnuts and Deception

Other books in the Peridale Café Series:

Chocolate Cake and Chaos
Shortbread and Sorrow

PANCAKES AND CORPSES

BOOK 1

CHAPTER 1

B aking was Julia South's therapy. As she squeezed more lemon juice into the buttercream icing, and avoided looking at the divorce papers sitting on her kitchen counter, she was grateful for that therapy more than ever.

"Good morning," she said to her smoky grey Maine Coon, Mowgli, as he strutted into the kitchen from the garden. "Hungry?"

Mowgli jumped onto the counter to greet her, making sure to cover the envelope containing the divorce papers with his muddy paw prints. Julia licked buttercream off her finger, and tickled appreciatively under his chin. He purred and rubbed his head against her, making her realise she wasn't just grateful for baking this morning.

Julia emptied a pouch of cat food into Mowgli's bowl as he softly purred and circled her feet. She tickled his head one last time before washing her hands and returning to her baking, just in time for the oven to beep.

Julia pulled out the lemon sponge cake and probed it

with the end of a knife, delighted by how perfectly cooked it was. She removed it from the tray and set it on a cooling rack so it would be ready for the freshly made lemon buttercream icing. Julia had been working on the recipe for her new lemon sponge cake for the best part of the week, and she was sure she had found the right balance between tangy and sweet with her latest batch. Even if she approved of the cake, it wouldn't make its way onto her café's menu until her customers had taken their turns sampling it.

Leaving the cake to cool, Julia turned her attention to the thick envelope again. She reached out to pick it up, but stopped herself. Ever since it landed on her doormat three days ago, it had been sitting untouched in the same spot on her kitchen counter. She knew she needed to open it eventually, but she didn't want to ruin her Saturday morning, so she shook out her curls and wandered in to her bedroom.

Julia lived in a quaint, two-bedroom cottage in the tiny village of Peridale, in the heart of the Cotswolds. She had been born and raised in Peridale, and it had been her home until she met her soon-to-be ex-husband, Jerrad, at the age of twenty-one. She had moved to London to be with him, where she lived until two years ago, when Jerrad politely informed her that they would be divorcing so he could marry his blonde twenty-five-year-old secretary, Chantelle. She had entertained the idea of staying in the big city to make it on her own, but the lure of home had been too strong, so she sunk her life savings into the tiny cottage.

She quickly dressed and assessed herself in the mirror. She brushed flour out of her brown curls as well as the creases out of her mint coloured 1940s style dress. It covered the tops of her arms, nipped in at the waist, and flared out into a skirt that stopped just below her knees. She had twenty pounds on Chantelle, as well as ten years in age, but Julia didn't care; she had never been happier.

After icing the lemon sponge with the buttercream, she boxed up the cake, and scratched Mowgli's cheek. He was sitting on the white envelope, hiding it from view with his fluffy behind. She liked to think he was hiding it on purpose, so she thanked him with a quick kiss on the head.

"See you later," she called to him, as she flung her handbag over her shoulder and grabbed her car keys. "Be good!"

The cool February sun shone down pleasantly on Julia as she hurried across her immaculate garden. A couple of the daffodils had sprouted early, adding some much needed bursts of yellow after a long and bitter winter.

She ducked into her vintage aqua blue Ford Anglia, dumping her handbag on the back seat, and her cake on the front. As though it was a small child, she pulled the seatbelt across the box before slotting her keys into the ignition. The car eased into first and she set off down the winding lane towards the heart of the village.

Julia's cottage was one of the last cottages on the edge of Peridale before the winding lane sprawled onto miles and miles of uninterrupted countryside past her cottage and beyond Peridale. She passed the next cottage dotted on the lane, and waved to Emily Burns, who waved back as she indulged in a spot of early morning gardening. The next cottage on the road had been empty for almost a year since Todrick Hamilton died. Julia usually cast her attention to the other side of the road as not to stir up the still raw emotions of losing her elderly neighbour, but today she looked at Todrick's cottage because there was a large white van parked up outside it blocking the road. She slowed down until she could go no further, and pulled on the stiff handbrake. The door to the cottage was wide open, with furniture and boxes littering the small, messy garden.

Leaving her keys in the ignition and cake on the passenger seat, Julia got out of her car and walked over to the low stone wall surrounding the garden. As she did, a tall man ducked through the front door, shielding his eyes from the sun. He was wearing faded denim jeans with a simple white t-shirt. His hair was dark, with flecks of grey prickling the edges of his hairline. Julia would have put him in his late-thirties if she were a betting woman. The stranger dropped his hand and looked in her direction, and Julia was taken aback by how handsome he was. He hooked his thumbs into his jeans and walked towards her, an easy smile on his face and a slight pinch between his brows.

"Can I help you?" he asked, his voice deep and husky.

"I need to get through," Julia said, casting a finger to the van, suddenly feeling flustered.

"No problem" he said, his smile widening. "You local?"

"I live just up the road."

"I guess we're neighbours." The stranger walked over to the open gate and instead of going straight to the van, he walked over to Julia with an outstretched hand. "Barker. Barker Brown."

"Julia South," she said, accepting his firm handshake. "Welcome to Peridale. The clouds have cleared for your first day of village life."

People in Peridale talked about the weather a lot, which was a sign of not much else happening. Julia tried to avoid the subject at all costs because it was all she heard all day in her café, but she was a Peridale girl, born and bred, so the weather seemed to be her default conversation setting.

Barker nodded his thanks of her welcome and let go of her hand. Her comment about the weather didn't start the conversation she had hoped. Barker smiled at her, but it didn't seem like a friendly smile. He seemed slightly amused, and Julia couldn't help but feel judged by her new neighbour. Julia could practically smell the big city on him.

Barker pulled the van into a curve in the road, and Julia just stared for a moment, wondering what could have brought the man to the village. She hadn't spotted a wedding ring, but she knew it could easily be in his pocket. Trying not to overthink it, she jumped back into her own car. Barker climbed out of the van, walked back, and leaned his hand against the top of her car. Julia reluctantly rolled her window down.

"I'll see you around, Julie," Barker said, slapping the roof of her car.

"It's *Julia*."

"Right," he said with a nod, as though it didn't matter to him either way. "Bye."

Barker turned around and headed back into his cottage without a second look back at her. If it hadn't been for the car slowly pulling up behind her, she didn't know how long she would have stared at the cottage before driving away.

Julia tried not to be a judgemental person, but nothing about Barker seemed to fit Peridale. She couldn't put her finger on exactly why, but the man left a sour taste in her mouth.

Julia pulled up into the single parking space in the tight alley between her café and the post office. Grabbing her cake and handbag, she squeezed out of the car and walked around to the front door. Her café was situated in the perfect place, right in the middle of the only shopping street in the village, which directly faced the village green. A terraced row of cottages sat on the opposite side of the green, one of which was owned by her Gran, Dot. St. Peter's Church and the small cemetery filled one of the other sides, with The Plough pub on the other.

Julia walked into her dark café, instantly noticing something was wrong. She put her handbag and cake down on the nearest table and hurried across to the counter. Not for the first time that month, her cake stand had been ransacked, with only the crumbs left behind as evidence of yesterday's baking. She checked the backdoor, but it was still locked and there were no signs of forced entry.

"The cakes were gone again this morning," Julia said to her sister, Sue, who turned up for her usual Saturday shift to help out in the café. "Every last one."

"How many times is that now?" Sue asked as she secured her pale pink apron in place.

"Four," Julia said as she pulled a fresh batch of chocolate chip cookies out of the oven.

"I keep telling you to go to the police."

"For stolen cakes?" Julia slid the warm cookies onto a cooling rack and started shaping the next batch. "Do you think people will mind that I'm only selling cookies today? It's the quickest thing I could think of to fill up the display case."

"People will love whatever you put out there. Everybody knows you're the best baker in Peridale," Sue said as she cut herself a slice of Julia's new lemon sponge cake. "Maybe it was rats?"

"How would a rat get up to the top shelf in that display case?"

"Super rats?" Sue said seriously with a shrug before taking a bite of the lemon sponge. "Ugh, this is so good. You're ruining my diet."

Sue had been on a constant diet for as long as Julia could remember, despite her younger sister having a svelte figure that most women would kill for.

"Who breaks into a café and only takes the cakes?" Julia mumbled under her breath as she moulded a ball of dough into a flat disc.

"Stop leaving the cakes in here overnight," Sue said through a mouthful of lemon sponge. "They'll soon get the message."

"I have a feeling it's somebody who needs the food."

"Call the police."

"I don't have any evidence."

"I think it's time for some cameras," Sue said as she licked buttercream icing from her fingers, before casting a finger into the corners of the rooms. "It's also time to hire some real staff. You know I've enjoyed helping you out on the weekends, but I can't keep turning down the extra shifts at the hospital for much longer."

Julia's stomach squirmed. The 'HELP WANTED' sign had been in the window since the beginning of the year but it hadn't generated much interest. Most people in Peridale either owned their own small business in the village, or they commuted to the bigger towns for work. The rest were retired, which suited Julia and her café. She was never short of customers wanting a slice of cake, a cup of tea, and a friendly chat.

When the cookies were finished, Julia flipped the sign from '*Sorry! We're closed*' to '*Come on in! We're open!*' and it wasn't long until her first customer and closest neighbour, Emily Burns, walked in, still wearing her gardening gloves.

"Cup of tea when you're ready, Julia," she said as she sat down at the table nearest the counter. "And a slice of whatever that cake is on the counter. Smells delicious."

Julia made up a small pot of tea and cut a slice of the lemon sponge, while Sue finished making the cookies for the day in the kitchen.

"The cake is on the house," Julia said, setting the plate in front of Emily. "It's a new recipe I'm working on, and honest feedback is welcomed."

"You haven't disappointed me yet!" Emily exclaimed. "Have you seen our new neighbour?"

Emily asked the question so casually, but Julia knew Emily had probably been peeking over her garden wall to witness Julia's interaction with Barker. If talking about the weather was the number one topic of choice in Peridale, gossiping about fellow villagers was the second. Julia wasn't much of a gossip, but it was rare she wasn't one of the first to find out the latest information, thanks to her café.

"I had a brief conversation with him this morning," Julia said, taking up a seat across from Emily and pouring a cup of tea from the pot. "He's called Barker Brown. I think he's from the city."

"Oh really?" Emily mumbled, her eyes widening at the new information. "He's rather handsome. If only I was twenty years younger."

"I hadn't noticed," Julia lied, adding a splash of milk and a spoonful of sugar to her tea. "Do you know why he's here?"

Much to Julia's disappointment, Emily shook her head as she took her first bite of the lemon sponge. Her eyes widened even further than before, and then clenched shut as she savoured the citrusy tang of the cake.

"Oh, Julia!" Emily exclaimed. "You've really outdone yourself with this one! I think this might be my new favourite."

"Thank you," Julia said quickly, wanting to get back to the topic of their new neighbour. "I'm not sure about Barker. He seemed a little smug."

Julia sipped her own tea as she tried to figure out why the man had had such an effect on her.

"The handsome ones usually are." Emily sighed regretfully. "Maybe he's retired young."

"Maybe," Julia agreed, not really believing it. "He doesn't strike me as the type of person who would choose a place like Peridale to retire."

They both finished their tea and Emily settled her bill to get back to her gardening. Julia knew she would try to strike up a conversation with Barker, if only to extract some information worth gossiping about on their next meeting. Even though Julia wouldn't usually be privy to joining in, she was more than intrigued by his sudden arrival.

The moment she resumed her place behind the counter, the bell above the door rang again. This time, it was Roxy Carter, an old friend from school. They had been the only two girls from Peridale village in their class at the local comprehensive, Hollins High School, so they struck up a close friendship that had lasted long into adulthood. Roxy now worked as a teacher in Peridale's only school, St. Peter's Primary School.

"Good morning, Roxy," Julia said with a smile as Roxy

approached the counter. "What can I get you today?"

"Huh?" Roxy mumbled, staring at Julia as though she had no idea where she was.

Roxy frantically ran her fingers through her red hair, tucking it messily behind her ears. Her eyes were sunken in and her skin pasty, as though she hadn't slept well for days.

"Is everything okay?" Julia asked.

Roxy blinked hard at Julia and glanced up at the chalkboard menu on the wall behind her.

"Latte to go please," Roxy said, shaking her head heavily. "I'm fine, just a little tired. You know what it's like."

Julia dug out a cardboard cup from underneath the counter and walked over to the coffee machine, not taking her eyes away from Roxy. Roxy chomped on the edges of her nails and jumped when the coffee machine hissed into life. Julia didn't need to ask again to know Roxy wasn't '*fine*'.

"Why don't you take a seat and I'll bring it over to you?" Julia offered.

Roxy nodded and picked the table closet to the counter, just like Emily had. Julia poured the steamed milk into the coffee and pressed the plastic lid securely in place. She placed the cup in front of Roxy, who stopped drumming her fingers to pick up the cup. She took a deep sip, not seeming to notice it was hot.

"Are you sure you're okay?" Julia asked softly, reaching across and resting her hand on top of Roxy's. "You seem a little on edge."

Roxy tried to feign a smile, but her bottom lip wobbled to the point where Julia reached into her dress pocket for her handkerchief. She pushed it across the table to Roxy, who gladly accepted it and dabbed the inner corners of her eyes.

"I'm just being silly," Roxy said, trying to force a laugh. "Ignore me."

"Silly is okay," Julia said reassuringly. "A problem shared is a problem halved."

Roxy smiled genuinely this time and pushed the handkerchief back to Julia, but Julia didn't pocket it straight away, just in case it was needed again. A car sped past the café and Roxy almost jumped out of her skin.

"Oh, Julia," Roxy whispered, leaning in low across the table. "I've ruined everything."

Before Julia could ask what she had ruined, a loud clatter, followed by Sue's loud cursing, came from the kitchen.

"Stay here," Julia said. "I'll be back in two seconds."

Roxy nodded and looked down at her coffee, her eyes glazing over. Julia hated to leave her, but Sue sounded like she was in trouble, and Julia's mind went straight to her mystery cake burglar.

"What's wrong?" Julia asked, dashing through the beaded curtains to the brightly lit kitchen. "I bet they heard that halfway across the village."

Sue used the counter to help herself up from the floor, where two metal trays of cookies and fresh dough surrounded her.

"I saw a spider," Sue moaned, pushing her thick brown curls from her eyes. "It ran right across the counter!"

"Is that all?"

"I could have died!"

Julia chuckled and sighed. She leaned over and picked up the mess as her sister straightened herself out.

"If only Mowgli was here," Julia said as she scraped the dough into the bin. "He loves chasing spiders."

"You know I'm allergic to cats."

"You're not allergic, you just don't like them," Julia teased. "If you see it again, call me to catch it, instead of throwing my cookies on the floor."

Julia patted her little sister on the shoulder and walked back into the café. Roxy was still there, but she wasn't in her seat. She was standing by the door with Gertrude Smith, the elderly organist from St. Peter's Church. Roxy was clutching Gertrude's arms and her face was screwed up as though she was about to say something unsavoury. They both looked over to Julia, and Roxy immediately let go of Gertrude and stormed out of the café, leaving behind her latte.

"Quite rude!" Gertrude exclaimed as she straightened out the sleeves of her coat. "What a *horrible* girl!"

"Is everything okay?" Julia frowned, looking from Gertrude to the latte.

"That girl is *unhinged*!" Gertrude cried, loud enough so that the whole village could hear. "*Unstable!*"

Gertrude came into the café every morning at ten for her usual pancakes and tea, even if Julia had to pretend she didn't notice the regularity of the organist's visits. The one time Julia had attempted to surprise Gertrude by having her order ready for her at ten, Gertrude had made sure to give Julia quite the dressing down, telling Julia she shouldn't be so presumptive. That had been over a year ago, and even though Gertrude claimed she might have wanted to order something else on the day Julia had pre-empted her order, she still hadn't ordered anything other than her usual since.

"Four pancakes drizzled with honey, with fresh

raspberries and blueberries, and a cup of tea," Gertrude called across the café as she took her usual seat at the table next to the window. "And when I say fresh, I mean *fresh*!"

Julia smiled and nodded, biting her tongue. She had just enough blueberries and raspberries delivered to her café every morning, just for Gertrude's order. Sue didn't understand why Julia bent over backwards to please such an intolerable woman, but Julia knew her livelihood balanced on the knife-edge of her reputation, and a negative comment from Gertrude would spread like wildfire around the tiny village in a matter of hours.

After making the pancakes and tea, Julia carefully set them in front of Gertrude. She usually turned her nose up at the food, as though she didn't return everyday, but today, she stared out of the window, completely distracted. Julia cleared her throat and Gertrude jumped, looking down at her food. Julia usually hurried away, but she hovered.

"Yes?" Gertrude said through pursed lips. "Can I help you?"

Julia's cheeks burned and her mouth turned dry. She looked out of the window at the village green, which had filled up with young children enjoying the first day of the weekend.

"Is there something happening between you and Roxy Carter?" Julia asked, as bravely as she could.

"I don't see what business that is of yours, *girl*!"

And with that, Julia scurried back to the kitchen, to vent to Sue.

"Somebody is going to kill that woman one day," Sue whispered, peeking through the beads as Gertrude tucked into her pancakes. "Mark my words."

CHAPTER 2

The rest of Julia's day went by a lot smoother than her morning had. Her lemon sponge cake was a hit with everybody who tasted it and she sold out of all of her cookies.

During the week, Julia had to invent little jobs to kill the time between customers, which was why she loved Saturdays so much. Along with her usual daily customers, she also got to see her weekend customers and converse with the tourists and groups of ramblers enjoying the Cotswolds.

An hour before closing, her Gran, Dot, hurried into the full café, wearing her usual stiff white shirt, buttoned up to her chin that was secured in place with an ornate antique brooch. She looked around at the faces, smiling at the villagers she knew and narrowing her eyes suspiciously at the ones she didn't.

"Have you heard about the new man?" Dot asked the second she reached the counter. "It's causing quite the scandal!"

"Hello, Gran," Julia said. "Cup of tea?"

"No thanks," Dot said, glancing over her shoulder at the full café. "You know how I hate big crowds, love. Did you hear about the new man?"

"Do you mean Barker Brown who moved into the cottage on my lane?"

"So you *have* heard," Dot sighed, clearly disappointed that she hadn't been the first to break the news. "Why didn't you tell me?"

"That I'd met my new neighbour?"

"You've spoken to him?" Dot's eyes widened. "What did he have to say for himself?"

"Not a lot. His van was blocking the road so I asked him to move it. We introduced ourselves and spoke briefly."

"Spoke about what?" Dot urged.

"The weather," Julia lied, not wanting to admit he had ignored her weather based conversation starter. "What was I supposed to talk to him about?"

"About why he bought Todrick Hamilton's cottage at auction for half of the asking price!" Dot cried, loud enough to catch the attention of the people in the café. "Todrick's daughter, Samantha, is said to be furious. She wasn't getting any offers, so she put it up for auction, expecting to get a decent amount. *No!* That slime from the city came in and scooped it up for nothing."

"So he is from the city?"

"That's what Emily Burns says."

"Emily got that information from me," Julia said with a soft laugh. "I was only speculating."

"Well, it's all the village has been talking about all morning. I heard he was a business tycoon who had come in to buy up all of the companies and turn us into some kind of tourist hot spot! Can you imagine?"

The tourists in the shop frowned at Dot, who was now directing all of her statements loudly into her listening crowd.

"Where did you hear that?" Julia asked.

"Well, it's what I suspect!" Dot cried, snapping her fingers together. "I better go. I've got topside of beef in the oven. You and your sister are having supper at mine tonight."

Julia didn't argue. Even if she had plans, she would have to cancel them. It didn't matter how old she or Sue got, they couldn't ignore a supper summons from their Gran.

Without another word, Dot turned on her heels and teetered back out of the café, her navy blue pleated skirt floating behind her. Julia hoped she would have just half of her Gran's zest for life when she reached her eighties.

"We're having supper at Gran's tonight," Julia said, poking her head through the beads. "Oh, hello, Johnny. What are you doing here?"

Julia left the full café and walked through to the kitchen, where Johnny Watson was talking in low whispers with Sue. Johnny was a reporter for the local newspaper, *The Peridale Post*. Julia had been on an unsuccessful date with him when she first moved back to the village. They had gone for coffee outside the village where she had decided they would be better suited as friends. Sue was insistent that Johnny still held a candle for Julia, but she brushed off her sister's unfounded gossip.

"Julia," Johnny said nervously, his cheeks reddening. "It's you I came to see."

Sue looked awkwardly at her, as though she knew something Julia didn't. When Sue looked down at the piece of paper in Johnny's hands, Julia followed her, and her heart sank.

"Is everything okay?" Julia asked, trying to keep her smile.

"I tried to stop them from printing it," Johnny said. "I really did try, but they wouldn't listen to me."

"Print what?"

"Maybe it's better she doesn't read it," Sue said.

"Read what?"

Johnny looked down at the paper in his hands. He seemed to be toying with his conscience for a moment before handing the paper over to Julia. She looked at Johnny, who looked apologetically at her as he shifted his glasses, before looking down at what was causing her sister to look so uncomfortable.

"'*Local Café Is A Constant Disappointment*'," Julia said, reading the headline of what appeared to be a review. "'*Two stars*'. This is about my café?"

"Oh, Julia," Sue said, placing her hand on Julia's shoulder. "It's just somebody's opinion."

"Who wrote this?" Julia asked as she scanned through the review. "'*Awful atmosphere*,' '*bland food*', '*amateur baking*'!"

Julia's heart sunk to the pit of her stomach, and she cast the paper onto the counter.

"I have no idea," Johnny said, looking as upset as Julia felt. "Our old reviewer, Mark Tanner, retired last month and we put out an ad for somebody to take his place. We only had one reply, and it came with the condition they would have full anonymity, even from us. We didn't have much choice. This is only their third review, but they haven't given one above a two-star. They gave Rachel

Carter's art gallery a one-star review, saying '*the only art the gallery could offer you was something to toss on the fire on a cold night*', and they gave Bob and Shelby Hopkins a two-star for The Plough, saying it was '*the worst pub in the Cotswolds*' and that their home brewed beer tasted like something '*left over in the sink after washing up*'. I've been fighting this all week, but my editor thinks it adds spice to the paper. When I found out it was going to print tomorrow, I came straight here to warn you."

Julia stared down at the paper, numb and shaken. She had always been confident with her café and what she served in it. When working in London, she had worked in a factory, bulk baking bland cakes for retail for most of her marriage, which was why she had tried so hard to create something that was the opposite of that.

"It's tomorrow's fish and chip's paper," Sue said encouragingly. "Don't let it get to you."

Julia tried to smile, but the corners of her mouth wouldn't turn upwards. She racked her brain for whom she could have upset for them to write such a bitter review.

"Thank you for warning me," Julia said to Johnny. "Can I keep this?"

"Only if you're sure. Like Sue said, it's tomorrow's chip paper."

Julia wanted to agree but she knew how long a single topic could circulate the village when there was nothing more interesting to talk about. If the weather held up and didn't rain, it would be the only thing to gossip about, aside from the new arrival. She doubted anything could eclipse such a juicy review of the village's only café.

"Do you know anything about who it could be?" Julia asked as she scanned the review, not really taking the words in.

"They only correspond by letter, but it's always hand delivered in the dead of night," Johnny said as he put his hands into his coat pocket. "It's always signed '*Miss Piston*', but we think it's an alias, because there's nobody in this village with that name."

Julia thanked Johnny again, and he left through the backdoor. Sue attempted to take the review away from Julia but she read it over and over, absorbing every word. She was only pulled from the writing when the bell on the counter rang.

For the rest of her work day, Julia attempted to smile through her hurt, but it wasn't enough. Every customer who knew Julia could tell something was wrong, but just like Roxy had with her, she lied and said she was fine. None of them believed her, which was why she was glad when half-past five rolled around and she could lock the door and flip the sign.

As Julia cleared away the plates, she could feel the sympathetic eyes of her sister watching her.

"People in this village will know it is all lies," said Sue. "You're the best baker in Peridale! Whoever wrote this was just jealous."

"Maybe."

"Don't let it get to you."

"I'm not."

"Liar," Sue said as Julia walked past her with a stack of plates and cups. "Whoever Miss Piston is, they're probably really unhappy and that's why they have to bring other people down."

Julia dumped the dishes in the sink and filled it with hot, soapy water. As she cleaned the plates and cups, Sue wiped down the tables, leaving her to her own thoughts. She imagined opening up on Monday morning after being closed tomorrow. She knew people wouldn't avoid the café, in fact, she'd probably be busier than ever, but she knew every customer would be clutching a copy of the newspaper, all with their own thoughts and opinions about the review. They would all be waiting for her reaction from the moment they read it.

"At least we've got Gran's topside of beef to take your mind off of it," Sue said as they pulled on their coats. "I just need to call Neil and let him know not to expect me home until late."

Sue hurried over to the phone behind the counter, leaving Julia to flick off the lights. She buttoned up her pale pink pea coat in the dark as her sister called her husband. If she didn't feel obligated, she would have cancelled supper at Gran's to go home to Mowgli and curl up with a good murder mystery to take her mind off the review, even if she did have her divorce papers taunting her.

As she waited for Sue, she reflected on what a strange day it had been. She thought back to Roxy, and her peculiar interaction with Gertrude. She made a mental note to call Roxy when she got to her Gran's, just to make sure she was okay.

"I asked Neil if he knew any Pistons," Sue said as she weaved back through the tables. "No luck, but he said he'll check the records at the library tomorrow."

Julia's brows pinched together, but not at her sister, at something she had said.

"Pistons," Julia murmured.

"Huh?"

"Organ pistons!" Julia cried, pushing her keys into

Sue's hands. "Lock up and tell Gran I'll be there in twenty minutes. I think I know who wrote that review."

Before Sue could ask any questions, Julia hurried across the village to confront the local organist.

Gertrude Smith's cottage had always been a topic of discussion. Julia remembered the terror it inflicted on her when she had to walk past it on her way home from St. Peter's Primary School as a small girl. It was a small cottage, not dissimilar from her own, but it had been swallowed up by so much creeping ivy, only the door and two windows were visible under the low hanging thatched roof. The small walled-in front garden was equally overgrown, and despite many villagers confronting Gertrude about it over the years, she refused to change a thing, insisting it was '*God's will*' to let the plants grow as naturally as possible.

As a thirty-seven-year-old woman, Julia agreed that the cottage was an eyesore in the otherwise spotless and orderly village, but it still inflicted the same childhood fear in the pit of her stomach.

Gertrude's cottage was in the middle of a row of six other small cottages. It didn't just stand out for the lack of a well-kept garden, it was also the only cottage on the street without a single light on in the house.

Julia stayed in the safety of the streetlight, staring at Gertrude's cottage. It didn't look like she was home, so Julia decided she was going to leave her conversation with Gertrude until Monday morning, when Gertrude would no doubt be in for her raspberry and blueberry pancakes to see the aftermath of her review. In the glow of the streetlight, she pulled out the review and read over it again, noticing how she was getting increasingly more wound up with each re-read. She looked up angrily at the cottage and noticed a shadow dart past the window.

Inhaling deeply, Julia unhooked the gate and waited for Gertrude to flick on a lamp, but the cottage remained in darkness. Julia glanced up and down the dark street, but it was completely empty. She could hear the six o'clock news playing on the television of one of the neighbours, but aside from that, there was an eerie silence she hadn't experienced before in the village she loved so much.

Julia walked down the short garden path, stepping over the plants that had snaked across the stone slabs. She reached the front door and rapped her knuckles against the old wood. The door opened upon impact.

Startled by the movement, Julia took a step back and peered into the cottage, wondering why Gertrude would leave her front door open.

"Gertrude?" Julia called into the dark. "It's Julia, from the café."

Julia heard sudden movement and the smash of glass, followed by more of the eerie silence that was making her feel so uncomfortable.

"Gertrude?" she called out again, pushing on the door and opening it fully. "Do you need some help?"

There wasn't a response, so Julia hesitantly stepped over the threshold and into Gertrude's living room. The inside matched the outside, with dark floral prints lining the walls, equally dark colours for the flooring, and an array of photographs and ornaments among the bulky cluttered furniture.

Julia almost called out again, but she stopped herself. She walked through the open double doors to the dining room. The broken window caught Julia's attention, as did the almost complete lack of glass on the table underneath it.

Holding her breath, she turned, wanting to run straight for the street, but an open door leading off from the dining room caught her attention. Through the shadows, she noticed a figure sitting in a chair. A relieved sigh left her lips and she relaxed for a moment. Squinting into the dark, it looked like whoever was in there was hunched over the desk writing something in the dark.

Julia pushed on the door, and it opened slowly. A strip of moonlight shone from the smashed window, illuminating the room. Even without the light, she had recognised Gertrude's tightly roller set hair, but she hadn't spotted something large and sharp jutting out from between Gertrude's shoulder blades.

Julia inhaled deeper than she thought she could as the moonlight glittered against the tiny part of the knife that hadn't been sunk into Gertrude's flesh. Her eyes flitted to Gertrude's glossy wide eyes and her slightly ajar mouth. Gertrude was still clutching a pen in her pale fingers. Julia attempted to scream, but no sound left her trembling lips.

Knowing there was nothing she could do for Gertrude, Julia ran back through the cottage and into the safety of the streetlight.

"I need the police," Julia said frantically into her phone as she choked back the tears. "There's been a murder."

CHAPTER 3

Dot's cottage was one of the few constants threading through Julia's life. It had been there for the little girl who had struggled with the death of her mother, and it had been there for that same girl when she was in her thirties and her marriage had broken down. Julia appreciated her Gran's opposition to change. Dot still had the same eleven-inch black and white television she had always had, the same floral sofa she refused to replace, and the same collection of ceramic cats, which Dot dusted every day, looking out from her mantelpiece.

Julia moved the beef around the gravy on her plate, and wondered why for the first time in her life the cottage wasn't providing that same safety and comfort.

"You need to eat something, love," Dot said calmly, resting her hand on Julia's. "You need to keep your strength up."

"I can't stop thinking about that knife," Julia said. "It was so big."

"That poor woman," Sue said, who also appeared to be struggling to eat. "You'd be pushed to find anybody who liked her, but that's no way to die."

"You reap what you sow in this life," Dot said, tapping her finger on the wood. "Let this be a lesson to all of us. Gertrude was a nasty piece of work, I'm just surprised it's taken this long for somebody to do her in."

Julia and Sue both looked wide-eyed at each other, before turning to their Gran, who pursed her lips without apology.

"Let's not pretend she wasn't the woman who wrote those nasty things about your café, Julia!" Dot stabbed her finger down on the piece of paper on the table. "Utter rubbish!"

There was a knock at the door. Glad of the distraction, Julia jumped up and hurried down the dark hallway. She passed a mirror and her pale complexion caught her attention. She was sure the colour would never return to her cheeks.

Inhaling deeply, she opened the door. A tall man loomed in the doorway, facing out towards the village green. Julia cleared her throat and the man spun around. It took Julia a second to recognise the man as her new neighbour, Barker Brown. He had swapped his faded jeans and white t-shirt for a well-fitting suit and a beige overcoat, which was turned up at the collar. His face was just as handsome.

Barker frowned down at her, with the same amused smirk from earlier in the day.

"Julia South?" Barker asked, checking a notepad in his hands, as though he hadn't remembered her name from their first conversation.

"Yes?"

"Detective Inspector Brown." He reached out his hand, a dark twinkle in his eyes. "I hear you discovered the body of a Mrs. Gertrude Smith. May I come in and ask you a few questions?"

Julia sat in the middle of the comfortable sofa and Detective Inspector Brown filled up one of Dot's tiny armchairs. He looked around the small cottage with the same amused smirk Julia had come to know him by. It made her stomach squirm uncomfortably.

"Tea!" Dot exclaimed, hurrying in with a tray, containing what Julia knew to be her finest china teapot and cups.

Dot set the tray on the table and retreated to the back of the room, where she stayed until Barker cleared his throat. She scurried back through to the dining room, where she and Sue would no doubt be pushing glasses up against the wall to overhear every word.

"You told the officers on the scene that you were walking home and saw a shadow in the window, and the open door?" Barker asked after consulting his small notepad. "Long way to walk home, isn't it? Forgive me because I don't know my way around the village yet, but isn't your cottage on the opposite side?"

Julia shifted in her seat and picked invisible lint off of her mint coloured dress, wondering why she had lied about her intentions behind visiting Gertrude. She pulled the hem past her knees and straightened out her back, deciding honesty was the best policy.

"I was going to see Gertrude to ask her a question," Julia said, avoiding admitting to her lie. "I saw the figure and I assumed it was Gertrude. I walked up to the door and I knocked, but the door swung open, and then I heard glass smashing. I thought she might be in trouble, so I called out for Gertrude, but she didn't respond, so I went inside to see if she was okay. I saw the broken window and I decided I was going to get out of there, to call the police, and that's when I saw her body."

Julia tried to stay strong but she felt the tears welling up in the corners of her eyes. She plucked her handkerchief from her pocket and quickly dabbed them away, not wanting to appear weak in front of the detective.

"I understand it's a difficult time for you," Barker said, completely devoid of any emotion. "What can you tell me about the shadow you claim to have seen?"

Julia was taken aback by the insinuation that her story wasn't true. It suddenly struck her that she was possibly a suspect.

"I don't know," Julia said, trying her best to focus on the blurry image in her mind. "It was dark. There were no lights on in the cottage. I just saw movement, called out, and then I heard the glass smash. Perhaps they were going to leave out of the front door, and then they saw or heard me so they panicked and escaped through the window?"

"Why don't we leave the speculating to the police?" Barker arched a brow and appeared to be concealing his amused smirk. "You said you were going to ask Gertrude a question. What was that question?"

Julia told him all about how Johnny Watson had visited her café to tell her about Miss Piston's venomous review, and how she had made the connection between piston and organ.

"Organ?"

"Gertrude plays the organ at the local church," she said. "*Played* the organ. She's done it for as long as I can remember."

"So you put two and two together and discovered a body?" Barker mumbled, and Julia was unsure if the question was rhetorical or not. "Is there anything else you can tell me about Gertrude Smith? Do you know who could have done this?"

Julia's mind flashed straight to Roxy Carter, and their meeting in her café that morning. She couldn't believe she was considering one of her oldest friends could be capable of murder, but it was something she was considering. She decided she would tell Detective Inspector Brown this piece of information, but only after she had had a chance to speak with Roxy herself.

"Gertrude comes into my café every morning at ten," Julia said. "She has four pancakes with honey, raspberries and blueberries and a cup of tea."

"I was looking for something less *trivial,*" Barker said with a sigh. "About her relationships or her affairs."

Julia pursed her lips and adjusted herself in the seat once more. She wanted to give the Detective a piece of her mind, but she was aware she was the only person who had any real information about the murder and she was her own alibi, so she bit her tongue.

"She has a son. William."

"Any friends?"

"Gertrude wasn't the type of woman to have friends," Julia said. "She was deeply religious and she didn't suffer fools gladly."

"So you're saying she had enemies?"

"I wouldn't go that far," Julia said, disliking how

Barker could so easily twist her words. "I just know that she's upset a lot of people in this village over the years."

"And you're one of them," he added.

"I suppose I am," she said, narrowing her eyes. "But not enough to murder her."

Detective Inspector Brown stood up, his head almost hitting the beams in the low ceiling. He pulled a card out of his inside pocket and handed it over to Julia. It contained his name, title, phone number, and the address of the village police station. She suspected they were freshly printed.

"You'll have to stop by the station tomorrow to make an official statement, but I'm satisfied with what you've told me," Baker said, sounding anything but satisfied. "If you think of anything at all, give me a call. I'll see myself out."

Barker opened the living room door, and Dot fell into him. She jumped back, straightened out the pleats in her skirt and smiled politely.

"Thanks for the tea," he said, before turning back to face Julia. "Oh, and Julie, try not to find any more dead bodies, will you?"

"It's Julia."

"*Right,*" Barker said, a small smile tickling his lips as he turned. "Goodnight."

Detective Inspector Brown left the cottage, but his presence lingered, as did his smile. Julia looked down at the business card and ran her fingers over his name. She resisted the urge to shred it into a million pieces. Barker had seemed more interested in point scoring than actually getting information from her. Tucking the business card into her dress pocket, she tried to figure out why that was.

"You're blushing," Sue said, jabbing Julia in the ribs. "I

think you like him."

"Like him?" Julia scoffed. "The man is practically intolerable."

"But quite handsome," added Dot, seemingly forgetting her own gossip from earlier in the day. "Quite handsome *indeed.*"

Julia couldn't bring herself to disagree with her Gran.

Later that night, Julia curled up by the fire in her cottage with Mowgli at her feet. She sipped a cup of her favourite peppermint and liquorice tea and grabbed her ingredients list notepad from the side table.

She flipped past a list of things she needed to pick up to make a chocolate orange fudge cake and turned to a fresh page. She bit the lid off the pen and wrote '*Gertrude Smith*' in the centre of the small page. She circled the name until the ink tore a hole in the paper and ripped through to the next page.

After taking another sip of her tea, and letting the sweet liquorice coat her throat, she reluctantly drew an arrow from the circle and wrote '*Roxy Carter*'. She didn't want to think her oldest friend could be capable of murder, but she knew she had to prove otherwise.

"You're barking up the wrong tree, Barker," she whispered to herself as she carefully closed the notepad.

CHAPTER 4

Peridale was a small village, so church attendance was slightly higher than most of the United Kingdom, but that didn't explain the circus Julia was witnessing at St. Peter's Church for its Sunday service.

"Everybody in the village has turned up," Dot whispered into Julia's ear as they shuffled into the crowded church. "There are only four reasons people have turned up today and three of them are connected to Gertrude's death!"

"Isn't that why we're here?" Julia whispered back. "I wouldn't have been here if you hadn't let yourself into my cottage this morning and shook me awake. I thought you were the murderer coming to get rid of the only witness!"

"I'm here every weekend!" Dot said, pursing her lips as she adjusted her finest church hat. "I come to pray. I'm a very religious woman, you know."

"Don't lie, Gran," Sue said, who was linking arms with Dot on the other side as they tried to find somewhere to stand. "You're usually fast asleep in bed when Sunday service is happening."

"*Shhh!* Not in God's house," Dot said, pointing up to the church's high ceiling. "What *He* doesn't know won't hurt *Him*. I'm here in spirit and I pray in my dreams."

"What do you pray for?" Sue asked.

"That He saves your souls, and that He brings a new man into Julia's life." Dot said, so loud that the people in the back row of the pews turned.

"I do *not* need a new man," Julia whispered, thinking instantly of the unopened divorce papers that were still sitting on her kitchen counter, waiting for her signature. "What are the four reasons that you think people are here?"

"Well," Dot said coyly, obviously glad Julia had asked. "I've given this a lot of thought. The first reason is that people are here to ask for protection from the murderer on the loose. The second is that the murderer is here asking for forgiveness and everybody is waiting for somebody to slip up."

That thought had crossed Julia's mind and it was one of the reasons she had rolled out of bed and crawled into her clothes. She had held Mowgli as close as he would allow last night, and the sun had already started to rise by the time she finally fell asleep. The image of the knife sticking out of Gertrude's back hadn't allowed her brain to stop trying to piece the puzzle together, no matter how tired she was.

"The third reason," Dot continued. "People are here to see who is taking over Gertrude's organ playing duties."

"I hadn't thought of that one," Sue gasped. "I wonder who it is."

"My money is on Amy Clark," Dot said, tapping her finger on her chin thoughtfully. "Everybody knows she's been after Gertrude's position for years. Gertrude is the far superior organist, which is why she hasn't missed a Sunday service in over forty years. She once dragged herself out of bed with the most terrible flu and still played amazingly. I wouldn't be surprised if Amy Clark was thanking God on her knees when she found out the news about poor Gertrude, God rest her soul."

"You've changed your tune from last night," Sue said, rolling her eyes.

"Not in the Lord's house," Dot said, nodding to the large statue of Jesus hanging from the cross at the front of the packed church. "The fourth reason is that people are genuinely here for the Sunday service."

Julia had to admit she wasn't one of them. She wasn't particularly religious, although she did believe something was out there, she just hadn't figured out what yet. The only times she attended church services were for christenings, weddings, funerals and Christmas Eve mass. She looked around the church, smiling to people she recognised, knowing most of them had only shown up for the first three of her Gran's four reasons.

A fifth reason had also compelled Julia to attend the service, but she decided to keep it to herself. She wanted to see if Roxy Carter would turn up. When she had finally fallen asleep in the early hours of the morning, she had been plagued by a terrible nightmare of Roxy standing over her with a large knife, ready to strike her down.

Julia had already scanned the faces of the attendees sitting in the pews and Roxy Carter's bright red hair hadn't jumped out at her. She was naturally ginger, so when she applied the red dye over the top, it made it look like her hair was made from pure flames. Julia had always admired

Roxy's bravery to go for such a bright colour, and even though Roxy pulled it off with ease, Julia couldn't see herself doing the same.

Turning her attention to the people still filing into the packed church, her heart skipped a beat when she noticed Roxy's sister, Rachel, followed by their mother, Imogen Carter. Julia waited for Roxy to follow Imogen, but she didn't. Her heart skipped another more intense beat when Detective Inspector Brown waltzed in behind them.

Julia quickly turned her attention to the front of the church, just in time to witness Amy Clark shuffling out of Father David Green's vestry. Julia didn't want to be cynical, but even from her distance she could see what could only be described as the second smuggest smirk she had seen all weekend. She glanced to Barker Brown, the owner of the first, who was standing four people away from her, looming inches above everyone around him. Even though he too was staring ahead, she could feel him looking at her out of the corner of his eye.

Amy Clark walked over to the organ and unbuttoned her coat. She was wearing a bright pink woollen cardigan, a diamond brooch twinkling from its breast pocket, with a pale blue pleated skirt, tan tights and a pair of sensible black shoes. Her usually wild and frizzy hair had been pristinely set into neat curled rows, making Julia wonder if the hairdresser had opened specially for Amy that morning for her big appearance.

The second Amy sat down on the stool and cracked her fingers, the frantic whispering started. Julia watched as heads turned and eyes widened when her fingers touched the organ's keys. The whispering turned to talking and then to almost shouting as *All Things Bright and Beautiful* bellowed through the pipes. The noise from the congregation didn't fall until Father David walked out of his vestry with a sad smile on his face.

"Not as good as Gertrude," Dot said rather loudly above the music. "Wolf in sheep's clothing. Amateur stuff!"

Father David delivered a lengthy and heartfelt eulogy for Gertrude, which caused more than a couple of people to clutch their tissues and hankies to their eyes. At one point, Father David even looked like he was going to shed a tear, but he held himself together. He ended his speech by commenting on the impressive turnout, and how he hadn't seen such a full church in his twenty years of service. The hint of sarcasm in his voice caused more than a couple of people to squirm in their seats, and if Julia had been sitting, she would have been one of them.

The service was longer than Julia had expected and it wasn't until almost an hour later that they were walking out of the church. The weather had perked up from the morning's clouds, but even though the sky was as clear as could be, it still felt like there was a dark cloud hanging over the village.

Dot and Sue walked arm in arm towards the church gates, but Julia told them to go ahead without her. Both of them looked back at her suspiciously, but they didn't object. She waited until Rachel and Imogen Carter exited and she caught their eyes through the crowd.

When they cut through and walked in her direction, she realised they also wanted to speak to her too.

"Julia, sweetheart," Imogen said softly, resting her hand on Julia's. "I hear you found the body. Terrible business all of this, isn't it?"

"It really is," Julia said, sighing heavily. "I was

wondering if you've seen Roxy recently?"

"Why?" Imogen asked, clearly confused. "Should I have?"

Julia tried to keep her smile firmly on her face as she stared at Imogen, wondering if she should tell her everything she had witnessed the morning before. She decided against it.

"I just wanted to catch up with her, that's all," Julia lied, widening her smile so much she was sure it looked fake.

Imogen nodded, patted Julia's hands and said her goodbyes. Rachel hung back and told her mother they would meet in The Plough for lunch later that afternoon. Imogen waved to them both and scurried off, leaving Rachel and Julia alone outside the church.

Rachel Carter was the complete opposite of her sister Roxy, but still as sweet. Instead of having red hair, her hair was onyx black and her features slender. Rachel was one of the few people in the village who left to pursue a university education, although she came back around the same time Julia did to put her fine art degree to good use by taking over the management of the local art gallery.

"Roxy told me about the argument with Gertrude Smith in the café yesterday morning," Rachel said in a hushed voice, glancing over her shoulder to make sure the passing crowd wasn't listening. "She was in a state."

"Have you seen her?"

Rachel shook her head, and grabbed Julia's arm and pulled her into the shadow of the large oak tree on the church grounds. When she was satisfied they were out of earshot of the lingering attendees, she looked deep into Julia's eyes.

"I haven't seen her since yesterday morning," Rachel said, biting into her orangey red lipstick, which caught Julia off guard with its bright hue. "She came to my gallery around half past ten yesterday and she was really worked up. She was babbling and she looked like she hadn't slept – I couldn't really understand what she was saying, but I managed to get it out of her that she had an argument with Gertrude. I tried to get some more information out of her but she vanished as quickly as she arrived, saying she needed to go and find some money. She seemed pretty desperate."

"Money?" Julia asked. "Why would she need money?"

"She earns a good wage working at the school," Rachel said, shrugging. "But she's been acting strange for weeks. It's been getting progressively worse. We usually meet each other for lunch during the week, but she keeps missing it, saying she's forgotten, but you know Roxy, she has an elephant's memory, which is why she makes such a good teacher."

"She was the same when I saw her. She came into my café as if she didn't know where she was," Julia said, trying to steady the nerves in her voice. "I sat her down and she told me she was in trouble. Next thing I know, she's got her hands on Gertrude, and then she stormed out."

Rachel clasped her hand over her mouth and closed her eyes. She stayed like that until Julia rested her hand on Rachel's shoulder. Rachel was a couple of years older than Roxy, but Julia was sure if she had been in the same class as Rachel at school, she would have been as good of friends with her as she was her sister.

"Mother called me late last night to tell me about Gertrude," Rachel whispered when she finally dropped her hand and opened her mouth. "I jumped straight into my car and I went to Roxy's house. She wasn't in, so I let myself in using my key. Things were all over the place and half of her clothes were missing, like she'd just packed in a hurry."

"This is worse than I thought," Julia mumbled, almost to herself. "Have you told Detective Inspector Brown any of this?"

The recognition in Rachel's eyes of the new DI's name sent a shudder down Julia's spine.

"Not yet," Rachel said. "But he stopped us both outside the church when we were coming in and asked us if he could ask some questions. Mother invited him to lunch at The Plough and he accepted."

"Don't tell him anything," Julia said. "He's looking for somebody to pin this murder on."

"So you don't think Roxy did it?" Rachel said, a frown forming between her brows.

"Do you?"

"I'm not sure. The evidence seems solid."

Julia didn't agree. Despite her nightmare the previous night, she had come to the conclusion that her friend couldn't possibly murder somebody, no matter how much trouble she was in. She knew she was missing most of the important jigsaw pieces, and she was determined to find them.

"I need to talk to Roxy first," Julia said, pulling out her ingredients notepad and a small pencil. "Do you have any idea where she might have gone?"

Rachel stared through Julia for a moment as she thought, but she shook her head and sighed.

"She's been quite friendly with Violet Mason recently. Maybe she's gone to stay with her?"

"Violet?"

"Roxy's new teaching assistant. She moved to the village a couple of months ago and she's renting a room in Amy Clark's cottage. Aside from you, Violet is the only friend my sister has."

Julia knew that to be true because she had always assumed she was Roxy's only real friend, which was why she was so surprised to hear about the existence of another. Roxy had always been very particular about who she gave her time to, something Julia had always admired, because Julia had always found herself to be too trusting. She wasn't hurt that Roxy had found somebody else to share her time with, she was glad of it, but she was hurt Roxy hadn't introduced her new friend, or at least talked about her.

She drew an arrow from Roxy's name in her notepad and added '*Violet Mason – Amy Clark's cottage*' next to it. Rachel peered over the top of the notepad but Julia snapped it shut before she could figure out what she was writing.

"Just remembered an ingredient I need to pick up for a devil's food cake," Julia said with an awkward laugh.

Rachel narrowed her eyes, but she didn't question Julia. The two parted ways and Julia hung back to examine her notepad. She noticed she now had three names written down in connection with Gertrude's murder. She connected a line from Amy Clark's name to the main circle, wondering if wanting to take over the organ playing was a strong enough motive for murder. She decided to add a question mark next to Amy's name, but she drew a circle around Violet's because she wanted to speak to her next.

"Wouldn't be interfering in my murder investigation, would you?" Detective Inspector Brown appeared from nowhere, causing Julia to jump and snap her notepad shut.

"Writing anything good?"

"Just a shopping list."

"For one of those cakes you bake?" Barker asked, displaying the smirk she had come to dislike. "I hear your baked goods are quite popular in this village."

"You've been asking people about me?" Julia asked, folding her arms across her chest and holding Barker's gaze.

"All part of the investigation."

Julia didn't think Barker suspected her of murder, but she did suspect that toying with her had become his new favourite thing to do in the village. She wouldn't be surprised if he had hung back, just to make that little dig.

"I hope it's going well for you," Julia said, sidestepping, only for Barker to do the same and block her way.

"Stay away from my witnesses," Barker commanded, his tone changing from playful to serious. "I don't know what you're up to, Julie, but leave this case to the professionals."

"It's *Julia*, and I don't know what you're talking about."

"I know about the altercation between Gertrude and a Miss Roxy Carter in your business yesterday morning." Barker's smugness immediately returned. "Gertrude luckily told her son before she was murdered, meaning I want to talk to Miss Carter."

"Isn't all of that classified information?" Julia said, pleased that she was able to match his smugness. "I don't know anything about any of that."

Barker faltered for a second but he held his stare. The amount he underestimated her radiated from his body, making her only want to find Roxy Carter before he did even more.

"Judging from the way you were talking to her sister, I'd say you know Roxy," Barker said, glancing down at his watch as though the conversation was starting to bore him. "If you have any knowledge of her whereabouts, I'd like to know."

"Have you checked her house?"

Barker's smug smirk turned upside down in an instant. Julia knew he was trying to catch her out, but she couldn't help feeling she was already a step ahead of the man, and that pleased her.

"Classified," he said.

"Well, if you'll excuse me, I've got one of those cake things to go and bake," Julia said, stepping around Barker and walking away. "Good day, Detective Inspector."

Julia walked towards the church gates and pocketed her notepad, and without needing to turn around, she knew Barker was watching her. Instead of going to her Gran's house or to her own cottage, she crossed the village green and unlocked her café door because as it happened, she did have a cake to bake. She pulled out the ingredients for an angel cake and got to work.

CHAPTER 5

"Angel cake!" Amy Clark exclaimed. "My favourite! It's so good of you to remember that, Julia!"

Amy stepped to the side and let Julia into her cottage without question. Julia had always been proud of her talent for remembering people's favourite cakes, especially in situations when she needed to use her baking skills as a form of bribery. It was a talent her mother had also shared and she used to quiz Julia on people's favourite cakes when they used to spend their Sundays baking together. She could only remember Amy mentioning that her favourite cake was an angel cake on one occasion, almost three months ago when she had visited the café and spotted a freshly baked one in the display case.

Julia handed the cake over to Amy, who hurried off to the kitchen to slice two pieces and make them a pot of tea. Julia showed herself into the living room, and even though she had never been inside of Amy's cottage before, it looked exactly as she expected. Everything was either a saccharine shade of pink or blue, and all of the ornaments cluttering the surfaces were of animals that all had an element of cute comedy to them. Julia was assessing a figurine of a juggling cat that looked spookily like Mowgli. She tried to imagine Mowgli standing on hind legs and juggling, but the thought disturbed her; she preferred her furry friend on all four feet.

"This is as good as I remember," Amy muffled through a mouthful of cake as she hurried into the living room brandishing a tray containing a pastel pink teapot and two powder blue teacups. Julia wondered if Amy had matched her outfit to her décor, or if it had been the other way around.

They both sat on the couch and Amy poured tea into two cups. She added four cubes of sugar to her tea before passing the dish along to Julia, who opted for one.

"I just wanted to stop by and congratulate you on your excellent organ playing today," Julia said, trying to inject as much sweetness and light into her voice. "You really have a knack for it."

Amy looked genuinely taken aback by the compliment, not seeming to notice the over-enthusiastic nature of Julia's tone. Amy rested her hand on her heart and smiled pleasantly, looking on the verge of tears.

"Thank you," Amy said, nodding, as though she really were holding back tears. "You know, I was terribly nervous."

"You couldn't tell."

"I've waited all my life to get up there and perform like that," Amy sighed, and she stared off towards the comedy figurines on the mantelpiece, although she appeared to be looking through them. "It's sad that it's only under *these* circumstances that I had the chance."

The lack of remorse in Amy's voice didn't go unnoticed. She had wondered if her Gran had over egged the rivalry between the two ladies, something Dot did with most village gossip, but this time it appeared to be the truth.

"It's so sad what happened to Gertrude," Julia said, hoping to glean some information from Amy. "I still can't get the image of her out of my head. Even though I only saw the outline of her body, it's something I can't seem to shake."

Once again, Amy didn't show a flicker of emotion. She leaned forward and picked up her cup, taking a sip as though Julia had just commented on the weather. She swirled the tea around in the cup and busied herself by picking a piece of lint off of her pink cardigan.

"I imagine those things do stay with you," Amy said after what felt like an age of awkward silence. "It was surprising."

"We were all surprised."

"I think we're crossing wires here," Amy said, a strained smile contorting her lips. "I am only surprised this didn't happen sooner."

The coldness of Amy's words took Julia by surprise so much that she reached out for her tea and took a sip in hopes it would warm her. Julia stopped herself from pushing the subject further, instead choosing to divert the conversation to the topic that had brought her to Amy's sickly sweet cottage.

"Is Violet home?" Julia asked as casually as she could muster.

"Violet?" Amy tilted her head as though thinking. "I don't think so. I could check if you want? I didn't realise the two of you were friends."

"Oh, yes," Julia said enthusiastically. "Well, we have a mutual friend in Roxy Carter."

The mention of Roxy's name mustered up a reaction from Amy that Julia hadn't been expecting. She hadn't been expecting any reaction at all, so when she saw Amy's features tighten and her jaw grit, it surprised her. Amy sipped her tea through strained lips, and then forced a smile forward.

"The last I saw of Violet was when she left this morning. I was going to ask her to come to the service with me, to watch me play, but she was rather insistent that she wanted to find William Smith."

"William Smith?" Julia asked, a little puzzled.

"That's what I said," Amy said, suddenly a little more animated now that they were both back on the same page. "I told her he wouldn't want to see anybody after finding out his mother had been murdered in her own home. I suppose he's feeling guilty after their huge argument. I wouldn't be surprised if that was the last time they spoke to each other."

"Argument?"

Amy suddenly tightened up again, even more than she had at the mention of Roxy's name. Her entire body turned stiff and the teacup started to shake in her hands. Tea spilled over the edge and onto her pale blue pleated skirt. It took her a moment to react, but when she did, it felt like an overreaction.

"Silly me!" Amy cried, jumping up and setting the teacup on the tray. "What am I like?"

She hurried over to her sideboard and pulled a tissue out of the tissue box, which looked to have been wrapped in the same pink and blue floral wallpaper as the walls. She dabbed at the stain for a moment before busying herself with rearranging the figurines that were neatly placed up on it. It was obvious she was hoping Julia wouldn't push the subject further.

"What argument?" Julia repeated again.

"It's nothing," Amy said dismissively, waving her hand clutching the damp tissue. "It's probably nothing."

"Probably nothing?"

Amy sighed and returned to the sofa and sat next to Julia, but a little closer this time. She leaned in and glanced around the cottage, checking that the figurines weren't eavesdropping on their conversation.

"I was at Gertrude's cottage last night and I heard them both arguing," Amy said in a hushed tone. "He was screaming at the top of his lungs and she was just taking it. Gertrude wasn't the type of woman who would just lie down and accept defeat but she didn't bite."

"What was he saying to her?"

"I didn't hear much, I was in the other room." Amy paused and glanced around her tiny living room, before adding, "He called her selfish, I remember that much. He repeated it over and over – '*You selfish witch! You selfish witch!*' – I remember what he said just before he stormed out."

Amy stopped talking and lifted her hand up to her mouth, as though she had just realised something serious. Julia reached out a hand and rested it on Amy's knee, and she smiled appreciatively.

"Go on," Julia urged.

"He said – '*I'll make you pay for what you've done*' – and then he left."

Julia's eyes widened and her mouth suddenly became dry. She let the words sink in and replayed them over and over in her brain, as though she had heard them first hand. She thought back to last night, and wondered if the figure she had seen could have been William, Gertrude's own son, fleeing from the scene of a murder.

"Amy?" Julia said calmly, inhaling deeply.

"Yes, dear?"

"Why were you at Gertrude's house last night?"

In an instant, Julia knew her question was one too many. Amy's body tightened up again and convulsed so hard, it looked as though she was about to have a seizure from holding in her outburst so tightly.

"I really must get on with my gardening!" Amy cried, her voice shrill and cracking. "We're going to be losing the light soon and I have lots to do. Thank you for the angel cake, Julia. I'm sure I'll be enjoying that for the rest of the week. Now, if you don't mind, I'll see you out."

Julia felt the wind rush past her as the door slammed behind her. She fished out her notepad, flicked through the recipes and paused on what had become her official investigation page.

She added a single ring around Amy's name and crossed out the question mark. Next to it, she wrote '*William Smith*', and drew two arrows, one to Gertrude Smith, and another to Violet Mason.

Julia suspected if she had any chance of tracking down Roxy Carter, it was through Violet Mason.

CHAPTER 6

J ulia had another night of restlessness, once again down to Gertrude, but this time over her words, rather than her death. She had stayed up for half of the night hoping they wouldn't print the damning two star review of her café, and the other half trying to figure out how to deal with the aftermath.

Standing behind her counter she let out a long yawn, and looked down at the morning's edition of *The Peridale Post*, not wanting to open it any more than she wanted to open the divorce papers still burning a hole on her kitchen counter.

As expected, the front cover and most of the inside material was filled with news of Gertrude's death. A picture of Gertrude covered the front page, but it was a picture Julia barely recognised. Not only did she look youthful and exuberant, she was smiling. There was an arm around her neck, but the rest of the picture had been cropped out. It was difficult to imagine Gertrude ever being a happy, young woman, and she wondered if that had been reality, or just a single moment captured in a photograph to paint a different picture after her death.

She selfishly skipped past the pages of tributes, and the many more pages speculating about the murder and the evidence, to the reviews section of the newspaper. She ran her finger along the page, ignoring the four star review of a local band's concert at the church hall and a new cookbook from somebody who once lived in Peridale forty years ago. When she saw the picture of her café taking up half of the bottom page, her heart sank more than it ever could.

Julia's dream to own a café was something she couldn't trace back to a single point, it was just something she always knew she had wanted to do. Baking with her mother had always been her favourite thing in the world. She died when Julia was just twelve-years-old, and everybody expected the grief to make Julia give up baking altogether, but it had the opposite effect. She baked even more, studying her mother's old handwritten recipe books until she had them down to memory, and then tinkering with the recipes and putting her own flair on things to make them her own. She had always looked at her owning a café as a way of preserving her mother's memory and giving her a legacy.

Marrying young and moving to London derailed Julia's dream, but it never dampened. Even in her lowest lows working on a production line in a soulless baked goods factory, the glimmer of hope that she would one day do things her own way kept her going. The day she returned home to find her bags on the doorstep and the locks changed was the day she knew she had to chase that dream.

Looking down at the grainy washed out picture of her café, she felt that dream shatter for the first time in her life.

All the heart she had poured in over the last two years had been sucked out in an instant, and all that was left behind were Gertrude's final bitter words about the place that painstakingly served her fresh blueberries and raspberries on her pancakes for two years. If Julia's mother's legacy was Julia's café, Gertrude's legacy was the words she had left behind.

"Morning, Julia," Johnny Watson said as he walked into the café clutching a copy of the morning paper in his hands, no doubt the first of many. "I wanted to check up on you before you got busy."

"After people read this, I doubt they'll be coming anywhere near here again."

"Don't say that," Johnny said, his soft smile comforting. "The taste buds don't lie and there's not a single person in this village who doesn't like what you bake."

"Apparently there was one." Julia pointed to the picture in the newspaper. "*Miss Piston.*"

"There'll be a new review next week and everybody will forget all about this one. Look at Rachel! Her gallery is doing fine after her scathing review last week."

Julia realised she hadn't told Johnny who the woman behind the reviews was. She almost didn't because she didn't want to prematurely turn the conversation around to what was likely to be a constant talking point for the months ahead, but with Dot, her sister and Detective Inspector Brown all knowing the truth, it was bound to get out sooner or later.

"I don't think you'll be getting another review anytime soon," she said.

"Why not?"

"Because I think '*Miss Piston*' was Gertrude Smith."

Johnny smiled for a moment, as though not knowing if she was being serious or joking, and then his brows tensed together as he pieced the jigsaw together on his own.

"*Piston!*" Johnny cried, snapping his fingers together. "Why didn't I think of that before?"

"I only figured it out right before the murder. That's why I was the one to discover Gertrude's body. I was going there to – well, I don't know what I was going to do. I certainly wasn't going to put a knife in her back, although she did the same to me, metaphorically speaking. I wanted to give her a piece of my mind, or maybe just try to reason with her, to make her see sense. I hoped if I could say the right thing, she would pull the review, or at least amend it. I shouldn't be saying any of this. It's not right to speak ill of the dead."

"Just because she's dead, it doesn't mean she's suddenly a saint," Johnny said with a smile so soft it made Julia's heart skip a beat. "Your café will survive this. You'll see."

Johnny reached out and rested his hand on Julia's, which was on top of the photograph, trying to block out all view of it. She looked down at her hand, and then quickly up at Johnny. Their eyes locked for a second, but that connection broke when the bell above the door signalled the arrival of a new customer.

Julia's relief at the interruption was short lived when she saw Barker Brown strut into her café. Johnny gathered his things, adjusted his glasses and muttered his goodbyes, his cheeks blushing all the while. Julia tried to remember why she had dismissed a second date so quickly.

"Is that your boyfriend?" Barker asked smugly.

"No," Julia snapped, her own cheeks blushing. "What

do you want?"

"Is that any way to speak to a paying customer?" Barker folded his arms across his chest, and scanned the chalkboard menu behind Julia's head. "More selection than I thought for such a small place. That review in the paper didn't mention your broad range of coffee and tea."

Julia felt Barker lean on the metaphorical knife that Gertrude had already planted between her shoulder blades. She had expected people to avoid her café, or even offer pity or sympathy, but she hadn't expected somebody to rub salt in the wound.

"What do you want?" Julia repeated again, not even trying to sound polite.

"It's not like you've got customers banging down the door to get in," Barker said, glancing over his shoulder to the door. "I'll have a large Americano and a scone with all the trimmings."

Detective Inspector Brown turned on his heels and chose the table under the window. Julia glanced at the clock and noticed that Gertrude should have been coming in any moment to take that seat. She had more than once stopped people from sitting there to save herself from the wrath of her most difficult customer, but now she wished she hadn't tried so hard.

Instead of rushing Barker's order, she took her time, making sure to perfectly grind and percolate the beans, not wanting the coffee to be too weak or too bitter. Even if she knew he would have some snarky comeback no matter what she served, she wanted to try and impress him. He was the type of person who could get under somebody's skin with just one look and he was well and truly under Julia's. When she ignored the obvious contempt she felt for Peridale's newest DI, the strange bubbling she felt in her stomach called out to her. It was a similar feeling she had felt when Johnny had put his hand on hers.

Pushing those childish thoughts to the back of her mind, she spooned jam and cream into one of that morning's fresh scones and carefully placed it on one of her finest plates.

When she set the order down in front of Barker, he looked up from the paper he was scribbling on. He seemed caught off guard long enough to not instantly apply his smug face, instead showing the softer version that Julia had first found so handsome, but not handsome enough to distract her from what was written on the paper. Her eyes instantly honed in on the scribbled note '*changing her will???*' in the margin.

"Working on anything important?" Julia asked.

"It's –,"

"Classified," she interrupted. "Say no more."

That told Julia everything she needed to know. He quickly flipped the paper upside down so she couldn't read anymore, but she didn't need to. She was in no doubt that the papers pertained to Gertrude's murder.

With her new information, she walked as quickly as she could while still remaining natural, and she pulled her small ingredients notepad out of her apron. She flipped it open under the counter and squinted down at it, resenting the fact that her eyesight wasn't what it had been in her twenties, and that she was probably going to need glasses soon. She pulled out her pen, flipped over the page, added a bullet point and wrote down exactly what she had seen on Barker's paper.

She muttered the three words aloud, forgetting she

wasn't alone. She snapped the notepad shut and looked up, expecting Barker to be hovering over her, but he wasn't. He was still in his seat and his face was screwed up as he chewed a mouthful of his cream and jam scone. Julia allowed herself to smile because it was a face she had grown to enjoy seeing in her café. It was the face of surprised delight. Seeing Barker enjoying her scone almost made her forget about her feature in the morning paper.

Detective Inspector Brown settled his bill and left the café without saying another sarcastic word to Julia. She hoped her baking had softened his edges, but she knew he would be back to his default setting the moment the delicious fresh baked scone was a distant memory. She made a mental note to bake him something special and take it to his cottage so he could keep reminding himself that she wasn't to be underestimated. If not to impress him, then to keep him on her side so she could pry useful information from him. Even if the Detective Inspector had beaten her to a vital clue, she suspected she had more pieces of the puzzle than he had.

The rest of the day was surprisingly quiet for Julia. Out of the handful of customers she did have, only two of them mentioned the review, and they were words of encouragement, not pity. The others were more interested in her discovery of Gertrude's body, a detail that hadn't been reported in the paper, but had quickly circulated the village via different and more powerful channels. It seemed the rest of the villagers were either exhausted from their unusual trip to church, or too scared that a murderer was on the loose.

At half past five, Julia closed the café and she set off towards Gertrude's cottage, but this time she was in search of her son, William Smith.

The addition of crime scene tape to the outside hadn't helped the eeriness of the cottage. The blue and white tape that had been strung across the gate had been snapped, and was fluttering wildly in the early evening breeze.

Julia looked into the cottage and unlike her previous visit, she saw a light, and it looked like it was coming from the study. There was a police car parked up the road, letting her know it was still an active crime scene, but a quick glance in the wing mirror let her know the officer was busy reading what looked to be an adult magazine.

Julia opened the gate and hurried down the garden path. She knew she was probably breaching a dozen different laws, but the door being unlocked made her feel a little less like she was breaking and entering.

As she tiptoed through the semi-dark cottage, she caught her reflection in a passing mirror and she barely recognised herself. It was only last week her biggest worry had been her divorce, and now it was trying to figure out a murder case because she was convinced the DI in charge wasn't capable of doing so.

Pausing outside the study where the light was emitting from, she glanced to the cottage's open front door, knowing she could turn back. The rustling of paper prickled her ears, compelling her to go forward. She pushed on the study door, which let out an almighty creak, as it swung open.

A hooded shadow, much like the one she had seen in the window, was huddled over a box, digging through a box of paperwork. Despite the creaky hinges, the hooded figure didn't turn around, and continued to dig. Julia cast an eye around the study, avoiding the chair she had found

Gertrude in. There was an obvious sign of a frantic search for something.

Inhaling deeply, Julia summoned her courage and knocked loudly on the wooden door she was standing next to.

"Hello, William," she said confidently.

The figure spun around and froze, like a police spotlight had just found them in the dark. Julia felt pleased with herself for a moment, until she saw an icy strand of blonde hair fall from under the hood.

"Who are you?" A thick Eastern European accent belonging to a woman asked.

Julia was at a loss for words, but when she finally found her voice, she realised there was only one woman the mysterious figure could be.

"Hello, Violet."

CHAPTER 7

Violet tore down her hood and stared at Julia, clutching a brown envelope in her hands.

"How do you know my name?" Violet asked, her voice dark and harsh, telling Julia that despite her youthful face, she was a woman who had lived life. "Who are you?"

"I'm a friend," Julia said, holding out her hands. "I'm a friend of Roxy's. Roxy Carter. She might have mentioned me."

Hearing Roxy's name softened Violet's expression and she dropped her hands to her sides and looked down at the envelope in her hands.

"The cake lady?" Violet asked. "I've heard lots about you."

Julia wasn't familiar with European dialects, but she would have placed Violet from Russia, judging by her thick, deep accent, beautiful striking features and white as snow hair. Her eyes were dazzling blue, piercing and twinkling through the dark. There was a hardness to her looks, but also an undeniable beauty and strength.

"I'm looking for Roxy," Julia said, jumping straight to the point. "Do you know where she is?"

"I was hoping to ask you the same thing," Violet said. "I have looked everywhere and I cannot find her."

Julia's stomach clenched. She believed Violet, which only condemned Roxy even more. For a moment, she dropped her guard, but she remembered where she was, and that neither of them should be there.

"Is that the will?" Julia asked.

"Will?" Violet asked, visibly confused. "I know nothing of a will. I found what I came for and now I must go."

She tried to push past Julia, but even though Julia wasn't taller than the beauty, she was wider. Julia held out her hand for the envelope but Violet moved her hand away and retreated back into the shadows, clutching it tightly to her chest.

"This does not concern you," Violet said sternly. "Let me leave."

"I don't think you understand the seriousness of what is happening here," Julia pleaded. "A woman has been murdered and I think our friend is the prime suspect. I need to find her and prove her innocence."

"Roxy would not hurt anyone."

"I don't think the police think that. She was seen on the morning of the murder arguing with Gertrude in my café. I witnessed it."

"This was separate," Violet said, clearly knowing the crucial information about what trouble Roxy was in. "I need to destroy this evidence before the police find it."

"Evidence?"

"Please, let me go." Violet's voice cracked, and Julia

could tell whatever was in the envelope meant a great deal to either Roxy or Violet, or both.

Before either of them could negotiate any further, Julia heard footsteps behind her, and she felt Detective Inspector Barker Brown looming over her before she saw him.

"Well, well, well," Barker cried. "You just can't help yourself, can you Julie?"

"It's Julia," she snapped. "Pronounced Juli-*ah*."

"Of course," he said. "You're under arrest. *Both* of you."

Julia turned around to see Violet casually drop the envelope on the floor without Barker noticing. When she did, two photographs fell out of the top and it took all of Julia's energy not to gasp in shock and cover her mouth. Instead, she turned back to Barker and held her hands high enough for cuffing so that he didn't notice her kicking the photographs under the desk.

"That won't be necessary, Julia," Barker said with so much smug satisfaction, it made Julia wish she had given him one of the misshapen scones. "That is, if you're both going to come quietly?"

Both women nodded so Barker led them out of the house and towards the waiting police car outside. Julia wondered if the officer had put his magazine down long enough to spot the light in the house and call for backup. Before she could wonder any longer, Violet hopped the small garden wall and disappeared into the night. Barker started to chase her, but she was as nimble as a gymnast and vanished in seconds. Julia suppressed her pleased smirk.

"Perhaps the handcuffs are necessary after all, Baker." Julia said, holding her wrists up once more.

"It's Barker."

"Of course."

Julia sat in the interview room and went over her story for the third time. She had never been arrested before, so she decided to tell Barker the truth about what had taken her to Gertrude's house once more. She told him about Amy revealing the argument, and wanting to ask William some questions about his mother's murder.

"You realise how incredibly stupid it was to visit a crime scene?" Barker said, drumming his fingers on the written statement he had taken. "You could have put yourself in danger."

"I wasn't thinking," Julia said, bowing her head.

"Who was that woman?"

"I don't know," Julia lied.

"Why do you care so much about solving this case?"

Julia stopped herself from telling him it was because she wanted to outsmart him and prove some unspoken theory that he was wrongly underestimating her, but she knew it was more than that.

"I know you suspect my friend, Roxy Carter, of murdering Gertrude, and I want to prove that she didn't."

"She's the most obvious suspect we have at this time."

"And sometimes self-raising flour is the most obvious choice for a cake but it doesn't mean it's going to give you the best results."

Barker smirked at her baking analogy, but it wasn't the usual smirk, it was a softer one that was filled with an ounce more compassion than usual.

"You really love all of that baking stuff, don't you?" Barker asked, sounding genuinely interested.

"It's my life."

Julia realised how pathetic that might have sounded, but it was true. She had baking, her café, Mowgli, and her friends and family, which was why she needed to find out the truth about Roxy Carter, innocent or guilty.

"Who do you think murdered her?" The same genuine interest was present again.

"I don't think it's that simple," Julia said. "We're missing vital pieces of the recipe for the murder."

"Not everything is about baking."

"For a simple sponge cake you need flour, eggs, butter and sugar, all in equal quantities," she said, already feeling like Barker was losing his interest. "For a murder, you need a victim, a weapon, the means and a motive."

"And a murderer," Barker added, the smugness returning.

"The cake is the result of the ingredients, as is the murderer." Julia smiled, proud of herself. "We have the victim and the weapon, Gertrude and the knife. We even have the means, that she was alone in her cottage in her study, presumably trying to change her will, from what I gathered from your notes. The only thing we don't have is the motive."

She realised what she had seen in Violet's photographs would give Roxy the perfect motive, but that was another piece of information she would keep until she spoke to Roxy.

"Since you've come this far, I might as well tell you Gertrude called her lawyer the afternoon of her death to change her will and disinherit her son." Barker said without pausing for breath. "She arranged a meeting for first thing on Monday morning, but as we know, she never made it."

"Disinherit William?" Julia mumbled almost to herself.

"Why would a mother disinherit her own son?"

"I have no idea, but that's what I want to find out, because I think that's the motive right there. This is classified! You can't breathe a word of this to anyone."

"Why are you telling me this?"

Barker paused and scratched at the back of his head. Julia was certain she noticed a slight blush forming on his cheeks.

"Because I trust you to keep quiet," Barker said, appearing to choose his words carefully. "You don't seem as interested in gossip as the others."

Julia was surprisingly touched. Knowing she had earned a pinch of Barker's trust made her chest flutter more than she had expected. Trying not to focus on the fluttering, she turned her thoughts to William, and she racked her brain for everything she knew about William, but her knowledge was sparse. She knew he was an only child, and that his relationship with his mother was frosty. He was a banker in the city, but he travelled back to the village on occasion to visit his mother. She had seen him speeding past her café more than once in his sports car, with the window down and a cigarette in his hand. He had once come into her café, glanced at the menu, pulled a face, and walked straight out again. The basic information she had didn't paint a very nice picture, but did it make him a murderer?

A knock at the door derailed her train of thought and a young female constable popped her head into the interview room.

"DI, there's a visitor for Julia at the front desk," Sarah said, sending a sympathetic smile in Julia's direction. "It's her sister, Sue."

"I'm in the middle of an interview."

"She doesn't want to see her, she just wanted me to pass this through." Sarah produced the cake box Julia had requested her sister bring during her one phone call, and she was delighted it had made it past the front desk.

Sarah placed the box on the table and hurried out of the interview room, leaving Barker to peel back the lid with an amused look flooding his sharp features.

"It's a double chocolate fudge cake," Julia said, peering inside at the perfect cake that had been chilling in her fridge. "I bake when I'm stressed, so I made it last night."

"And you used your one phone call to call your sister to bring it here, and not to call a lawyer?"

"Yes."

"Why?"

"I doubted you'd had much time to eat since that scone this morning," Julia said. "What with you solving a murder case and all."

They both shared a smile for a moment and for the first time, it felt like their humour was on the same page. Julia knew the effect her baking had on people, so she was glad to see it having that desired effect.

"That's very kind of you," Barker said softly. "And you're right, I haven't eaten since that scone this morning. I didn't think anything would compare."

Julia was touched by the compliment, which he delivered without a hint of irony or sarcasm. He ran his finger along the glossy icing and dropped it into his mouth.

"Wow," he said. "How did you know chocolate cake was my favourite?"

"Lucky guess."

"Did you hope you could feed me up so I would drop

the charges?"

"I would never," Julia said, faking an offended gasp. "Did it work?"

"Oh, I was never going to put you through the system," Barker said with a casual shrug as he took another mouthful of the icing. "I just wanted to scare you."

"But you took a statement. You wrote four pages."

"All part of the experience. Did it work?"

"Maybe," she admitted. "A little."

"For what it's worth, I don't think you're the murderer, but I need you to promise me you're going to stay out of this investigation and leave it to the professionals."

"Okay."

"That's not the same as a promise," Barker said in a low voice, leaning across the table.

"Promise."

Her words seemed to satisfy Barker, even if her fingers were crossed under the table. She didn't like the thought that she was lying to a man she had just mentally upgraded from an enemy to an acquaintance, but if she didn't want to see Roxy Carter behind bars, it was what she needed to do.

"Do you know anything else?" Barker asked after he finished his second slice of chocolate cake. "Any last words before I let you go?"

"That depends," Julia said. "What do I get in return?"

Barker smirked and leaned across the table.

"What do you want?" He asked darkly.

Julia leaned across the table and smiled tenderly at him for a second before saying, "Information about Amy Clark."

Barker Brown switched back to Detective Inspector mode, darted back in his chair, and assessed Julia from across the table. She wondered if she had undone the progress her baking had done, or if he was considering what she had just said.

"I have some information on Amy Clark," he said casually, glancing over to the door. "But it depends what you've got for me."

Julia thought about the photographs, wondering if she could give the DI some useful information without putting Roxy even more in the frame.

"Check Gertrude's bank account for suspicious transactions," Julia said carefully. "I have a feeling she was blackmailing one or more villagers."

"Is this just a hunch?" He asked, his brow arching.

"Yes, but a good one. Amy Clark admitted to being at Gertrude's cottage where she overheard a conversation between William and his mother in which he called her selfish. It is common village knowledge that Amy and Gertrude are sworn enemies, so they wouldn't be meeting up for tea and biscuits."

"Is that all you're basing this on?"

"Just check," she said firmly. "Follow the money back. It might lead you to the murderer, it might not, but it's information."

Barker Brown evaluated what she had said for what felt like a lifetime, as he tried to decide if what she had told him was useful or not. Julia knew there was a possibility he was going to take her information and not share what he knew about Amy Clark; she couldn't blame him if he did.

"Amy Clark has a criminal record," Barker said. "I'm only telling you this because I think it might link to what you've just told me. I had lunch with Roxy's mother and sister to try and get some information and they mentioned

Amy's rivalry with Gertrude so I did a little digging and I found some pretty dark stuff from her past."

"How dark?" Julia found herself leaning in without even realising.

"Amy did twelve years in prison for assisting in a bank robbery back in the seventies." Barker said quietly. "And now that you've told me about possible blackmail, I have to consider that Gertrude knew about Amy's criminal past and was using it against her. All of this is public record, but it's a case of joining up the dots."

Julia didn't know what she had been expecting, but she hadn't been expecting something so huge. She felt a couple more of the pieces slot into place and she was happy somebody else was in Barker's mind other than Roxy.

When Barker finally let her go with another warning to stay out of trouble, she left him alone with the double chocolate fudge cake and set off home. On her walk up the lane, she spotted a hooded figure sitting on the stone wall outside her cottage. Julia wasn't scared or surprised to see Violet there.

"You were an easy woman to track," Violet said. "Easier than Roxy. You saw the photographs?"

"I did."

"So you know that me and Roxy are lovers." Violet said, bowing her head.

"I figured that part out, yes." Julia sat on the wall next to Violet. "Was Gertrude blackmailing Roxy about those photographs?"

Violet nodded and started crying.

"That horrible woman was taking pictures of the church and Roxy was visiting her father's grave. She was upset, so I put my arms around her and I kissed her. We promised each other we would keep our relationship a secret. Roxy was so scared of a scandal at school and we were scared of losing our jobs, the one thing she loved the most. Gertrude got the pictures by accident, but the next day, she arrived at Roxy's house with them and told Roxy if she didn't pay her five hundred pounds a week, she would send the pictures to the head teacher."

"Why would she do that?" Julia mumbled, staring into the dark.

"Because she was the devil, and I'm glad she was murdered, but I promise you Julia, it wasn't me or Roxy."

"It's okay," Julia wrapped an arm around Violet's shoulder and squeezed tight. "Who you love shouldn't be a crime."

"Even if we were a man and woman, Roxy is my superior and my mentor," Violet said, holding back the tears. "We would both lose our jobs either way. We tried to end things, but we couldn't."

Violet started crying properly and Julia's heart broke for them both. Any sympathy she felt for the smiling, youthful version of Gertrude on the cover of *The Peridale Post* vanished in an instant.

Julia invited Violet inside for a cup of tea but she declined. They parted ways, and after Julia fed Mowgli, she crawled into bed with her notepad. She put a line through Violet's name and three question marks above Roxy's. She needed to find Roxy before it was too late.

She flipped the page and added '*blackmail*' under the note about the change of the will, along with Roxy and Amy's name in brackets. Julia would have put her life savings on Gertrude blackmailing more than just the two of them.

Julia closed the notepad and rested it on her nightstand. She flicked off the lamp and slid into her soft, satin covers. The second her head rested on the pillow, she knew she was in for her best night's sleep since before the murder. Her last thought before she drifted off was if Barker had finished the rest of the chocolate cake.

CHAPTER 8

J ulia was more than happy to see more of her regular customers' faces on Tuesday. She didn't realise how much she enjoyed her café being part of their lives and their routines until it wasn't. Julia had almost forgotten all about the review until she saw a copy of the newspaper clutched in Rachel Carter's hands when she came into the café during a quiet period after lunch.

Rachel pulled out a chair at the table nearest to the counter, and Julia got to work making her usual vanilla latte with an extra shot of espresso. Rachel was the only customer, so Julia took advantage of the moment and decided to take a break. She made herself a cup of peppermint and liquorice tea and sat across from Rachel.

"You too," Rachel said, pointing at the review. "I thought I'd never work again, but it turns out people in this village are rather forgiving."

"Still doesn't feel nice, does it?"

Rachel closed the newspaper and sipped her latte. Julia noticed the slight purple smudges under her eyes.

"At least Gertrude can't spread more of her poison," Rachel said after taking another sip. "You're not just a master of cakes, Julia. Your coffee is the best I've ever had too."

Julia smiled and the compliment almost blindsided her from what Rachel had just said.

"How do you know it was Gertrude?" Julia asked as she sipped her hot tea.

"I figured it out," Rachel said with a small laugh. "Piston? Hardly *subtle,* is it? And besides, there aren't many people in the village who were as wicked as that woman."

Julia couldn't disagree with that. After finding out that Gertrude had been blackmailing Roxy for five hundred pounds a week, Julia had run out of excuses not to agree with all of the nasty things people were saying about her. Julia knew if Gertrude hadn't been murdered, she probably would have forgiven her for the review and kept serving her pancakes, but that was the type of woman Julia was. She doubted Rachel would have been so quick to let Gertrude step foot in her gallery.

"I had an ulterior motive for coming here, aside from your excellent coffee," Rachel said, leaning in and lowering her voice. "I'm beginning to really worry about Roxy's disappearance. I can't help but think the police are trying to pin this on her, and the longer she stays away, the easier that's going to be."

"I have a feeling the police might be looking in other places at the moment."

"Oh?" Rachel seemed genuinely surprised. "Where?"

"Amy Clark and William Smith," Julia said quietly. "I

think Gertrude was blackmailing Amy, and Amy swears she heard William arguing with his mother the morning of her murder. It wasn't just your sister who was on Gertrude's bad side."

"Blackmail?" Rachel asked, not sounding at all surprised. "Did you manage to find Violet?"

"I did."

"So I assume you *know*?" Rachel said, sipping her latte again. "About the true nature of their relationship?"

"You knew?"

"Of course I knew," Rachel said, sounding a little amused. "Roxy is my sister. She confided in me about everything, including Gertrude blackmailing her. I only found that out on the day of the murder. When Roxy came to my gallery, she asked me for money, saying Gertrude was blackmailing her, and that she had exhausted her small pot of savings. I was quite shocked."

Julia listened but she didn't react. She sipped her peppermint and liquorice tea as she noticed the sudden change in Rachel's story about that conversation. Julia could have sworn Rachel had said Roxy was babbling incoherently when she visited the gallery. She decided against mentioning the inconsistencies.

"What time did you say you went to Roxy's cottage?" Julia asked, diverting the conversation.

"About six," Rachel said. "Maybe a little after. It was after I closed the gallery. Why?"

"I'm just trying to establish a timeframe. By the time I got to the cottage, it was about quarter to six. Roxy's cottage is on the other side of the village, which means there was no way she could have gone home, packed and vanished before you got there."

"Unless she packed her things before?" Rachel added.

Julia sipped her tea again, trying not to react. Despite Rachel's worries that the police were trying to pin the murder on her sister, she didn't sound as though she fully believed her innocence.

The conversation quickly switched to idle village gossip before Rachel finished her latte and left the café, leaving behind her copy of *The Peridale Post*, which Julia tossed straight into the bin.

She was only alone in her café for less than a minute when a sports car pulled up outside, its brakes screeching as it slammed to a halt. William Smith jumped out and headed straight for Julia's café, and from the stern expression on his face, he didn't look like he wanted a cup of tea and a friendly chat.

William was a tall, slender man who looked to be in his mid-forties. He still had a thick head of hair, which was suspiciously absent of grey hairs, and his face was handsome and clean-shaven. His pale grey suit looked to be designer, as did the chunky gold watch on his wrist.

"Julia South," William said coldly as he opened the door. "I want a word with you."

Julia straightened her back and put both of her hands on the counter. William's face was full of anger and rage, but Julia was determined not to match that.

"Can I help you?" she asked. "Perhaps a cake, or a nice cup of coffee?"

"You know very well I don't want a cake or a damn coffee!" William slammed his hands down on the counter. "What were you doing at my mother's cottage last night? One of the neighbours saw you being carted off into a police car, and another fleeing the scene. Your accomplice to *murder*, no doubt?"

William failed to take a breath. His face burned amber and a vein at his temple bulged violently out of his skin.

"Why don't you just sit down, and calm down?" Julia suggested. "If you want to talk to me like a reasonable adult, I'd be more than happy to."

"*Reasonable?*" He choked on the word. "You *murdered* my mother!"

"I certainly did not!" Julia cried, her tone matching his. "Now, you can sit down, or you can leave!"

William looked to the table nearest the counter and he reluctantly sat down, making sure to make as much noise as possible. Julia had never had children, but she expected this was how teenagers acted when they didn't get their own way.

Julia sat across from him and waited for him to visibly calm down.

"I didn't kill your mother," Julia said calmly. "I went to the cottage to find you, actually. I thought you might have been there. I wouldn't have gone in, but I saw a light on, and I assumed it was you. Obviously, it wasn't you, nor was it my accomplice. I'm sorry about what has happened to your mother, but I'm trying to figure this out as much as everybody else."

William suddenly started crying, and Julia was quite taken aback. She offered him her handkerchief, which he gratefully accepted. When the blubbering finally stopped, he inhaled deeply, his face redder than ever.

"The last thing I said to her was that I hated her," William said, his voice finally calm and a reasonable volume. "If only I had known what was coming."

"None of us knew."

"I didn't have the best relationship with my mother. We never saw eye to eye on anything. I was always much closer to my father, God rest his soul." William paused to wipe his nose with the handkerchief, and Julia made a mental note to wash it before pocketing it again. "Despite all of this, I never thought her final action in life would be to spite me."

"The change of the will?"

William nodded. He didn't bother to ask how Julia had found out.

"Now the police seem to think I killed her!" William cried. "It's absurd. We might not have liked each other, but I still loved her. I thought she loved me somewhere deep down, but this just proved she didn't."

Julia decided there and then that William hadn't killed his mother. He had been the main suspect in her mind, but seeing how fragile the man was about his relationship with his mother, she knew he could never have been the one to sink the knife into her back.

"Do you know who your mother was going to leave her inheritance to?" Julia asked.

"No. That's why I went there. She called me to let me know I was being disinherited. That was the type of woman she was. I left work, jumped in my car and drove straight there."

"And what time was that?" Julia pulled out her recipe notepad and pencil out of her dress pocket, and flipped to the notes page.

"About five," William said. "I was gone by ten past. I knew there was no making her see sense. She had two women in her living room, and they were all drinking tea like nothing was happening. The truth is, I don't even need whatever she's leaving behind. I moved to the city and I made my own money, but it's just the biggest slap in the face."

"Two women?" Julia asked, her pencil primed over the paper.

"Yes, two," William said certainly. "One dressed in pink and blue, and one with red hair."

"How red?"

"What?"

"How red was her hair?"

"Faded," William said with a shrug. "It was greying."

Julia flipped the page to her list of suspects. She crossed out William's name and scribbled down 'Imogen Carter'. Rachel might not have inherited her mother's ginger hair, but Roxy had.

"You mentioned your father," Julia said. "When did he die?"

"Three years ago," William said heavily. "He had a heart attack and that was it, he was gone. His wife still hasn't come to terms with it."

"Wife?" Julia asked, completely puzzled.

"My mother and father divorced in 1978," William said. "He had a lucky escape."

When Julia was alone in her café again, she scribbled down two notes. The first was 'why was Imogen Carter at Gertrude's cottage with Amy Clark?' and the second was 'find out more about what happened in 1978', both of which she hoped to figure out in her next visit.

After baking a box of cinnamon swirls, she set off across the village to Imogen Carter's home.

CHAPTER 9

I mogen Carter's house was unusual in Peridale, in that it wasn't a cottage, and it was quite modern. Julia had always marvelled at the strange glass construction as a child, and she always loved going to Roxy's house for supper after school.

Julia remembered how much life the house had when she was a child, but now it looked sterile and cold. Imogen's husband, and Roxy and Rachel's father, Paul Carter, passed away when Roxy and Julia were teenagers, and now Imogen lived in the house alone. It looked more like a glass prison than an inviting home these days.

The doorbell rang throughout the house and Imogen Carter answered the door, with rollers in her faded ginger hair. She clutched a white silk robe across her body, which looked thinner than Julia remembered.

"Julia, dear," Imogen said with a shaky smile. "So nice to see you. Come in. Do I smell the distinct scent of your cinnamon swirls?"

"The very same."

"You're an angel, Julia," Imogen beamed as she accepted the box. "I haven't been eating much, so these will go down a treat."

Julia followed Imogen across the shiny white floors of the grand entrance, which had a large domed window in the ceiling looking up at the pale blue sky above. They walked through to the living room, which was as sterile as Julia remembered. Everything was white, including the carpets, and Julia knew they wouldn't last two seconds in her cottage with Mowgli's muddy paws.

"Please, sit," Imogen offered as she tightened the tie of her silk robe. "I'll make us up some tea. I have some of that peppermint and liquorice tea you like so much."

"That would be lovely."

Imogen hurried off to the kitchen, leaving Julia alone in the living room. She was scared to sit down on the white leather couch, in case the dye from her peach coloured 1940s style dress somehow leaked and injected some much needed colour onto the blank canvas.

The only colour in the entire room came from the select pictures in glass frames, which were displayed neatly on the mantelpiece, all pointing forty-five degrees to the right. Julia spotted herself with Roxy as little girls in their yellow summer school dresses. She smiled. A slightly older Rachel was in the background of the picture, pulling a face behind Roxy's back, as the two girls grinned unaware. A part of Julia yearned for those simpler days.

She heard the kettle ping and decided to sit on the couch. The leather creaked underneath her, as though it was never used, and was just for show. An opened envelope caught her attention on the gleaming glass coffee table. She recognised it as a bank statement because she was with the same bank. Julia chewed the inside of her lip and looked in the direction of the kitchen. She couldn't see Imogen, so she quickly pulled the letter from the envelope.

Julia knew she was invading her friend's mother's privacy, but she was only looking for one piece of information and she could ignore everything else. She ran her finger down the '*PAYMENTS*' column, and snapped her fingers together when she saw a five hundred pound payment to Gertrude Smith. She heard the jingle of china cups on a metal tray, so she quickly stuffed the paper back into the envelope and sat back on the couch.

"I'm afraid I haven't heard from Roxy if that's why you're here," Imogen said as she set the tray on top of the envelope. "I'm beginning to really worry. The school even rang me to ask if I knew where she was. It's not like her to miss work. She loves that place. I hope nothing bad has happened to her."

Julia suddenly realised she hadn't even considered that Roxy could have faced the same fate as Gertrude. Her stomach turned and she pushed that thought to the back of her mind.

"I'm sure she's fine," Julia said, unsure of whom she was trying to convince. "She'll be in touch when she's ready."

"I hope so," Imogen said with a heavy sigh. "I haven't left the telephone's side. It's not like Roxy to take off and not get in touch."

Julia knew that much to be true. Roxy was the type of friend who would call, or send a text message every day of her holiday, just to let you know she was doing okay and having a fun time.

"Do you go to church every Sunday?" Julia asked.

"Church?" Imogen said with a confused smile. "Oh, not really. I was only there because the women at my book club called and said it was going to be eventful. I don't know what they were expecting to happen, but the most we got was Amy Clark's mediocre organ playing."

Julia was surprised Imogen had been the one to bring up Amy Clark because that's where she had been hoping to steer the conversation. Julia picked up her cup and took a sip of the peppermint and liquorice tea, wondering the best way to broach the subject.

"Are you friendly with Amy Clark?"

"Not really," Imogen said casually. "She's quite garish with all of that colour."

If Amy's pastel pink and blue cottage was the opposite of Gertrude's eerie dark cottage, Imogen's white and glass house was the opposite of both of them.

"So you weren't at Gertrude's house with Amy, an hour before she was murdered?" Julia asked, taking a sip of her tea.

Imogen's eyes popped open and she choked on the cinnamon swirl she had just taken a bite of. She quickly chewed and swallowed, covering her mouth with her hand.

"Where did you hear that?" Imogen asked, not denying it.

"William told me he saw two women when he went to visit his mother. I only knew Amy was there, and his description led me to you."

Imogen took a sip of her black coffee and set it back down, taking her time to adjust it so that the handle was exactly parallel to the lines of the tray. She tilted her head and observed her handiwork, as though it was the most important thing in the world.

"I was there. What of it?" Imogen said.

"Why were you there?"

"What business is that of yours?" Imogen snapped, revealing a different side of the woman Julia had known since childhood. "It's not a crime to visit a neighbour. I didn't kill her."

"Did your visit have something to do with Gertrude blackmailing Roxy?" Julia asked.

"What?" Imogen mumbled. "Gertrude was blackmailing Roxy as well?"

Julia frowned and tilted her head. She suddenly realised she had crossed wires.

"As well?" Julia asked. "You mean to say Gertrude was blackmailing you too?"

Imogen tried to laugh off the suggestion, but only for a split second. Her expression quickly turned grave and she pursed her lips and rested her hands on her lap. She stared sternly at Julia, and then down to the tray, as though she was seeing through it to the bank statement below it.

"Why was Gertrude blackmailing Roxy?" Imogen whispered, her eyes glazing over.

"I don't know why," Julia lied carefully, not wanting to out her friend's secret lover. "I just know that she was. Her friend, Violet, confirmed that's why Roxy has been so stressed, and I suspect that's why Roxy has gone into hiding. I also suspect she was blackmailing Amy Clark too."

"Roxy didn't kill Gertrude," Imogen said. "And neither did I!"

"How long was Gertrude blackmailing you?"

Imogen sighed and collapsed back into the couch. She rested the back of her hand against her forehead and exhaled dramatically. Whatever had been going on had clearly drained Imogen, just as much as it had Roxy, but the mother seemed better than the daughter at hiding the truth.

"Only a couple of weeks," Imogen said after a moment's silence. "It came out of the blue. Gertrude turned up on my doorstep one night. It was quite the surprise, so I invited her in, and she said if I didn't send her five hundred pounds a week, she would –,"

"Reveal your secret?" Julia finished the sentence for her.

"How do you know about the adoption?" Imogen cried, sounding more surprised than ever.

"I didn't," Julia said, suddenly putting her cup back on the table. "I just think that Gertrude knew something about Roxy and that's why she was blackmailing her, and I think she knew something about Amy, and that's why I suspect she's also a victim of Gertrude's blackmail."

Imogen sunk further into the white leather and began to sob. Julia offered her the freshly washed handkerchief, which she snatched out of Julia's hands and dabbed her eyes with.

"Nobody can know about this," Imogen said. "I don't even know how that *witch* found out. I made sure to cover my tracks perfectly. I didn't leave a trace."

"Know about what?" Julia asked, leaning forward.

"Roxy and Rachel are adopted," Imogen said with a wild sob. "Neither of them knows."

Julia clasped her hand over her mouth and her eyes widened. She didn't know what she had been expecting, but it wasn't that.

"But you and Roxy look so much alike," Julia said, unsure of why her mind went straight there.

"I got lucky with her," Imogen said, before blowing her nose on the handkerchief, which would need it's second wash of the day. "Rachel not so much. I found out very young that I couldn't have children and it was all I ever wanted. I couldn't swallow the thought of going through life not knowing the joy of being a mother. It was my late-husband's idea to adopt. I wasn't so sure because I didn't think I could love another person's child as though it were my own, but the second I held Rachel in my arms for the first time, I knew she was mine. It was a bond I had never known before. I adopted Roxy two years later and it was the same. It was so perfect, I didn't want to admit I didn't give birth to them. I didn't want anybody questioning who their real mother was, because it was me. I was raising them, so they were my babies. My husband and I swore we would never tell the girls the truth. I was going to take that secret to my grave, until Gertrude turned up that night. I was so shocked that she knew, and so devastated that she was going to tell my girls the truth, I signed the cheque there and then and I've been bank transferring the money to her since, once a week. I don't even know how she found out. She said something about not being the only one with a secret child and that's when she left."

Julia wanted to pull her notepad out to scribble down every last detail, but she stopped herself. Instead, she sat next to Imogen and pulled her into a hug. The woman sobbed for minutes without talking, before finally pulling away and drying her eyes one last time.

"You can't tell them," Imogen pleaded, clutching Julia's hands tightly. "Promise me you won't tell them."

Julia knew the girls had a right to know where they had come from, but it wasn't her place to reveal that truth to them. As she looked into Imogen's eyes, she saw desperation and heartbreak, and it was something Julia could empathise with, but hadn't experienced herself. She had always assumed she was going to have children of her own one day, but now that she was alone at thirty-seven, she knew the clock was ticking. Jerrad had convinced Julia that they should wait until later in life and she had somehow gone along with it. Looking back, she knew Jerrad had just been stalling for as long as he could until he had the guts to end things.

"I won't tell them," Julia said. "But maybe you should."

"This secret goes to the grave with Gertrude Smith," Imogen said, a strange smile filling her lips. "Nobody needs to know a thing. It's like it never happened."

Imogen resumed eating her cinnamon swirl as though nothing had actually happened. Julia left soon after that and scribbled down two new notes to her list. The first was '*Roxy and Rachel are adopted*', and the second was '*Gertrude's secret child?*'. She didn't know how either thing was connected yet, but she had a feeling they were. She flipped back to her suspects' page and drew a big arrow from Imogen to Gertrude.

CHAPTER 10

J ulia pushed her peas around her plate. She wasn't particularly hungry, but her Gran had gone to the effort of cooking for her, so she'd tried her best to eat as much of the homemade cheese and onion pie, peas and mash as she could. The summons to supper had come on Julia's walk home from Imogen's immaculate prison, so Julia ran home to feed Mowgli, and headed straight to her Gran's, where Sue was already waiting for her.

"I was thinking of having my birthday party at the gallery this weekend," Sue said after sipping some of her white wine. "We could have some food, and some drinks. I could invite some girls from the hospital and we could make a real night out of it. I know I'm only turning thirty-two, but it's a reason to party. What do you think, Julia?"

"About what?" Julia mumbled.

"A party at the gallery."

Julia stared from Sue to Dot, wondering if there was something she had missed. She shook her head and dropped her fork onto the plate, and pushed it away, finally giving up on trying to force-feed herself.

"Yeah, sounds like fun," Julia said, nodding enthusiastically while also staring at the table and still deep in thought. "I'm sure Rachel will appreciate the business."

"A party is just what this village needs," Dot exclaimed. "I'll invite the girls from poker club, if that's okay with you, Sue?"

"Poker club?" Sue said with a laugh. "And that's fine by me."

"Me and some of the girls got a little bored of the weekly trips to bingo, so we meet here on Fridays and have a little tipple."

"Isn't that illegal?" Sue asked.

"Probably," Dot said, rolling her eyes heavily. "What isn't these days? As long as Julia doesn't tell her new Detective Inspector boyfriend, we'll be okay."

"He's not my boyfriend," Julia mumbled, breaking out of her trance to look at her Gran. "We barely like each other."

"Sue told me about you giving him a cake."

"I thought I was being arrested."

"He must like you if he let you off," Sue offered as she sipped her wine again. "He is rather handsome Julia, wouldn't you agree?"

"I haven't noticed," she said dismissively. "Gran, did you know Gertrude when she was married?"

Dot looked taken aback by the question. She scrunched up her face for a moment, before pushing up her tightly permed curls and nodding.

"Of course," Dot said. "I've lived in this village my whole life. The pair of them moved here when Gertrude was pregnant. You're going back some forty-odd years though. They divorced years ago."

"1978?" Julia asked.

"It must have been," Dot said with a nod. "Why the sudden interest in Gertrude's husband?"

"It's just something William said," she mumbled as she tapped a finger rhythmically against her chin. "Do you know what their marriage was like?"

"Unhappy!" She said without a second thought. "She publically humiliated that man every chance she got! I'm not surprised he went looking elsewhere. He always looked so browbeaten and miserable."

"He cheated on her?"

"Old Frank?" Dot laughed. "Oh, yes! Constantly. Gertrude wouldn't admit it if you had asked her, but this village talks, and we have eyes. He was seen messing around with many women when William was a little one. He filed for divorce eventually, although Gertrude insisted she kicked him out, but nobody believed that. She was alone after that."

"Are you sure she was alone?" Julia asked.

"I'm pretty sure," Dot said. "Why is this important? Do you think it's got something to do with the murder? Last I heard, old Frank died of a heart attack a couple of years ago. You're barking up the wrong tree with that one."

Julia couldn't shake away what Imogen had said about Gertrude's secret child. It seemed important and vital to finding the murderer, but she couldn't quite piece together why.

"So there's no chance Gertrude had another child after William?" Julia asked.

Dot laughed and shook her head. Sue was staring at Julia across the table, frowning and clearly confused. She shot her a look that said '*why do you care?*', so Julia waved her hand and turned back to their Gran.

"Something like that wouldn't be kept a secret in this village!" Dot said. "It's impossible. She was pregnant when she arrived to the village, but never again. She had William when she was in her forties, and William was about ten-years-old when his father left, so if she had another child in her fifties, that would have been a miracle!"

The drumming of Julia's finger on her chin increased as her mind worked overtime.

"What about Frank?" Julia asked. "Did he have any children after he left Gertrude?"

"He was just as old as she was, so I don't think so," Dot said, clearly getting irritated by Julia's line of questioning. "Why is this important?"

"I haven't figured that part out yet."

"You need to let this go, sis," Sue said, reaching across the table to grab Julia's hand. "You're getting yourself into dangerous situations. I'm worrying about you."

"It's bigger than me," Julia said. "There's a murderer on the loose and if I don't find them, who will?"

"The police?" Sue said, laughing as though it was an obvious statement. "Detective Inspector Brown?"

"He doesn't see the bigger picture," Julia sighed. "He's a typical man. Thanks for dinner, Gran, but I should get home. It's been a long day and I have baking prep to do for the morning."

"But I have trifle in the fridge!" Dot cried. "You can't go yet!"

Julia knew the trifle would have been store bought. Her Gran was her father's mother, so the baking gene was on the other side of the family, not that it had passed to

Sue. Sue was okay when it came to measuring and putting things in the oven, but she lacked Julia's finesse and skills to bake truly delicious treats.

After taking her plate through to the kitchen, Julia slid into her pink pea coat, kissed her Gran and sister on their cheeks, and headed out into the night. She inhaled the night air, appreciating the slight chill. She hoped the walk home would unlock something vital in her brain. She felt like she had all the pieces of the puzzle and the sooner she put the pieces in the right order, the sooner she could get back to worrying about baking, instead of the murder.

Julia put her hands in her pockets and looked in the direction of her café. Even in the dark, it filled her with pride. She tried to imagine the life she had had back in London, but it felt like it belonged to somebody else, which only made her wonder why she was so reluctant to sign the divorce papers sitting in her kitchen. She didn't want Jerrad, nor did she really want him to suffer. The relationship with the secretary he had left her for hadn't lasted longer than six months and he had gone through two other women since. He was welcome to that life, she just couldn't help feeling he had taken the easy way out, and she had been forced to start her life all over again. She was grateful for that now, but a little part of her, the part that was stopping her from signing the papers, wanted to put a little obstacle in the way of what Jerrad wanted.

Her thoughts snapped right back to reality when she noticed movement in her café. She thought it was her imagination, or the dark playing tricks on her, so she hurried across the village green. When she saw the definite outline of somebody emptying the contents of her display case, she knew she was witnessing her mystery cake thief in action.

Julia turned back to her Gran's cottage, and then to the local police station up the road, but she decided she was going to confront the thief alone.

Instead of going for the front door, she crept along the alley where she usually parked her blue Ford Anglia, and to the small stone yard behind her café. She saw the beam of a flashlight moving around behind the counter as she carefully stepped into the café. Being as careful as possible, she closed and locked the back door.

Julia crept across the kitchen and to the beaded curtain separating it from the front of her café. She peered through the beads and watched the tiny, slender figure chomping down on a slice of her latest addition, the lemon sponge cake that she had perfected over the weekend.

"Enjoying that?" Julia asked.

The figure spun around, and to Julia's surprise, it was a girl, and not just any girl, a teenage girl. She dropped the cake and scooped up her bag, but she seemed frozen to the spot. The girl looked from Julia to the front door, assessing her exit route.

"It's okay, you're not in trouble," Julia said softly when she saw how alive the fear was in the girl's eyes. "Why don't you sit down and I'll cook you something proper?"

The girl raised an eyebrow and glared at her as though she was mad, but to her surprise, she slowly walked around the counter and sat in one of the seats, not taking her eyes away from Julia. After flicking on some of the lights, Julia left the girl sitting in the chair and staring around the café, and she went into the kitchen to see what she could throw together. The only other food she served other than her cakes was toast and pancakes, so she put as many slices of bread into the toaster as she could, and set herself to making scrambled eggs with some of her cake ingredients.

She set the food in front of the girl, who under the light looked like she needed a good wash. The girl looked down at the food and up to Julia before she grabbed a slice of bread, scooped up as much of the eggs as possible and crammed it into her mouth. Despite the knife and fork Julia had placed next to her, she repeated the grabbing and scooping with her dirty fingers and black nails until the plate was empty. It was obvious she hadn't had a decent meal in a while.

"What's your name?" Julia asked when she sat across from the girl.

The cake thief looked to the beaded curtain and Julia knew she was considering her escape, but she turned to Julia and looked down her nose at her, as though deciding she was going to toy with Julia.

"What's it to you, lady?" The girl asked.

"How can we have a conversation if I don't know your name?" She said. "I'm Julia."

Julia held her hand out, even though the girl's fingers were dirty and now covered in butter and egg grease. The girl stared down at their fingers before slapping her hand into them.

"Jessika with a *k*," she said proudly. "Everyone calls me Jessie."

"Well, Jessie," Julia said as she discreetly wiped her fingers on the edge of her dress under the counter. "Do you mind telling me what you're doing in my café, and how you got in here?"

Jessie stared at Julia through narrow slits, as though she was trying to figure out if Julia was a woman to be trusted or not. Julia pushed forward her friendliest smile, and Jessie smiled back a little.

"You should really get a good security system," Jessie said looking around the café. "The back door is too easy to pick. You're lucky it's me and not some of the others."

"Others?"

"Homeless folk," Jessie said, as though it were obvious. "They're not all honest people like me."

"Honest people don't break into people's cafés and steal."

"It's not stealing if it's food," Jessie said. "Not really. I just really like your cakes, lady."

Julia was touched by the compliment.

"How old are you, Jessie?"

"Old enough," she snapped back.

Julia chuckled. She liked Jessie's spirit. It didn't seem that Jessie was going to give Julia that information, so Julia had to guess for herself. She had dark hair and pale skin, which was covered under a layer of grime and dirt. If Julia had to guess, she would have guessed the girl wasn't any older than eighteen.

"Why are you homeless, Jessie?" Julia asked.

"Because I am."

"Don't you have parents?"

"Dead." Jessie said in a matter-of-fact voice. "Died when I was a baby. Been in the system ever since."

"So you ran away from a care home?"

"Foster parents," Jessie said, and Julia sensed a hint of anger deep in her voice. "They're not even looking for me. Been gone for three months."

"I'm sure they are looking for you."

"They're not, lady," Jessie snapped. "They just care

about the money. Got some more of that new lemon cake stuff? It's good."

Julia smiled and nodded. She went into the kitchen and pulled the cake out of her fridge. She cut a slice bigger than she had ever cut before and took it through to Jessie, who was scratching furiously as the back of her thick, unwashed hair.

Jessie devoured the cake in record time, even licking her fingers afterwards. Julia knew she couldn't just sit by and let this child go back out into the world in such a state, so she came up with a plan in that moment.

"How would you like to come to my cottage and shower? I'll even give you a bed for the night, if you want to take it."

Jessie stopped licking her fingers and scowled at Julia. She stared down her nose again, her eyes scrunched up as she thought about what Julia had just offered.

"What's the catch?" Jessie asked, folding her arms across her chest. "There's *always* a catch."

"No catch." Julia held up her hands and sat back at the table. "That's the offer. Take it or leave it."

Jessie wrinkled up her face again, but it seemed the offer of a hot shower and a bed was too much to pass up. She shrugged and picked up her bag, and waited for Julia to lead the way.

After locking up the café, they walked up to Julia's cottage in silence. Jessie jumped at every small sound, making Julia wonder how many nights the poor girl had spent outside alone. Had she slept rough through the long winter?

Jessie spent almost an hour in the shower, emptying Julia's boiler out of every last drop of hot water. She didn't mind. When she walked past the bathroom to see if Jessie was okay, she heard her singing a song Julia recognised off the radio, and it put a smile on her face.

After her shower, she sat in front of the fire, which Julia had got going just for her guest. With a towel tucked under her armpits and another in her hair, she sat shivering in front of the flames. Without the layer of grime on the girl's face, she looked even younger than Julia had first thought.

"Why are you being nice to me?" Jessie asked out of the blue, jolting Julia from reading her Gertrude notes over and over.

"Everybody deserves kindness," Julia said.

Jessie smiled and bowed her head. She bid Julia goodnight and headed off to the guest bedroom Julia had made up for her. If Sue or Dot found out about her houseguest, they would think she was irresponsible for letting a homeless thief into her home. If it had been another person, Julia might have agreed, but she saw Jessie for what she was; a lost girl who enjoyed her cakes and needed an ounce of compassion.

Mowgli curled up in her lap, as she sipped her fresh peppermint and liquorice tea. When she heard loud snoring coming from the guest bedroom, she pulled out her laptop and balanced it on the chair arm, and for the first time since the murder, she researched something other than Gertrude Smith.

CHAPTER 11

When Julia popped her head into the guest bedroom on Wednesday morning, she wasn't surprised to see Jessie had already left. The bed had been perfectly made, and the towels had been neatly folded at the end of the bed. She wondered if she would ever see Jessie again, or if that was the end of her stolen-cake mystery. Now that Julia knew the truth, she wasn't sure if she was happy she had cracked the case.

On the other hand, she was eager to crack the murder case. A good night's sleep had reenergised her efforts to find the killer, and she had woken up with a possible theory about Gertrude's secret child.

Julia pulled the red velvet cake out of the oven and placed it straight onto the cooling rack. Mowgli ran in from the garden, his fur covered in dandelion spores. He shook them off before jumping up onto the counter to pad towards her, adding more muddy paw prints to the already covered divorce papers.

"What do you think, Mowgli?" Julia asked as she

stroked under his chin. "Do you think I'm being silly by not signing this and getting it over with?"

Mowgli purred and bounced up to butt her face. Julia wanted to believe her cat was telling her she should open and sign the papers in her own time, but she knew he was just hungry.

After feeding Mowgli, and icing the red velvet cake with butter roux icing, she hopped into her blue Ford Anglia and set off towards the village. She only got a couple of metres before Emily Burns jumped out into the road waving her arms. Julia slammed her foot on the brakes, and they screeched out, stopping inches away from Emily. She didn't seem to notice how close she had come to being hit because she scurried around to Julia's door and waited for her to roll down her window.

"Have you heard the news?" Emily asked as she pulled her gardening gloves off. "William Smith has been *murdered*!"

"Murdered?" Julia gasped, her hand drifting up to her mouth. "Are you sure?"

"I've had four people call me already this morning to tell me!"

Julia knew the Peridale gossip network could spread false information in a heartbeat, but she doubted something so serious would make its way around the village so quickly if it weren't true.

"I need to go," Julia said, winding her window up before Emily Burns could engage in conversation.

She sped down the winding lane faster than she had ever driven before. As she passed Barker's cottage, she slammed on her brakes again when she saw him pushing his arms into his camel coloured trench coat, a slice of burnt toast clenched between his teeth.

"Is it true?" Julia asked as she jumped out of her car. "That William has been murdered?"

"Good morning to you too, Julia," Barker mumbled through the toast, before tossing it into the grass and wiping the butter and crumbs from his lips with the back of his hand. "Where did you hear that?"

"Is it true, or not?"

Barker unclipped his gate and walked around Julia and towards his car.

"It's true what they say about small villages," Barker muttered under his breath, a smirk already forming on his lips. "I only just found out myself and yet the gossips are already talking. Yes, it's true."

The smirk quickly dropped when he seemed to remember that the gossip in question was about a dead man.

"Was he stabbed, like his mother?" Julia asked.

"That's need-to-know information."

"If somebody found his body, that information will be all around the village in no time, if it isn't already."

"That's just it," Barker said as he ducked into his car. "One of our officers was walking home past the village green when they saw Amy Clark leaning over the body, soaked in William's blood."

Detective Inspector Brown slammed his car door. Julia knocked on the window and he pressed the button and the glass slid down.

"You've arrested Amy Clark for William's murder?" Julia asked.

"Not just his murder, Gertrude's too. You were right to be suspicious of Amy Clark," Barker said as he twisted his key in the ignition. "You've done your part, Julia. Get to your café and carry on with your life. I'm sure you'll have plenty of customers today who all want to use your business as a gossip hub."

With that, the window slid up and Barker sped off down the winding alley, taking the corners dangerously sharp.

The entire drive to the café, Julia was trying to understand why she didn't feel relieved that somebody was in custody for both murders. Amy Clark had been one of her prime suspects. She had the means, the motive, and the opportunity, and she had been caught red handed at the scene of a second murder, but something didn't sit right with Julia. She wondered if it was because it felt like an anti-climax to her investigation. Had she really expected to walk into the station with her little notepad, having figured out the murder? It felt like something that would wipe the smile off Barker's face, but she knew it wasn't realistic.

Julia drove past the village green and her heart sank. A crime scene tent had been erected in the middle of the green, and crime scene tape had been wrapped around it. Men in white body suits came and went as the early risers of the village stood around the edges of the grass, whispering amongst themselves. She spotted her Gran as one of those villagers, but she was so deep in her gossiping that she didn't notice Julia's unique car driving by.

Even though she hated to admit it, Detective Inspector Brown was right. Now that the murderer was behind bars, she could get back to focusing on her café. The double homicide would give Peridale plenty to talk about for months to come, but she knew the village would move on and get back to normal eventually.

Julia pulled up at the opening of the small alley between her café and the post office where she always parked her car, but despite the '*STRICTLY NO PARKING*' sign on the side of her café, there was already a car there. Sighing, Julia killed the engine and jumped out, hoping the driver was still inside. As she walked to the car, she quickly recognised it as William Smith's sports car.

Turning to look at the white tent, she wondered if William had parked his car here before walking to his death. The thought turned her stomach. The police hadn't seemed to notice the victim's car parked in the shadow of her café. She considered calling the station right away, but she couldn't resist a peek of her own through the tinted windows.

Careful not to touch anything, Julia cupped her hands as close to the window as she could, and peered inside. It was a typical man's car, covered in old food wrappers from motorway service stations, and old newspapers. She spotted that week's copy of *The Peridale Post* on the floor of the passenger seat, underneath a sausage roll wrapper. In the cup holder, there were two white coffee cups from a chain coffee shop, which naturally made Julia's hairs stand on end. She didn't know how anybody could drink such over-processed, over-sweetened nonsense. Red lipstick on the rim of one of the cups caught Julia's attention. She thought she recognised the shade as belonging to somebody in particular, but she wasn't sure if she was over thinking things.

Using her black cardigan to stop the transference of her fingerprints, she tested the handle, and to her surprise, the car door was unlocked. It seemed that when William parked, he didn't think he would be away from his car for very long. It upset Julia that he hadn't known he was walking to his death. She hadn't known much about the man, nor had she really liked him, but after seeing him cry about his emotionally unavailable mother, she couldn't help but feel saddened that he had succumbed to the same fate.

Julia ducked into the car to get a closer look at the cup. Without the tint of the windows, she unmistakably knew she had seen that particular orangey shade of red lipstick before, because only one woman had features so striking to pull it off. She also picked up on the distinct whiff of a badly made vanilla latte. Using her cardigan again, Julia ripped off the cardboard lipstick print and pocketed it, vowing to hand it over to the police after she had gone to talk to the owner of the fresh print.

After leaving a hastily written '*back in twenty minutes*' sign in the café window, she jumped back in her car and drove across the village to the art gallery, and when she saw it was closed, she redirected to Rachel Carter's cottage.

CHAPTER 12

R achel Carter's cottage was similar to Julia's, in that it was on its own winding lane leading out of the village. The cottage was traditional on the outside, with its low roof, small windows, and old stone, but the inside showed that Rachel had inherited her mother's tastes for minimal, clean living.

"Julia," Rachel exclaimed when she opened the door. "I was about to call you."

"You were?" Julia said as she stepped into Rachel's cottage. "I can't stay long, I haven't opened the café yet. I just wanted to ask you a question."

"So you're not here about Roxy?" Rachel asked, her eyes narrowing.

"Roxy?"

"She turned up this morning," Rachel said. "She's in my guest bedroom sleeping. She was in quite a state."

Julia followed Rachel down the hallway to the guest bedroom, where Roxy was fast asleep on top of the bed. Her skin was pale and she looked frailer than Julia had ever seen her look before. Julia's initial feelings of relief were quickly replaced with more sinister ones. She had so many questions she wanted to ask Roxy, but she couldn't justify waking her up. She didn't know where she had been since Saturday, but it didn't look like she had been relaxing in a spa.

"I suppose you've heard about William?" Julia asked, already pulling the lipstick printed piece of cardboard out of her pocket.

"Mother called at the crack of dawn," Rachel said as she led Julia through to the sitting room. "Quite sad."

Despite Rachel's declaration of sadness, she didn't appear at all to be sad. Julia would have gone as far as to say that Rachel seemed rather indifferent to the news. She wondered if she had jumped to conclusions about the lipstick. Rachel was wearing the same orange tinted red she had worn to church on Sunday, but Julia knew it wasn't impossible that somebody else in the village would own the same shade, or even somebody outside the village.

"Your lipstick is nice," Julia said.

"Thank you," Rachel said with a smile. "Roxy bought it for my birthday. I wasn't sure if it would suit me, but people seem to like it. It's quite unique."

"Did you know much about William?" Julia asked, quickly redirecting the conversation.

"No more than the usual," Rachel said suspiciously, her eyes tightening. "The flash car, job in the city. Did you come here to ask me about William Smith? If so, it's a wasted journey. What's that you've got in your hand?"

Julia looked down at the lipstick print and suddenly wondered if she had taken herself on a fool's errand. Her gut had told her to ask Rachel about it, so she decided that's just what she was going to do. When her gut told her a cake recipe needed a touch more butter, or a dash of cinnamon, it was rarely wrong.

"I found this in William's car," Julia said, handing the piece of cardboard over. "It is parked in the alley next to my café and the door was open. I recognised it as the shade you wear. Like you said, it's unique."

Rachel accepted the piece of cardboard, her expression barely flickering. She held it up to the light for a moment, before tossing it onto the clutter-free glass coffee table, crossing one leg over the other and resting her hands on her knee.

"It's mine," Rachel said sternly.

Julia was taken aback by the quick admittance.

"Do you know how it came to be in William's car?"

"Of course I know," Rachel said with a small laugh. "Because I was in his car. Listen, Julia, I might as well be honest with you, not that it's *any* of your business. William and I have been seeing each other romantically. It was never serious and it was never going to be. He came into the gallery a couple of months ago to buy a painting, and we went out for coffee after. When he came back to the village, we met up. Ever since his mother's death, his moods have been frantic, and it was becoming exhausting, so I asked him to meet me late last night. He picked me up after the gallery closed and he drove me to one of those awful motorway service stations. Nobody can make vanilla lattes like you can. I broke it off and then he dropped me off, and that was the last I heard from him."

"Have you told any of this to the police?" Julia asked, picking up the torn piece of cardboard. "You were one of the last people to see him alive."

"It's not important," Rachel said. "I don't know why

he hung around in the village. Our relationship was nothing more than a fling. It meant nothing to either of us. He wasn't even bothered when I told him we should call it off. In fact, he agreed it was probably for the best."

Julia thought back to the blubbering mess she had comforted in her café and wondered if that same man would have been okay with any slight rejection. She wasn't so sure.

Before she could ask more questions, Roxy skulked into the sitting room, rubbing her red raw eyes. When she spotted Julia, she immediately burst into tears and wrapped her arms around her neck.

"I've been so worried about you," Julia whispered into Roxy's ear. "Where have you been?"

"I've been so stupid, Julia," Roxy said, sobbing against her shoulder. "So stupid."

When Roxy calmed down, they sat next to each other on the sofa. Once again, Julia was wondering if her friend could be capable of murder, and she was surprised when she couldn't come to a definitive answer.

"Where have you been?" Julia repeated. "Why did you leave the village after Gertrude's murder?"

"Oh, Julia," Roxy sobbed into a tissue. "I had no idea Gertrude had been murdered. I ran away because of – *because of -*,"

Roxy's voice trailed off and she continued to heavily sob.

"I know about the blackmail," Julia said. "I know about Violet too. The *truth* about you and Violet. I've met her and she told me everything."

"She did?" Roxy peaked up through the soaked, almost shredded tissue, glancing awkwardly to Rachel. "That's the reason I left. I couldn't stand the thought of ruining her career as well as my own. That morning before I came to the café, Gertrude came to my home, demanding more money than ever. She wanted one thousand pounds as a final payment, and she would leave me alone. I didn't have *that* kind of money! I teach six-year-old children for a living. She'd emptied my savings and I was desperate. I hadn't been sleeping and I felt completely lost. I thought about asking my mother for the money, but I knew that would mean telling her everything, and I couldn't bring myself to do that. When I left the café, I went home and packed my things. I jumped on a train and I went to stay with an old friend from university, Beth. I've been sleeping on her sofa, trying to figure out my next move. I knew I needed to get as far away from Peridale as I could, that way Gertrude couldn't find me. I thought maybe she would forget about the final payment if I weren't around to remind her. I thought if I left Peridale, Violet would be safe. She would keep her job, and everything would work out okay for her. It's silly really. I wasn't *thinking*. I had barely slept a wink for weeks."

"Why did you come back today?" Julia asked, a hard lump rising in her throat.

Roxy wiped away the last of her tears and she sat up straight. She brushed her considerably faded red hair out of her face and turned to look Julia dead in the eyes. Julia wondered if she was looking into the eyes of a killer.

"Beth was on the computer, reading the news. She saw an appeal from the police asking for information about a murder in Peridale. She called me over and I read all about Gertrude, and how she had been stabbed, and that they were looking for me for questioning. I got on the first train back, and I came straight here. I was going to go straight to the police, to explain that I wasn't even in the village when Gertrude died, but I crashed out."

"So you don't know about William Smith?" Julia asked softly. "Gertrude's son?"

Roxy frowned, her eyes narrowing to slits. She opened and closed her mouth, but she didn't make a sound.

"He's been murdered, Roxy," Rachel said. "Stabbed like his mother."

"What?" Roxy said, shaking her head. "*No, no, no*! I didn't do it, Julia, *I swear*! I know what it looks like, but I didn't do it!"

"It's okay," Julia said. "They've arrested Amy Clark."

"Amy Clark? The church lady?" Roxy asked, looking just as confused. "Why would she do such a thing?"

"Gertrude was blackmailing her too," Julia said. "It's a long story, but you don't have to worry. Just stay here. Don't leave Peridale again. Just *stay* here."

Julia stood up to leave, but Roxy grabbed her hand and dragged her back down to the sofa.

"Don't leave me," Roxy pleaded. "Please."

"I need to," Julia said with a soft smile, prying Roxy's fingers off of her hand. "I'm going to go speak with Amy."

Julia kissed Roxy on the cheek and headed towards the door. Rachel followed her, softly closing the door to the sitting room.

"Are you going to tell Detective Inspector Brown about my relationship with William?" Rachel asked quietly as they hovered near the front door.

"I think it's important he knows, if only to establish a timeline before his death."

Rachel nodded, considering what Julia had said, before

applying a small smile.

"I understand," Rachel said. "It's better he hears it from me. If you're driving to the station, can I ride with you?"

"What about Roxy?"

"She'll be okay," Rachel said, glancing back to the sitting room door. "She'll probably just fall asleep again. By the way, your sister called last night about having her birthday party at the gallery tomorrow night."

And just like that, the conversation switched from murder to birthday parties. When Rachel started talking about balloon colours and bunting, Julia tuned out, and instead turned her thoughts to how she was going to convince Detective Inspector Brown to let her talk to a suspected murderer.

CHAPTER 13

Peridale police station was a tiny place. It usually dealt with petty crime and local squabbles between neighbours, not double homicide cases. From the moment Julia stepped inside and asked to speak to Detective Inspector Brown, she could tell the station's resources were being stretched to capacity.

While she waited for Barker to appear, Rachel told the man behind the desk that she knew about William, and he told her to take a seat. Instead of sitting next to Julia, Rachel sat on the opposite side of the station's waiting room and busied herself with reading a magazine.

"Julia, whatever it is, I don't have time for it," Barker huffed as he marched towards her.

"I need to speak to Amy Clark," Julia said. "It's urgent."

As expected, Barker laughed at her, his head shaking heavily.

"Impossible!" Barker cried. "She's currently being interrogated about these murders. I've got my boss breathing down my neck to solve this double homicide. I thought I was moving to this village for an easier life, but this is more complicated than any case I've worked in my entire policing career."

"I don't think Amy did it," Julia whispered, standing up so that she was level with Barker. "If I can just speak to her, I think she can tell me something that will point us straight to the real murderer."

Barker stared down at her, as though trying to decide whether he should laugh or cry. Julia held her stance and darkened her stare, to let him know she was being deadly serious. Just when he was about to say something, an officer ran towards him and pushed a piece of paper into Barker's hand.

"*Dammit!*" He cried, screwing the paper up in his hands. "Her alibi checks out."

"Alibi?" Julia asked.

"She said she was shopping at a supermarket outside the village. I didn't believe her but the supermarket has confirmed that she was seen on the security cameras and was spotted by several members of staff at the time of the murder. Who travels out of town at five in the morning to go shopping?"

"A woman who doesn't want her fellow villagers to know she doesn't shop locally because she prefers the choice and price of the chain supermarkets," Julia said calmly. "Please Barker, all I need is five minutes with her."

Amy looked equally confused and relieved to see Julia when she walked into the investigation room. Barker sat on a chair in the corner and motioned for Julia to sit across from

Amy, who was clutching a weak looking plastic cup of tea in her shaking hands.

"I didn't do it," Amy whispered as she sipped her tea. "Oh, Julia, I *didn't* do it."

"I know," Julia said soothingly. "I believe you. I think you can help me figure out who did though."

"I don't know anything!" Amy cried as she pulled her powder pink cardigan together. "I was just driving home from CostMart when my headlights caught the poor man's white shirt on the village green. The sun had only just started to rise, and I thought he was a drunk, so I got out and told him what for. When he didn't move, I walked over and that's when I saw the knife, and that it was William. *Oh, Julia! It was awful!* The poor man was still alive. I held him and I screamed out for help, and that's when the officer found me. I know how it looks, but I swear to God, I didn't kill that poor boy."

Julia wanted to tell Amy that her alibi had cleared, but Barker had made her swear not to. She wondered if he still suspected her and that she would confess with a little more pressure. Julia knew they could interrogate her for the next ten years and she would never confess.

"I know Gertrude was blackmailing you about your past," Julia said. "You weren't the only one. She was also blackmailing Imogen and Roxy Carter."

"I knew about Imogen," Amy said, a frown forming in her crinkled brow. "But why Roxy?"

"That's not important right now," Julia said. "You have known Gertrude for a long time, haven't you Amy?"

Amy sighed and nodded.

"Can you believe we used to be friends? When I – *when I* – oh, you know the truth about my past. When I was

released from prison, I knew I wanted a fresh start away from anybody who knew me as Amelia Clarkson. I was born Amy Clark, but that was the name I went by when I -
"

"Robbed banks?" Barker jumped in.

Amy shot him daggers across the room before turning back to Julia.

"Those were the days," Amy said with a soft sigh. "I know it wasn't right, but I haven't felt as alive as I did when we were on a job. It's almost as though it happened to another woman in another life, but those memories are what keep me warm at night. My mother said I got in with a bad crowd, but I was the leader of that crowd. I deserved every year in prison that I served, and I wouldn't change a second of it. I found God when I was in prison. I used to play the organ at the Sunday service. When I moved to Peridale, that's what me and Gertrude bonded over. We were thick as thieves for the longest time, until I found out she was blocking me from ever playing the organ at service. It was Father Wentworth back then, and Gertrude had him wrapped around her little finger. I always thought she had an eye for him, but she would never be unfaithful to her Frank, even if he didn't pay her the same courtesy. She wouldn't let me play the organ just once. Not *one* time. She could *never* share. We went from being friends to enemies and that's how it stayed. When she died, all I could think was '*it's my time to shine*'. I asked God to forgive me for even thinking that, but I knew Gertrude had gotten what was coming to her."

Julia almost felt bad for always viewing Amy Clark as the old lady who liked to wear colours associated with newborn babies. She had seemed like an old lady for as long as Julia had known her, and Julia had never even considered that she had lived a life before that.

"Did Gertrude have any other children after William?"

"Gertrude?" Amy laughed. "*Impossible*! By the time Frank left, she was already too old. Why do you think that?"

"I don't, I was just checking to make sure my theory was correct," Julia said, glancing over to Barker, who was sitting on the edge of his seat staring curiously at her. "What about Frank? Is there any way he got one of the women he was having an affair with pregnant?"

"One of the women?" Amy said with an amused smile. "There was only ever one. Martha Tyler. She was Gertrude's only friend, but Gertrude treated her as badly as she treated Frank. She was younger and prettier than Gertrude. She must have noticed her husband had an eye for another woman. Martha and Frank fell madly in love. Martha confided in me that she was going to run away with Frank and start a new life. I *encouraged* it. I saw how Gertrude treated Frank. Their marriage had been dead for years before the divorce. Separate bedrooms, you know what I'm saying. Gertrude couldn't handle being left for another woman, even if she had caused it herself, so she spread the rumour that Frank had been cheating on her with multiple women. That became the truth. It was easier to admit that he had been unfaithful, rather than admit that he had fallen in love with somebody who appreciated him."

"So Frank and Martha married?" Julia asked.

"That's the strange thing," Amy said, tapping her finger against her chin. "They never made it down the aisle. Before they ran away with each other, Martha called things off and vanished. Frank was devastated but he didn't stay with Gertrude. He left Peridale and he eventually met somebody else. I never met Frank's new wife, but he seemed happy. He would fill me in on details of his new life with his annual Christmas cards, but they trailed off eventually. I didn't see him again until his open casket at his funeral. I feel like I'm the only one left from the old gang."

"And Martha?" Julia urged. "What happened to her?"

"That's another strange thing," Amy said, looking off wistfully into the corner of the room. "About a month ago, Martha turned up in Peridale. She visited me at my cottage and it was as though no time had passed. She even looked the same, just older. Her hair was as black as it had always been. I was always so jealous of it. She told me she was dying, and she wanted to make peace with the village before she left. She died a week later and I went to the funeral, but I didn't recognise anybody there. I asked Gertrude if she wanted to come, but she refused to even say Martha's name, so I went alone. The blackmail started the day after the funeral."

Julia's mind was buzzing, and the theory her dreams had pushed forward had only been strengthened with Amy's new information.

"Well that was useless," Barker said as he walked her back through the station. "Just an old lady reminiscing about the good old days."

"Yes," Julia agreed, biting her tongue. "Will she be released?"

"We've got twenty-four hours to charge her, but with that alibi, it doesn't look like we can. Is there anything else I can do for you, or can I get back to my job?"

"There's one thing, actually," Julia said. "If I wanted to see if a person had been reported missing, how would I go about that?"

"You want to report a missing person?" Barker asked.

"No, I want to see if somebody else has," Julia said as she reached into her handbag to pull out her notepad. "A girl in her late teens."

She ripped off the page where she had written down everything she knew about Jessie.

"Is this connected to the case?" Barker asked as he skim read the information.

"No, but it's important to me," Julia said. "Is there anything you can do?"

Barker folded the small piece of paper and pocketed it, giving Julia his word that he would check the missing persons database and get back to her with what he found.

"By the way, William Smith's car is parked in my space next to the café," Julia said as she left. "You might want to get somebody to move it."

Julia quickly drove home, leaving her car outside her cottage. She hurried down to her café, which had been closed an hour after opening time. A small crowd had gathered outside, and they cheered when Julia pushed through them to unlock the door. She told them a lie about waking up late and quickly fastened her apron around her waist, and got to work.

When her sister appeared during a quiet period after the lunchtime rush to pick up a vanilla slice and a cappuccino, Julia pulled her into the kitchen.

"I need three blank invitations for your birthday party tomorrow night," Julia whispered quickly. "I'm going to need them to figure out who killed Gertrude and William Smith.

CHAPTER 14

After work on Thursday, Julia put a box of cakes, along with a blanket and a note for Jessie in the stone yard behind her café. On Friday morning, she was happy to see that her café hadn't been broken into and the box, blanket and note were gone.

A little after opening, her first customer of the day was Barker Brown. He ordered a shot of espresso and two slices of toast and sat at the table nearest the counter.

"Amy Clark was released last night," Barker said as he tucked into his golden buttery toast. "Back to square one."

"Not quite square one," Julia said, hovering behind the counter and focusing on wiping away something that wasn't there. "Did you find anything about the missing girl?"

"Jessie?" Barker mumbled through a mouthful of toast as he pulled a folded sheet of paper from his pocket. "Or should I say, Jessika Rice. Sixteen years old, been in the care system her whole life. She has a criminal record longer than my arm. Breaking and entering, theft, resisting arrest, breaching the peace, you name it, this girl has done it. She was reported missing after disappearing from her thirteenth foster home, taking two hundred quid with her on the way. She sounds like a piece of work."

Julia took the paper from Barker and scanned over it. She wasn't too bothered about the long list of crimes, but she was happy to see that Jessie had been honest about her name. That told Julia more about the girl, who she couldn't believe was only sixteen, than any files on a computer would.

"Thank you, Detective Inspector," Julia said, slipping the paper into the pocket of her pale yellow dress. "I really appreciate it."

"Friend of yours?"

"Not yet."

Barker tossed back his espresso, licked the butter from his fingers and left. He gave Julia another vague warning of staying out of trouble, to which she waved her hand. Julia wasn't alone for long before Roxy Carter walked into the café, looking much better than the last time Julia had seen her.

"On the house," Julia said as she set a latte and a chocolate brownie in front of her.

Roxy smiled appreciatively and took a bite of the brownie. She closed her eyes and licked the chocolate from her lips, as what looked like intense pleasure washed across her face.

"I thought I would never taste your brownies again," Roxy said. "I don't know what I was thinking running away."

"Have you spoken to the police?"

"The new DI came around this morning," Roxy said. "Brown, or something. Quite handsome. Have you met him?"

"I have," Julia said, wondering if there was anybody in the village who didn't find Barker handsome. "Have you spoken to Violet yet?"

"Only on the phone. I'm going to see her next, but I needed some caffeine for courage. I don't even know where to begin apologising to her, for dragging her into this, and then running away. All it took was a good night's sleep to see how foolish I was."

Julia pulled two of the three envelopes from her pocket and placed them next to Roxy's plate.

"Invitations to Sue's birthday party tonight," Julia said. "One for you, and one for Violet."

"I'm not sure I'm up to it," Roxy said, assessing the invitations with caution. "Rachel told me about it, but I don't know if I can show my face."

"The sooner you do, the sooner people will get the gossiping out of their systems and move on," Julia said. "Besides, it's a good place to debut your new relationship. It's better to do it now while there's plenty of other gossip floating around. People will hardly notice."

Roxy thanked her and pocketed the invitations. Julia hurried back into her kitchen, exhaling a huge sigh of relief that her plan was working. She pulled out her notepad and flipped to the list of notes she had made last night. She crossed off Roxy and Violet's names and circled Imogen's, having already decided she wanted to drop that invitation off herself.

Julia spent the rest of the day rushed off her feet struggling to keep up with the amount of customers coming through the door. News of Sue's party had spread, and the people with invitations were expressing their excitement, and the people without were either asking Julia for permission, or inviting themselves. Julia knew the gallery could hold as many people that were going to turn up, and if her plan worked, the more people in the village to witness things, the better. She didn't want there to be any wiggle room on the facts when it was all over.

Julia pulled up outside of Imogen's white and glass house, and peered through the windows. She could see Imogen sitting in her silk robe, watching television. Julia wondered if word of the party had spread this far out into the village yet.

With her invitation in hand, Julia walked up to the house and pressed the doorbell. When Imogen answered the door, she looked less pleased to see Julia than the last time she had been there.

"I hope this won't take long," Imogen said. "My show is about to start."

"I just wanted to drop this by," Julia said, passing Imogen the envelope. "An invitation to Sue's birthday party tonight. I know it's short notice, but I know she would love to see you there."

"*Tonight?*" Imogen said with a wrinkle of her nose as she brushed her fading red hair out of her face. "I'm not sure I'm very much up to it, Julia. I heard Roxy was back, but she hasn't been in touch. Sometimes I wonder if those girls know the truth about where they came from. They've been growing further and further away from me recently."

"I'm sure they're just busy with everything else that has been going on," Julia said reassuringly. "Roxy told me herself she wanted to see you at the party."

Julia felt bad telling a white lie, but Imogen's face lit

up. She looked down at her robe and sighed heavily, before tossing her head back and nodding.

"Fine!" Imogen cried, waving her hands. "But I need to start getting ready right *this* minute if I'm going to be anywhere near presentable for the party!"

Julia left Imogen to pamper herself, and she went back to her own cottage and did the same. She changed out of her pale yellow dress, which was full of coffee stains and flour, and she slipped into a simple black dress, in her usual flared 1940s style. She spent more time than usual sorting her hair out, creating a victory roll in the front and pinning the curls up in the back. Berry red lipstick, black mascara and rose-tinted blusher completed the look, along with her mother's understated diamond earrings and necklace; the only things Julia had inherited, aside from her baking skills.

After slipping into some uncomfortable black heels that Sue had bought her two years ago, she stepped in front of the floor length mirror, which she usually rushed by in the mornings, her appearance being the least of her worries.

Julia caught herself off guard. She barely recognised the woman staring back at her. Gone was the café owner who loved to bake, and in walked a striking woman. Everybody always said Julia looked like her mother's twin. She had never seen it much herself, until she was looking at herself done up in the mirror. The last time she had put this much effort in to her appearance had been Sue's wedding, almost ten years ago.

Pleased with her efforts, Julia hurried downstairs, fed Mowgli, and headed for the door. On her drive down the winding lane towards the village, she spotted Detective Inspector Brown sitting on a rusty, wrought iron bench under his living room window reading some papers. To her surprise, he looked up when he heard her car's old rattling engine, and he stood up. Julia slowed down and pulled up next to his car.

"Julia, you look -," Barker mumbled as she got out of the car. "New dress?"

"Just something I had in the back of the wardrobe," she said. "Nice tuxedo."

"Your sister invited me to her birthday party tonight, so I thought I would make an effort."

"She did?" Julia said through almost gritted teeth.

"She was quite insistent."

"That's my sister, alright," Julia said, wondering why she hadn't seen her sister's meddling coming. "Reading anything interesting?"

"Case notes," he said regretfully. "Trying to see if there's anything I've missed, but it's all just a blur. Half of me wants to stay in tonight and go over everything, but I know the break will give my brain a chance to recharge, and it will be a good chance to meet some more of the locals."

Julia thought back to the man who had arrived in Peridale almost a week ago, and she couldn't imagine that same man having any interest in meeting the local residents. It seemed more than just Julia's double chocolate fudge cake that had softened his edges. Even with the double homicide case to contest with, she knew not many could resist being sucked into village life.

"Well, I'll see you there," Julia said, turning back to her car. "I promised Sue I would help put the finishing touches to the party."

"Want to go together?" Barker asked suddenly. "If I stay here, I'll only keep reading the same sentence I've been reading for the past twenty minutes, plus, knotting balloons is a special talent. We'll take my car. I don't trust the look of yours."

"There's nothing wrong with my Ford Anglia!" Julia said, stroking the bonnet. "She's vintage."

"She's *something*."

Barker pulled his keys out of his pocket and unlocked his car. Julia picked up a pile of paperwork on top of the seat and tossed it into the back. As she did, the file flipped open, and her eyes honed in on the police report made by Rachel Carter yesterday at the station. Something in the first sentence caught her eye, so she grabbed it and screwed it up into her fist before Barker saw.

With the paper clenched tightly in her fist, they drove to the gallery, and Barker's side-glances to her didn't go unnoticed. She was glad she was wearing makeup, or he might have noticed her face burning up as she concealed a smile.

CHAPTER 15

I t turned out Julia and Barker weren't needed at all to help get things ready for the party. When they walked into the gallery, everything was as it should be. Sue and her husband, Neil, were sipping champagne, along with Dot. They all turned and spotted Julia at the same time, and she detected their eyes widening when they noticed who she was accompanied by.

"This place looks amazing," Julia said as she looked around at the bunting and balloons decorating the white spaces between the art. "You've done a really lovely job."

"I took the day off work," Sue said as she leaned in for a kiss. "You look amazing, Julia."

"Doesn't Julia look beautiful, Detective Inspector?" Dot asked, casting her champagne flute in Julia's direction.

Julia wanted the ground to swallow her up, and she could feel Barker wishing the same. Her Gran was many things, but subtle wasn't one of them.

"She does," Barker agreed, scratching at the side of his head. "Any more of that champagne?"

"This way, mate," Neil said, wrapping his arm around Barker's shoulders. "You like football?"

Neil and Barker walked off towards the food and drink table, leaving Julia with her sister and Gran. She fixed her attention on an abstract painting of what she thought was St. Peter's Church from the village, hoping they wouldn't interrogate her.

"Tell me *everything!*" Sue squealed. "I knew you two would hit it off! I *knew* it!"

"Thanks for the heads up on his invite," Julia whispered. "And there's *nothing* to tell. I was driving past his cottage and he suggested we take the same car. I thought you would need an extra pair of hands to help with the decorations."

Sue rolled her eyes, clearly not believing Julia. Even Julia wasn't sure if she believed herself. She glanced over to Barker, and the flutter in her stomach was too strong to be ignored.

"I never thought he could look more handsome, but that tuxedo has proved me wrong," Dot whispered, before sipping her champagne.

"I hadn't noticed," Julia said, hearing the lie in her voice. "How long before people arrive?"

"About fifteen minutes?" Sue said. "Gran, why don't you go and grab Julia some champagne?"

Dot tutted as she turned on her heels to shuffle off towards the men. Rachel appeared from her office with a phone crammed against her ear. She waved and smiled to Julia as she headed for the front door.

"So," Sue urged. "Did you get your invitations out?"

"I did."

"And you know who the murderer is?"

"I think so."

"You only *think* so?" Sue whispered desperately. "I gave you permission to ruin my birthday party on the one condition that you were sure."

"I found something earlier," Julia said, pulling the screwed up piece of paper from her handbag, making sure Barker wasn't looking over. "A police report Rachel Carter filed about William Smith. She told me they were having a secret affair, so I told her to tell the police. I don't even think she realises it, but she's pointed me to the murderer in the first line of her statement."

Julia smoothed the paper out against her dress and handed it to her sister. She read over the first couple of lines, her brow furrowing.

"*But -,*"

"Yes," Julia jumped in.

"So that means -,"

"It does."

"Are you going to -,"

"Tell Detective Inspector Brown?" Julia took back the paper and folded it up as small as it would go before stuffing it back into her bag. "Why ruin the fun? Either way, he'll have his murderer in jail and I -,"

"Will have proven Barker wrong," Sue jumped in, finishing Julia's sentence for her. "If you didn't like him, you wouldn't care so much about proving yourself."

"I need you to do something for me later on."

"Is it legal?" Sue asked suspiciously. "You've been getting up to all sorts recently."

Julia told her what she wanted her to do, but before she even agreed to helping with Julia's plan, the first guests arrived and Sue rushed off to greet them. Dot returned with champagne for Julia, and a small plate of buffet food that she had taken from under the foil covered plates.

"Tonight's going to be a long night," Dot mumbled through a sausage roll. "You know how I hate parties."

"I'm sure tonight will be a night to remember, Gran," Julia said softly before sipping her champagne. "You'll see."

An hour into the party and Julia was worried her invitations hadn't worked. Just when she was about to call Roxy to check up on her, she walked in hand-in-hand with Violet, with Imogen trailing behind. The befuddled look on Imogen's face told Julia that Roxy had told her the true nature of her relationship with Violet. People immediately started to stare and whisper, but neither Roxy nor Violet seemed affected.

"You made it," Julia said as she walked across to them. "You all look beautiful."

"Blimey, Julia!" Roxy cried. "I almost didn't recognise you."

Roxy was wearing a floor length, red satin dress, which beautifully complimented what looked like freshly dyed red hair. Imogen was wearing a body-hugging white wrap dress, which cut off just above the knee. Her faded hair had been curled and pinned back, and she had a white shawl wrapped around her arms. Violet was the one who had undergone the most dramatic transformation. When Julia had seen her under the black hood, she had known she was beautiful, but she hadn't realised how beautiful she really was. Violet's icy blonde hair was slicked back off her face, giving her striking features room to shine. She had opted for a floor-length glittering silver dress, which was low-cut in the front, and had a slit running from the bottom of her right foot, all the way up to the hip. She looked as though she had been pulled from the pages of a high fashion magazine, and Julia doubted Peridale had ever seen anything like it.

"It's nice to see you again, Julia," Violet said, her accent as thick as Julia remembered. "You look very beautiful."

"Nothing compared to you," Julia said, blushing under her makeup. "But thank you."

"Where are the drinks?" Imogen muttered, then headed off to the table at the back before Julia had a chance to answer.

"She's still processing it," Roxy said when they were alone. "I think she's mourning the loss of ever having any grandchildren. What with Rachel turning thirty-nine and still being single, I think she had her hopes pinned on me finding a nice man, and instead -,"

"You found me," Violet beamed, kissing Roxy on the cheek. "We will give her grandchildren, don't you worry about that."

Julia left them alone. She was happy for them, but their new love reminded her of how things had been when she had first met Jerrad. He had promised her their love would last a lifetime, and that he would give her everything she wanted, including children. Julia tossed back her champagne, wondering why she had believed a man like him.

"Good party," Barker said when they met at the buffet. "I was right about the night off reenergising me. I feel ready to come at this case with fresh eyes tomorrow."

"I'm sure you'll find the murderer in no time," Julia said as she tossed a strawberry into her mouth.

"Is that Amy Clark?" Barker whispered, squinting into

the crowd. "That woman has some nerve."

Julia turned to see Amy Clark making her way through the crowd, which was parting like the Red Sea around her. She shuffled forward sheepishly, and when she caught Julia's eye, she headed straight for her. It didn't matter that Amy Clark had been released, news of her arrest would have travelled around the town, and an arrest was as good as guilty in most people's eyes.

"I knew I shouldn't have come," Amy whispered as she brushed down the front of her pink and blue dress. "I should go."

"Life is too short to miss out on parties," Julia said as she handed a glass of champagne to Amy. "Enjoy yourself. People will get bored soon."

"Are you sure about that?" Amy said with a nervous laugh. "I'm sure people will know about my past soon, and then I'll be chased out of the village."

Julia couldn't imagine anybody chasing a lady in her eighties out of the village, but she knew how scary the thought of being the subject of the villagers' gossip could be. She had experienced that first hand.

"The only people who know about that are you, me, and Detective Inspector Brown, and we're not going to tell anybody, are we?" Julia said, staring up at Barker with a raised eyebrow, who stared down at her confused, so she gave him a swift and sharp kick in the shin with her heel.

"No, we won't," Barker said. "You deserve a second chance."

Amy thanked them both and joined the line of people queuing up at the buffet. Julia wasn't very hungry, so she ditched the plate of food she had gathered up. Her and Barker walked out to the garden behind the gallery.

Twinkling lanterns shone brightly against the ebony sky, sending a warm glow over the beautiful flowers. They sat on a bench at the bottom of the garden, enjoying the silence for a moment, listening to the chatter and the music as it floated out from the gallery.

"I misjudged this village," Barker said after ditching his food. "It's not what I had expected."

"Why did you come here in the first place?" Julia asked.

"I was bored of the city," Barker said with a soft smile. "Bored of the same crimes. I wanted a change of pace. When the idea of transferring to a small village came up, I took it with both hands."

"And you got two murders in your first week."

"What a welcome that was," Barker chuckled softly. "It's unlike any place I've ever been before. Despite everything that's happened, the people here are full of so much life. My last birthday, four people turned up to my party, and they were all from work. Everybody in the village has come to celebrate with your sister."

"I think most of them have come to see if there's any news about the murders," Julia said. "If gossiping was an Olympic sport, Peridale would take gold."

"I've noticed that. Makes my job difficult. Half of the village know things before I do."

Julia thought about all of the things she knew that she still hadn't told Barker. For a moment, she felt guilty for withholding the information, but she knew if she revealed everything she had figured out to the Detective Inspector, he might dismiss some parts as trivial and focus on the wrong thing. If everything went to plan, all of the dirty laundry would be out in the open before the night was over.

"I think you'll do just fine here, Detective Inspector," Julia said with a smile. "It can take a while to adjust from the city, but you'll be part of the furniture in no time."

"You've lived in a city?"

"I spent twelve years of my life away from this village," Julia said heavily. "Worst decision of my life."

"Well, I'm glad you're here now," Barker said.

Julia turned to look at him, and their eyes locked, as did their smiles. If it hadn't been for the look in Barker's eyes, she might have taken his comments as throwaway. She didn't notice she was leaning in to kiss him until her eyes closed. Through her lids, she felt the Detective Inspector doing the same, but before their lips met, a sneeze cracked through the silence like a whip.

Julia pulled away as quickly as she had leaned in, to see her Gran tiptoeing across the grass.

"Hay fever," Dot mumbled apologetically.

"I should be -," Barker whispered.

"We were just -," Julia added.

Dot smirked and turned on her heels. She shuffled back into the gallery, chattering to herself, no doubt exclaiming what a good couple they would make. Julia turned to Barker, sure that her makeup wasn't hiding her embarrassment this time. Neither of them spoke, instead choosing to awkwardly laugh. They headed back into the gallery in silence and quickly split up.

Julia caught Rachel talking with her mother, so she moved in closer and joined their conversation.

"Have you seen Roxy?" Imogen asked. "I feel like I've been saying that a lot recently. I don't know what's gotten into that girl."

"I haven't," Julia said. "Maybe her and Violet have

gone out for some air?"

Imogen pursed her lips at the mention of Violet's name, which she followed up with a heavy roll of her eyes. She walked away, leaving Julia and Rachel alone.

"She'll get over it eventually," Rachel said. "She's from a different generation."

"Love is love," Julia said. "They look more in love than I ever was with my husband. Have you ever been in love, Rachel?"

"Do you mean with William?" Rachel chuckled. "It wasn't love, it was just a casual thing."

Before Julia could delve more into Rachel's relationship with William Smith, Sue hurried over, visibly out of breath.

"Something's happened in the other room," Sue panted through short breaths. "I think you need to come and see this, Rachel."

Rachel looked from Sue to Julia, clearly panicked. They both followed Sue into the other gallery, which was separated by a door labelled '*closed for the party*'. From her visit to the gallery, Julia knew the second room in the gallery contained some of the more valuable works Rachel had on display. The second they walked in, it was apparent what had happened, even though the lights were dimmed to almost darkness. The biggest painting in the centre of the main wall had been slashed right down the middle.

"The Georgia O'Keefe!" Rachel cried, clutching her hand over her mouth. "Who could have done this?"

Julia looked desperately to her sister, who shrugged.

"I came in here to make a phone call away from the noise and I just found it like this," Sue said quietly. "I'm so sorry, Rachel. Was it valuable?"

"Priceless," Rachel whispered, her voice choking. "I

studied Georgia O'Keefe at university, and this was the crown jewel in my collection."

Julia turned her head to look at the two halves of the slashed painting. She knew Georgia O'Keefe painted flowers, but she was struggling to see the beauty in the art. She was more accustomed to seeing the beauty in her baking.

"I'm calling the police," Rachel said as she reached into her bag to pull out her phone. "This isn't acceptable. This is worse than murder!"

Julia eyed to Sue to leave them alone, so Sue hurried back to the door, her heels clicking on the wood flooring. When they were alone, Rachel hugged the phone to her chest as she ran her fingers along the frayed edge of the canvas.

"It's not even a clean cut," she whispered. "It's beyond repair."

"Are you sure?"

"I'm positive," Rachel said. "I don't understand why somebody would do this."

Julia glanced around the empty gallery as she reached into her pocket for the paper. She pulled it out and unfolded it, her hands shaking. Rachel turned around and looked down at the paper in Julia's hands, but she was far enough away that she wouldn't be able to read it in the low light.

"When you made your statement to the police about your relationship with William did you tell them everything you told me?" Julia asked, keeping her voice low so the rest of the party wouldn't hear them.

"Excuse me?" Rachel said, her face screwing up. "What does that have to do with my painting being ruined?"

"Nothing," Julia said, passing the paper over to Rachel. "I just didn't expect Sue to go to such extremes when I asked her to come up with a reason to get you in this room so that I could follow you in."

Rachel looked at Julia and then down at the paper. She read through it expressionless, before tossing it. Julia watched the paper flutter down to the floor, the slither of moonlight shining in through the tall windows casting it's shadows into the darkest corners of the room. It hit the floor weightlessly, but Julia was sure she heard it crack through the hefty silence.

"You just can't help yourself, can you Julia?" Rachel's features suddenly darkened as she reached into her handbag to pull out something shiny and silver. "You should have stuck to baking."

Julia stared down at the knife and was surprised by the sudden lack of fear. She was so overwhelmed with the amazement that her theory had been correct, it blinded every other basic human emotion, but she suspected looking into the eyes of a killer would do that to a person.

"How long have you known you were adopted?" Julia asked calmly, not taking her eyes away from the shimmering blade, which seemed to be growing with every second. "Is it the same time you found out that Gertrude's ex-husband, Frank, was your real father, and that William was your half-brother?"

Rachel slowly clapped her hands together, the knife blurring from side to side. She dropped her hand and let out a low, chilling laugh.

"You figured out *all* of that from my false police report?" Rachel said, glancing down to the report she had made, claiming that somebody had stolen her mobile phone. "Aren't you a clever one, Julia South? I always thought you were wasted in that café."

Julia spun around as Rachel circled her, the knife swaying from side to side. Taking a moment to compose her thoughts, Julia blinked slowly before taking a step back from Rachel.

"Amy Clark told me Martha Tyler came to Peridale to find peace with the village she once called home, but I think she came to find somebody she had said goodbye to thirty-nine years ago. Martha had been having an affair with Frank Smith, and I don't doubt that she loved him, but I think Gertrude discovered that Martha was pregnant before Frank did, and she scared Martha away. Of course, I don't know for certain that Martha was pregnant, but it's the only thing that makes sense to me, the only thing strong enough to tear people apart and force them into making bad decisions. I suspect Gertrude knew something life changing about Martha, and she used it against her to drive her husband's pregnant mistress out of the village, in hopes of saving her marriage. Of course, it didn't work, and Frank married somebody else, leaving Martha to raise a baby on her own. Maybe it was too much for her to be a single parent, or maybe she couldn't stomach the thought of raising Frank's baby on her own, so she gave the baby up for adoption. That baby was you. I figured that out when Amy Clark mentioned Martha's black hair, I was just trying to figure out if you were really capable of murder. Just as Imogen and Paul Carter were looking to adopt their first child, you were brought back to Peridale. How ironic that Gertrude wanted to get rid of you, but you came back here. I would say it was a cruel twist of fate. I doubt Gertrude figured out who you were until Martha tracked you down and told you her secret before she died. I suppose it came as a shock to you that you were adopted, and you were looking for somebody to blame, and Gertrude was that woman."

"She denied me ever knowing my real parents!" Rachel cried, tears welling up in her eyes. "My real mother and father could have been a part of my life if it wasn't for that witch!"

"After you found out the truth about your birth, you went to Gertrude and I think you blackmailed her."

"I wanted to make her pay!" Rachel said with a dark laugh. "She *deserved* to *suffer!*"

"Little did you know, in order for Gertrude to pay you, she used the secrets of your own family to blackmail them in return. She was lining your pockets with money from your sister and mother, but I suspect you didn't know that at first. Of course, you were clever enough to keep all of the blackmail out of the banks, so nothing would ever be traced back to you."

"It wasn't until she wrote that nasty review of my gallery in *The Peridale Post* that I found out. She thought she could ruin my business and run me out of town, but it only made me angrier. I went to her cottage, saw the pictures of Roxy and Violet, and she told me about the blackmail. I found out the truth when I met Martha, so when I found out she was also blackmailing Imogen I put the pieces together, so I went to confront her. She said she was going to disinherit William and leave everything to me. She said she felt guilty about what she had done. *Ha!* I didn't believe her. I spent a little time with my real mother, but it was too late. It wasn't enough to make up for those lost thirty-nine years. She thought I would blame her, but I didn't. There was only *one* woman I blamed. I panicked, so

I picked up a knife and I drove it into her back. It was the only thing I could do! Her money didn't make up for what she had done to me. I always knew I didn't fit in, but I found out far too late in life to do anything about it. She robbed me of a life I should have had! Gertrude told Martha that Frank knew about the pregnancy, and that he didn't want anything to do with the baby. She believed her and left. Frank never found out about me because of Gertrude."

"You never had a secret affair with William," Julia said. "Instead, you killed your half-brother."

"He was going to go to the police!" Rachel cried, shaking the knife in Julia's face. "He called the lawyers and his mother had been stupid enough to give them my name over the phone! They wouldn't tell the police, but because William was the heir to Gertrude's estate, they revealed the nature of the phone call. When he confronted me, he suspected that I had some information on his mother. I was blackmailing her, and that's why she was blackmailing people herself. He was so furious, so I told him the truth. At first, he was happy to find out he had a half-sister. He told me he had always resented being an only child. Resented that his mother had waited so late in life to have him, and yet here I was the whole time. William told me his dad, Frank, had always wanted a daughter too. What good was that information to me? It was all *too* late. His happiness didn't last long when he figured out what I had done. He wouldn't listen. He got out of the car and started walking to the police station, so I did what I *had* to do."

"You murdered your half-brother in the middle of the village green and you let Amy Clark take the blame."

"Nobody saw me!" Rachel said, almost pleased with

herself. "And Roxy was at home to be my alibi. I was there when she arrived and fell asleep, and if the police ever suspected me, she'd tell them I was there when she woke up. Everything fell into place perfectly. Even you didn't notice it was me when you saw me at Gertrude's house! You almost caught me, so I smashed the window and made a run for it. I went to Roxy's house instead, and I saw that she had gone. By then, I knew the truth about Roxy's lover, but I knew nobody else did, so if she had run away, it would make her look guilty."

Julia was speechless. She stared at Rachel, a woman she had known since childhood, but she didn't recognise her. She had always been a little distant and cold, but she had never suspected she would be capable of murder, or willing to let her own sister take the blame.

"You're sick," Julia said.

"Oh, shut up, Julia!" Rachel yelled, raising the knife above her head. "You always were a little know-it-all!"

She struck the knife down, but Julia grabbed Rachel's wrist. They wrestled for what felt like an age, and the blade floated dangerously close to Julia's face. She expected to see her life flash before her eyes, but she didn't. Instead, she felt an intense feeling of survival she had not experienced before. She was suddenly reminded of all the things she had to live for, and she wanted to live for them. She needed to live.

"You would have let them arrest me?" Roxy's voice floated around the corner of the gallery, her lipstick smudged and her hair messy. "Rachel, I can't believe what you've done."

Rachel turned and watched Roxy and Violet walk towards them from the shadows, just long enough for Julia to knock the knife out of Rachel's hand with her handbag. She turned to Julia, but Julia wasn't going to take any chances. With strength she didn't know she possessed, she pushed Rachel into the wall and brought the slashed Georgia O'Keefe painting down around her body.

"Get Detective Inspector Brown!" Julia told Violet as she kicked the knife away. "*Hurry!*"

CHAPTER 16

The entire party crowded outside the gallery and watched as Detective Inspector Brown escort Rachel towards the flashing lights of the police car. Julia was surprised by how she wasn't putting up a fight.

Julia couldn't begin to imagine what it would feel like finding out you were adopted after thinking you knew where you came from for thirty-nine years. She could imagine how resentful Rachel had felt towards the woman whose meddling had caused her to live a lie, but she couldn't imagine that feeling ever driving her to murder. She couldn't imagine Gertrude knowing she had signed her own death certificate decades ago with her desperate attempts at saving her broken marriage.

"I'm sorry you had to find out like this," Julia whispered to Roxy. "If I'd have known you were there -,"

"If I wasn't there she would have tried to kill you," Roxy said, wrapping her fingers around Julia's. "I had missed Violet so much, so we broke away from the party to

– you know. I would like to say that I always knew I was adopted deep down, but I didn't. My mother and father are the people who raised me, not two strangers who created me. I don't know why Rachel couldn't see that. How did you figure out it was Rachel, and not me?"

"Rachel told me that you told her about Violet when you went to visit her the morning of the murder, but I figured out that you probably didn't visit her at all."

"I didn't," Roxy said. "How did you know that?"

"When I went to Rachel's cottage to ask her about the lipstick, you talked about the blackmail and running away, but you never once mentioned that Violet was your lover. You were being very conscious about your words, so I suspected that Rachel had found out about the relationship from another source, and there was only one woman in the village who knew."

"Gertrude!"

"Exactly."

"I don't know what to say," Roxy said with a heavy sigh. "My own sister would have watched me go to prison."

"I would never have let it get to that," Julia whispered, pulling Roxy into a hug. "I figured this out to stop that from happening."

When Roxy finally let go, she thanked Julia and walked towards her mother, who was sobbing on the edge of the road, while being comforted by Violet. Despite everything, Julia knew they were going to be okay.

"How did you piece it together, Julia?" Amy Clark asked loudly enough to grab the attention of the watching crowd, who all turned their attention from the police car to Julia.

"It all came down to the lipstick," Julia said. "I saw a

lipstick stain on a coffee cup in William Smith's car and I knew the unique shade belonged to Rachel. Gertrude and Frank divorced in 1978, so when I suspected Martha Tyler had a secret baby, and that Martha had been in Peridale a month ago, I knew the murderer had to be that baby, and had to be somebody who was thirty-nine. Looking back, Rachel was the only person I spoke to who never denied killing Gertrude or William."

"But why would she do such a horrific thing?" Dot asked as she glared at the police car as it drove away.

"She was just a lost girl who didn't feel like she fit in," Julia said. "Gertrude symbolised that pain, and William just got in the way."

An hour later, Julia was standing behind her counter in the café with most of the village crammed into the tiny space. Her till was filled with what she suspected to be record takings, and the place was bursting with more life than the busiest Saturday at the height of summer. She felt like Gertrude's two-star review was already a distant memory.

The bell above the door rang out and another person wrestled their way through the thick crowd to the counter. Julia smiled when she saw it was Detective Inspector Brown.

"Can I have a word?" He said, his expression stern.

Julia took him through the beaded curtain to the kitchen, and she leaned against the steel counter in the middle.

"Next time you have vital information about a murder case, I'd appreciate it if you told me before you approach the suspect," Barker said, his tone firm, but his eyes and smile soft. "You could have gotten yourself killed."

"I was fine."

"I'm being serious, Julia," he said, shaking his head as he paced in front of her. "When I found out she had a knife, my heart sank. She wouldn't have hesitated to make it a third murder."

Julia knew he was right, but she was touched that he seemed to care more about her wellbeing than she did. In that moment, she had been running on adrenaline, but it had taken multiple sugary teas in the café to calm her nerves.

"How is she doing?" Julia asked.

"She's currently confessing to everything," Barker said, and he stopped pacing and leaned against the counter next to her. "How were you so certain it was her? Rachel Carter wasn't even on my radar! I was trying to find an accomplice of Amy Clark. I was *so sure* she had something to do with it."

"I wasn't completely certain until I approached her, but this was the final nail in the coffin," Julia said as he pulled Rachel's police report from her dress. "I stole this from your car. When I came to speak to Amy Clark yesterday, Rachel came with me because she told me she had been having a secret affair with William Smith. I found evidence that she had been in his car, and she claimed to have broken things off hours before he was murdered. When I saw the police report in that file on your passenger seat, and I saw that she had reported a stolen mobile phone, I knew she had lied to me. On the surface, she seemed like the only person without a motive, but Amy Clark's story allowed me to piece history together to figure out what happened in the present. You heard the same information as I did in that interview, but sometimes it takes a close ear to the ground and a finger on the pulse of the village to really *listen* to the information you're being told."

Barker turned to her and for a moment he looked angry, but his expression softened and he smiled, their eyes locking like they had in the gallery's garden.

"I really underestimated you, Julia," Barker said. "You did something I couldn't do myself. You ignored the obvious and you listened to people's stories."

Hearing what Julia had wanted to hear all along didn't fill her with the same happiness she had expected. She realised she hadn't just been trying to prove Barker wrong about her, but to prove him wrong about the village she loved so much. For that, she felt she had succeeded.

"Did you just come here to tell me off?" Julia said, glancing back through the curtain at the busy café.

"Actually, there was something else," Barker said, sucking the air through his teeth. "How would you like to grab a coffee sometime?"

"Coffee?" Julia asked. "I own a café."

Barker dropped his head and laughed softly.

"I'm trying to ask you out on a date, Julia," he said quietly, his cheeks flushing.

"Oh, I know," Julia said.

"So?"

"I'll think about it."

"You'll think about it?" Barker said, arching a brow. "Is that all I get?"

"Yes," Julia said, nodding sternly. "I'll think about it."

Barker pushed the air out of his lungs and shook his head once more. He smiled at Julia and nodded, before turning on his heels and walking back through the beaded curtains. When she was alone, Julia allowed herself a moment to let the grin spread from ear to ear. She intended to go on that date with Detective Inspector Brown, she just wanted to let it eat away at him for a couple of days, just like it had with Julia when they first met.

"I love a happy ending," said Sue when the café finally closed just a little after midnight. "Promise me you won't get involved in another murder case?"

"I'll try not to."

"That's not the same as a promise."

"None of us know what's around the corner," Julia said. "Although Barker asked me out on a date."

"And you said yes?" Sue gasped, clutching her hand over her mouth. "I *knew* he liked you!"

Julia thought back to the almost kiss at the gallery earlier in the night, and she was surprised her Gran hadn't already told Sue. Perhaps that was one piece of gossip she would keep to herself until Julia was ready.

"I didn't say yes," Julia said. "But I will."

"That's still a happy ending in my eyes," Sue said as she leaned in to kiss Julia on the cheek. "I'm going to go home and snuggle up to my husband and let him know he's the luckiest man in the world to have somebody like me, and not somebody like Rachel Carter as his wife. Goodnight, love."

"Goodnight," Julia said.

"Oh, and thank you for not telling the police I was the one who slashed the painting," Sue said as she walked through the beaded curtain. "I saw that awful flower and I was sure it was worthless."

She watched her sister walk through the messy café, and for the first time since Julia had opened the café, she was going to leave the clearing away for the morning because there was something else she needed to do for things to truly be a happy ending.

Julia almost fell asleep in a chair in the dark corner of her stone yard behind her cafe, so when she saw the shadowy figure creeping through the night, she bolted upright and forced herself to wake up.

"Hello again, Jessie," Julia said.

Jessie sprung up from picking up the box of cakes Julia had left as bait. She glanced from the gate to Julia, but she didn't run. Julia opened the back door of her café and invited Jessie into the light.

After pulling down her hood and letting her dark hair fall forward, and eating an entire victoria sponge, Jessie sat back in her chair and looked around the café, a lot more at peace than she had seemed before.

"I have an offer to make you," Julia said. "It's a little different from the last one."

"I'm listening," Jessie said, staring down her nose the way she did.

Julia pulled out the chair across from Jessie and sat down. When she put her hands on the table and locked them together to stop them from shaking, she realised she was more nervous now than she had been hours earlier staring at Rachel's glittering blade.

"The room you stayed in at my cottage," Julia said, looking Jessie directly in the eyes. "It's of no use to me and I rarely have guests. How would you like to rent it?"

Jessie arched a brow and immediately started laughing. She shook her head and leaned across the table at Julia, her dark hair falling over her hazel eyes.

"Don't you remember, lady? I'm homeless. I don't have money."

"I know," Julia said, nodding carefully. "That's why I'm offering you a job here, in my café. I'll pay you a fair wage, and I won't charge much for the room, just enough for the upkeep. We'll have to contact social services, but I'm sure we can come to some sort of arrangement."

Jessie stared at Julia, and she wasn't sure if she was going to burst out laughing again, or make a run straight for the door; she did neither. Instead, she stared down her nose directly at Julia for the longest time.

"You mean – *like* – foster me?" Jessie said.

"If that's what it takes, and if it's okay with social services, then yes."

Julia had come up with this plan the night Jessie had slept in her guest bedroom, she just hadn't been sure she wanted to go through with it until tonight. Roxy's words had made her see that family is who you choose to be with, not who you are forced to. Jessie hadn't found a family, and Julia hadn't had the children she thought she would, but she could see the good in Jessie, even if Jessie couldn't.

"I'm not good," Jessie said. "I've done stuff."

"I know," Julia said, pulling out the piece of paper Barker had given her earlier that day. "All of this, it will need to end. That is my only condition. You treat me with respect, and you get it right back. What do you say?"

Jessie didn't say anything. She jumped out of her chair and wrapped her arms around Julia's neck. It took Julia a moment to realise what was happening, but when she did, she wrapped her arms around Jessie and hugged the girl she doubted had been hugged for a long time.

"Thanks, lady," Jessie whispered.

"Is that a deal?"

Jessie pulled away, tear streaks marking her dirty cheeks. She nodded furiously and held her hand out. Julia accepted it, and she was surprised by the strength of Jessie's grip.

Julia didn't know what the future held, but for the first time since arriving back in Peridale, she didn't feel like she had a weight looming over her. She knew that when she got home, the first thing she would do was face reality and open her divorce papers.

Julia pulled the '*HELP WANTED*' sign out of the window and looked down at it. She glanced over to Jessie, who was tucking into more cake. It was going to take a lot of hard work to get Jessie ready for working in the café, but if she enjoyed baking cakes as much as she enjoyed eating them, Julia knew they would be just fine.

"Come on, Jessie," Julia said as she opened the door. "Let's go home."

LEMONADE
AND LIES
BOOK 2

CHAPTER I

J ulia awoke to the sound of banging again. She stared at her bedroom ceiling, darkness suffocating her vision. She tossed and turned, clutching at her eyes, forgetting she was wearing an eye mask. The first hints of the oncoming sunrise were slipping through the darkness. It was earlier in the morning than she would like to acknowledge.

Yanking off her eye mask, she looked at the dark beams in her small cottage's low ceiling. Another low thud echoed through the darkness to remind her why she had awoken.

Julia tossed back her satin duvet and slid her feet into the warm sheepskin slippers her gran had given to her for Christmas. She stood up, her knees creaking more with each day. A quick glance in the mirror at her pale pink nightie and her wild curly hair reminded her that she was only thirty-seven. She wouldn't have to start worrying about her knees giving way for another couple of years, or so she hoped. She thought of her octogenarian gran, who was still darting around the village like a woman in her twenties.

She hurried along the hallway, a chill brushing against her exposed legs. Her grey Maine Coon, Mowgli, was softly purring in a fluffy ball on the doormat, unaware of the night-time disturbance.

Julia stopped outside of her guest bedroom, which was currently being occupied by her new sixteen-year-old lodger, Jessika, who went by the name Jessie. Julia had never expected to take a young girl into her home, but she also hadn't expected to find that same girl breaking into her café and stealing cakes on a regular basis. Julia could have taken the homeless girl to the police, but she decided to do the kinder thing. She gave the girl a home, and a job helping out in Julia's café.

Hovering her knuckles over the wood, she almost knocked, but she decided against waking Jessie. She knew how dangerous that could be for a sleepwalker.

Julia pried open Jessie's bedroom door as silently as she could, which wasn't easy in the centuries old cottage. She felt the entire timber frame scream out, a piercing creak cracking like a whip through the silence. In the corner of her eye, Mowgli looked up from his slumber, before tucking his nose back under his paw.

Jessie had been living with Julia for nearly a month but the sleepwalking was new. This was the fourth time it had woken Julia. She had felt useless to help her young lodger at first, but after a quick internet search, she was more equipped to deal with the situation.

She made out the shadow of Jessie through the dark as she delicately and rhythmically pounded her head against her wardrobe door. Her long, dark hair hung over her face, contrasting against her stark white nightie, making her look like she had crawled out of the screen of a horror film. Julia wasn't scared; she was just an ordinary girl after all.

Julia did the only thing she could do. She placed her hand between Jessie's forehead and the wood, softening the blow. As though she could consciously sense the change, the movement stopped, but she didn't wake. Without saying a word, Julia guided Jessie back to her bed, which she climbed back into with ease. It hadn't been as simple the night before.

After tucking Jessie back in, Julia gazed down at the girl, wondering how she had survived living on the streets for so long. Jessie hadn't talked much about it, so Julia hadn't asked, but it didn't mean she wasn't curious.

Julia turned and spotted a book on Jessie's nightstand. The cover and title made her smile. She picked up '*Baking For Beginners*' and flicked to the front page. It seemed that Jessie had borrowed it from Peridale's tiny library without Julia's knowledge. In the weeks Jessie had been working in the café, she had been clearing tables, washing up, and assisting in Julia's baking. Julia could sense Jessie was itching to get her hands properly stuck into baking her own creations.

When she seemed at peace in bed, Julia placed the cookbook exactly where she had found it. She backed out of the room, cautiously closing the creaking door. She walked past her own bedroom and straight into the kitchen. She dropped one of her favourite peppermint and liquorice teabags into a cup and filled the kettle.

She flicked on her under-counter lights and pulled up a stool. The cat clock with the flickering eyes and swishing tail told her it was a little after six. Letting out a slow yawn, she knew she would pay for her early start later in the café. Saturdays were always the busiest days but at least she had

Jessie's help now.

Julia cast her eyes to the white envelope sitting on the corner of her counter. The divorce papers enclosed within had been read over and signed, and the envelope resealed ready for posting to her solicitor. She wanted to post them, but just like a bad cold, she was finding it difficult to get rid of them.

The moment they were with her solicitor again, she would be divorced. Considering she didn't much like her soon-to-be ex-husband, she should have been happy about finally cutting ties from him, but happiness was an emotion that evaded anything surrounding the break up. More than anything, she felt she had failed, not just her marriage, but herself. She had changed so much and abandoned her village to join her husband, Jerrad, in London. Twelve years later, she found her bags on the doorstep along with a note telling her he had changed the locks because he was in love with his secretary, who was ten years Julia's junior and twenty pounds lighter around the middle.

Two years later, Julia now owned her small cottage on the outskirts of Peridale, the village she had grown up in. She had opened her own café in the heart of the community, and now she had a lodger, as well as her cat. She felt she was truly content with her life, which didn't explain to her why she was clinging onto the envelope.

Tossing back the last of her tea, she cursed herself under her breath. She promised herself today would be the day she dropped them in at the post office.

No more excuses.

Jessie woke with her alarm clock at eight. The sun was high in the clear sky and Julia was already washed and dressed for work. She had also already made good progress with her usual morning baking to fill the display cases in her café.

"This was on the doormat," Jessie grumbled as she scratched her hair, flinging a lavender envelope on top of the divorce papers. "I had the craziest dream last night."

"Oh?" Julia asked, avoiding Jessie's still half-closed eyes. "What about?"

"It's already gone," Jessie said with a shrug. "What are you baking?"

"I'm trying to perfect Sally and Richard's wedding cake recipe," Julia said, pushing a finished cupcake in front of Jessie. "I just can't seem to get the balance right."

Jessie took a big bite out of the cupcake. Julia didn't have to wait long for the verdict. Jessie immediately spat the mixture back into the cake casing and pulled a face that reminded Julia of the time Mowgli licked chilli powder off the counter.

"Oh, God. What's in that?"

"Cinnamon, orange and rose," Julia said with a heavy sigh, looking at the dozen cupcakes she had just baked, hoping to be able to sell them in the café. "I might just have to tell Sally it can't be done. Was there too much rose?"

"There was too much everything," Jessie said, shaking her head, looking down at the cupcake with disgust. "Who wants a cinnamon, orange and rose wedding cake, anyway?"

Julia had to wonder. She was often people's first port of call when they wanted a wedding cake but didn't want to pay the out of town bakery prices. Julia prided herself on her baking, humbly accepting that she was the best baker in the village, but even she sometimes got it wrong. She had quickly learned she could count on Jessie to tell the truth. She was a girl who did not mince her words.

"Can I have one of your fancy teabag things?" Jessie asked as she wandered over to the kettle. "And some painkillers? My head is banging."

Julia fished two painkillers out of her designation junk drawer in her kitchen, and slid them across the counter to Jessie. She thought about telling her about the sleepwalking, but she didn't want to alarm her. Julia was hoping it would stop before it got too serious, but from her research, it could be a recurring problem that usually intensified when somebody was under extreme pressure or stress. Julia thought giving Jessie a home and a job had taken that stress off her young shoulders. Had she given her too much responsibility too soon?

Julia sat at the counter and pulled a corner off one of the cupcakes. As usual, Jessie had been right about the overpowering flavour. It wasn't often her baking found its way straight into the bin, but these were nowhere near the high standard the villagers of Peridale expected from her café.

Jessie put a cup of peppermint and liquorice tea in front of Julia, and pulled up the chair next to her. Julia turned her attention to the lavender coloured envelope, suddenly realising it was far too early for the postman to have made his way up to her cottage.

"You found this on the doormat?" Julia asked as she picked up the envelope.

"That's what I said."

Julia turned it over in her hands. It had no stamp, and it was simply addressed to '*Julia*' in such ornate and delicate lettering it resembled art.

"Who hand delivers letters this early in the morning?" Julia wondered aloud.

"A nutter. I'm going for a shower. I smell like Mowgli after he's been rolling in the garden."

Leaving her tea unfinished, Jessie shuffled to the bathroom, and it wasn't long before rushing water and the sound of Jessie's singing floated through the cottage. Julia smiled to herself. She had come to enjoy Jessie's company more than she had expected.

After taking a sip of her hot tea, Julia tore open the tight seal of the envelope, the overpowering scent of lavender filling her nostrils. She winced. Her mother had hated the smell of lavender and Julia had inherited that quirk. As she pulled the letter out of the envelope, Mowgli jumped up onto the counter. He sniffed the unfinished cupcake, then the letter; he turned his nose up at both.

"Alright, I get it!" she said, tickling under Mowgli's chin. "It's awful!'

The heavily scented letter appeared to be an invitation, handwritten in the same ornate lettering as her name on the envelope. She scanned the invitation, her eyes honing in on the signature at the bottom. Her stomach knotted when she saw '*Katie Wellington-South*'.

Starting back at the top where her own name was, she read through the detailed invitation:

Dear Julia,

It gives me great pleasure to invite you to Peridale Manor for a very special garden party, where I, Katie Wellington-South, and my dear husband, Brian South, will be making an exciting announcement.

Please arrive at Peridale Manor at noon on Sunday March 11th. You are welcome to bring one guest.

We look forward to your attendance, and we cannot wait to share our very special news with you.

With hugs and kisses,
Katie Wellington-South

Julia didn't know how many times she read over the invitation, picking over every word, trying to decode what secrets were going to be revealed at the '*very special garden party*'. She didn't like where her imagination was taking her.

"Katie Wellington-South?" Jessie mumbled as she read the invitation over Julia's shoulder, breaking her from her thoughts. "Who's that?"

"My father's wife," Julia said, pushing the scented paper back into its envelope. "She's inviting us to a garden party tomorrow."

"Don't you mean your step-mother?" Jessie asked as she rubbed a towel through her dark hair. "I've been with enough families to know your dad's missus is your step-mum."

"Katie Wellington is *not* my step-mother," Julia said quickly. "Come on, get dressed. We're going to be late to open the café."

Jessie rolled her eyes and headed off to her bedroom, leaving Julia to read over the note again. When her sister and gran both called one after the other asking if she too had received an invitation, she was only surprised it had taken them so long to call.

"Are you going?" Sue had asked.

"Are you going?" her gran had asked.

Julia had given them both the same response.

"I don't know."

And she didn't. As they drove towards the centre of Peridale village with the morning's bakes carefully fastened in on the backseat, Julia drummed her fingers on the steering wheel, wondering what kind of announcement could be so important that it needed a garden party to make it. In the depths of her mind, she heard the sound of a baby crying, and every hair on her body stood on end.

It wasn't until she was pulling into her parking space between her café and the post office that she realised she had, once again, forgotten to pick up the divorce papers off the kitchen counter.

CHAPTER 2

J ulia was surprised to find herself at Peridale Manor the next morning. Looking up at the sandstone bricks of the old enormous manor house, she felt comfort in knowing most of the village had also received hand delivered lavender invitations. One of the many perks of owning a café was that Julia didn't have to seek out gossip, it usually found her.

"You've never spoken about your dad before," Jessie said carefully, appearing to sense Julia's tension. "Are you close?"

"Not anymore," Julia said, her fingers tightening around the Victoria sponge cake she had baked that morning. "Should we ring the doorbell? I'm surprised more people aren't here yet."

Julia checked her silver wristwatch, wondering why she had thought it was a good idea to get there an hour early. She had hoped to ease herself into the day, but she hadn't expected to be the only one to show up so soon.

"Maybe we should wait in the car for more people to

show?" Jessie suggested, hooking her thumb back to Julia's vintage aqua blue Ford Anglia, which was sitting quietly on the gravel driveway.

"That might look a little odd."

"And standing on the doorstep doesn't? What's so bad about your dad and his missus anyway?"

Before Julia could answer, Jessie jabbed a finger on the ivory doorbell. It tinkled throughout the house, bouncing off the various wooden and marble surfaces that Julia knew lay beyond the front door. Jessie unapologetically winked at Julia, and stuffed her hands into the pockets of her scruffy jeans. She had refused Julia's offer of driving to the late-night mall out of town to buy a dress for the occasion.

The door opened and Julia was relieved not to see Katie or her father. Instead, the flushed and frowning face of someone she assumed was the housekeeper greeted them.

"Yes?" the short, dumpy woman snapped, her fierce eyes darting from Julia to Jessie, then to the cake tin. "The garden party doesn't start for another an hour. You'll have to come back later. We're not ready."

Julia knew most faces in the village, but she didn't recognise this one. The woman's lined skin and pulled back wiry hair made it obvious she should have taken her retirement long ago. Charcoal black lined her bulging eyes, making them look like they could pop out and roll down the driveway at any moment.

"She's family," Jessie said, offense loud in her voice. "The Lord of the Manor's daughter. Isn't that right, Julia?"

"Mr. Wellington?" the woman snapped, looking Julia up and down, her wide eyes somehow continuing to widen. "Mr. Wellington only has one daughter, and *this* is certainly not her."

Julia was glad there was nothing wrong with the elderly woman's eyesight. She would hate to be mistaken for Katie Wellington.

"What Jessie was *trying* to say, is that I'm Brian's daughter," Julia said, applying her best smile and offering forth the Victoria sponge cake. "Mr. South?"

"I know whom you're talking about," the woman snapped, shaking her hand, then stepping to the side. "You had better come in. Funny, I never knew he had a daughter."

"He's got two," Jessie said, stepping over the threshold without wiping her feet on the doormat. "Nice gaff you've got here."

"The correct thing to say would be '*he has two daughters*', not '*got*'. And it is a '*manor*', not a '*gaff*', whatever that means," the woman said bitterly, hurrying Julia into the house so she could close the door. "You really should teach your daughter proper English."

"She's not my mum," Jessie said casually as she spun around on the spot, looking up at the crystal chandelier in the centre of the grand entrance. "Are they real diamonds?"

The old housekeeper grumbled under her breath, then disappeared into the depths of the house, leaving Julia and Jessie standing at the foot of the sweeping mahogany staircase. Through an open door to the kitchen, Julia could see caterers and waiters running around making final preparations for the garden party. It was all a little excessive for Julia's tastes, but it seemed like the right amount of extravagance for Katie Wellington-South.

Julia turned in time to see her dad ducking out of a room as he buttoned up his cufflinks. He didn't seem to have noticed her. She didn't doubt that he thought she was just another member of staff blending into the walls. When he spotted her, his eyes bulged as wide as the housekeeper's.

"Julia," he said, the surprise loud and clear in his voice. "You came."

Brian walked across the mahogany floorboards, his Cuban heels clicking with each step. His skin was tanned and weathered, nodding to his numerous holidays a year. Glistening oil slicked his greying, but still thick black hair off his face. Some of that hair prickled his broad chest, which could be seen through his open collar. It seemed to be open an extra button lower every time Julia saw him. A chunky gold watch, which she didn't doubt was twenty-four karat, hung from his wrist, and the cufflinks he was fiddling with looked to be solid diamonds. He looked just like the man Julia had come to know as her father, but nothing like the man who had worn comfortable jeans and moth-eaten jumpers she still held onto in the depths of her memories.

"I made a Victoria sponge cake," Julia said meekly, her cheeks burning scarlet.

"My favourite," he said, ducking in for a quick kiss on Julia's cheek, filling her nostrils with his overpowering musky aftershave. "You've always remembered that."

He accepted the cake tin and cast it onto a table, which was creaking under the weight of a vase overflowing with white lilies. Brian's eyes wandered over to Jessie, and it was obvious he was immediately judging her well-worn red Converse, ripped up skinny jeans and baggy jumper. The hairs on the back of Julia's neck stood defensively on end.

"This is Jessie," Julia offered before he asked. "She's been staying with me for a while."

"Like a lodger?" he asked, one of his dark brows darting up. "Is money tight? You know you only have to -,"

"She's also working in my café," Julia interrupted, not wanting to get onto the conversation of money. "Aren't you, Jessie?"

"Mmhmm. Was homeless before Julia took me in."

Julia enjoyed the shock in her father's eyes, but it also broke her heart. The man she was clinging onto in her mind wouldn't have looked at somebody in need like that.

"How is that little café of yours doing?" he asked, turning his attention back to Julia.

"It's doing fine. Very busy, in fact."

"I keep meaning to pop in," he said. "I'm always hearing good things."

Julia knew he wasn't going to '*pop in*', just as much as he did. Ever since she had returned to Peridale and told him that she was going to open a café, he had treated her dream with amusement, as if the whole thing was nothing more than a hobby to keep Julia occupied and distracted while her divorce raged in the background.

"This announcement must be something pretty big if you've invited the whole village up here," Julia said, eager to discover the truth.

"Any excuse for a garden party," he said with an uneasy laugh. "You know what Katie is like. I can't stop and chat. I promised her I would check on how things are going outside. Is your sister coming?"

"She's coming later with Gran."

"Mum's coming?" he said, his eyes glazing over a little. "Of course. I'll see you later. Jessie, it was nice to meet you."

"Yeah," Jessie said, her dark eyes narrowing to slits as her arms folded tightly across her chest. "So nice."

Brian hovered for a moment, his eyes briefly meeting

Julia's. His heels let out a small squeak against the freshly polished wood as he turned and headed in the direction of the garden. When they were alone, Julia and Jessie looked at each other, neither of them seeming to know what to say.

"Well, he seems like a real old -,"

"Maybe coming here wasn't a good idea," Julia interrupted, cutting Jessie off before she let out an expletive. "Every time he sees me he looks like he's going to throw up."

"I noticed that too," Jessie agreed as she sucked the air in through her teeth. "Will there be food at this thing? I'm starving."

In the next hour the rest of the villagers arrived, including Julia's sister and gran. They mingled in the entrance hall sipping champagne and eating tiny canapés, which were being handed out by handsome men in tuxedos carrying silver trays.

"I wanted proper food," Jessie mumbled under her breath. "Not this posh finger stuff."

"I'd usually tell somebody your age not to be so ungrateful, but I'll agree with you there," Dot, Julia's gran, said as she nibbled at the edge of a canapé. "What is this?"

"Smoked salmon," Sue said, tossing one whole into her mouth. "I quite like it."

Dot shot Sue a sharp look as she pushed up her tightly wound curls at the back of her head. She peered around at the faces in the crowd looking as uncomfortable as Julia felt. If Julia felt like her relationship with her father was strained, it was nothing compared to her gran's.

"I didn't raise him this way," Dot muttered under her breath. "All of this excess is bad for the soul. It will rot him from the inside out."

"You know it's all *her*," Sue said, grabbing another smoked salmon canapé off a passing tray. "She's a *Wellington*."

"And he's a *South*!" Dot said, her lips pursing tightly. "Your grandfather would turn in his grave if he knew your father had married into this ghastly family. All of this for a silly announcement? It's beyond belief!"

Sue caught Julia's eyes, and for a moment, both of the sisters knew what the other was thinking. They quickly looked away, neither of them wanting to acknowledge the elephant in the room.

"I heard she was pregnant," said Emily Burns, who lived in the cottage next to Julia's. "It's been all around the village."

"I heard they were getting divorced," added Amy Clark, the village's organist at St. Peter's Church.

"Who has a party to announce a divorce?" Emily bit back. "That's preposterous. Mark my words, it's a baby! Evelyn from the B&B said so, and she has the sight, you know."

"A baby at his age?" Amy said, rolling her eyes. "Rubbish."

Julia caught Sue's eyes again, and it was only when she saw her own worry in her sister's eyes that she realised she had stopped breathing. She shook her head and let out a long breath, her cheeks flushing red. Dot and Jessie were both staring at her with worry in their eyes.

"Will you excuse me?" Julia said, already turning around. "Nature calls."

Before any of them could say anything, Julia pushed through the crowd and hurried up the mahogany staircase, and straight into the bathroom. She remembered where it was from her infrequent visits to the manor house. She slammed the heavy door into its frame and dragged the lock across. It nipped the skin on her left index finger. She cried out and crammed the bloody cut in her mouth, closing her eyes and trying to calm herself.

She walked over to the mirror hanging over the sink and assessed her reflection. Her cheeks were plump and naturally rosy, framing her delicate nose and wide green eyes. Her brows and lashes were dark and shapely, matching her dark curly hair in hue. She rarely wore makeup, but today she had opted for mascara and a little berry lipstick. It was the only thing stopping her from splashing cold water on her face.

Since she had read the invitation, she had only been able to think of one thing. It had been spinning around in her mind, tormenting her every waking thought. She had hoped she was overthinking things, but she saw the same worry in her sister's eyes. Hearing Emily say the words she had been afraid to say out loud made her stomach tighten.

Could her father be having another baby? She wanted to laugh at the suggestion, but she knew it was more than possible, what with Katie being the much younger one in the relationship. She had always wondered if this was where things were heading for her father and his new wife. It hadn't seemed like a possibility until yesterday.

She looked her reflection dead in the eyes and asked why she was so bothered if he was to have another baby. Her mind answered instantly, and much quicker than she had expected.

Julia was now the same age her mother had been when she had died. As a twelve-year-old girl, she hadn't realised just how young thirty-seven was, but as it looked back at her in the mirror, she knew she had so much life left in her. Her father had lived his life, and now that he was in his early-sixties, the thought of him bringing another life into the world, a possible brother or sister for Julia, sounded outrageous.

She immediately felt jealous of this invented younger sibling, who would no doubt benefit from her father's years of making mistakes. When her mother died, her father was physically there, but he wasn't mentally, leaving Julia and Sue's gran to pick up the pieces and raise the girls as if they were her own children.

Their father danced around the country dealing antiques, rarely visiting Peridale, and growing more and more distant from his daughters. He would bring them extraordinary gifts from his travels, but eventually they faded away. It hadn't taken Julia long to realise they were just a smoke screen for his lack of caregiving. With Sue being the younger daughter, it took longer for her bubble to burst, which explained why she was more defensive of his actions than Julia cared to be.

By the time he finally moved back to Peridale and settled, Julia was living in London and Sue was already married. He was a stranger to both of them, and their interactions had become nothing more than polite exchanges when they happened to see each other. He was a shadow of the caring and loving man Julia remembered from before her mother's death. She wondered if Sue even remembered that version of their father.

Turning her attention back to the present, Julia shook her curls out and acknowledged that the announcement could be one of many things. She washed her hands, dried them on a fluffy towel adorned with the Wellington family crest, and headed back to the door, her heels clicking on the exposed floorboards.

At the top of the grand staircase, she was surprised when she didn't hear the chatter of the party below. It seemed they had moved through to the garden without her. She didn't mind. It would give her a little longer to gather her thoughts. Just as she was about to descend the staircase, a raised man's voice ricocheted down the hallway, catching her attention. She turned to look in the direction of the voice, her foot hovering over the top step. It was coming from a slightly open door at the end of the hall. She listened to the raised voice, not quite able to make out what he was talking about. She would have left it, but she heard the distinct high-pitched squawk of Katie Wellington-South, and it sent a familiar shiver running down her spine.

Peridale village was renowned for its gossipers, and even though Julia rarely engaged in the gossiping, the intrigued villager within her itched to know what the shouting was about. Backing up the hallway, she slowly crept towards the open door.

"This has nothing to do with you!" Katie screamed, her shrill voice piercing through the air like nails down a chalkboard. "This is my decision!"

"This has everything to do with me!" the man cried back, matching her volume.

If Julia had recognised the man's voice as her father's, she would have promptly retreated because she didn't want to overhear something so private. As it happened, she didn't recognise the man, so she crept closer.

"You're always interfering!" Katie yelled. "Always trying to ruin things for me. You're never happy unless I'm miserable."

"Miserable?" the man cried, laughing sarcastically. "You don't know the meaning of the word! You have everything! Dad has let you live in this house all your life, and yet I was tossed out at eighteen to be shown the harsh realities of the world. What did you do? You messed around with your stupid modelling career, and then when that didn't work, you ran back to Daddy and held your hand out. What did Dad do? He tossed every coin you could catch at you. And now *this*! Are you really that bored that this is what you want to do with your time?"

"I need something too, Charles!" Katie cried. "I'm stuck here all day, going out of my mind looking after Dad. He can barely get out of bed these days. Do you know how difficult it is for me?"

"Am I supposed to feel sorry for you?" Charles cried back. "Because I don't. I *never* will. You're still the spoiled little brat you always were. It never mattered that I was the oldest. You've always been his little princess, regardless of what you do. All you care about is getting your hands on my inheritance."

"That's not true!"

"So why are you doing this? This is all I'll have when he's gone. This house was my ticket into the green. Do you know how difficult it is running my own business? People aren't buying like they used to, but you wouldn't know that. You're up here, playing with *his* millions, while I'm struggling to keep my own roof over my head."

The arguing stopped for a moment. Julia thought she was about to be outed. She heard footsteps heading towards the door, but they turned back as if someone was pacing. Reaching into her handbag, Julia pulled out a small compact mirror, and placed it against the edge of the open door. She fiddled with the angle for a second before she landed on Katie, and then on the man, who she was sure she recognised.

"The old man will never give me the house now," Charles said, shaking his head. "You've got him right where you want him."

"It's not like that, Charles."

"It's always like that with you, Katie," Charles said, before turning around, his eyes almost looking straight at Julia in the mirror. "You're no sister of mine."

Julia jumped back into the shadow of a doorway just in time. She stared into the mirror, pretending she was fixing her hair. Charles stopped and looked directly into her eyes, before shaking his head and running down the staircase, taking them two at a time.

Julia heard the click of Katie's impossibly high heels heading towards the door, so she ran as quickly as she dared back into the bathroom, resting her ear against the wood until she felt it safe to venture out. The last thing she wanted was for Katie to take her anger out on her, or even worse, try and engage her in a conversation.

When the coast was clear, Julia left the bathroom, made her way down the staircase and towards the garden, the knot in her stomach only growing tighter with each step. Everything she had heard from the Wellington siblings had only confirmed her suspicions about the '*big announcement*'.

CHAPTER 3

J ulia joined Jessie, Sue and Dot in the garden. They were all sipping large glasses of freshly squeezed lemonade, which were being handed out on trays. Julia grabbed one and crammed the straw in her mouth, needing the sugar rush.

"Where have you been?" Dot asked, glancing around the crowded garden. "I was about to send out a search party. Everybody in the village is here!"

"I got lost," Julia lied, hoping that would wash.

Her gran arched a brow, letting her know it certainly didn't wash, but she didn't push it. Julia wondered if her gran could sense the worry in Julia's eyes, and she was just choosing not to acknowledge the baby shaped elephant in the room because she couldn't bear the thought of it being true.

"Detective Inspector Brown is over there," Sue whispered in Julia's ear after jabbing her in the ribs. "He's talking to psychic Evelyn."

"I wonder if he's asking her when you'll say yes to him

asking you out on a date?" Dot added, standing on tiptoes to look over to where Barker was, as though she would be able to hear what he was talking to Evelyn about. "It's been nearly a month since he asked you. '*Maybe*' won't cut it forever, you know."

Julia's cheeks blushed. She took a long sip of the lemonade, which tasted as fresh as a summer's day. Barker caught her gaze across the crowd and sent a little wave in her direction. A smile took over her face as she sent a small wave back.

"Your face has gone all red," Jessie said unsubtly. "Are you feeling okay?"

"She's in *loooove*," Sue said, making sure to drag out the word for as long as possible.

"Give it a rest, will you?" Julia said, dropping her hair over her face. "I wouldn't exactly call it that."

Julia didn't know what she would call it. Barker had moved to the village just over a month ago, and his first week had been spent butting heads with Julia as she interfered with Gertrude Smith's suspicious murder case. When Julia figured out the murderer before Detective Inspector Brown had a chance to, he seemed to gain newfound respect for her, and he asked her out on a date. Julia's response had been '*maybe*', and even though she knew she did want to go on a date with the tall, dark and handsome Detective Inspector, saying '*yes*' hadn't seemed so easy.

"Good afternoon, ladies," Barker said as he approached them, clutching his own glass of lemonade. "Lovely day for it, don't you think?"

"Quite," Dot said. "How's the detecting going?"

"Trying to keep the village safe," Barker said, his

charismatic smile beaming from ear to ear. "I've been trying to get this one to ditch the café and join the force after her turn at playing detective."

"Hear that, Julia?" Sue said, her brows darting up and down as her lips hovered over her straw. "Barker thinks you're good enough to go pro."

"I'm going to barf," Jessie mumbled under her breath after loudly sucking the last of her lemonade from her ice filled glass. "I'm going to get a refill."

"We'll come with," Dot said, grabbing Sue's arm and dragging her with Jessie. "Have fun, you two."

Julia smiled awkwardly as her family disappeared, leaving her alone with Barker. For a moment, they silently stood and observed the garden party unfolding around them. When they both seemed ready to talk, they turned, and tried to speak at the same time.

"Ladies first," Barker said, with a small laugh.

"I don't think detective work is for me," Julia said, her finger playing with the top of the green and white straw jutting out of a lemon wedge in her glass. "I'm much more suited to baking cakes."

"You do make a mean double chocolate fudge cake," Barker said, nodding in agreement. "But you also ran circles around me when it came to finding Gertrude Smith's killer."

Hearing that made Julia swell up with pride. Part of the reason she had been so invested in finding the murderer before Barker was because he suspected her friend, Roxy Carter, of committing the crime, and another part felt underestimated by Barker, and she wanted to prove herself.

"So how did you score yourself an invitation to this thing?" Julia asked, eager to shift the focus of the conversation.

"Katie dropped by the station with invitations for all the boys," Barker said, sipping his lemonade. "She seemed quite keen that I come."

"Katie?"

"Do you know her?"

Julia awkwardly sucked her lemonade, glancing around the crowd. She spotted Jessie, Sue and Dot all watching eagerly. Dot sent over two thumbs up, which Sue quickly dragged down and mouthed her apologies.

"She's married to my dad," Julia said bluntly.

Barker choked on his lemonade and stared down at her, eyes wide as the housekeeper's, and as amused as her father's. "Seriously? But she's so – *young*."

"You think?" Julia agreed, chewing the inside of her cheek.

"Doesn't that mean she's your step-,"

"Don't say it," Julia held her hand up. "I've had enough of that from Jessie."

They both laughed, and paused to suck their lemonade. Eager to change the subject again, Julia edged the topic to something more intriguing.

"Any interesting cases?" Julia asked.

"You know I can't talk about them," Barker said. "There is something I wanted to ask you, actually. Remember that night in your café when I asked you out on a -,"

Barker's sentence was stopped midway when a collective cry rippled through the crowd. Everybody turned at once to look for the epicentre, which became very apparent, very quickly. Two men appeared to be brawling in the middle of the crowd, causing people to edge forward to form a circle around the fight. Peridale could pretend to be as civilised as the next village, but Julia knew the second something exciting was happening, no matter how low-brow, everyone wanted to be able to give their own eyewitness account.

"Out of the way!" Barker cried. "I'm police!"

That threat alone parted the sea of people. Julia took advantage of the parting and stuck close to Barker, her own curiosity getting the better of her. They both broke out into the clearing, where one man had another pinned to the ground. Julia instantly recognised both of the struggling men. The man writhing in the grass was Charles Wellington, the brother who had been arguing with Katie not so long ago. The man on top was Richard May, a local man who Julia was trying to create a cinnamon, rose and orange wedding cake for.

"How could you?" Richard cried out, his fist ready to strike Charles' face. "You're a little swine! I'm going to have you!"

"We'll have less of that," Barker called out, scooping Richard off Charles as if he weighed no more than a bag of flour. "Calm down! There are children here."

For a moment, the red mist didn't fade from Richard's eyes, until he looked around and saw the sea of scared and confused faces. He pushed his long, messy hair out of his red face, then tore free of Barker's grip. He doubled back through the crowd and disappeared.

"What was all that about?" Dot whispered in Julia's ear, appearing from nowhere. "Who's that on the ground? I know that face."

"Katie's brother," Julia mumbled, almost without realising. "I remember him from the wedding."

"Oh yeah," Sue said, also appearing from nowhere. "He got drunk during the reception and started swearing at Katie. My Neil was one of the men who had to drag him out."

Barker held out a hand for Charles, but it was ignored. Charles stumbled up to his feet, and tossed his hands defensively over his head, casting his sharp eyes around the crowd of waiting faces.

"What are you all looking at?" Charles screamed out, with the same anger Julia had heard earlier. "*Huh*?"

People jumped back as if he were a rabid animal ready to attack, even though he had been the one being attacked by Richard. Charles smoothed out his icy blonde hair, and pushed his way through the crowd, disappearing into the house.

"What could have gotten into Richard like that?" somebody in the crowd mused.

"I heard he was having trouble with Sally," another said. "Right before the wedding, too."

"I'm supposed to be making their wedding cake," Julia thought aloud.

The chatter wore on along with the afternoon. Just when Julia finished her third sickly sweet glass of lemonade, and thought the point of the garden party had long since been lost, a long nail tapping on a microphone echoed through the crowd.

"Who in the world is *that*?" Jessie asked, barely able to contain her laughter.

"That's Katie Wellington-South," Julia said.

Jessie looked from Julia, then back to the woman teetering along the stage in platform shoes as she continued to tap her red nail on the microphone.

"You're kidding me?" Jessie said. "*That's* your step-mum?"

"She's not our step-mum," Sue jumped in. "And we wish we were kidding."

They all stared at Katie, whose platinum blonde hair had been blow dried into a curly mane, thicker and longer than naturally possible. Her makeup, as usual, was bright and could be seen right at the back of the crowd. Her shirt was typically tight, cutting off above her pierced navel, and straining over her ample and artificially enhanced bosom, which sat abnormally high under her chin. As she opened her plump, glossy lips to smile, her impeccably white teeth gleamed out, brighter than the sun in the cloudless sky. A couple of people seemed shocked by the woman's appearance, but most of Peridale already knew Katie Wellington-South and her ways.

"Is this thing on?" she mumbled, her squeaky voice causing static across the airwaves. "Brian, am I transmitting?"

Brian, who was standing just off to the side of the stage gave Katie two enthusiastic thumbs up. He was standing behind a wheelchair, which contained a barely conscious Vincent Wellington, who was hardly recognisable behind his oxygen mask. Julia knew he wasn't much older than Dot, but he seemed twice as old as any person she had ever met.

"Welcome, one and all," Katie squealed, casting her beaming clown-like grin at the audience, shielding her eyes from the sun. "Can you all hear me in the back?"

There was a mumble and nodding of heads as everybody peered to the back of the crowd. Julia noticed the same perplexed and entertained looks in people's eyes.

"Thank you all for coming here on such short notice," Katie squealed, not seeming to realise the purpose of a microphone. "I hope you've all been enjoying the canapés and our special Wellington family lemonade recipe, passed down from my great-great-grandmother, Bertha Wellington."

The woman in front of Julia let out an audible yawn. The man beside her checked his watch. Just like Julia, they hadn't come for a history lesson, they had come to find out the mystery behind the announcement.

"I'm sure you're all wondering why you are here today," Katie said. "It's because my husband and I have some *very* exciting news to share with you all. Isn't that right, Brian? Why don't you come up here?"

Katie motioned for Brian to join her. He shook his head and held his hands up. Katie didn't seem to get the hint, so she teetered over to the stairs at the side of the small stage and dragged him up. He waved awkwardly into the crowd as they walked across the stage together. One person tried to start a slow round of applause; it didn't catch.

"Hello everyone," Brian mumbled into the microphone Katie had crammed in front of his mouth. "Thanks for coming up here today."

Katie wrapped her arm around his waist, and Brian did the same. Their age gap was never more apparent than when they were standing side-by-side.

"How old *is* she?" Jessie mumbled, still clearly shocked.

"She's the same age as me," Julia said as coolly as she could. "She's thirty-seven and he – *my father* – he is sixty-two."

Jessie's eyes shot open, and her hand clamped over her

mouth to contain the laughter. Julia was glad their age gap amused her, because all it did for Julia was turn her stomach. She would never forget the day she found out over the phone from her gran that her father was marrying a woman the same age as her. At first she had thought it was one of her gran's twisted jokes, but she wasn't that lucky.

"So, our big announcement," Katie said, letting out a small squeal of excitement. "We're very pleased – *no*, not pleased. What's the right word, baby?"

"I'm going to throw up," Sue mumbled. "This is unbearable."

"We're over the moon?" Brian offered, looking a lot more uncomfortable than Katie did with the microphone in his face.

"*Yes!*" Katie agreed. "We're *over* the moon to announce that we are turning Peridale Manor into a luxury spa!"

Katie squawked and bounced up and down on her dreadfully high heels, looking out expectantly into the crowd. Julia turned to Sue, both frowning at one another. Julia wiggled her finger in her ear, wondering if she had heard that right.

"Is that it?" Dot rolled her eyes, passing her lemonade to Julia. "Hold this. I've been clinging onto my bladder since she got up onto the stage. Fill me in on what I miss."

Dot trundled through the crowd and back into the house. Julia and Sue both turned back to the stage, where Katie had stopped bouncing, and was staring disappointedly into the sea of puzzled faces.

"Not the reaction I was expecting," she mumbled quietly into the microphone. "Let me say it again. We're turning Peridale Manor into a luxury spa!"

"We heard you the first time!" a man heckled from the

crowd.

"You called us up here for *that*?" a woman cried. "We thought you were *pregnant*!"

"Pregnant?" Katie laughed, her hand dancing over her exposed midriff. "God, no. With this figure? *No*. My husband and I, with the permission of my father, are turning this great manor into a spa. We'll offer luxury beauty treatments and weekend packages for the ultimate relaxation experience!"

Katie stared into the crowd again, but she seemed to be angering people more with each word that left her glossy lips. Julia didn't care what else happened, she was just glad her pregnancy fears had been her imagination playing tricks on her.

"How are we supposed to afford that?" Amy Clark, the elderly organist, called. "We're regular folk with regular jobs in these parts."

"Well, people will come from out of town to stay here for the weekend," Katie said, a small awkward laugh escaping her lips. "It's a *good* thing! Think about how all of the businesses in town will benefit from the extra tourism."

"It'll attract rich *yuppies*!" the same man from earlier cried. "They'll treat our village like their playground!"

Katie opened her mouth, but nothing came out. The crowd was growing more restless with every passing second. She dropped the microphone to her side, and started whispering into Brian's ear. He whispered something back, and she nodded. She clicked her fingers at a tuxedo-wearing waiter who was hovering by the side of the stage. He hurried over, crammed a hard hat over Katie's enormous hair, a heavy fluorescent jacket over her revealing outfit, and helped her switch from her platform stilettos to heavy work boots.

Now that the free food and lemonade had dried up, the chattering in the crowd grew louder and louder. People seemed less happy to stand around listening to Katie talk now that the cat was out of the bag. Katie looked out from under her yellow hardhat and lifted the microphone up to her lips again, seeming to sense the unrest.

"If you would all like to follow me in an orderly fashion, I'd like to show you the construction on our brand new outdoor pool, which will be open to all Peridale residents free of charge during the week."

The mumbling died down a little. The sound of a free swimming pool seemed to ease the villagers.

"What about weekends?" somebody cried.

"Well, of course there will be a *small* charge at the weekends. Now, if you would all like to follow me."

A couple of people started to boo the charade, but Katie was either choosing not to listen, or she couldn't hear it under the heavy hardhat. She started walking towards the steps, assisted by Brian, who was carrying her shoes like a butler. Before she reached the edge of the stage, an invader snatched the microphone out of her hand and took the spot where she had been standing. The crowd suddenly grew silent.

"You hear *that*, little sister?" Charles called out through the microphone. "The people of Peridale don't *want* your spa. They don't *want* you to turn this *great* manor into a circus."

For the first time all day, there was a cheer. Some people were even clapping. It seemed they had short memories and couldn't remember the same man fighting on the ground not too long ago.

"This manor is a *symbol* of this town and it *shouldn't* be touched. Who's with me?"

Charles turned the microphone into the crowd, and a rapturous cheer crackled through the large speakers. Julia assessed Charles with caution. The argument she had heard earlier suddenly made more sense, and she was sure the intention behind Charles' sudden bout of village pride wasn't inspired by historical preservation.

"You ruin *everything*!" Katie screeched, her shrill voice traveling throughout the grounds without the aid of a microphone.

"This house will become a spa over my dead body," Charles said firmly, before dropping the microphone and pushing his way off the stage.

The entire crowd moved towards Charles, hoping to catch a glimpse of his next actions. He disappeared around the side of the house, quickly followed by a crying and shrieking Katie, and Brian, who tried to calm his wife. Vincent was still sitting by the side of the stage, staring into space. He didn't seem to have a clue where he was or what was going on.

"Your family is nuts!" Jessie exclaimed excitedly. "What was all that about?"

Julia almost mentioned the argument she had eavesdropped upon earlier, but decided against it. There were too many pairs of ears listening for a scrap of real gossip to explain what had just happened.

"Should we go after them?" Sue asked, standing on tiptoes to look over the crowd.

"Let's leave them," Julia said, resting a hand on Sue's shoulders, pushing her back into the grass. "They'll sort it out."

Out of nowhere, a dozen men carrying trays filled with more canapés and lemonade dispersed through the crowd. The rumbling calmed, and the free food and drinks went down a treat. Even Julia was growing to like the taste of the Wellington family lemonade. She thought she sensed a dash of grapefruit mixed in with the lemons and sugar, and made a mental note to try such a mix in a cake.

"A spa in Peridale?" Barker said as he made his way over to Julia. "I'm not so against the idea myself. I like a massage as much as the next man."

"You city folk," Sue said, rolling her eyes. "Full of your airs and graces. I wouldn't mind the free pool though. I hate having to drive out of the village in the summer when I want an outdoor swim."

"What do you think, Julia?" Jessie asked. "For or against your nutty step-mum's spa?"

Before Julia could correct Jessie about her use of the word '*step-mum*', the crack of shattering glass pierced through the air, silencing everything. It just so happened that Julia was facing the right way to see a man bursting through an upstairs window of the manor house, surrounded by a flurry of glass shards. He travelled noiselessly to the ground, his arms floating above his body, but not reaching out for air as Julia expected a man falling from a second story window would.

Julia heard the thud of his body hit the grass. She was in no doubt that the man was dead. Suddenly realising who the man could be, she dropped her lemonade and pushed through the crowd, not needing Barker's police credentials to do the work for her.

With Sue hot on her heels, she burst through the ring of shocked faces that had gathered around the face down man in the grass. When Julia saw the icy blonde of Charles Wellington's hair, she instantly felt guilty for feeling relieved that it wasn't her father.

"What have I missed?" Julia heard her gran call through the crowd. "What are you all huddled over for?"

CHAPTER 4

J ulia looked up at the broken window, along with many others, all seeming to want to find a clue worthy of gossiping about. The only remnants of the window were tiny, jagged shards around the perimeter of the frame. Charles had fallen through the window with some considerable force.

"He's dead," Barker whispered quietly as he checked the man's pulse. "Julia, can you call for an ambulance?"

Julia scrambled for her phone, her heart pounding in her chest. Pushing the phone into her ear, she turned to see the shock on her gran's face as Sue told her what had happened. Jessie was staring down at the body, her mouth opening and closing like a fish out of water.

Minutes later, an ambulance and two police cars were speeding towards Peridale Manor while Detective Inspector Brown attempted to clear the scene. In a village where everybody needed to know everything about everyone, it was a task easier said than done.

"What's everyone crowding around for?" Julia heard

Katie's shrill shriek call across the garden. "Will somebody *answer* me?"

People dropped their heads and guiltily backed away from the body on the ground. A path cleared for Katie to stumble forward, still in her heavy work boots, jacket, and yellow safety helmet. She saw the limp body of her brother on the ground, and her wide eyes scanned the crowd as tears gathered along her heavily coated lashes.

"*No!*" she whimpered, burying her head in Brian's chest as inky mascara streaked down her rouged cheeks. "*No!*"

Brian stared ahead at the body, his eyes wide and unblinking as he comforted his sobbing wife. As her pained screeches grew louder, the thinner the crowd around the body became.

The uniformed officers got to work securing the scene and successfully brushing away the remaining villagers. Julia, her gran, Sue and Jessie all hung back, and it was obvious none of them knew if they should also leave. Julia heard her gran mutter something about being related when an officer approached them, which seemed to give her a pass to stay and stare. Julia on the other hand had something more important to do when she caught Barker slipping away from the madness and into the house.

"I need the bathroom," Julia whispered to Sue as she slipped away.

Taking the mahogany staircase as carefully as she could, she crept up them for the second time that day. When she reached the top step, she spotted Barker at the end of the hallway, crouched under the broken window. The noise from the garden fluttered through the curtains of the empty frame.

"I'd say he was pushed," Julia said as she approached Barker. "Quite hard too, if you ask me. Knocked the entire window out of its frame."

"You know you can't be up here, Julia," Barker mumbled as he inspected a stray shard of glass that had fallen inwards. "It's a crime scene."

"I won't touch anything."

Julia crept forward, scanning the hallway for anything out of the ordinary. The lavishly decorated walls were lined with ornate landscape paintings in heavy gold frames. Ornaments on tall stands sat under the paintings, illuminated by sconces jutting out of the walls.

"This stand is empty," she thought aloud, summoning Barker up from the ground. "If you look, there are three display stands on each side of the wall, between the window and these two doors, all containing an ornament, but this one is empty."

Barker looked from a vase to an ornate figure of a glass ballerina on the two stands on either side of the empty one, but Julia's frustration started to bubble when she noticed familiar dismissal in his eyes.

"That's hardly a clue, Julia," Barker said, turning his attention back to the window. "Who says there was anything on that plinth?"

Julia stared down at the empty stand, noticing a definite wobbly line in the centre, indicating that something had been there. She crouched down so that she was eye-level with the stand, and under the bright light, there was an unmistakable layer of dust everywhere, apart from the centre where whatever had been taken had stood.

Julia pulled out her phone and snapped a quick picture of the shape etched in the dust while Barker's back was turned.

"I'm calling this a crime scene, so you need to leave."

"Yes, sir. Good luck with the investigation."

"You've got that look in your eyes again," Barker moaned. "Please, Julia, I *implore* you to leave this one to me."

"What is this look people keep talking about?"

"It's the same look you had when you were trying to outsmart me by finding Gertrude Smith's murderer before I did."

Julia concealed her smile as she turned on her heels, not wanting to remind Barker that she had outsmarted the Detective Inspector by finding the murderer before he had.

As she walked along the hallway and back towards the staircase, she looked down at the floor, the nervous bubbling in her stomach growing louder each time she spoke to Barker. She was sure he was about to re-ask her out on that date in the garden before Charles and Richard's fight, and this time she was sure she would have said yes. While she looked down, she spotted muddy boot prints barely visible on the oak floorboards. Glancing over her shoulder, she concentrated on the floor as Barker spoke on the phone. The boot prints ran all the way down the hall, stopping just before the window. They then trailed back into the bathroom where Julia had hidden earlier. The door was open so she glanced inside, noting that the boot prints suddenly vanished in front of the bathtub, almost as if somebody had sat on the edge of the bath and removed their boots.

Julia thought about attracting Barker to the boot prints, but he had told her to stay out of his investigation. If he were worth his Detective Inspector badge, he would notice the faint footprints and come to his own conclusions. Julia decided she would let Barker get on with his investigation, but that didn't mean she wouldn't get on with her own. She pulled her recipe notepad out of her bag, flipped past a page of ingredients for a new chocolate orange scone she wanted to try, and scribbled down everything she had just learned.

Back in the garden, Julia re-joined her gran, Sue and Jessie just at the very moment a stretcher covered in a red blanket was hoisted into the back of an ambulance.

On the edge of the stage, Katie was still sobbing into Brian's arms, while Brian watched the stretcher, still unblinking. Vincent Wellington gawked at the grass from behind his oxygen mask, unaware of what had just happened to his son.

"If I get like that, I want you girls to put me out of my misery," Dot said when she noticed Julia looking at the wheelchair-bound old man. "Take me out to a farm, and put a bullet in my back. I won't stop you."

"*Gran!*" Sue whispered, slapping Dot's arm with the back of her hand. "A man has *just* died!"

"I'm just saying!" Dot protested, rubbing the spot where Sue had just tapped her. "That's no life. I'm not surprised he agreed to let Katie turn this place into a spa. She probably asked over dinner while a nurse dribbled soup down his chin. Poor man wouldn't have had a clue what he was agreeing to."

When Dot finished talking, neither Julia nor Sue spoke. Instead, they looked uncomfortably at each other, both hearing truth in their gran's statement, but also not wanting to give her permission to keep ranting at the scene of a man's murder.

"Should we say something?" Sue whispered to Julia, as they both looked over to their father. "Poor man looks in shock."

"I think we should leave it," Julia whispered back.

"He's still our father, Julia."

Julia's heart twitched in her chest. She knew that was true, but the unblinking coldness of his eyes had shaken her to her very core. It was the exact same look that had taken over him when Julia's mother had been lowered in the ground all those years ago. Sue probably didn't remember, but it was etched in Julia's memory like a red-hot stamp on a cow's backside. She particularly remembered how he had spent the entire day wordlessly staring into the distance, ignoring his two distraught daughters.

They watched on as officers wrapped crime scene tape around the spot where Charles Wellington had been. Julia knew it wouldn't be long before the forensics team turned up to document every detail of the scene. For now at least, there was nothing to be gained from lingering around at Peridale Manor.

After driving back into the village, Julia and Jessie parted ways from Dot and Sue, heading back up the winding lane leading to Julia's cottage. When they were alone, Julia noticed a similar vacantness in Jessie's eyes. It hadn't gone unnoticed that she hadn't said a word since the garden party had turned sour. Julia had just been waiting until they were alone before attempting to talk to her young lodger.

"I'm sorry you had to see that," Julia whispered, nudging Jessie softly with her arm. "It's never easy seeing your first dead body."

"That's not my first," Jessie said with a shrug, facing away from Julia.

"Oh. Right."

Julia was rendered speechless by the lack of emotion in Jessie's voice. She knew people could become detached when talking about death, but Julia hadn't expected somebody so young to be so weathered towards it. She wondered if she should push the subject, but like talking about Jessie's time on the streets, Julia knew it was probably best to wait for Jessie to voluntarily open up than pry for information.

"If you ever want to talk, I'm here," Julia offered, pulling her house keys out of her handbag as they climbed out of Julia's vintage aqua blue Ford Anglia.

Jessie didn't say anything, instead choosing to nod as she chewed the inside of her lip. Julia unhooked her peeling white garden gate. As they walked towards her old cottage with its low thatched roof, she decided they were going to spend the afternoon baking, if only to keep both of their minds occupied.

CHAPTER 5

Monday morning in Julia's café was usually the quietest time of the week. It was when she spent her time deep cleaning the kitchen, and checking which ingredients were starting to run low. On the Monday morning following Charles Wellington's death, it became very apparent that her deep clean and stock check would have to wait.

For as long as Julia had owned the café, this was the first Monday morning in Julia's memory that there was a small cluster of residents waiting as she pulled her Ford Anglia into her small parking space. At first, Julia had thought the villagers just wanted to use her café as a base to hear all of the latest gossip regarding the recent death, but it turned out they had created a connection between Julia and Charles and they intended on using it.

"Has your father said anything yet?"

"How is your father doing?"

"I'm so sorry for your loss, Julia. Your family must be going through such a difficult time."

"Were you close to Charles?"

"How's Katie holding up? Poor woman having to see her brother like that."

By lunchtime, Julia was tired of repeating over and over that she knew no more than anyone else because she wasn't close to her father, and she had only met Charles once previously at her father's wedding. For most people, this didn't settle their insatiable thirst for more information, so they continued to quiz her regardless, certain she must be hiding something.

"Has your father called?" Dot asked, after hurrying in a little after one, her hands filled with bags of shopping. "He hasn't called me. The *cheek* of the man!"

"Why would he have called?" Julia poured Dot a cup of tea. "I doubt he even has my number."

"He's your *father*! You *deserve* to know what's going on," Dot said, dumping her bags at the table nearest the counter, which was where people usually sat when they wanted to talk with Julia as she worked. "I haven't heard a thing since yesterday! Everyone is talking, but nobody knows a thing."

Julia set the cup of tea in front of her gran, along with a bowl of sugar cubes, and a small jug of milk. Dot dumped four lumps of sugar and half of the milk into her tea, once again defying the doctor's warning of age-related Type 2 diabetes.

"I bet it was Richard," Dot exclaimed suddenly after taking a deep sip of her hot tea, the cup barely pulled away from her lips. "It *has* to be! We all saw that fight between him and Charles right before he was pushed to his death."

"But why would Richard May want to kill Charles?" asked Roxy Carter, who was in the café on her lunch break from the local primary school. "You can't accuse people of murder without any proof."

"What more proof do you need?" Dot cried, stamping her finger down on the table. "You *saw* Richard trying to bash Charles' face in, didn't you?"

"I heard him and Sally had called their wedding off," Roxy said, taking a bite of one of Julia's brownies. "Maybe Richard was just taking his frustration out on the wrong person?"

"Or *maybe* he was getting ready to murder him!" Dot insisted. "Mark my words, young girl. The truth *will* come out with the dirty laundry."

Roxy's face turned a deep shade of red as she stared down at her brownie. Julia wasn't sure if her gran knew what she had just said, but the hurt was written all over Roxy's face. It hadn't been long since Roxy's romantic relationship with her teaching assistant, Violet, had been used to blackmail her by Gertrude Smith, thus putting her in the frame when Gertrude was murdered. Julia loved her gran, but along with the rest of Peridale, her first reaction was often an overreaction. It wouldn't be long until her gran's declaration of Richard's guilt spread around the village as fact, as it had done with an innocent Roxy.

After closing the café at the end of a long day, Julia sent Jessie back to the cottage with the house keys, leaving her to drive up to Peridale Manor alone with a beef casserole secured in the passenger seat. Pulling up alongside a lone police car, she secured her handbrake, casting an eye to her casserole, which she hoped would serve a dual purpose.

Julia unbuckled her seatbelt and pulled her keys out of the ignition. She opened her small black handbag, pulled out her small ingredients notepad, immediately flicking to the notes she had made. She had written a long list of things she wanted to find out. The first point, which she had circled multiple times, was to talk to Katie and her father.

Julia knew they would be too distraught to think about food, so she had baked a casserole out of concern, but she also hoped it was a valid excuse for visiting uninvited.

"Yes?" the surly housekeeper grumbled through a crack in the door after Julia rang the doorbell. "The Wellingtons aren't taking visitors."

Julia applied her kindest smile and pushed forward the casserole. The dumpy woman with the heavily lined eyes and pulled back wiry hair sourly looked Julia up and down.

"I was here yesterday," Julia offered.

"So was half the village, sweetheart," the woman snapped, her bulging eyes rolling. "Clear off."

"I'm Brian's daughter," Julia said, wondering if the housekeeper really didn't remember their meeting yesterday.

"Oh," the woman said with a heavy sigh, opening the door and stepping to the side. "I remember. You brought that insolent child with you."

Julia bit her tongue, knowing the venomous housekeeper could easily deny her entry if she wanted to. Taking her chance, she stepped over the threshold and into the grand entrance hall.

"I didn't catch your name yesterday," Julia said.

"That's because I didn't give it. I'll fetch Mr. South for you. Stay here."

The housekeeper shuffled away and headed towards the staircase, looking over her shoulder at Julia as she went. Julia smiled at her, which only seemed to anger the woman more. When she reached the top of the staircase and turned along the hall, Julia let out the breath she had been holding in, and took a couple of steps forward. She wondered what could have happened to the housekeeper to make her so bitter.

Julia placed the casserole on the lily filled table. The tin containing her Victoria sponge cake was still there, seemingly untouched from the previous day. Julia walked along the entrance hall towards the open door of the kitchen. Through the large windows above the stove, people moved back and forth. At first, she thought they were police officers, until she realised they were builders.

"Julia?" Katie called from the top of the staircase, the surprise loud and clear in her voice. "What are you doing here?"

Julia turned on her heels and scooped up the casserole dish as Katie made her way down the stairs. Julia hadn't expected to see Katie. She had assumed she was going to be curled up in bed, grief-stricken and distraught after her brother's death. Instead, she was as put together as always, her makeup thick and her hair voluminous. She was wearing all black, perhaps as an outwardly sign of mourning, but her stomach and chest were still poking through the sparse material.

"I made you a casserole. I didn't think you would want to be cooking today."

Katie stared down at the gravy and beef mixture through the plastic wrap, her lips pursed into what was obviously a fake smile.

"You know we've got our housekeeper, Hilary, for that," Katie said, awkwardly accepting the dish. "I'm sure your father will enjoy this. I don't eat meat on Mondays."

"Oh," Julia said, narrowing her eyes at the strange

woman who was the same age as Julia but different in every possible way. "I was hoping to speak to my father. Is he around?"

"He's at the station," Katie said as she walked through to the large and immaculate kitchen. "He's making a statement."

"A statement?" Julia asked, hurrying after Katie. "At the station?"

"I didn't want more police up here," Katie said as she pulled open the giant double doors of her fridge before balancing the casserole on wrapped trays of leftover canapés from the garden party. "The sooner things get back to normal, the better. Can I get you a drink? Perhaps some lemonade? There's plenty left over."

"That would be lovely," Julia said, not really wanting to sit and chat with Katie, but knowing it would give her a reason to stick around and find out what she wanted to know. "It really is good lemonade."

"Thank you," Katie said, a grin spreading from ear to ear as she rested a hand on her chest. Julia was amused to see a small streak of lipstick on Katie's teeth. "Do you really mean that?"

Julia nodded. Katie looked on the verge of tears for a moment, but she shook out her white blonde hair, and pulled a huge jug of the lemonade from the fridge. She poured two large glasses before sitting across from Julia, facing away from construction in the garden. As Katie busied herself stirring the lemon wedges and ice with her straw, Julia peered through the window and watched a team of workmen dig out what she suspected was going to be the pool Katie had wanted to show her unimpressed guests.

"I see work is still going ahead."

"No time like the present," Katie said, staring blankly, and yet somehow deeply into Julia's eyes. "There is lots of work to get done. The pool is just the start. We're converting the spare bedrooms into luxury guestrooms, each with their own bathroom. It was murder trying to get planning permission for all of this, but my father called in some favours from the council."

"It all seems rather grand," Julia said, trying to fake interest. "You must have been thinking about this for a long time."

"It's always been a dream of mine," Katie said. "Like that little café of yours."

Julia gritted her teeth and smiled. She could tell Katie viewed her café the same way her father did. Using what was left over from her lifesavings after buying her cottage hadn't been an easy decision. Julia had known there was every chance her venture would fail, and she would be left broke with no income. Luckily, her cakes had hit the spot with the villagers, unlike Katie's idea for a spa. Julia looked at the wealthy woman examining her nails as if they were the most important things in the world. Julia wondered if she had ever had to worry about anything serious in her entire life.

"Any idea what time my father will be back?"

"No," Katie said, glancing to the giant station clock on the wall. "He's been there since this morning."

Julia glanced at the clock. It was nearly six in the evening. The police weren't taking a statement from her father; they were interrogating him.

"Where was my father when – when *it* happened?" Julia asked, her finger circling the lemonade glass.

Katie's expression tightened, as did her eyes. The caked

on makeup creased into her fine lines, revealing her true age. Julia was glad she had lived a life without the shackles of makeup because she was sure it had allowed her to age a little more naturally.

"He was with me. After my brother ruined everything, we came inside to find him. We couldn't find him, so we went into Brian's study. He gave me some whiskey to calm my nerves. When I'd calmed down, we came out and – and saw *him*."

Julia thought for a moment that Katie was about to crack and start shrieking again, but she composed herself, showing more self-restraint than Julia had previously thought the vapid woman possessed.

"Did anybody see you together?"

"You sound like the police!" Katie said, her shrill voice suddenly rising at a rate that made Julia's arm hairs jump up. "Me and Brian were together. Now, if you *don't* mind, my father needs his medication. Hilary will show you out."

Julia hadn't realised Hilary was standing in the doorway, waiting to usher Julia out of the manor. She practically dragged Julia away from her lemonade, and tossed her outside. Standing in between the police car and her own vintage automobile, she pulled her notepad out of her bag, considering tearing out the notes she had made, so she could go home and forget about the whole thing. She ran her finger along the points she had made, pausing at '*Establish Katie and Dad's alibi*'. Julia pulled out her small metal pen and twisted out the nib to draw a big question mark over the word '*alibi*'. If she hadn't learned that her father had been at the station all day, she might have believed Katie's story about drinking whiskey in the study, but something wasn't sitting right with Julia.

Instead of walking towards her car, she cast an eye back at the manor, and when she was satisfied that she wasn't being watched, she crept around the side of the house, past the crime scene. A white tent had been erected and was being guarded by a lone officer. Julia sent a smile in his direction, but he didn't send one back. Walking past the crime scene, she made her way beyond the stage, which was still there from the day before, and towards the construction site she had seen through the kitchen window. She knew Katie would easily spot the yellow polka dots on her navy blue dress if she looked out, so Julia knew her time to investigate was limited.

"*Julia?*" a familiar voice called to her across the construction sight. "Julia, over here."

Julia looked past the construction workers to see Joanne Lewis standing by a car. Joanne worked in the village's charity shop, making her a regular in Julia's café. She was a tall, slender woman in her early-forties, with an elongated face and high forehead. Her tightly wound brown curls had been cut just above her jawline, making her face look even longer. Julia had always thought her hair would complement her face more if she let it grow out a little, but she was too kind to point that out.

"Joanne, what are you doing here?" Julia asked after weaving her way through the construction workers, who appeared to be packing up for the day as the blue sky turned pink.

"My Terry got the contract for this spa job," Joanne said, casting an eye over to the manor.

Julia looked over to the builders, instantly spotting Terry's bald head and potbelly hanging over his faded jeans. He was reading something from a clipboard on the steps of a builder's cabin. When Julia had first moved to the village, she had called on Terry's building expertise to help fit the kitchen and counter in her café. Terry had heavily discounted the work because Julia was a local, and she had thought favourably of him since.

"I didn't see you at the garden party yesterday," Julia said.

"I was back here with the boys. We were expecting Katie to bring the crowd around to see the progress on the digging, but – well, you know what happened next. We were waiting when we heard the glass shatter."

They both smiled awkwardly at each other, neither appearing to want to talk about the death. Julia was sure this was the first villager she had encountered all day who didn't want to gossip, and she was glad of it.

"I'm sure Terry is pleased to get such a big contract," Julia said, wanting to fill the sudden awkwardness.

"He's managing the whole project," Joanne said proudly, her face lighting up. "It couldn't have come at a better time."

Before Julia could ask why the timing was good, Joanne's teenage son, Jamie Lewis, walked towards them, covered in mud and wearing a yellow hardhat.

"Hello, Jamie," Julia said, smiling at the teenager. "I didn't realise you had finished with school already."

"Dropped out," he said with a shrug, followed by a heavy yawn as he got into the car without saying another word.

Julia looked to Joanne who was maintaining her smile, even if it did look uncomfortable and strained.

"He was always going to end up in the family trade," Joanne offered, her tone sounding like an excuse, rather than an explanation. "He was never really good at exams, so we spoke to the school. They agreed to let him leave with our permission to start his building apprenticeship early. He'll get a qualification from it in the end. I hear you've taken in a young girl off the streets?"

Julia sensed the urgency in Joanne's voice to quickly divert the topic of conversation away from her family. Julia hadn't told many people about what she had done for Jessie, but word had somehow still spread all over the village, and everybody seemed to have their own opinions on the situation, and they weren't shy about telling Julia about them.

"She's a good girl," Julia said. "Same age as your Jamie I think."

They both looked into the car as Jamie tapped away with his thumbs on his phone. In a way, he reminded Julia of Jessie. She wondered if all kids that age were allergic to talking.

"You should get her on an apprenticeship at the local college," Joanne suggested. "They help out with their wages, and you get them trained up. I'm sure I saw a baking apprenticeship in the prospectus. I'll drop it around to yours if you like?"

"That would be kind of you," Julia said. "Thank you."

"Are you adopting Jessie?" Joanne asked, still obviously wanting to keep the focus on Julia rather than herself. "I heard you were."

"You did?" Julia asked, wondering why she was surprised that false information had somehow spread around the village without her knowing about it. "I've spoken to her social worker, but I'm waiting on a letter about the next steps."

"It's a big responsibility taking on a troubled kid," Joanne said, pulling her car keys out of her pocket as Terry walked towards them, also covered in mud. "I better go. I've got a stew on a low light back home. I'll drop that college prospectus off sometime this week?"

"Thank you," Julia said, stepping away from the car.

She smiled at Terry Lewis, but he blanked her completely and jumped into the car. Julia wondered if she had misjudged the man.

Joanne gave Julia a little wave as she ducked into the car. Julia waved back, peering through the windows as Terry and Jamie both tapped silently away on their phones, the mirror image of each other. Julia's day had been long and exhausting, but she couldn't imagine how difficult a day of digging was on the mind and body.

As she drove through the darkening village, she was far too tired to think of anything related to Charles Wellington. Her mind was securely fixed on a cup of peppermint and liquorice tea, a bubble bath, and a good book.

CHAPTER 6

J ulia woke to her alarm, groaning as she rolled over, wishing she could have another hour in bed. Jessie had woken her again with the sleepwalking in the early hours of the morning, but after she had stopped Jessie climbing into the shower in her night clothes, she crawled back into her own bed and fell straight back to sleep.

Over breakfast that morning, neither of them spoke much, and Julia wondered if Jessie knew about her sleepwalking. Either way, Jessie didn't mention it, so Julia didn't push it.

When they arrived at the café, Julia was glad to see there wasn't a gossiping crowd waiting for her to open up. She left Jessie in charge of the counter and started on her deep clean, which would give her time to think, away from the few customers.

Unluckily for Julia, her thinking time was interrupted when Sally Marriott came into the café, requesting to speak to her. When she noticed her red raw eyes and dishevelled appearance, Julia took Sally through to the kitchen.

"I suppose you've heard," Sally mumbled as she dabbed her nose with a shredded tissue. "Richard has called off the wedding."

No sooner had the words left Sally's lips did she double over, her mousy hair hanging over her eyes as she sobbed her heart out. Julia pulled the useless tissue from Sally's grip and replaced it with her own handkerchief from her dress pocket, which Sally gratefully accepted.

"I had heard, but I didn't want to assume it was true," Julia said softly, her hand rubbing the back of Sally's shoulders.

Sally paused her sobbing to smile at Julia, but the smile quivered and the tears resumed almost instantly. She was a young woman in her mid-twenties and even through her upset, Julia could still see the natural English rose beauty radiating underneath. She had always admired Sally's looks from afar, and along with the rest of the village, had been surprised when she announced that she was marrying Richard May, who despite being handsome, was twenty years her senior.

"I thought I should tell you not to bother with the wedding cake," Sally said, sniffling into the handkerchief as the tears calmed down. "You can keep the deposit."

"I wouldn't dream of it," Julia said, already pulling her purse from her handbag, which was hanging from a hook on the wall. "Besides, I was having trouble making a cinnamon, rose and orange cake work."

Sally laughed softly, and Julia was glad to see a little lightness appear in her face before another flood of tears took over. She pushed the deposit she had taken into Sally's blouse pocket, sending a soft wink to the jilted girl. Julia knew what it felt like to have a man pull the rug from under her feet, and she knew how expensive starting out on your own could be.

"I should have seen it coming," Sally said, drying her eyes for the final time before inhaling deeply and looking up at the fluorescent lights in the kitchen's ceiling. "My mother always did say I wanted what I couldn't have."

Julia rubbed Sally's shoulder sympathetically, wondering if what she had heard about Sally 'carrying on' with another man was true.

"Maybe there's a chance you'll reunite?"

"There isn't," Sally said, letting out a bitter laugh. "He's already cancelled the venue and told his parents it's over. He's so angry. I'm such a stupid girl. I tried to talk to him at Peridale Manor yesterday, but he refused to talk to me."

"You were at the garden party yesterday?" Julia asked. "I didn't see you."

"I only went to find Richard, but he wouldn't speak to me. I wanted to talk to him, to explain, but he pushed me away and he left. And then I heard about – *about* -,"

Sally didn't finish her sentence. Her sobbing started afresh, harder and heavier than ever before. Julia took Sally into her arms, and the crying woman clung to her like a baby to its mother. Through the beaded curtain, Julia could see Jessie and the few customers, her gran being one of them, all staring into the kitchen to see what was happening.

When Sally finally pulled away and handed back Julia's handkerchief, she shook out her mousy hair and composed herself.

"I've still got to see the florist and the dressmaker," Sally said, her bottom lip trembling, but no tears appearing.

"All I ever wanted was the fairy tale wedding."

Julia knew she should tell her that she was still young and there was still time, but her own experience of the so-called fairy tale had jaded her. Instead, she wanted to tell Sally that it was overrated, and even if she walked down the aisle with Richard, *'till death do us part'* could really mean *'until I leave you for my young secretary'*. Julia decided neither were appropriate, so she offered Sally a drink and a cake on the house, both of which she declined. Julia let Sally leave out of the backdoor to avoid getting caught up in being questioned by the villagers.

"So?" Dot asked, looking at Julia expectantly along with the other villagers. "What did she say?"

"Whatever she said was said to me in confidence."

"Didn't you find out if the rumours about her and Charles Wellington having an affair were true?" Dot asked, her eyes wide and her mouth practically salivating.

"It wasn't my place to ask."

There was a loud groan from the watching crowd, and they quickly dispersed, some of them sitting, and some of them leaving as if they had only come for the gossip. Julia wondered if they had seen Sally entering the café and decided to follow her. How many people would suddenly find themselves in the florist and dressmakers?

After Dot told Julia and Jessie that they were having dinner at her house that afternoon because she had some lamb chops that needed to be eaten, Julia retreated back to the kitchen and pulled her notepad from her bag.

Flipping to a fresh page, she wrote Charles' name in the middle and circled it. She reluctantly drew an arrow from Charles and added her father's name. Less reluctantly, she drew another arrow and wrote Katie's name, followed by a line connecting the two. Next, she added two more arrows and two more names, which were also connected. She stared at Sally and Richard's names, adding a question mark next to the latters.

After witnessing the fight between Richard and Charles, the village had come to the conclusion that Charles was somehow involved in Richard calling off his engagement to Sally. After seeing Sally and looking into her eyes, Julia felt like she had all but confirmed this to be true. She traced over the question mark next to Richard's name, wondering if a broken heart could drive a man to commit murder.

At the end of the workday, Julia and Jessie drove back to her cottage to pick up a pecan pie that was chilling in her fridge. Her gran didn't specifically ask Julia to bring dessert, but if she didn't they would be eating something that came out of a packet.

As the first signs of night started to tickle the pale sky, they pulled up outside of Julia's cottage. Julia killed the engine and unbuckled her seatbelt, while Jessie continued to stare blankly ahead, not seeming to notice they had even stopped.

"Is everything okay?" Julia asked softly, making Jessie jump. "You've been quiet today."

Julia didn't want to mention she had noticed Jessie growing increasingly quieter over the past week, although it hadn't gone unnoticed that it had started around the same time as the sleepwalking.

"I'm just tired," Jessie said with a shrug. "It's nothing."

"Am I working you too hard at the café?"

"It's nothing like that. Like I said, I'm just tired."

Julia smiled softly at Jessie, who strained to smile back. Jessie was filled with so much passion and energy, so she hated seeing her young lodger's fire being dimmed. Julia had never wished to read another person's mind as much as she did in that moment.

They got out of the car and walked towards Julia's cottage. Further down the lane, her elderly neighbour, Emily Burns, was pruning her immaculate rose bushes. She spotted Julia and vigorously waved her over.

"Let yourself in," Julia whispered into Jessie's ear. "Emily is waving to me, and if I don't go and talk to her, I have a feeling she's going to hack my door down with those pruning shears."

Jessie accepted the keys, letting out a small laugh, and Julia was pleased to see her smiling again. She watched Jessie unlock the cottage door and walk into the darkness, stepping over a large stack of letters as she did.

"Good evening, Emily," Julia said as she approached Emily's low wall. "Your roses are looking exceptional."

"That's so kind of you to say, Julia," Emily said as she yanked off her gardening gloves. "You'll never guess what I heard earlier today."

Julia wondered if she should start to guess, but she decided saying nothing was the best option. No matter how she approached the topic, Emily would divulge everything she wanted to say.

"I heard something quite interesting walking back from my hair appointment this afternoon," Emily said, pushing up her greying curls for emphasis. "I don't usually pass Richard and Sally's cottage, but I fancied stretching my legs seeing as it was such a lovely day. Well, I say it was a lovely day, but it was ruined by the screaming and shouting that was coming from Richard and Sally's, or should I just say Richard's cottage, if the rumours of Sally's infidelity are to be believed."

Julia smiled and listened, not wanting to add that she knew those rumours were true.

"It was so loud, I practically heard every word. Your name came up more than once."

"My name? Are you sure?"

"It's a small village, Julia," Emily said, leaning over her freshly pruned rose bush, her eyes twinkling devilishly at being the one to break the information. "Unless there is another Julia who bakes cakes, I'm more than sure it was you."

"What were they saying?"

"Oh, nothing much," Emily said, waving her hand. "That wasn't the interesting part. Sally was crying about how she had visited your café to cancel her wedding cake order, but she was telling Richard how it wasn't too late and that you were an understanding woman. The poor girl was begging for his forgiveness, mind you, I never thought they were suitable. My own husband was older than me, but those two always seemed odd. If you ask me, I'd say Sally was after Richard's money. You know he inherited a fortune from his father? Richard Senior was a lance corporal in the army, and he was a thrifty saver. The money had barely hit Richard's account when Sally started sniffing around."

"What did you hear that was so interesting?" Julia asked, wanting to get to the point.

Emily could barely contain her smile. She looked up and down the lane to make sure it was clear, before leaning so far into the rose bush that the thorns snagged and tugged at her blouse.

"Sally told Richard that she loved him, and nobody else," Emily whispered. "Richard replied by saying, and I quote, '*you think because he's dead, I'm going to forgive you?*'"

Emily leaned back and pulled the thorns out of her blouse. She brushed down the stray strands and folded her hands over her chest, far too pleased with herself to care about the state of her garment. When Julia didn't respond, Emily's smile turned to a frown, and she leaned in again.

"You know what that means, don't you?" Emily whispered again, her eyes darting up and down the lane. "Sally was having an affair with Charles Wellington, and Richard found out, that's why they were fighting at your step-mother's garden party."

"She's not my step-mother," Julia found herself saying. "It's been lovely chatting Emily, but my gran is expecting me for dinner. Have a lovely evening."

Before Emily could engage Julia in more gossiping, Julia turned on her heels and walked as quickly as her legs would take her back to her cottage. If she hadn't just discovered that Sally had been at the garden party, the news of the affair wouldn't have bothered Julia so much, but her mind was spinning so quickly, she didn't immediately notice that the stack of letters on her doormat was thinner than when Jessie had opened the door. Julia crept down the hallway, and peered into Jessie's open bedroom door, just as Jessie was folding a letter and cramming it back into an envelope. She opened her wardrobe, curled the letter up, and crammed it down into one of her boots.

Julia stepped back, not wanting Jessie to know what she had just seen. Julia didn't know what was contained within that letter, but she was more than sure it was linked to Jessie's sudden shift in mood.

"Ready?" Julia asked, stepping forward again when she heard Jessie close the wardrobe door.

"Do you mind if I stay here and get an early night?" Jessie asked, forcing forward what appeared to be a fake yawn. "Dot won't mind."

Julia almost protested, but stopped herself. She thrust forward her kindest smile and nodded, telling Jessie where the rarely used takeaway menus were if she got hungry later. Reluctantly leaving her alone in the cottage, no doubt leaving her to pour over the contents of the mysterious letter, Julia fed Mowgli, grabbed her pecan pie, and drove back into the village.

CHAPTER 7

Julia could barely get a knife through Dot's lamb chops, but she battled through, smirking across the table to Sue every time one of their knives slipped from the tough meat.

"That was delicious," Sue said after finishing and pushing her plate away, sending a wink to Julia. "Your homemade mint sauce really complimented the lamb."

"Homemade?" Dot scoffed as she cut her last piece of lamb in half, her tiny arms working double speed. "You know I don't have time for that nonsense. Me and some of the girls had our second weekly book club meeting just before you girls got here. I barely had time to throw the chops into the frying pan."

Julia wanted to ask how she had managed to cook them twice through if she hadn't had time, but she held her tongue.

"Book club?" Julia asked. "Is that new?"

"Well, our poker club was rumbled by your boyfriend," Dot said, rolling her eyes as she started to gather the plates.

"I simply asked him the laws regarding gambling in the privacy of one's home, and he took quite the exception to it. Started asking all of these questions, so I told the girls it was better if we switched things up for a while until he stopped sniffing around."

"What book are you reading?" Sue asked.

"Fifty Shades of Grey," Dot said casually. "It was the only book in the charity shop with enough copies for all of us."

Sue and Julia both bit their lips at the same time to stop their laughter from bursting out. Whenever Julia thought she had her gran figured out, she would say something that would prove her wrong.

After the plates were cleared away, Dot brought Julia's pecan pie from the fridge, along with a small bowl of clotted cream. She served up three generous slices, leaving one for Julia to take home to Jessie.

"Delicious as always Julia," Dot mumbled through a large mouthful. "I'm not usually a fan of that American food, but I have to say that this is quite lovely."

"Just something I'm thinking of putting on the menu," Julia said. "Read about it in a cookbook Jessie got from the library and it intrigued me."

"Jessie can read?" Dot asked, a brow darting up. "I thought she was raised on the streets?"

"*Gran!*" Sue cried.

"What?"

"Don't be so mean!" Sue said, shaking her head at Julia. "Jessie is a lovely girl."

"Did I say otherwise?" Dot snapped. "I'm just stating facts. The girl was raised on the streets, wasn't she Julia?"

"She was living on the streets for about six months,

Gran. Before that, she was living with foster parents."

"Poor girl," Dot said. "It's not like she's had the best life. I doubt her education has been consistent throughout her life. How is she? I'm surprised not to see her with you tonight."

Julia crammed her mouth full of pecan pie, wondering if she should reveal her worries to her family. She decided if she told them, they might be able to give her advice on what she should do.

"She told me she was tired, but she's hiding something from me," Julia said after licking clotted cream from her lips. "She's been sleepwalking too."

"You used to sleepwalk," Dot said. "Scared the wits out of me at first."

Julia stared ahead at Sue, not realising that her gran was talking to her.

"I used to sleepwalk?" Julia asked, her brows pinching together as she dropped her fork, suddenly no longer hungry. "I don't remember that."

"Well, you wouldn't. I never told you. It was right after your poor mother died. You used to get up in the dead of the night to sit by the window, staring out. I thought you were a burglar at first. You almost got a ceramic cat bashed over your head the first time I caught you."

Julia stared down at her pecan pie, wondering why she had no memory of this. She looked at Sue, who shrugged. It was possible her gran was just confused, but Julia doubted she would make up such a thing.

"How long did it last?" Julia asked, her voice low, almost ashamed.

"You grew out of it eventually," Dot said, tapping her finger on her chin as she thought. "In fact, I could have sworn it only happened in the times when your father was away. Yes, that's right. I remember telling him that you were getting up and looking for his car to pull up outside. I think you eventually realised his trips home were getting less frequent and it seeped through to your subconscious."

Julia tried to conjure some memory of it happening, but nothing came forth. She thought of her twelve-year-old self sitting by her gran's sitting room window in the dark, staring out at the village green waiting for something that would never come. Her chest tightened.

"I find it best to just confront things head on," Sue said carefully, seeming to recognise the hurt in Julia's expression. "Just ask her what's on her mind. Even if you don't think she wants to talk about it, she might just need a little coaxing."

Julia couldn't touch her pecan pie after that, so when Sue and her gran finished, she cleared the plates away herself, and took her time washing them in the small kitchen sink. When she was finished, she joined them in the sitting room for tea. Julia sat in the armchair furthest from the window, finding it difficult to look in its direction.

"Has your boyfriend said anything about this murder case?" Dot asked after blowing and sipping tea from her small china cup.

"Barker isn't my boyfriend," Julia said, hearing the bite in her voice. "I haven't seen him since the garden party."

"I'm surprised how little information is floating around the village," Dot said, scrunching up her face and staring hopefully at the small red telephone in the corner. "You would think somebody would know something? Did you know Joanne Lewis' husband was working on Katie's silly spa idea?"

"Where did you hear that?" Sue asked, clearly not having heard that information herself.

"I saw Terry at the garden party," Dot said, her eyes suddenly narrowing as if she had just landed on some information she had forgotten she possessed. "Well, I saw him on my way back from the bathroom. It was right before I came out and saw you all huddled around the body."

"You saw Terry in Peridale Manor?" Julia asked, her ears pricking up. "Upstairs?"

"I used the downstairs bathroom," Dot said, shaking her head. "You don't suppose I was in the house at the same time that poor man was pushed from the window, do you?"

"It's possible," Julia said, sipping her tea and leaning forward. "What did Terry say to you?"

"I was just asking what he was doing in the house," Dot said, tapping her chin once more. "Yes, that's right. He was wearing work boots and he stood out like a sore thumb in that house. He had just come in from the garden for some water. He told me he had gotten the contract for the work, and that he was digging out the pool. I told him how ridiculous the spa idea was, and then I came outside, and well, we all know what happened next."

"Which direction was he heading in?" Julia asked.

"Direction?" Dot asked with a frown. "Why does it matter? The kitchen, I think."

"Not the staircase?"

Dot thought about it for a moment, looking from Sue and Julia, her mouth opening and closing. She seemed frustrated by all of the questions.

"It might have been," Dot said, tugging at the brooch fastened to her collar under her chin. "I'm an old woman.

My memory isn't what it was, girls. The staircase and the kitchen are in the same direction, so maybe."

"I visited Peridale Manor yesterday," Julia said quietly as she stared ahead, her mind working overtime. "Katie told me that Dad was being questioned by the police, and that he had been at the station all day. Then I saw Joanne Lewis, and she told me about Terry getting the contract."

"Your father was being questioned?" Dot asked, her frown deepening. "Why?"

"I don't know yet," Julia said dismissively. "What I do know is that Joanne specifically told me her and Terry were both outside at the time of Charles' death."

"Oh," Dot said, her hand drifting up to her mouth. "*Oh!* Have I just uncovered something?"

"Perhaps," Julia said, not wanting to get her gran excited. "He could have quickly gone back outside again. Wrong place, wrong time."

Sue sighed and pinched between her brows. Julia could sense what was coming next.

"Julia," Sue started, looking her sister deep in the eyes. "Why do I feel like you're investigating this?"

"Because I am," Julia said, already reaching for her pad to scribble down what Dot had just revealed. "I think the police are trying to pin this murder on Katie or Dad."

"Do you think either of them did it?" Dot asked, her voice suddenly small.

"I don't know," Julia said. "Either way, I want to know, and if they are arrested, I want to be absolutely sure there is no room for error."

Dot's eyes widened excitedly, but Sue sighed again and shook her head. Julia knew her sister was just worried about her. She didn't understand Julia's need to find out all of the facts. Julia didn't understand it much herself, it was just a drive she had within her. It was a similar feeling she had whenever she tasted one of her cakes and she was trying to put her finger on why it didn't quite taste right.

"I'll keep an ear to the ground," Dot exclaimed, snapping her fingers together as she ran towards the phone. "In fact, I'll start calling around to see if people have heard anything."

Julia wasn't interested in idle village gossip, she was interested in finding out the truth about what had led to somebody pushing a man out of a window at a garden party. Somebody had murdered Charles Wellington, and her list of suspects was growing by the day. She added '*Terry Lewis*' alongside Katie and her father, and Sally and Richard. Flipping back a page, she added '*find out if Terry had a connection to Charles*'.

Dropping her notepad back into her bag, she quickly finished her tea and made her excuses to go home so she could shut herself in her bedroom with her notes and her thoughts.

CHAPTER 8

On Julia's drive back up to her cottage, she was so distracted that she almost didn't notice Barker getting out of his car. She slowed down, pulling up behind him. When he spotted her, a smile spread across his face, which had the ability to make Julia forget what had been swirling around in her mind.

"Evening," Barker said, leaning his hand heavily against the top of her car as she rolled down her window. "Bit late to only just be closing the café, isn't it?"

"Dinner at Gran's," Julia said. "I could say the same about you. I suspect the investigation is keeping you all busy."

Barker pursed his lips, and he almost seemed disappointed in Julia for heading straight to the investigation. She tightened her fingers around the steering wheel, inhaling deeply, trying to rid her mind of it for a moment.

"Can I invite you in for some tea?" Barker asked, glancing awkwardly back to his cottage. "Or some coffee?"

Julia heard the nerves in Barker's voice, and they mirrored the ones that had suddenly sprung up in her stomach. She peered past Barker's car into the dark, imagining her cottage in the distance.

"Do you have peppermint and liquorice tea?" Julia asked.

"They make that?" Barker asked, a brow darting up. "I have black tea."

"Good job I carry my own," Julia said as she reached into her handbag to pull out an individually wrapped teabag.

Julia jumped out of her car and followed Barker through the dark, and into his cottage. It was small and similar in layout to Julia's, but everything else was completely different. Where Julia's cottage was neat and tidy with appropriate furniture for a period building, Barker's home was messy, filled with stacks of boxes he still hadn't unpacked, and glossy furniture that would have better suited an apartment in the city.

"I've been meaning to unpack those," Barker said when he caught Julia staring at the brown boxes. "It's been a bit busier than I expected."

They walked through to his small sitting room, which was equally as messy. Pizza boxes and coffee cups cluttered the table, along with paperwork and golfing magazines. Barker turned on a couple of lamps, gathered up the papers, and cleared the shiny leather couch for Julia.

"I had a cleaner at my last place," Barker said, his cheeks blushing. "I've been meaning to find one in Peridale. Either that, or I adjust to cleaning up my own mess."

"You're a busy man," Julia said, not wanting to shame him for the mess. "There is a cleaning agency in the village.

I'll see if I can get their number for you."

"That would be great," Barker said as he accepted Julia's wrapped teabag. "Make yourself comfy. I'll get the kettle on."

Barker hurried off to the kitchen, ducking so he didn't hit his head on the beams. Julia couldn't decide if the cottage didn't suit Barker, or if Barker didn't suit the cottage. He had been living in the village for over a month now. It already felt like he had been there as long as everybody else, but looking at his glossy furniture and packed boxes reminded Julia how different he really was.

"Smells delicious," Barker said, sniffing Julia's tea as he walked back in clutching two mismatching mugs. "I've always been a coffee man myself."

"Two sugars?"

"You remembered," Barker said with a nod. "Impressive."

"It's a talent," Julia said, accepting her mug. "Or a curse. Depending on how you look at it. There's not a villager's order in the café that I seem to be able to forget, even if I wanted to."

Barker sat in an armchair across from Julia and stared ahead at the blank TV, which Julia noticed hadn't even been plugged in. She remembered moving into her own cottage, eager to unpack everything to feel right at home as quickly as possible. Adjusting from the city to Peridale had taken her minutes, not months, but she had been born there. She wondered what it must feel like to come to such a small village and be thrown into its hustle and bustle with no time to acclimatise.

"I heard you were interviewing my father," Julia said, trying and failing to drop it casually into the silence.

Barker smirked as he sipped his steaming hot coffee. He reached out and placed the coffee mug on top of a golfing magazine before leaning back in his chair to rest his fingers over his creased white shirt and tie.

"I don't like to rule anybody out," Barker said. "For what it's worth, I don't think he did it."

"Did his feet not match the footprints you found?" Julia asked, again trying and failing to sound casual.

"How do you know about those?"

"I noticed them when I was at the manor."

Barker narrowed his eyes on Julia, a smirk tickling his lips. He sighed and rubbed his eyes heavily with his hands before sitting straight up and leaning against the chair's arm. The armchair didn't look particularly comfortable, but neither was the couch under her.

"You don't miss a trick, do you, Julia?"

"I try not to."

"No, his feet didn't match those boot prints, not that we've found the boots yet," Barker said. "It doesn't mean he's innocent. Those boot prints could have been made at any time before the murder."

"Actually, between about midday and the murder," Julia corrected him. "When I went to the bathroom earlier in the day, the boot prints weren't there."

"And you only just think to mention this now?" Barker asked, his nostrils flaring.

"You told me to stay out of things," Julia said quietly before taking another sip of her tea. "I'm just doing what you told me."

Barker stared at her, and for a moment he appeared angry, but his scowl turned into a warm smile. He let out a small laugh and shook his head. Leaning his arm on the chair and resting his head on his knuckles, he stared at Julia.

"Did you manage to figure out what was missing from the plinth next to the window?" Julia asked.

"Katie couldn't remember what was there," Barker said. "Neither could your father. Vincent Wellington barely knows what day it is. I don't even think he realises his son has died."

"It's a sad situation," Julia said. "It's no life to have."

"I can't help but feel your step-mother is taking advantage of his state."

"She's not my step-mother," Julia quickly added. "She just happens to be married to my father. We're the same age, you know?"

"She looks much older," Barker said with a small wink. "Did you know she used to be a glamour model? When I was investigating the house, I was surprised to see very explicit pictures of her hung all over her bedroom."

"Sounds like Katie," Julia said. "Self-indulgent and superficial to the core. She told me she was only doing this spa thing because she was bored."

Julia recognised the venom in her voice, forcing her to sit up and sip her tea. She thought back to what her gran had told her about her sleepwalking, and the lingering resentment towards her father bubbled stronger than it had in over two decades. That resentment had found a new target in Katie, and she hated herself for being that way.

"One of my officers saw you snooping around Peridale Manor yesterday," Barker said, seeming to sense Julia's thoughts.

"And what makes you so sure that was me?"

"I gave them your exact description and told them to watch out for you," Barker said. "Even I didn't expect you to jump so quickly into this one."

"I was visiting my family."

"The family you're not even that close to?" Barker asked, leaning forward a little. "I asked your father about his relationships. He filled me in a little."

"You were asking my father about me?" Julia asked quietly, her brow reflectively arching.

"It was just routine. We ask all sorts of questions to establish a profile of somebody. He didn't say much, just that you two weren't close."

Julia sipped her tea, wondering if that was true, or if Barker had purposefully asked her father questions about her to try and figure her out. As the sweet liquorice coated her throat, she wasn't sure if she should be offended or flattered.

"My father's feet are quite big, aren't they?" Julia asked suddenly.

"Yes? Why?"

"Size twelve?" Julia asked. "Maybe eleven?"

"Eleven," Barker said, his eyes narrowing. "Why do you ask?"

"Because I'm just trying to establish the size of the boot prints found at the scene. If they didn't fit my father, I'm guessing they were smaller, rather than larger? I'd say size thirteen, even for a man, is a little on the large size. I'd also say it wasn't a ten either. It's possible to fit your foot into a boot one size smaller, even if it will be a little uncomfortable. The way you said my father's foot didn't fit makes me think it didn't fit by a long way because you sounded rather disappointed that your obvious suspect didn't quite fit into the frame, which was why you suggested the boot prints may be unrelated, even though we both know they were. So, my guess is that the prints found at the scene were either a seven, or an eight? From my memory, they didn't look much smaller than that, which means the murderer has either size seven, or eight feet, or maybe even a little smaller, but not too much smaller. Just like you can fit your feet into a size smaller, you could fit your feet into boots a little bigger, but not too much bigger because boots that large would be too heavy to produce such clear footprints if the boots drastically didn't fit a person. Am I thinking along the right lines here, Detective?"

Julia paused to sip her tea and enjoy the look of complete shock that had slowly spread across Barker's face. She had stitched together the theory in the back of her mind over the last couple of minutes, but it made complete sense to her.

"If this was a couple hundred years ago, you would have been burned at the stake for being a witch," Barker said, his eyes widening. "You know that, right?"

"I'll take that as a compliment, and also that I was right."

"I didn't say that."

"But you didn't correct me," Julia said, her hands closing around the warm mug. "If I had been wildly wrong, you would have tried to correct me, Detective Inspector. I know you're not a man who puts a lot of stock into his pride, but you are a man, which means you like to be right."

"What makes you think I don't put stock into my pride?" Barker asked, his eyes widening as though he really were sitting in the company of a witch.

"Because if you were a proud man, you wouldn't have

invited a woman into your cottage when it looks like this," Julia said as she rested her half finished tea on the cluttered coffee table. "Thank you for the boiled water."

"You're leaving already?" Barker jumped up, his head almost hitting the low ceiling.

"Jessie will be wondering where I am. Unless you want to sit around for the rest of the night discussing the finer details of your case?"

Barker let out a small laugh of disbelief, and Julia revelled in the fact that she had clearly trumped him more than once. When she had first met Barker, she knew he underestimated her, and even though she knew he no longer did, she still enjoyed being one step ahead of him. Just like when she was following somebody else's recipe for a cake she had never baked before, she liked to guess the next step before reading it. More often than not, her logical thinking proved her right.

"You're an extraordinary woman, Julia Smith," Barker said as he led her towards the front door. "I can easily say I have never met a woman quite like you."

"Should I take that as a compliment?" she asked as she fished her car keys from her pocket.

"I'm not quite sure," Barker said as he leaned around her to open the front door. "What I am sure of is that I'm going to ask you out on a date, and this time I won't take no for an answer."

Julia stepped out of his cottage, dropping her curls over her face to conceal her sudden blushing.

"I wasn't intending to say no."

"I'll pick you up tomorrow at seven," Barker said.

"I look forward to it," Julia replied, the butterflies in her stomach swirling around so hard that they were crashing into one another. "One more thing, Detective Inspector. Size seven, or size eight?"

"I'm sorry?"

"The boots. Seven or eight?" Julia said, her fingers gripping around her keys. "For my own piece of mind."

"That would be telling, wouldn't it?" Barker said, his usual smug smirk returning at being able to trump Julia back. "Goodnight, Julia."

Julia walked casually back to her car, and set off up the lane. Just before Barker's cottage faded from view, she glanced back in her rear-view mirror to see Barker still standing on his doorstep, looking towards her car. The man she had only known for a month was making her feel excited in a way that her husband of sixteen years had failed to.

Back in her cottage, she was disappointed to see Jessie asleep on top of her bed, not because her lodger had fallen asleep, but because she appeared to be pretending to have done so. It only confirmed to Julia that there was something she didn't want to talk about.

Julia made a mental note to investigate two things; she wanted to revisit Peridale Manor to speak to her father, and she wanted to check Jessie's wardrobe to see what she was hiding.

CHAPTER 9

J ulia left Jessie in charge of the café the next morning for the first time so she could visit Peridale Manor alone. Dark clouds circled above the house as she drove towards it, blocking out the blue sky Julia had awoken to. In Julia's mind, the dark clouds had been circling all morning. She couldn't shake the feeling she was being lied to by more than one person.

"Julia," her dad exclaimed after Hilary let her into the house, putting up less of a fight this time. "I wasn't expecting to see you today. Can I get you a cup of tea, or coffee?"

"Tea would be lovely," Julia said as she reached into her handbag to grab a teabag. "I've brought my own."

"Peppermint and liquorice?" he mumbled as he read over the label. "How – *unusual*. I'm sure it tastes more delicious than it sounds."

Julia's father handed the teabag to Hilary, who eyed it disdainfully. Brian stepped to the side and let Julia lead the way through the house to the grand sitting room.

"This is one of the rooms we're turning into a treatment room," he said as he sat on an uncomfortable looking antique sofa. "It has beautiful views of the grounds, although I dare say it's going to rain today."

Julia looked out of the floor-to-ceiling windows where she could see a team of four working on the new pool. It appeared they were getting ready to pour concrete into the foundations they had dug.

"Is Katie home today?" Julia asked after Hilary brought through their tea on a heavy silver tray.

"She's gone to London for the day for a shopping trip with some of the girls, to take her mind off things. You know what it's like."

Julia didn't know what it was like. She didn't have a brother, but if she did, she couldn't imagine a shopping trip taking her mind off his murder. She tried to imagine the pain she would feel if Sue were taken from her so cruelly, but it was impossible to summon.

"She seems to be coping quite well," Julia said as she sipped her hot tea. "Were they close?"

"Not as close as she would have liked. He was rather jealous of her."

"Jealous?" Julia asked, remembering the argument she had overheard between them. "Because she is Vincent's favourite?"

Brian's lips quivered, appearing confused by Julia's knowledge of their relationship. She busied herself by blowing on her hot tea, wishing she had kept that information closer to her chest.

"Parents don't have favourites," he said with a small shrug. "We just love our children differently."

Julia attempted to ignore the irony in what he had just

said. If Vincent cared differently for each of his children, Brian cared equally indifferently for his own.

"This isn't my first time here to talk to you," Julia said, resting her tea on the edge of the awkwardly shaped antique sofa. "I was here two days ago, but you were busy."

"Katie mentioned your visit," he said, giving a non-convincing smile. "I suppose she told you where I was? The police were simply just trying to eliminate me because I live here."

"And did they eliminate you?"

"Of course they did," he said with a small laugh, the suspicion on his face growing. "You don't think I could push a man from a window, do you?"

Julia didn't know what to think. She didn't like the thought of her father committing a murder, but she didn't know the man sitting in front of her as much as he was pretending. She remembered what Barker had told her about the boots not fitting, so she shook her head and reached for her tea.

"And Katie?" Julia asked, wanting to steer the conversation towards the purpose of her visit. "Have they eliminated her yet?"

"It's not as simple as that," he said, leaning forward to rest his elbows on his knees. "Why do I feel like I'm being interrogated by my own daughter?"

"I'm just curious. I was here. Everybody was here. We all just want to figure this out as much as I suppose you do."

"There's no *supposing* about it," he said, his voice growing a little darker. "Charles and I never particularly saw eye to eye. There was a reason it appeared Vincent favoured his daughter. Charles was a loose cannon, a troublemaker some might say. Vincent's money is old family money, but there's less of it left than people assume. If Charles had had his way, he would have gambled away every penny the moment he inherited his share of Peridale Manor and it's dwindling fortune. When Katie suggested to her father that they turn this place into a spa, he was happy to consent. Of course, this was before his last stroke. He doesn't talk much these days. In fact, he doesn't do much at all. If he knows his son is dead, he's not grieving. Charles wasn't a nice man, nor was he kind to his sister or father. He lived recklessly, surfing from couch to couch. He burned through his trust fund in a matter of years and had been living off hand-outs from his father. Katie is an entrepreneur. She is invested in giving this old place a purpose. She has vision, unlike her brother. She saw the Wellington name becoming a brand so future generations would reap what she had sown. All her brother cared about was getting his cut and wasting it."

"Future generations?" Julia choked, her minty tea catching the back of her throat. "I didn't think Katie or Charles had kids."

Brian squirmed uncomfortably in his seat, telling Julia everything she needed to know. She remembered how scared she had been of the announcement, and how relieved she had been when her fears had been proven wrong.

"I wasn't going to tell you girls until it was official," Brian said with a heavy sigh. "We're trying for a baby, but it's not easy. We're having – *complications*."

"A baby?" Julia mumbled, her cheeks burning red. "Don't you think you're -,"

"Too old?"

"Maybe just a little."

Brian exhaled heavily, leaning back in his chair. He

stared ahead at Julia with sadness in his eyes, and for a brief moment, Julia thought she saw years of regret flash through them. In that split second, Julia was looking at the father she was still clinging to in the back of her mind.

"We have a lot to offer a child," Brian said in a rehearsed way. "The Wellington name must continue somehow."

"You're not a Wellington," Julia found herself saying without thinking about it. "You're a South."

"Well, the baby would be a Wellington-South. You get the idea."

"I do," Julia said, her jaw gritting tightly. "Very clearly."

At that moment, as if on cue, the heavens opened. Heavy rain pounded down on Peridale Manor, scattering the workman like ants. Julia and her father sipped their tea in silence as they listened to the pitter-patter of rain echo throughout the old manor.

"Was there anything else, Julia?" her father asked as he stood up. "I have a meeting at noon with some old antiques contacts to ask about furniture for the spa."

Julia finished her tea, and placed it back on the silver tray. She followed him in standing, knowing she had dozens of unanswered questions, but she was unable to think of anything other than a tiny screaming baby who would be her brother or sister.

"There was one thing," Julia said, gathering her thoughts, trying to think of what was the most important. "After Charles was pushed, I noticed something had been taken from one of the display plinths next the window. Do you know what was there?"

"Ah, yes. The detective asked me that too," he said

with a small nod, his finger napping his chin. "I'm afraid I don't. Katie doesn't either. This house is so big and full of so much junk, neither of us can recall what was there. Vincent would probably know, but it's almost impossible to get a word out of the poor man. Is it important?"

"I'm sure it's not," Julia lied, not wanting to let him know that she thought the missing item was a possible murder weapon. "Can I use your bathroom before I go?"

"Of course," he said as they walked back through to the grand entrance hall. "It's upstairs, second door on the left."

Julia hurried up the staircase, feeling her father's eyes on her with every step. She turned the corner, and walked towards the bathroom, making her way further down to hall. The broken window had already been replaced, making it feel like nothing had happened at all. The display plinth was still empty, but the dust had since been polished away. Julia knew there was one overlooked person in the house who would know exactly what had been there, but she was sure that Hilary wouldn't be so quick to offer Julia any information.

After a minute passed, Julia turned to walk back towards the staircase. If her father had been there, she would have had to make her way back downstairs and abandon her plan. Luckily, he wasn't, so she hurried along the hallway, her tiny kitten heels clicking loudly on the polished mahogany floorboards.

The layout of the manor was a mystery to her, with dozens of different doors lining the long hall. Very soon, those rooms would be full of spa visitors enjoying whatever Katie had to offer them.

Along with the murder, the spa was also a popular topic of conversation in her café at the moment, with most of the villagers firmly against it, even if they were offering free use of the pool to residents during the week. As a business owner, Julia was undecided. The new tourists in town would likely give her profits a little boost, but the thought of the village changing in any way made her tummy ache. While the rest of the world was constantly shifting and evolving, Peridale had stayed as it always had, and that's why she loved it.

Ignoring all of the other doors, Julia went straight to the room Katie and Charles had been arguing in, on the morning of his death. On her way, she caught a glimpse of Vincent sitting in front of a TV in his wheelchair. She thought they locked eyes, but she decided it was her imagination playing tricks on her.

After knocking softly on the wood, Julia crept into the room when there was no reply. She realised instantly that this was her father and Katie's room. The nude portraits of Katie that Barker had spoken of littered the walls. Julia wasn't a prude, but the narcissism made her feel uneasy. The wallpaper behind the portraits was blood red and ink black damask, giving the room a seedier feeling than the rest of the manor.

Ignoring all of this, Julia went straight to the walk-in closet to find exactly what she was looking for. The floor was lined with hundreds of pairs of designer heels. Julia didn't understand what a woman could do with so many pairs of shoes. She owned a couple of pairs of work shoes, some flat and some with small heels depending on how she felt, and a single pair of black high heels, which she had only worn once, despite Sue buying them for her years ago.

Julia plucked a shoe out at random to look at the size printed on the sole. Just to be sure, she picked up a couple more shoes to check they were all the same size, which they were. They were all size eight, which was an above average size for a woman Katie's height, but not uncommon.

Leaving the shoes exactly where she had found them, Julia turned and walked back into the bedroom knowing her father could walk in at any moment. On her way past the window she looked out into the rain. The heavy clouds circled above, making it look as though it was virtually dusk, not nearly noon.

She then noticed a yellow light in the darkness. Squinting, she spotted the builder's cabin stationed at the far end of the garden. Next to the cabin, the rain was bouncing off the roof of a car she immediately recognised as Joanne's. The Lewis house had been next on Julia's list, so she hurried out of the bedroom and down the stairs, ready to kill two birds with one stone.

"Ah, there you are," her father said, appearing from a door when she reached the bottom of the stairs. "I thought you had already gone."

"Women's troubles," she said quickly, knowing he wouldn't ask any more questions. "Dad, can I ask you something?"

"Of course you can," he said, suddenly looking nervous.

"Where were you when Charles was pushed from the window?"

Brian pursed his lips and folded his arms across his chest, appearing to be considering if he should tell Julia. She knew she was going out on a limb, but he had told her the truth about him and Katie trying for a baby, so it was worth a shot.

"I was in the grounds looking for Katie," he said, his

eyes dark and piercing. "After Charles ruined her speech, she ran off looking for him. When she didn't find him in the house, she ran off into the grounds before I could stop her. I went looking for her, but I couldn't find her, so I went back to the house where she was drinking whiskey in my study. She said she couldn't find him so she looped around and came to find me, but needed something to calm her nerves. Then we came out, and that's when we saw what had happened."

"Is that what you told the police?" Julia asked.

"I told them the truth," he said with a firm nod. "I know what you're trying to suggest, Julia. Katie didn't kill her brother."

"I should get going," Julia said, setting off towards the door. "I've left Jessie in charge of the café."

Brian walked her to the grand entrance, opening the door for her. They stood and looked out into the rain for a moment. He looked as if he might say something, but he didn't. Julia wondered if he knew he had just told her that Katie's alibi was a lie, therefore putting her alone in the house at the time of her brother's murder. Were those boot prints really the boots Katie had put on in front of a crowd of people? Even if they were the right size, Julia didn't want to rule anything out yet, even if the evidence was mounting up.

Julia hurried through the rain towards her car, the shower instantly soaking her through. She flicked on her headlights, watching as the rain bounced against the gravel driveway. Her father lingered at the front door, so she started to reverse slowly into a U-turn. When he finally closed the door, she looped around and pulled up next to Joanne's car.

CHAPTER 10

Julia jumped out of her car and walked past Joanne's, the rain continuing to stick her dress to her skin. Through the yellow light piercing the closed blinds, there were two figures, one of them pacing back and forth. Julia crept up the couple of steps towards the door of the cabin. She was about to knock, but through the din of the rain, a woman's voice floated through. Pressing her ear up against the white plastic door, she recognised the voice as Joanne's.

"You should be glad he's dead!" Joanne cried. "He's done us all a favour. Without this job, we'd be ruined."

"Joanne, just -," said a man, who she recognised as Terry.

"Don't tell me to calm down! You gambled away our future. You gambled away your son's future. We're hanging on by a thread, and this job is the only thing that is coming to save us. When was the last time you got us a job like this? *Huh*? You haven't in *years*. You got us into this mess, so you can fix it."

"Joanne, just listen -,"

"*Terry!*" she shrieked. "There's nothing you can say to make this better. I'm tired of this. I'm going, and if you know what's good for you, you won't follow me."

Julia quickly ducked under the window and darted around the far side of the building, pushing her body up against the cabin wall. She heard the door open and seconds later, Joanne's engine roared to life. Holding her breath and closing her eyes, she stood frozen against the wall as the rain pelted against her. She didn't dare breathe until Joanne's car drove past her and sped away from the cabin.

Not wanting to chance being caught by Terry, she walked around the back of the cabin, her tiny heels sinking into the mud. The suction of the mud pulled off her left shoe, her bare foot planting in the sludge, her toes dancing in the filth. Hands outstretched and water in her eyes she bent down to pick up her shoe, but she fell forward, landing hands and knees in the mud. It took all her power not to cry out.

She touched the heel of her shoe, so she pulled it out of the mud, deciding it was better to carry it back to her car. Soaked and filthy, she tiptoed through the torrent.

Keeping her headlights turned off, Julia reversed through the dark and drove quicker than she ever had, until she was pulling up outside of her cottage.

As she quickly showered so she could go back to the café clean and fresh, Joanne's words were circling around her mind.

'You should be glad he's dead. You got us into this mess.'

Julia hurried into her café under the protection of an umbrella. She wasn't surprised to see that it was almost empty, except for one customer. What she was surprised to see was Sally sitting at the table nearest the counter. When Jessie and Sally both turned to look at who had just walked through the door, they both looked extremely relieved to see Julia.

"I was beginning to think you would never come back," Jessie whispered to her as Julia hung her raincoat up in the kitchen. "There was a huge rush of people when the rain started."

"It's good practice," Julia said. "How long has Sally been here?"

"About twenty minutes," Jessie said as she looked down at Julia's dress. "You weren't wearing that when you left."

"It's a long story. I'll tell you later."

Julia adjusted her hair in the reflection of a knife, brushed down the creases in the blue dress she hadn't had time to iron, and walked through to the café and straight to Sally.

Julia noticed how different she looked from the last time she had seen her. It looked as though she had had a good night's sleep, her mousy hair was perfectly straight despite the rain, she was wearing a full face of makeup, and she was smiling. Julia sensed some nerves coming from Sally, but she understood them because she could guess what Sally was about to tell her.

"The wedding is back on," Sally said cautiously. "We've decided to give things another go."

"That's great news," Julia said, unsure if it was. "I suppose you're here to reorder your wedding cake?"

"You're a mind reader, Julia," Sally said, her fingers fumbling with her engagement ring. "Although can we just have a simple sponge this time? Richard never liked the idea of a cinnamon, rose and orange cake anyway."

Julia nodded, wondering if this second attempt at their engagement had come with some strict conditions. Looking into Sally's eyes, Julia sensed uneasiness in them, even if she was trying to hide it behind a smile. Her mascara and elaborate eye shadow were distracting, but not enough to hide the fact she had recently been crying.

"Forgive me if I'm talking out of turn, but I wanted to ask you a question about Charles," Julia said quietly, leaning across the table.

"Charles?" Sally's false smile suddenly dropped, and her bottom lip started to tremble. "What about him?"

Before Julia could say another word, her café door opened, and a dark figure walked in from the rain. They all turned to watch as Richard pulled his hood down, his eyes honing in on Sally.

"I've been waiting for you in the car," Richard said, his voice flat and empty.

"I was waiting for Julia to get back," Sally explained, the shake in her voice obvious.

"Have you asked her about the cake?"

"Yes."

"And told her you don't want that stupid flavour?"

"Yes."

"Then let's go," Richard said, his dark eyes landing on Julia as he reopened the door.

Sally pulled on her jacket, and without another word headed straight for Richard. Something red caught Julia's attention against the whiteness of her door. Richard's knuckles were covered in cuts, but they weren't fresh; they had started to scab over.

"What a weirdo," Jessie said loudly when they both left the café. "What does she see in him?"

"Sally dreams of the happily ever after. She will do whatever it takes to get it, even if that means sacrifice."

"I think women like that are dumb," Jessie said, smacking her gum against her tongue, which Julia had told her she wasn't allowed to chew behind the counter. "You wouldn't catch me dead bowing to a man like that."

"I did for a while," Julia said, holding her hand out under Jessie's mouth for her to spit out the gum. "When Richard attacked Charles at the garden party, did he actually hit him?"

Jessie reluctantly spat the gum into Julia's palm. She screwed up her face, thinking about it for a moment, before looking down her nose at Julia in the way she did.

"Nope," she said firmly. "Your boyfriend dragged Richard off before he got a chance."

"He's not my boyfriend," Julia corrected her as she tied her apron around her waist. "Although I do need to talk to him."

"Are you going to ask him on that date?"

"He already asked me again," Julia said, a smile spreading across her face, but then quickly vanishing when she remembered what day it was. "It's tonight!"

"Oh, please," Jessie said, rolling her eyes as she walked through the beads into the kitchen. "A moment while I vomit."

She let the excitement spread through her for a minute while Jessie was in the kitchen. She bit into her lip, wondering if she had anything suitable for a date in the back of her wardrobe.

CHAPTER 11

"Close your eyes," Sue demanded as she moved towards Julia with a small makeup brush. "Stop fidgeting!"

"It tickles," Julia said. "How much longer is this going to take?"

"Miracles don't happen without a lot of praying," Sue mumbled as she took a step back from Julia. "Needs more wing."

Julia attempted to look in the mirror that Sue had been blocking with her body since insisting on doing Julia's makeup. She had foolishly called her sister to ask for some advice on what she should wear, so when Sue showed up at her door ten minutes later clutching a trunk filled with more makeup than Julia knew what to do with, she instantly regretted calling her sister.

"Barker isn't going to be able to resist you when he sees you," Sue said, clearly pleased with her handiwork. "I've never seen you look so feminine."

"I don't know if that was a compliment or an insult."

"Both," Sue said. "Open your eyes and look at me."

Julia did as she was told. Her lids felt heavy under the weight of the eye shadow Sue had been precisely applying for the last twenty minutes, as did the rest of her face. She felt like she was wearing a mask; something she wasn't at all used to. She wasn't opposed to a little mascara or lipstick every now and then, but it wasn't practical to apply a full face of makeup before baking in the morning.

"Barker has seen me before," Julia said, trying her best to look past her sister to the mirror. "He knows exactly what I look like."

"There's nothing wrong with a little enhancement," Sue said as she dug in her trunk for more makeup. "A little highlight and I think we're done."

"I don't think my face can take anymore."

"It's the *final* touch. I promise. It'll just bring the whole thing together."

Sue swirled a clean brush in a compact of sparkly powder, which kicked up a small cloud of glittery dust. She dusted the powder on her cheeks, nose and cupids bow until she seemed satisfied that she had done her absolute most to make Julia look presentable for her date. When she was done, she stepped back, a proud grin spreading from ear to ear.

"You look like you're going to cry," Julia mumbled out of the corner of her mouth, scared to move in case the mask fell off.

"You look beautiful!" Sue said, clasping her hands together under her chin. "Oh, Julia. You look *so* beautiful."

Sue stepped to the side to finally let Julia see what she had done. Squinting in the dim light of her bedroom, Julia moved closer to her dressing table mirror. Her heart rate doubled in an instant.

"I look – I look-,"

"Beautiful!"

"*Like a clown!*" Julia cried, moving even closer to the mirror. "I don't even look like myself."

"That's the whole point!"

Julia closed one eye to get a better look at the black powder smoking up to her brow, unsure if it had been Sue's intention to make her look like a panda. Her cheeks were striped silver, pink and brown, bringing to mind Neapolitan ice-cream.

"I look like The Joker!" Julia moaned, pulling apart her sticky, red lips. "I look like a *clown!*"

"It'll look better when I've finished your hair," Sue said, already twisting Julia's wavy hair around the barrel of a curling iron. "Trust me."

Julia sat back in the chair and stared at her reflection, and for a moment she almost did submit to her sister's pruning. The heat of the curling iron sizzling against her scalp snapped her to her senses, and she sprang forward and out of the chair.

"This isn't me!" Julia said, clutching the small burn on the back of her head. "I'm sorry, Sue, but this isn't me."

Leaving her sister, Julia opened her bedroom door and walked through to the sitting room, where Jessie was flicking through the TV guide and drawing moustaches on the women. Julia needed an opinion she could trust, and she trusted Jessie's without question.

"Jessie?" Julia asked, resting her hands on her hips. "How do I look?"

Jessie mumbled her acknowledgment of Julia's presence but continued to perfect her moustache on a soap star's upper lip. Her tongue poked thoughtfully out of the corner of her mouth as she assessed her handiwork. Julia cleared her throat, and Jessie's head snapped up.

"Oh my God," Jessie spluttered loudly, not even trying to hold back her laughter. "What did she *do* to you?"

That was all Julia needed to hear. She turned on her bare heels and marched back into her bedroom.

"It's too much," Julia said as she looked around for her makeup wipes. "I have twenty minutes to look like myself before Barker is outside of my cottage."

"*Julia!*" Sue cried, pouting like she did whenever she didn't get her own way. "I've spent an hour working on that!"

Julia spotted the face wipes under her handbag on the corner of her dressing table, which was now cluttered with Sue's makeup. Julia couldn't believe all of those products were now smeared on her face. She had always wondered what she would look like under heavy makeup, and now that she knew, it wasn't something she would be doing again.

Julia reached out for the makeup wipes, but so did Sue. The sisters wrestled like girls a quarter of their age while Jessie snickered in the doorway.

"Let go!" Julia groaned, tugging hard on the makeup wipes.

Sue did let go of the wipes, but the force of it sent Julia falling back. She reached out for the dressing table to catch her, but her fingers closed around the soft leather of her tiny handbag. The bag followed her, and its contents fell to the ground, surrounding her. Jessie stopped laughing and helped Julia up off the ground, but Julia was already pulling out a wipe to clear her face.

"What's this?" Sue mumbled as she gathered up Julia's things.

Julia looked out of one of her eyes as she wiped the other. Sue was staring down at the page of suspects in Julia's small notepad.

"Dad? Katie?" Sue read aloud, turning around before Julia could snatch the notepad out of her hands. "Sally, Richard, Joanne and Terry? What is this, Julia?"

"Murder suspects," Jessie said, rolling her eyes. "Isn't it obvious?"

"Julia?"

"Like Jessie said," Julia mumbled quietly as she pulled a second wipe from the packet, the first looking like it had just been ran through the dirt. "Suspects for Charles Wellington's murder."

"You've been investigating, haven't you?" Sue sighed, her eyes soaking in every detail of Julia's notes on the next page. "Why can't you just leave this to the professionals?"

"Julia's the smartest woman I know," Jessie spat out, looking angrily down her nose at Sue. "She's better than any copper."

Julia smiled gratefully through the mirror at Jessie, who took a sheepish step back as though surprised by her own words.

"I don't think Dad did it," Julia said. "I just haven't crossed his name out yet. He told me he was out in the grounds when Charles was pushed, but Katie told me they were together in Dad's study. Dad found Katie in his study drinking whiskey, but I suspect that was after Charles was pushed. Katie's feet match the size of the boot prints found at the scene of the crime."

"Boots?" Sue cried, shaking her head and tossing the

notepad on the cluttered dressing table. "How do you know all of this?"

"I ask the right questions."

"And the other names?" Sue appeared in the mirror behind Julia as she wiped off the last of the eyeliner surrounding her lashes. "Why do you suspect them?"

Sue sat on the edge of the bed and stared at her. Julia could tell Sue was trying to appear angry, even a little concerned, but the curiosity was also there. If Julia didn't tell her, she knew Sue would rack her brains all night to piece things together. Julia almost didn't want to say a word. She wanted Sue to know what it felt like to have pieces of a puzzle swirling around in her brain.

"Sally and Richard were both at the garden party when Charles was pushed out of the window, but they weren't with the rest of us," Julia started as she examined her fresh face, glad to see herself again. "We all saw Richard fight with Charles, but we didn't see him actually strike Charles. When I saw Richard yesterday, his knuckles were cut, but the cuts weren't fresh. Sally told me when she arrived at Peridale Manor, she saw Richard in a state and he wanted to get out of there in a hurry. I don't know for sure, but I think we can all assume that Sally and Charles were having an affair, and that's why Richard attacked Charles."

"So you're saying Richard found Charles after the fight, hit him, and then tossed him out of the window?" Sue asked, edging closer to the end of Julia's bed.

"Not necessarily," Julia said as she applied a generous amount of her favourite moisturiser. "That's the obvious theory, but I have a feeling Sally is lying to me about something. She seems scared of Richard."

"Do you think she saw him push Charles?"

"Or he saw her and he's covering for her?" Jessie offered, sitting next to Sue. "You're right, she *did* look scared of him, but wouldn't you if somebody knew you had committed murder?"

"Exactly," Julia said, the smile in the mirror telling her that they were on the same page.

"And the others?" Sue asked. "Joanne and Terry? I thought Terry was just the builder?"

"Do you remember what Gran said about seeing Terry in the manor around the time Charles was pushed?" Julia said, turning in her chair to face them both. "I spoke to Joanne. She told me they were both in the garden waiting for Katie to bring everybody to see the pool being dug."

"Do you think she's lying?" Sue asked, her eyes widening in shock.

"She could be," Julia said, nodding in agreement. "Or she just remembered wrong. They weren't suspects until earlier today. I went to Peridale Manor to talk to Dad and I saw them both in the builder's work cabin, so I went to speak to them to ask some questions, but I overheard them arguing before I had a chance."

"About the murder?" Jessie asked, her brows furrowing. "That's a bit of a stupid thing to do."

"Not quite," Julia said, shrugging softly. "It's open to interpretation. Joanne told Terry it was a good thing that Charles was dead and that they were in a bad place financially. She accused Terry of getting them into a mess, and that he had to sort it out."

"Terry has a gambling problem," Sue said, snapping her fingers together. "Neil told me he had to throw Terry out of the library for using the computers to gamble. He said he was in there every single day placing huge bets and then getting really angry when he lost money. Neil didn't feel right about it, so he approached him and told him not to come in if he was going to use the library computers for that. He didn't exactly ban him, but he as good as did."

"That explains the money troubles," Jessie said, looking from Sue to Julia. "And why Joanne would say she is glad that man is dead. If they are really broke, getting that spa job would be a pretty big deal, wouldn't it?"

"But what does that have to do with Charles?" Sue asked.

"Aren't you listening?" Jessie asked with a roll of her eyes. "Charles wanted to stop the house turning into a stupid spa. If he succeeded, that broke builder and his missus would lose their contract and most of the money with it. With the Wellington dude out of the way, Terry gets to finish his work and make the money."

"It wasn't that obvious," Sue mumbled, looking from Jessie to Julia, hoping in vain that Julia hadn't already figured it out too. "It does make sense though."

"I'll know more when I speak to them both," Julia said, turning back to the mirror to apply a light coat of mascara.

"Or you could just leave it to Detective Inspector Brown and his team," Sue said. "They've probably already gotten this far."

"Perhaps," Julia said, knowing they hadn't. "But where's the fun in that?"

Jessie smirked at her in the mirror. Julia felt like she was getting closer and closer to figuring out the truth, but for now, she pushed it out of her mind so she could focus on her date with Barker. After applying a subtle berry lipstick, she climbed into one of her nicer dresses and some kitten heels.

"How do I look?" Julia asked, standing in front of Jessie and Sue.

"Like you always do," Sue said, the disappointment loud and clear.

"Good," Julia said, turning to the mirror to run her fingers through her naturally messy curls. "That's exactly what I was going for."

CHAPTER 12

Peridale's only restaurant, The Comfy Corner, was Julia's favourite place to eat when she wasn't at her café, so when they pulled into the small backstreet it was nestled on, her face lit up.

"I hope you don't mind keeping it local," Barker said as he pulled up outside of the small restaurant. "I don't know the area too well yet and this place came highly recommend from the boys at the station."

"It's perfect," Julia said, looking up at its twinkling sign. "They have the best carbonara this side of Italy."

Barker got out and walked around the car. Julia took the opportunity to look in the visor mirror. She wasn't a vain woman, but she also didn't want to have lipstick on her teeth. Before she could open the door, Barker pulled it open and offered his hand.

"Thank you," Julia said, getting out of the car without using his offer of assistance.

"Have I mentioned how beautiful you look yet?" Barker asked as he shut the car door behind her. "Because you do."

"Twice."

"Oh," Barker said, nodding his head. "Sorry. Can you tell I'm nervous?"

"A little," Julia admitted. "You don't need to be nervous of me, Detective."

"Are you sure?"

Julia chuckled softly and walked towards the restaurant's door. She found it endearing that Barker was nervous about their date. It meant he cared, and she liked that. She couldn't ever imagine her soon-to-be ex-husband, Jerrad, being nervous around her. He had always been collected and lacking in emotion to the point of being robotic.

"Evening, Julia," Mary Potter, the owner of the small restaurant said. "Are you here for your big date with Barker?"

"Word does travel fast," Julia mumbled under her breath, wondering how many people her gran had called that afternoon. "Table for two, please."

"The candles are already burning," she said with a soft wink. "Follow me."

Barker's hand settled into the small of Julia's back as they walked across the restaurant. It took her so much by surprise, her entire body turned rigid. It had been so long since a man had touched her, she had almost forgotten how nice it could feel.

"Perfect table for a date," Mary said when she stopped at a table tucked away in an alcove, and out of view from the rest of the restaurant. "We call it lover's corner. Can I get you any drinks?"

"Dry white wine," Julia said as she sat in the chair

Barker had just pulled out for her.

"Water for me," Barker said, patting his car keys. "Better safe than sorry."

Mary nodded and shuffled over to the bar. She was a gentle woman in her sixties, but she was also notoriously nosey. Most people in Peridale were, but Mary was nosier than most. Nothing got past the woman. She seemed to know things about people that were so secretive, villagers had accused her on more than one occasion of hiding secret recording devices around the restaurant. Julia didn't believe the rumour, but it was the reason her gran boycotted the place.

"It's quite charming in here," Barker said, looking around the comforting stone and oak interior. "You don't get places like this in the city."

"It used to be a pub. Dates back centuries," Mary said as she shuffled back with their drinks. "These walls could tell you some stories. Each brick tells a tale."

Mary set their drinks on the table, along with the menus she had nestled under her arm. She recommended the Peridale Pie, as she always did, and shuffled back to the bar.

"What's a Peridale Pie?" Barker whispered over the top of his menu.

"It's basically a cheese and onion pie with curry spices thrown in for good measure," Julia whispered back. "Mary's husband, Todd, is the chef and he's rather eccentric."

"Certainly sounds interesting," Barker mumbled as he looked through the leather bound menu. "As does everything on here. I never thought I'd see a Tennessee burger next to a beef wellington."

"It's rather eclectic, but everything is delicious."

They looked over the menu in silence for a couple of minutes and Julia settled on chicken liver pâté on toast for her starter, and the spaghetti carbonara for her main. Sue had warned her against eating messy food on the date, but Julia knew if a little carbonara sauce on her chin scared away a man, he wasn't worth keeping.

"Speaking of Wellington," Barker said. "I hear you were at Peridale Manor again yesterday."

Julia had assumed mentioning the case was off limits for their date, but now that Barker had brought it up, she wasn't going to dance away from the subject.

"I wanted to establish my father's alibi," Julia said. "Which I suppose you already know doesn't marry up with his wife's?"

"I do," Barker said with a quick nod as he snapped the menu shut. "What the heck, I'll try the Peridale Pie! Oxtail soup for starters too."

Julia closed her menu and glanced around the edge of the alcove. Mary was talking to her husband. She didn't doubt for a moment that they were discussing their date.

"I'm surprised you're not telling me to stay out of things," Julia said after a sip of wine.

"I've come to realise that no matter what I say you'll do what you want. I like that about you. You're a strong woman."

"Most men don't like a strong woman."

"I'm not most men."

"I've realised that, Detective," Julia said, holding back her smile. "You are certainly different than the usual Peridale men."

"Do you know that for a fact?" Barker asked, his eyes twinkling darkly in the soft candlelight. "Any skeletons in the closet that I should know about?"

Julia became flustered, but she was saved having to mention her divorce when Mary came to take their order. She fumbled with her hair, tucking it behind her ear. The last thing she wanted to talk about was her divorce.

Mary took their orders, complimenting them on their choices, and also recommending a dessert if they still had room at the end. When she hobbled away, Julia was glad Barker didn't immediately pick up where they had left off.

"Do you think your step-mother is capable of murder?" Barker asked, leaning across the table, his lips obscured by the flickering flame of the tall candle. "Off the record."

"Is she your prime suspect?"

"Isn't she yours?" Barker asked, his brows creasing as though there was no other option. "I'm assuming you've figured out her foot size matches, and we all saw her put on the boots."

"It certainly seems to make sense."

"But?" Barker sat back, a grin forming.

"There is no but," Julia said, shrugging softly. "I just like to keep all options open. When a cake isn't working, I don't throw in the first ingredient I can think of. I take my time, assess the flavours and really make sure I'm adding the right thing. Sometimes that first thought is right, but more often than not, it's wrong. You can always add, but you can't take away."

"So you don't think she did it?"

"I didn't say that."

"Well, obviously there's Richard," Barker offered, leaning back into the flame of the candle, appearing to revel in talking the case over with Julia. "I've interviewed him twice now, but aside from attacking Charles, there's nothing else. Sally says she was with him at the time of the murder."

"She did?" Julia said, a brow unintentionally arching. "She told me something different."

"You've interviewed her?"

"I'm making her wedding cake," Julia said innocently. "Which she cancelled, and then re-ordered. They're back together now, but when they were broken up, she told me she went to Peridale Manor to talk to him, saw him, then he left."

"She told me they both left and went home," Barker said, his eyes narrowing to dark slits. "Why would she lie?"

Before Julia could offer her theory, Mary appeared with Julia's chicken liver pâté on toast, and Barker's oxtail soup. They thanked her and she vanished again. They both started to eat, but Julia could feel Barker itching to discuss further.

"I sensed she was lying to me," Julia offered after cutting her toast slice in two. "Either story could be true, or both lies."

"She's hiding something. I just don't know what," Barker said before blowing a spoonful of his hot soup. "Do you think either of them did it?"

"Possibly," Julia said with a nod. "Have you considered Joanne and Terry Lewis?"

"Who?"

Julia contained her smirk. She took her time popping a piece of the pâté-covered toast into her mouth. She chewed slowly, enjoying Barker watching her intently as he messily slurped his soup.

"Terry Lewis is the contractor working on the spa conversion," Julia said when she felt she had left him to sweat it out long enough. "Joanne is his wife."

"Why do you suspect them?"

"They're having money troubles, and Joanne lied about Terry's alibi. She told me her and her husband were in the garden at the time of the murder but my gran saw and spoke to him in the manor."

"Have you ever considered your gran did it?" Barker teased. "Normally I wouldn't imagine a lady in her eighties throwing a fully grown man out of a window, but she's something else. She scares me. Did you know she was running an illegal poker club?"

"It's now a book club," Julia said with a small chuckle. "They're reading Fifty Shades of Grey."

Barker choked on his soup, his cheeks burning red. He dabbed at his lips with a cotton napkin and stared at Julia as if expecting her to say she was joking.

"This village is certainly colourful," Barker said as he resumed his soup. "Who do you think did it?"

"It's too soon to say," Julia said honestly. "It's not even been a week yet. There are still things to be discovered."

"Such as?"

Before Julia could answer, Mary reappeared to ask them both how their food was at the very moment they were mid-chew. They nodded and mumbled their satisfaction, turning down Mary's offer of drink refills. She knowingly smiled at Julia and mouthed something that looked like '*he's so handsome*' before leaving them once again.

"We still don't know what was taken from that display plinth next to the window," Julia said. "I feel like it holds the key to finding out the truth."

"I was sure that was unrelated until this morning,"

Barker said after taking his last mouthful of soup. "The autopsy came back and the coroner said there was a wound so severe on Charles' head that it was very likely he was dead before he was even thrown out of the window."

Julia finished the last of her pâté, but she didn't say anything. Barker looked at her, confused for a moment, before rolling his eyes and smiling.

"But you already knew that, right?" Barker asked.

"Didn't it strike you as odd that Charles was completely silent as he fell from the window?" Julia asked. "Have you ever heard of somebody silently falling to their death? Whatever was taken, I'm sure it was heavy enough to kill a man."

"Katie and your father are saying they can't remember what was there," Barker said with a sigh as he leaned back in his chair and glanced around the restaurant. "I don't believe it for a second."

"It is possible they don't remember," Julia offered, unsure if she believed her own words. "It's a big house."

"The one person who would know can't even speak. I tried to interview Vincent, but I got nothing."

Before Julia could tell him there was one person in the manor that would know what had been taken, Mary appeared to take away their plates. Instead of shuffling straight away, she lingered for a moment.

"Are you still selling that shortbread of yours?" Mary asked Julia, her eyes closing as she licked her lips. "My Todd is Scottish and he said you make it better than any Scot he's met. Simply divine."

"It's still there," Julia said. "I'll bring you some up soon."

"You're such a sweet girl," Mary gushed, turning to

Barker. "You've got yourself a good one here, Detective."

Barker smiled and blushed again, but he didn't say anything. When Mary finally left them alone, it seemed both of them had forgotten what they were talking about.

"So," Barker said, exhaling heavily. "Any men in Peridale I should watch out for slashing my tyres after they find out I've taken you on a date?"

Julia nervously laughed, her lips wobbling but unable to speak. She glanced around the alcove, hoping Mary was on her way back to cause further distraction, but she wasn't. Julia turned back to Barker, who was looking at her expectantly. Just when she was about to spill the beans about her estranged husband, Barker's phone rang loudly in his pocket.

"Bloody hell," Barker cried as he fumbled for his phone. "I told them not to call me. Do you mind?"

"Not at all," Julia said, relieved and grateful for the timing. "It could be important."

Barker excused himself and walked across the restaurant, only answering the phone when he was out of earshot from Julia. She watched as he paced up and down the empty restaurant, ducking out of the way of the low beams as he went. It hadn't gone unnoticed how handsome he looked in his dinner suit.

"That was work," Barker said, his voice grave and his eyes so wide, Julia knew what was coming. "There's been a break-in at Peridale Manor. I'm going to have to go."

"I'm coming with you," Julia said before tossing back the rest of her wine and standing up. "And don't argue, Detective. I'm technically family so you can't stop me. If you don't take me with you, I'll call a taxi."

For a moment Julia thought Barker might protest and

insist that she stay and eat her dinner, or go home, but he didn't. He sighed, and turned on his heels to head straight for the door. At that moment, Mary pushed through a door holding spaghetti carbonara in one hand and Peridale Pie in the other.

"We're going to have to go," Barker said apologetically, pulling a red fifty-pound note out of his wallet. "Keep the change."

Julia apologised as she passed Mary. Even the smell of her favourite dish at The Comfy Corner didn't tempt her to stay. She heard Mary mumble something about *'young love'* as she headed back into the kitchen.

CHAPTER 13

T he drive up to Peridale Manor was a silent one. When they pulled up outside, there was already a police car on the scene. They both jumped out of the car the second Barker put his handbrake in place.

The front door was open, and Katie, Brian and two officers were talking in the grand entrance. Katie was hysterically chattering in a luminous pink nightie while Brian held her, and the two young officers attempted to write down what she was saying.

"Julia?" Brian mumbled, his forehead furrowing. "What are you doing here?"

"I was with Detective Inspector Brown," she said. "There was no time to take me home."

Her father nodded, seeming to accept this without question. His pale face and blank expression didn't go unnoticed. It was the same face Julia had seen at the garden party after discovering Charles' body. Was it the face of a man who knew he was holding onto a guilty woman?

"Mrs. Wellington," Barker said, stepping in front of the two bemused officers. "I'm going to need you to calm down and tell me what exactly happened here tonight."

"Wellington-*South*," she bumbled through her tears. "There was a man. A man upstairs!"

"A man?" Barker asked, glancing suspiciously to Julia. "Can you be more specific?"

"A masked man upstairs," Katie said angrily through her sobs. "I was c-c-coming out of the bathroom and I saw a masked m-m-man all dressed in black. I screamed, and he ran away."

Barker looked even more suspiciously to Julia out of the corner of his eye. It was obvious he didn't believe her. Julia wasn't sure if she did either. The description of a masked burglar almost seemed cartoonish.

"And did anyone else see this masked man?" Barker asked, turning to roll his eyes at the officers. "Anyone to corroborate your story?"

"*Story?*" Katie shrieked, her voice echoing in every corner of the manor. "It's not a *story*, it's the *truth*!"

"Did you see this man?" Barker asked, turning his attention to Julia's father.

Brian awkwardly looked down at his hysterical wife, but he shook his head. Julia noticed his grip on her loosen.

"Was anything taken?" Barker asked, pinching between his brows.

"Well – *no*," Katie said. "I don't think so. I think I scared him off."

"And this burglar was alone? They didn't put up a fight?"

"They just ran down the stairs and out of the front door."

Barker audibly sighed, clearly frustrated with Katie. Julia knew exactly what he was thinking without needing to ask; she was thinking it too. It wasn't common for burglars to act alone, especially in such big houses, and she also knew they didn't tend to be unarmed or scared of a shrieking woman in her silk nightie.

Barker turned and started whispering with the two officers while Katie buried her mascara-streaked face in her husband's chest. Brian didn't put his arms around her, instead just staring into space. Julia realised nobody was paying her any attention, so she slipped away unseen and practically sprinted up the staircase.

Julia saw exactly what she wanted to see on the top step; the display plinth was no longer empty. A white marble bust was sitting on the display plinth. Just to be sure, she pulled her phone out of her handbag to check the picture she had taken on the day of the murder.

"Detective Inspector," Julia called over her shoulder as she took a second photograph of the plinth. "You might want to come and see this."

Barker and the two officers ran up the staircase, joining her in front of the bust.

"Look," Julia showed Barker the image of the missing marble bust on her phone, then she flicked to the one she had just taken in the exact same position. "*Earl Philip Wellington*. Born 1798, died 1865."

Katie and Brian joined them in the crowded hallway and they all stared at the bust.

"That's my great-great-great-great-grandfather," Katie mumbled through her sobs. "He built this manor."

"When I asked you what had been taken from this plinth, you claimed not to have remembered," Barker said sternly, the vein in his temple throbbing brightly. "Tonight when you claim a man broke into your home, this bust is suspiciously returned. As you know from my phone call earlier this afternoon, your brother was potentially killed by a blow to the head with a heavy object."

As Barker explained the situation to Katie, Julia leaned into the bust, detecting the unmistakable scent of heavy bleach. Whoever had returned the bust had made sure to clean it thoroughly first. She doubted even the best forensics team would be able to find a speck of blood or a fingerprint on the sterile marble.

"I just forgot," Katie protested, looking to Brian, her unnaturally shaped brows dashing up her shiny forehead. "It's a big house. You can't *prove* anything! You can't *prove* that bust was taken!"

"I have pictures," Julia said, stepping forward with her phone in her hands.

Barker's hand closed in around her arm and he pulled her back before she could turn the phone around. He leaned into her ear, his breath hot on her cheek.

"If anybody finds out I let you investigate a crime scene before I shut it down, I'll be in deep trouble," Barker whispered darkly.

Julia gritted her jaw as she looked down at the picture of the empty plinth on her phone. She was instantly offended that she wasn't allowed to show what she had found for the sake of Barker not getting in trouble at the station, but she relented and stepped back, mumbling that she had made a mistake.

"See, you *can't* prove it!" Katie said, grinning like a mad Cheshire cat. "You can't prove the bust was taken. It's your word against mine. We say it wasn't taken. Don't we, babe?"

Katie turned to Brian, who didn't say a word. He gulped hard, a cold sweat breaking out on his forehead, trickling down the side of his deeply tanned and lined face.

"Babe?" Katie asked, less sure.

Julia might not have been her father's biggest fan, but she didn't like seeing him in such a moral dilemma. She stepped forward again as she dropped her phone back into her handbag.

"There's one person who will be able to confirm if the bust was taken or not," Julia said, wanting to take the heat away from her father.

"My father can't even speak!" Katie cried. "The man had a stroke less than a month ago!"

Julia stepped to the side of Katie and looked straight down the dark hallway to the woman peeking through a door, and had been ever since Julia had called for Barker.

"Hilary?" Katie laughed, but her expression soon turned dark.

"Officer Galbraith, I want you to hold Katie in the kitchen," Barker said, his voice professional and calm. "I have a witness to speak with."

"You *can't* do this!" Katie shrieked.

"Calm yourself Mrs. Wellington, or I'll have you cuffed," Barker ordered, his finger in the woman's face.

"It's Wellington-South," she muttered, less confident this time. "Wellington-*South*."

Julia's father's study was a dark room lined with bookshelves bursting with hefty hardback volumes. The room was windowless and claustrophobic, each book adding to the suffocation. As Hilary carefully walked across the room to the chair in front of the desk where Barker was sitting behind the dimly lit lamp, Julia knew why he had picked this room above any other.

Hilary sat in the chair in front of the desk, her posture composed, her lips pursed, and her wiry grey hair tightly scraped into a taut bun at the back. Even though Julia was standing at the back of the room, she could imagine Hilary's darkly lined eyes bulging in the soft glow of the lamp.

"Hilary," Barker started, leaning back in the chair and resting his fingers on his chest. "Do you have a last name, Hilary?"

"That's none of your business," she said firmly, her voice breathy but stern. "I haven't done a thing wrong."

"Nobody is saying you have," Barker said, quickly leaning into the light. "Unless you want to tell me something?"

Julia held back laughter. She knew Barker was trying to scare Hilary into slipping up, but Julia found his interrogation techniques more comical than frightening. Hilary seemed to think the same because she busied herself with adjusting the hem of her skirt.

"Hilary Boyle," the housekeeper said reluctantly. "What does any of this nasty business have to do with me? I've already told you I was in the kitchen at the time of the murder and I have a dozen waitresses and waiters to tell you the same. I saw the poor boy fall from the window from within the house."

"I don't doubt that," Barker said, looking up at the ornate ceiling before looking right back at her, his eyes narrow and firm. "Did you know Charles well?"

"I've known that boy since the day he was born,"

Hilary said, her voice not wavering. "I knew he was trouble from the first time I heard him cry."

"And Katie?"

Hilary wavered for the first time. She shifted in her chair, glancing over her shoulder at Julia. Julia was still surprised Barker had let her sit in on the interview, but she was the only one he had allowed. She had promised not to say a word.

"She's just as bad," Hilary said softly. "If not worse. A rude, insolent child. If Mr Wellington hadn't lost his tongue, he would tell you the same."

"I gather you've been here for a long time?" Barker asked, his fingers drumming heavily on the desk. "Long enough to know the layout pretty well?"

"I know this house like the back of my hand," Hilary said, pride loud and clear in her voice. "Like it's a part of my own skin."

"And you clean it quite regularly?"

"Every single day."

"Dusting?"

"I beg your pardon?"

"Do you dust, Mrs. Boyle?" Barker asked, leaning closer into the light, shadows dripping down his chiselled face. "Ornaments, for example?"

"Are you questioning my credentials as a cleaner, Detective?" Hilary asked harshly. "Because I assure you, I'm the best this village has to offer! And it's *Miss* Boyle to you. I never married."

"I apologise, Miss Boyle," Barker said, holding his hands up. "I didn't mean to offend, I just wanted to check you knew this house and its contents. Have you noticed anything go missing recently?"

Hilary shifted once again in her seat, telling them both exactly what they wanted to know. She glanced over her shoulder at Julia before looking down to continue adjusting the hem of her skirt.

"I assume you're talking about the bust?" she asked. "I did wonder about that. It's not my place to ask. I assumed the brat had sold it to try and cover some of the costs of her silly idea to turn this fine manor into a tacky spa. You hear whisperings if you listen hard enough, and the money isn't flowing like it used to."

"You didn't think to mention this absent bust to the police?" Barker asked.

"Why *would* I?" Hilary snapped, clearly offended. "What does this have to do with *anything*?"

"That's confidential, Miss Boyle," Barker said firmly. "When was the last time you saw the bust?"

"Ten minutes ago when you dragged me from my room," Hilary said, resting her hands on the table and matching Barker's pose by leaning into the light. "I was just about to go to bed, you know. It's silver polishing tomorrow, and I like to get it done before breakfast. I assume, however, that you're asking when was the last time I saw the bust *before* I noticed it had gone missing. It was the morning of the garden party."

"Are you sure?"

"Of course I am sure," Hilary cried, the offence louder in her voice than ever before. "Are you trying to insinuate that I am going senile? I'm as sharp as a knife and as bright as a bulb, I'll have you know. That morning, Katie was being extra brat-like and she made me clean the entire house from top to bottom. I specifically remember because I forgot my marble polish and I had to run back downstairs to get it. Vincent – *I mean* – Mr. Wellington is very specific about cleaning things with the right equipment. He is very proud of this manor and its history. Before I could even get back upstairs to clean it, Katie sent me out to the garden with lemonade for the builders, and it never got done."

Having heard all he needed to, Barker thanked Hilary and stood up. He buttoned up his dinner jacket and headed straight for the door.

"You're going to arrest her, aren't you?" Julia asked.

Barker didn't say a word. He opened the door and walked swiftly across the entrance hall to the kitchen. Hilary stood up and adjusted her skirt, gazing menacingly at Julia. Seconds later, Katie's shrieks echoed throughout the manor, and Julia didn't need to look to know the two officers were dragging her towards the front door.

When Katie's cries grew more distant, Julia walked out of the study. First she saw Barker standing in the kitchen doorway talking quietly on his phone, then she saw her father standing at the top of the stairs, staring blankly down at the front door. He didn't protest, or say anything to help his wife, he just stared as though he was as mute as Vincent. Even from her distance, Julia noticed a tear rolling down his cheek as he turned away.

"Whose side are you on, girl?" Hilary asked bitterly as she walked slowly past Julia shaking her head. "You kids have no sense of loyalty these days."

Julia turned to Barker as he walked slowly across the hall towards her. He smiled uneasily at her, but she couldn't smile back.

"We did it," Barker said, letting out a relieved sigh. "How do you feel?"

"Not as pleased as I expected," Julia admitted, looking

to the spot her father had been standing as Hilary reached the top of the stairs. "It feels so unresolved."

"The truth will come out," Barker reassured her, resting his hand on her shoulder. "Her alibi was the only one that didn't check out. She was in the house at the time her brother was murdered, and she is the only person with such an obvious motive. I'm sure when forensics get their hands on the bust, they're going to find her prints and his blood. I'm sorry this ruined our date."

"As first dates go, this one was certainly different," Julia said, enjoying the feeling of Barker's hand resting heavily on her shoulder, his thumb touching the exposed part of her collarbone. "I'll let you take me home now, Detective."

CHAPTER 14

I t rained again all day, but that didn't stop people coming into Julia's café to gossip. She took almost record takings from the residents who wanted somewhere to sit and talk about Katie's arrest. The rain seemed to help keep them there hours longer than usual, and by noon it was standing room only.

When Julia finally shooed the last customers out of the café at the end of the day and flipped the sign, the forced smile dropped from her face and she rested her head against the door, completely exhausted. She hadn't been able to sleep much the night before because Katie's shrieking had rattled around her ears until the early hours. She was sure she only managed an hour of sleep before Jessie's head banging on the wardrobe door jolted her out of her exhausted slumber.

"You look knackered," Jessie said, letting out her own yawn as she started to clear away the messy tables. "I thought you would have slept better last night knowing that your step-mother who isn't your step-mother is behind bars."

Julia untied her apron and pulled it over her head, tossing it onto a table. She caught Jessie's yawn, and her mouth opened so wide she thought it was never going to close again. The bags under her eyes were practically ruched. All she could think of was her bed, however, there was somebody she wanted to visit before she could do that.

"Are you okay cleaning up on your own?" Julia asked, already grabbing her pink coat and umbrella from the hooks in the kitchen. "I'll lock the door. Just use the spare keys to let yourself out and lock up if I'm not back."

"Where are you going?" Jessie asked after dropping a pile of dishes into the hot soapy water she had just run.

"How do you feel about college?" Julia asked.

"College?" Jessie replied with a deep frown. "I wasn't any good at school. I failed all my exams."

"Joanne's son, Jamie, is on a building apprenticeship," Julia said as she pushed her arms through her coat. "He studies at college one day a week, but he works for the rest of the week. You're already doing that, so why not get qualified?"

Jessie screwed her up face before looking down her nose at Julia.

"You mean, like a certificate?" Jessie asked. "A real one?"

"As real as they come," Julia said, glad that Jessie wasn't dismissing it outright. "It'll look good for when your social worker visits if we're showing that you're settling into Peridale. This is just another way to do that."

The mention of her social worker stiffened Jessie in an instant, and her face turned bright red as though she had completely stopped breathing. Julia stared at her young lodger as she buttoned up her jacket, suddenly realising she hadn't heard from the social worker in a while.

"Yeah, whatever," Jessie said, spinning and picking up a dirty plate which she started to vigorously scrub.

"Joanne has a prospectus for the college so we'll have a look properly tonight," Julia said, grabbing her handbag and tossing it over her shoulder. "If you need anything, you have my mobile number."

Jessie nodded, her dark ponytail bobbing up and down. As she walked through the café towards the door, she wondered why Jessie was so scared of her social worker. When they had spoken on the phone, she had seemed like a pleasant lady, even if she had not sent out the paperwork she said she would.

Julia pushed up her umbrella the second she stepped outside, pulling it close to her head. Strong wind almost knocked her off her feet as she walked around the village green. The umbrella did little to protect her from being soaked by the sideways falling rain, which was tumbling so heavily it bounced off the road underfoot.

Julia was glad Joanne's cottage was only around the corner, nestled along with three other terraced cottages between The Cozy Corner and Peridale's tiny library. She hadn't realised how close the Lewis house was to the library, which made sense of Terry's gambling visits. She imagined Joanne had banned him from doing it in the house, driving him next door.

The houses were directly on the narrow winding road, meaning Julia had no protection from the rain as she stood and waited for somebody to answer the door. A car zoomed by, sending water cascading over her. A cold cry escaped her lips as the icy water soaked through to her figure, driving her knuckles harder into the thick door.

When the door finally opened, it was Jamie Lewis, not Joanne or Terry who answered.

"Is your mother home?" Julia asked, her teeth chattering as she clung desperately to her useless umbrella, her hands white and freezing.

"She's out shopping," Jamie mumbled, barely making eye contact with Julia.

"Will she be long?"

Jamie shrugged and looked over his shoulder to the roaring fire in the heart of the sitting room.

"Could I possibly come in to wait?" Julia said, forcing herself to smile. "I'm quite soaked through."

Jamie sighed, and Julia almost expected him to slam the door in her face, but he stepped to the side and let her in. Julia hurried in backwards, collapsing her umbrella as she went. Jamie closed the door behind her. For a moment she stood dripping on the doormat while she tried to catch her breath.

"Could I have something to warm me up?" Julia asked. "Some tea, perhaps?"

"Whatever," Jamie said with a shrug.

"Plop this in some boiling water," Julia said, pulling a soaked peppermint and liquorice tea sachet from her handbag. "Emphasis on the word *boiling*."

Julia's attempt at humour didn't crack a smile on the surly teenager's face. He snatched the teabag out of Julia's shaking fingers and lumbered off to the kitchen, leaving Julia to her own devices. She pulled off her coat, glad that her dress beneath was only wet at the back. Nestling on a footstool in front of the roaring fire, she hugged her body as the warmth surged through her frozen flesh.

Jamie returned, practically tossing her tea onto the side table next to her, splashing and soaking a stack of letters. Julia's eyes instantly honed in on the red writing on the top one, which read '*DO NOT IGNORE. IMPORTANT*'. She didn't need x-ray vision to know it was probably a credit card or loan company chasing a debt.

Jamie threw himself onto the couch and picked up a controller to resume playing the fighting game he had been playing before Julia interrupted. She watched as the character on the screen shot a man three times at short range, no doubt controlled by Jamie. She looked at the teenager, who didn't seem phased by the gore on screen. Julia wondered if Jessie had grown up in a conventional and stable home, would she be interested in the same things as other teenagers?

"I've actually come to ask your mother about apprenticeships," Julia offered, attempting to add something to the awkward silence other than the boom of the gun. "She told me you're doing one in building."

"Construction," he corrected her, his thumbs tapping away on the controller.

"Do you enjoy it?"

Jamie shrugged heavily, staring ahead at the TV screen like a zombie. Julia wondered if the purple bags around his eyes were from a lack of sleep or just from staring at the screen for too long.

"Is today your day off?"

"They rang up and told us not to come in today," Jamie muttered, his attention firmly on the game. "Probably 'cause of the rain. Can't pour cement in the rain."

Jamie didn't seem to have heard about what had

happened at Peridale Manor last night. She considered not telling him, but she was sure news would spread around the entire village by the end of the day.

"Katie Wellington-South was arrested last night," Julia said, picking up her mug and cupping it warmly in her hands. "For her brother's murder."

Jamie's thumbs stopped tapping and he paused the game. He turned to Julia, his brow stern.

"What?" Jamie snapped. "What does that mean?"

"It means that I don't know what is happening with the spa," Julia said. "I know your dad was relying on the work, but I don't know if the work will be there if she's convicted."

"My dad?" Jamie cried, his previously disinterested and quiet voice suddenly loud and full of passion. "You don't know the first thing about my dad, or what we're going through!"

"I'm sure you'll get another job," Julia offered, glancing to the letters on the side table. "I doubt this will change anything with your apprenticeship."

"My apprenticeship?" Jamie cried, tossing the controller onto the floor and suddenly standing up. "Do you think I *wanted* to do this stupid apprenticeship? I've only done it to help my dad. He needed the extra pair of hands for the spa job."

Julia put her tea back on the side table and stood up, preparing herself to tell Jamie she would come back later. At that very moment, the door opened and Joanne hurried in, her hands full of shopping bags, and her short curly hair soaked to her scalp.

"Julia," she cried, her teeth chattering. "What a surprise."

Joanne looked from Julia to Jamie, who was still standing there, his breathing suddenly erratic. Julia wasn't sure what the teen was going to do, but he turned on his heels and stormed off up the narrow flight of stairs. A door slammed, shaking the cottage.

"Boys at that age," Joanne said with an awkward laugh. "Full of hormones and testosterone. I tell him that game isn't good for his moods."

Julia hurried over and took some of the shopping bags out of Joanne's hands, which she gratefully handed over.

"I stopped by to grab that college prospectus from you," Julia said as they walked through to the kitchen. "Jamie was kind enough to let me in out of the rain to dry off."

"Of course," Joanne said, slapping herself gently on the forehead after setting the bags down. "You know what, I've been so busy that I completely forgot. I'll go and grab it for you. It's in Jamie's bedroom, I think. That's if he's speaking to me."

Joanne let out another nervous laugh and rolled her eyes. Julia pondered if this was what she had in store if she fostered Jessie. With the sleepwalking suddenly occurring, she wondered what else was around the corner.

Leaving the kitchen, she walked back through to the sitting room to pick up her tea. Glancing to the staircase to make sure she was alone, she curiously picked up the top letter to see if the one underneath it appeared to be a debt letter. Julia was shocked when she reached the bottom of a pile of ten and they all appeared to be quite serious letters from various companies. Peridale's residents might not have wanted the spa, but she knew the Lewis family needed it. Her heart hurt to think Katie had offered them a way to solve their problems, and then taken it away just as quickly.

She remembered a period of financial difficulty early in her marriage when Jerrad had racked up a serious credit card debt and hidden the letters from her for over a year. When she found them stuffed in a box of cereal he knew she didn't like, she ripped open each envelope like a women possessed. The only reason she had opened the box was because it had passed its use by date. The rage and upset she had felt back then flared up inside of her again as she carried her cup through to the kitchen. She could only imagine how much worse things were for Joanne.

Jamie's bedroom door slammed again, yanking Julia out of her thoughts. She jumped, her heavy cup slipping from her still shaking fingers. It tumbled silently to the ground, much like Charles had from the window. With a loud smash, it split into three large pieces, ricocheting fragments of porcelain across the tiled floor. Glancing up at the kitchen ceiling, she expected to hear Joanne's footprints running down to her, but she didn't.

Making a mental note to confess her crime and offer to replace the mug, Julia opened the cupboard under the sink and fished the dustpan and brush from in between two large bottles of bleach. Bending down, she quickly brushed up the mess from the terracotta tiles, making sure to get right under the shopping bags.

Looking back up at the ceiling, she heard Joanne and her son bickering in low voices about something, no doubt about how many computer games he played.

Julia stepped over the shopping bags towards the bin with the cup fragments balanced in the dustpan. The front door opened and closed again, letting the sound of the wind rattle around the small cottage. She popped open the bin and glanced over her shoulder to see if somebody had just arrived, or if Jamie had just stormed out. Deciding it was none of her business either way, Julia turned her attention to the bin as she poured the broken cup in with the rubbish.

She almost released the bin pedal under her foot, but something black, set against something white caught her eyes. Glancing over her shoulder, she leaned in further, making out the shape of another giant bottle of bleach buried in the rubbish, and on top of it, the black thing appeared to be made of fabric. Reaching inside, she fished it out, shaking off the broken cup pieces as she did.

As she held the balaclava up in front of her face, her heart sunk to the pit her stomach. She stared into the soulless eyeholes, and they stared back, mocking her for getting things so wrong.

"Oh, Julia," she heard from behind her. "If only you had left things alone."

Dropping the balaclava, she turned just in time to see Terry Lewis holding the hot kettle over his head. It struck the side of Julia's skull, and she was unconscious before she hit the shopping bags.

CHAPTER 15

J ulia was aware that she was travelling in a car before her eyes opened. She was also aware her ankles and wrists were tied before she tried to move them. Letting out a loud groan, she rolled her head against the headrest, a splitting pain piercing through her head as she watched the blurry streetlamps whiz by in the rain.

She thought she was dreaming, and any moment Jessie's head banging or Mowgli jumping on her chest would wake her. Her eyelids were so heavy, but she tried to force them open as the orange lights blurred by. They suddenly stopped. She felt the tyres underneath her change from smooth road onto something bumpier. She realised that she was in danger.

She attempted to speak, to cry out, but all that left her mouth was a muffled groan. She bit down, her teeth landing in something soft. Was she gagged? Opening her eyes properly for the first time, she let out a terrified cry.

"Shut her up!" the driver commanded.

A hand vanished behind Julia's head, pulling the gag

tighter into her mouth. Despite the pounding in her head, she turned to see Jamie Lewis sitting next to her in the back seat of the car. He blankly stared at her, emotionless and empty.

Julia shook her head and something hot and thick trickled down the side of her face. She attempted to lift her hands up to touch it, but Jamie yanked them back into her lap. She didn't need to put her fingers to the cut to know Terry's blow to her head had caused some serious damage. Her eyelids fluttered again, this time not from exhaustion, but from an intense wooziness. She tried to fight it, but against her own will, darkness claimed her.

Julia felt the rain on her skin before she opened her eyes. She felt the sensation of floating before she attempted to move her limbs. She assumed she was dead and entering the afterlife, but the pain in her head screamed out, letting her know that she was very much alive. She opened her eyes again and stared down into the darkness.

Frowning hard, she realised that she was being carried. She didn't know why, but the plod of the walk told her she was draped over Terry's shoulder. Instead of trying to make noise, she forced herself to stay silent, despite the intense pain and crippling fear.

"This has all gone too far," she heard Joanne hiss.

"She would have gone to the police," Terry said, and Julia could feel his words boom through his body and into hers. "We couldn't allow that. She wasn't just going to ruin our future, but our son's too. Is that what you want?"

"Of course not!" she snapped back.

"This wouldn't have happened if *you* hadn't been so useless," Terry said. "I'm tired of cleaning up *your* mess."

Julia waited for the person to reply, but they didn't. Without needing to open her eyes, she became aware of the presence walking two steps behind her. She wanted so desperately to see who it was, but she fought the urge to open her eyes.

"This is never going to work," Joanne moaned. "They're going to catch us."

"They're not," Terry bit back, his voice full of venom. "The bimbo is in jail and her other half is drowning his sorrows in a bottle of whiskey. He'll be asleep by now and I doubt anything is waking him. It's perfect."

"What about the old man?"

"He's had a stroke," Terry said with a dark laugh. "Even if he saw the whole thing, he wouldn't be able to say a word."

"Are you sure there's nobody else?"

"There's a housekeeper but she's old," Terry said, sounding irritated by Joanne's questions. "She'll be fast asleep."

"How are we even going to get in there?" Joanne asked, the worry loud and clear in her voice. "Oh, Terry, it's not too late."

"To do what?" he cried, his voice booming. "Hand ourselves in? Tell them the *truth* about what happened at the garden party? Is that what you want? *Huh*, Joanne? Is that what you *want*?"

"You know it isn't!"

"Then this is the only way," Terry said, readjusting his grip on Julia by tossing her in the air. "You know it is. Why did *you* let her into the house? You're an idiot, boy."

Julia realised the figure walking behind her was Jamie. Opening her eyes a fraction she looked down at his shoes.

Heavy mud-covered work boots; size eight if she had to guess. Closing them again, she realised where they were going and what was likely about to happen.

"Get the key out of my pocket, Joanne," Terry instructed. "It's under her foot. Be careful not to wake her. If she's still out, she won't be able to make a sound."

"She's already awake," Jamie mumbled.

"What?" Terry cried, tossing Julia up so that she landed hard on his shoulder. "For how long?"

"Couple of minutes."

Terry turned, sending Julia into a spin. She opened her eyes and caught Joanne whizzing by. She didn't need to see Terry striking his son because she felt the back of his hand hitting Jamie's cheek through her body.

"This is all *your* fault!" Terry sneered. "You're pathetic."

Terry turned and started walking even quicker towards the house. She could hear Jamie sniffling into his sleeve, muffling his cries the best he could. They were the sobs of somebody who had learned to hide them.

"Get the key," Terry ordered again. "Come on! *Hurry up*! This needs to be *now*!"

Julia felt Joanne rummage under her restrained foot to pull something out of his pocket. Julia looked down and the gravel had turned to grass. They had reached Peridale Manor.

She heard the click of a lock and they left the rain. Just from the tiles, she could tell she was in the kitchen. It was cold, which meant the heating had been turned off for hours, likely making it the early hours of the morning.

The ground came from under Julia as Terry tossed her over his shoulder and slammed her onto the table as though she were a bag of sand. He gripped the front of her soaked dress and yanked her up into a sitting position so they were face to face. She stared into his dark eyes, the stubble around his mouth was peppered grey like the edges of Barker's hairline. She remembered their date and she started to uncontrollably sob and shake.

"Listen to me!" Terry said, shaking her shoulders. "*Shut up*, woman! Joanne, pass me that knife."

Joanne snatched up a large knife from the counter at the very moment a crack of white lightning pierced through the dark rain. It illuminated the kitchen, showing the madness in Terry's eyes and the fear in his wife and son's.

"Are you going to be good?" Terry asked, pressing the cold blade of the knife against Julia's face. "Or do I need to do this the painful way?"

Julia forced her cries to stop. In that moment, a sudden calmness fell over her as she stared into Terry's murky soul.

"Find me something to drink," he shot over his shoulder at Joanne. "I need something to take the edge off."

Joanne hurried over to the fridge, pulling its heavy doors open. The light flooded the kitchen. Julia could see Jamie pacing back and forth, sobbing silently and shaking out of control.

"There's only lemonade," she called.

"I need something *strong*!" Terry cried. "*Dammit*, woman. Get me some alcohol."

Joanne rummaged through every cupboard until she found a bottle of cooking wine. That seemed to suit Terry perfectly. He pulled the cork out with his teeth, spat it out, and crammed the bottleneck into his mouth. Head tossed back, he gulped the dark wine like it was water, only stopping when he had drained every last drop. Eyes clenched, he bobbed his head forward as he panted for breath, his teeth and lips stained blood red.

"You're going to walk up those stairs," Terry said, pointing the knife in Julia's face, his large gut pressing against her knees. "And you're going to do it quietly, or else I kill every person in this house as they sleep. Do you understand?"

Julia nodded without thinking, making the dizziness return. She forced herself to stay with this world and not float through into the darkness between this and the next. She knew if she had any chance of walking out of the manor alive, she needed to stay focussed.

Terry quickly slid the knife down, making her think he was going to stab her. Instead, he sliced the restraints from her feet and dragged her off the table. Her ankles were weak and her head swirled from standing on her own for the first time. She caught her reflection in the dark kitchen window, the side of her face stained in scarlet.

"*Move*," he ordered, grabbing a fistful of the back of her dress and placing the knife dangerously close to her spine. "Come on. Walk."

Julia stumbled forward. She frantically looked to Jamie, but he was as with them as Julia had been during the second part of their car journey.

She took the steps as slowly as she could, trying to formulate a plan. She played up to her injury, staggering and grabbing the handrail. Terry's need for silence meant he wasn't going to hurt her until completely necessary, so as long as she kept her gagged mouth shut, she was keeping herself alive. She knew when she reached the top she would be walking towards the window like a pirate down the plank.

The moment Julia's shoe touched the top step, her body convulsed beyond her control. She wondered if the injury to her head was causing her to have a seizure, but she quickly realised it was out of sheer terror. She had stared down a blade before and expected death, but her life hadn't flashed before her eyes then. As she stared down at the polished mahogany floorboards, she saw everything before her. She thought of Sue, and her gran finding out she had been thrown from the same window as Charles Wellington. She thought of Jessie being cast back into the care system, and Mowgli back to the streets. She would never know what it would be like to finish a date with Barker, nor would she die divorced from the man she detested. Her café would gather dust, and her father would die an old man in prison after the Lewis family successfully framed the drunken man for her murder. The worse part was, she wondered if her father might even believe he did it. She didn't know how much of that whiskey he had drank, but she remembered how much he had drunk after her mother died, and it was a lot.

Thinking of her mother calmed her. It even sent a flicker of warmth through her body. She didn't know if she believed in a God, or in an afterlife, but the thought of possibly being reunited with her mother filled her with a swelling light. She had always known this day was coming and it had comforted her to think she might one day see her mother again, even if she hadn't expected it to be so soon.

The convulsing started again, and she looked up from the ground. She caught a man's eyes, but they weren't Terry's or Jamie's, they were much older and much blanker. She realised she was looking through a crack into Vincent Wellington's bedroom, where he was sitting under a blanket in his wheelchair in front of a silent TV. For a moment, she thought she saw those old vacant eyes widen, but before she could be sure, Terry pushed her on.

She turned her attention to the window. Its glass was fresh, but that wouldn't last long. Would death hurt? It wouldn't be like falling asleep, more like falling into a nightmare she wouldn't jolt from. She reconsidered if it was a nightmare, but it felt too real; the pain in her head felt too real.

Just thinking of the pain in her head made her ears burn with a deafening buzzing. She clenched her eyes and stopped, wanting to clutch her head. When she opened them, she realised the Lewis family could hear it too.

"What is that?" Joanne seethed through gritted teeth. "An alarm?"

"There wasn't an alarm when I put the bust back yesterday," Terry said.

Julia heard a door open, and then another. They all turned to see Brian and Hilary squinting into the dark, both disgruntled and half asleep.

"What the -," Brian mumbled over the alarm as he walked forward and flicked on a light. "*Julia?*"

Just hearing her father say her name immediately broke her. Tears flooded her cheeks, mixing with the blood and dripping through the gag so she could taste the mixture of iron and salt. Julia felt a renewed urge to survive this horrible night, so she ran in the only direction she could, towards the window.

Pushing her body up against the cold glass, she watched as Terry advanced on her brandishing his knife. Brian charged forward as Hilary stood screaming from behind her hands. Julia knew her father was never going to catch up to save her. She didn't want to fall onto the blade of a madman regretting so many years of her life, but she did. All she wanted was a hug from her dad.

"No!" a voice cried and a dark shadow appeared in front of her like a ghost, standing between her and the knife.

She heard a small whimper, but she didn't stick around to see what had happened. She leapt into her father's arms, her hands still restrained. Painful sobs escaped her throat and her father's lips pressed up against her forehead.

"It's all going to be okay," he whispered. "It's all going to be okay."

Julia realised she had been waiting to hear those words from him since the day her mother died.

Forcing back her tears, the sound of another's was drowning out the piercing alarm. She pulled away from her father to see Jamie and Terry stumbling towards the window. It looked as though they were hugging, but from the strained cries leaving Joanne's mouth, she knew something more serious had happened.

Jamie's eyes met her and they tensed, apologising in a way words couldn't. It was then she saw the blood dripping between them, and she realised exactly what had happened. Jamie had jumped in between her and the blade.

Julia noticed why it looked like they were hugging. Jamie was clutching onto his father's shirt as though the two were fused. With the strength of ten men, Jamie dragged his father with him through the window. The glass shattered and they both fell into the rain.

Unable to hold on anymore, Julia let the darkness take her as Joanne's screams rang throughout the whole of Peridale.

CHAPTER 16

J ulia's eyes shot open, instantly closing because of the bright daylight. She forced them open again, realising it wasn't daylight at all, but florescent tubes in the hospital ceiling.

"She's awake!" she heard her gran cry. "Sue, wake up! She's *awake!*"

Julia blinked hard, feeling like she had been asleep for years. Against the beeping, she heard Sue's groans as their gran woke her. Next to Sue, Jessie stirred from her sleep too.

"Huh?" Sue groaned, sitting up and rubbing her eyes. "What's happening?"

"She's awake!"

Sue, Jessie and Dot all rushed over to her side. Jessie clutched one hand, Sue clutched another and Dot rested her own hand on Julia's forehead, which she realised was bandaged up.

"How long have I been out?" she asked, her croakiness surprising her.

"Just a day," Dot said soothingly, her thumb rubbing over the bandages. "You gave us all quite a fright."

Julia remembered the blow to the head and everything that had happened following it. She remembered watching Terry and Jamie tumbling out of the window, and then fading into darkness in her father's arms. She knew it was all too bizarre to be a dream.

"Joanne?" she mumbled.

"She's been arrested," Sue said, squeezing Julia's hand. "You don't have to worry about them."

"The others?" she asked.

Sue looked to Jessie, who looked to Dot, who looked to Julia. None of them seemed to want to tell her what had happened.

"Terry died," Jessie said in a soft voice Julia didn't recognise. "Jamie is in intensive care."

"He survived?"

"He did it, Julia," Dot said. "Jamie struck Charles over the head. Joanne confessed everything."

"I know," Julia said. "I know why."

"It doesn't matter why," Sue said, squeezing Julia's hand again. "All that matters is you're safe, and that boy will leave this place in a box, or in handcuffs. Either way, he can't hurt you."

"No," Julia mumbled, coughing as she struggled for words. "He saved me. He stood in front of the blade."

They all looked from one to the other again, and she could tell they were wondering if she was under the influence of the heavy drugs she could feel pumping through her system. It was all so bizarre, she began to wonder that herself.

She was about to start explaining again, but the door

creaked open and Barker walked through, clutching a tray of plastic coffees.

"I thought we could all use some -," Barker said, his voice trailing off and his eyes meeting Julia's. "You're awake!"

"Barely," Dot said. "She's delirious. Thinks that dreadful Lewis boy jumped in front of his mad father's blade to save her."

"He did," Julia said, fighting off more coughing. "He is just a boy."

Dot, Sue and Jessie all backed away, making room for Barker to stand by Julia's side. He didn't hesitate in scooping up her hand and when he squeezed, she squeezed back.

"I was so worried about you," Barker said, his bottom lip trembling. "Why did you have to go snooping, hmm?"

"I didn't," Julia said, attempting to laugh but coughing instead. "Not this time. I went to get a prospectus for Jessie. For college."

Jessie looked guiltily to the floor, and Julia tried to tell her she didn't need to feel guilty, but she couldn't summon the energy to raise her voice loud enough to reach her across the room.

"You can explain later," Barker said, his hand clutching Julia's hand so tight she felt safe enough to forget what had happened. "All that matters is you are safe."

"The alarm?" Julia asked.

"It was Vincent's medical alarm," Barker said, with a small laugh. "He saw you and he *saved* you. He pressed the button and woke everyone up. The man is still in there somewhere."

"Katie was telling the truth," Julia croaked, her eyelids

fluttering. "The burglar was real – I found – *I found* -,"
Darkness took her once again.

CHAPTER 17

3 WEEKS LATER

Julia's first day back in the café was a surreal one. She was given more flowers and sympathy cards than she knew what to do with, and she recounted the tale of what had happened so many times it had started to feel like it had happened to somebody else. Even though they had all heard the story on the Peridale grapevine, there wasn't a dry eye or a gasp free mouth in her café that day.

A little after noon, Sally Marriott came into the café alone. All heads turned and watched as she walked towards the counter, her head bowed in silence. When she met Julia's eyes, she immediately broke out into tears.

"Oh, Julia!" she cried. "I feel like all of this is *my* fault."

"Don't be silly," Julia said as she took Sally into the kitchen to get her away from the eavesdroppers. "You didn't have anything to do with this."

"I just can't help but think if I hadn't lied to the police, or to you, maybe the truth would have helped them in some way."

Sally sat down and Julia made her a strong cup of coffee. Sally explained how when she had visited Peridale Manor, she had found Richard pinning Charles to the ground and punching him in the face. She told Julia that she managed to drag him away and convince him to come home with her so they could talk. As they were leaving, they saw Charles fall out of the window, so they quickly left the scene so they wouldn't be suspected.

"I understand," Julia said, resting her hand on Sally's jittery knee. "You don't have to feel guilty."

Sally sipped her coffee and attempted to smile, but Julia could sense sadness still deep within her.

"I really loved him, Julia," she said, nodding her head and holding back tears. "I thought Charles was the one. We met late last year at The Comfy Corner. Richard had stood me up and Charles was supposed to be meeting his sister because she wanted to tell him something, but she didn't show up. I suppose it was about the spa, but she decided against telling him so she could get on with things. If she had just told him, none of this would have happened. He wasn't as bad as people said. We got talking and he was so kind and sensitive in a way Richard wasn't. One thing led to another and – *well*, you know the rest. Richard found messages on my phone the night before the garden party, so he went up to the manor looking for Charles because he knew everybody in the village would be there. I was such a fool, Julia."

"Do you think marrying him is the best decision?"

"I've left him," Sally said, calming herself long enough to take a sip of coffee. "For good, this time. We were never right for each other. I was just in love with the idea of the fairy tale. Cinderella and her Prince Charming. He showed me attention and I fell in love with the fantasy. I'm sorry to cancel my wedding cake order again."

Julia smiled and stood up. She walked over to the fridge and pulled out a plastic box filled with small slices of cake. She peeled off the lid and offered it to Sally, who looked suspiciously at them before plucking one out.

"Cinnamon, rose and orange!" she exclaimed as she bit into it. "Oh, Julia! It's delicious! It's better than I ever could have imagined."

"Keep them," Julia said. "Those three weeks at home gave me plenty of time to practice. I had a feeling you wouldn't be walking down the aisle with Richard, but I wanted to perfect it for my own sake. Now that I have the recipe, you can ask me for that any time. I see where you were coming from. It is an unusual taste, but it's quite refreshing on the palette."

After Sally finished her coffee, she once again exited through the backdoor away from prying eyes. This time, Julia knew Sally was walking towards a better life for herself.

No sooner had Sally left did another unexpected guest arrive. Julia watched as her father walked into her café for the first time. He looked around the room, appearing surprised by what he saw. Jessie scowled at him over her shoulder as she sprayed cleaner on the cake display case.

"You've done a really nice job in here," he said as he walked towards the counter. "What do you recommend?"

"I have your favourite Victoria sponge," Julia said, already reaching into the counter for it.

"I fancy something different today," he said calmly. "It's time for a change."

Julia paused, her hand hovering over the Victoria sponge. She smiled at her father, and he smiled at her. She could feel the first page of their new story being written in that moment. She plucked out a chocolate brownie, added it to a plate with cream, and slid it across the counter.

"On me," Julia said. "How's Katie?"

"Recovering," he said as he ran his finger through the cream and dropped it into his mouth. "Her brother dying, being arrested, and then what happened to those two lads. It's all just hit her hard."

"I need to go to the manor to see her," Julia said, bowing her head. "To apologise for not believing her."

"I didn't either," he said, joining her in bowing his head. "I don't think she's forgiven me for it, but it will take time. I think we've all learned that time can heal old wounds."

"Or reopen them," Jessie chimed in as she scrubbed the front of the counter. "But it can heal them too."

Brian laughed softly and looked down at the brownie, then around the café, and then at Julia. She thought he might cry, but he collected himself and stared deep into her eyes.

"I'm proud of you, kid," he said.

He quickly finished his brownie and left, promising to go and speak to Sue. Julia hoped it wouldn't be the last time he stepped foot in her café.

"Jessie, can you watch the counter for me?" Julia asked as she pulled out a heavy white envelope she had hidden that morning. "I just need to nip next door."

"You got it, boss," Jessie said, saluting with a wink. "I held down this place for three weeks, didn't I? I think the folk around here are starting to warm to my cakes more than yours."

Julia smiled her thanks to Jessie, not wanting to tell her about the dozens of phone calls she had had since Jessie had been in charge, begging her to come back so they didn't have to endure Jessie's baking. It would take a little more practice before she was up to Julia's standards, but now that she was enrolled in her college apprenticeship, she was optimistic for the future.

With the letter clutched in her hands, Julia walked next door to the post office. She thought about how much this letter had been taunting her everyday while she had been at home, mocking her for not having had the guts to get rid of it sooner.

She wondered if that was how Jessie had felt, stuffing all of the letters from the social workers, who were trying to arrange a home visit, in various boots in her wardrobe, all of which Julia had discovered and read. It turned out Jessie's sleepwalking had been from her fear that if faced with the official decision of fostering her, that Julia would reject her. The second Julia told her that wasn't going to happen, they hugged it out and agreed that there would be no more letter hiding or secrets. Jessie agreed on the condition that Julia posted her divorce papers, but that was a condition Julia was more than happy to oblige. The sleepwalking had stopped, and the only thing waking Julia in the night was the banging of her own head when the painkillers wore off.

"First class," Julia said, dropping the heavy envelope onto the scales. "Recorded. I want to make sure this gets where it's going."

"That'll be three pounds twenty please, love," said Shilpa, the kind lady who ran the post office. "How's your head?"

Julia's fingers wandered up to the butterfly stitches keeping her healing cut together. She had figured out a way to style her hair so the work of Terry Lewis couldn't be seen even when the stitches were taken off later that afternoon.

"Healing," Julia said as she handed over the exact money in coins. "Can barely feel a thing."

"You've been through the wars, young lady," Shilpa said as she counted out the money. "Your tracking number is on your receipt. Take care, love."

And just like that, her divorce papers were gone. Out of her hands. She had expected to feel euphoric, like a weight had lifted off her shoulders, but instead she felt nothing. It made her wonder why she had dreaded this moment for so long. Jerrad was in her past now, and she had so much to look forward to in her future.

Against the advice of the doctors, Julia drove up to the hospital after the café closed. She was itching to have her stitches taken off, and she didn't fancy chancing her luck trying to make her appointment in time catching the buses.

"One, two, *three*," the nurse said as she peeled the stitches off. "Didn't hurt, did it?"

"I've been through worse."

The nurse smiled but she didn't question Julia. Unless she had read the lengthy articles about what had happened in *The Peridale Post*, she doubted the nurse would know. Julia was glad. She knew eventually the residents of Peridale would move onto something else, but until that time happened, people weren't letting her forget the ordeal she had been through.

After giving her some aftercare instructions and a prescription for a cream to help the scar fade quicker, Julia left the room but she didn't head for the hospital exit. Instead, she walked into the depths of the hospital to the room where Jamie Lewis was being kept.

Luckily for her, the officer on the door was one of the officers who had originally arrested Katie, so he knew exactly what had happened. He told Julia she could have five minutes, and that was all. She didn't need any more.

She slipped into the room and the noisy hospital corridor faded away. The small body in the bed rolled over, its eyes widening with recognition. He attempted to sit up, but handcuffs chaining him to the bed restricted his movement.

"How are you feeling?" Julia asked, unsure of what to say, and unable to look him in the eyes.

"Sore," he mumbled. "You?"

"Better."

Julia pulled up a chair and sat next to Jamie. She hadn't brought a card, or flowers, or grapes, but she was there, and she knew that was important. The boy would be going to prison for a long time, so she wanted to make sure he knew exactly how she felt.

"I understand why you did what you did to Charles Wellington," Julia said, looking in his eyes for the first time since he had thrown himself out of the window clutching his father, an image that had haunted her every night since. "I know what it feels like when everybody wants you to be one thing, but you want to be another."

"I never wanted to be a builder," Jamie said, looking hopelessly into Julia's eyes. "I wanted to be a comic book illustrator. I got into a really good college in London, but my dad told me I couldn't go. He said I had to be in his trade because they couldn't afford to send me to London, and they needed the extra hands."

"That wasn't fair of him," Julia said.

"I gave up my dreams to help him and he didn't care. When I heard Charles Wellington talking over the microphone about how he was going to stop the spa being built, I saw everything I had already lost. I ran into the house looking for him. Some guy was hitting him, but a woman came and dragged him away. Charles stumbled upstairs so I followed him. I didn't know what I was going to do. I thought I was going to talk to him, to convince him how other people in the village needed the spa, how *my family* needed the spa. Without that job, we were losing our house. I guess we've lost it now. The debt collectors were days away as it was. We were counting on that money to save us. My dad gambled away everything. Their lifesavings, the money my gran had left for my future. *Everything*. I hated him for it.

"Charles came out of the bathroom, and I tried to talk to him. He called me a dumb kid and he wouldn't listen to what I had to say. I panicked. I saw my father in him. I *cracked*. I picked up the bust and I hit his head. He fell so quickly. I didn't mean to kill him. I didn't mean -,"

"I know," Julia said, reaching instinctively out for Jamie's hand.

He held back the tears before continuing.

"I knew he was dead. I just knew it. My dad came looking for me and he saw what I had done. It was his idea to throw Charles out of the window. He picked him up, and tossed him like he was nothing. We cleaned up the blood and he took the bust. I ran into the bathroom and I panicked. I knew any minute somebody would rush upstairs to see what had happened, so I opened the window and I climbed down the drainpipe.

"And then I ran. I didn't stop running. I never thought I would stop running. My dad came home and he found me. He beat me. Then my mum came home. We didn't tell her. My dad told her that we had gone for some lunch together and it was best she just tell people we were all together when Charles was pushed out of the window. She didn't question him. She didn't find out the truth until my dad hit you. I wanted to keep her out of it, but it was too late.

"When I saw my dad about to stab you, I knew I had caused this. I couldn't let it happen again. I didn't think, I just jumped in front of him. I *wanted* to die. I *wanted* him to die. I *wanted* it all to stop. I thought it had worked. I remember looking up at the rain, and touching the knife handle, and then my eyes closed. When I woke up here, I didn't understand why I wasn't dead."

"There has been *enough* death," Julia said, squeezing his hand. "You took two lives, but you saved one. You already know you're going to prison, but you'll be a free man one day. You might even be out by the time you're my age."

"That old?" Jamie said, laughing through his tears.

"Less of the old," Julia whispered with a wink. "Take care of yourself, Jamie."

"You too."

"If you still remember me when you get out of prison, come and find me," Julia said as she opened the door. "I'll show you what old really means."

She doubted she would ever see Jamie again, but she hoped he would still be able to have a life one day, maybe even find happiness. He was just a child who was pushed to make a bad decision. Julia knew how easily that could have been Jessie on any different day. She looked back at him one last time, almost upset that she had discovered the truth.

"Julia?" she heard Detective Inspector Brown's voice call out down the hallway as she walked away from his room. "What are you doing here?"

Julia turned, a smile on her face and peace in her heart. Seeing Barker warmed her like the hottest July sun.

"Getting closure," she said.

"Did you get it?"

"I think so."

"I'm glad," Barker said, glancing over his shoulder to his colleague who was standing guard outside of Jamie's room. "I slipped him twenty quid and told him to let you in when you finally showed up."

"What made you think I would show up?"

"Because you're a good woman," Barker said, his smile easy and soft. "A good woman, who I still haven't taken on a proper first date."

"I hear the jacket potatoes in the canteen aren't half bad," Julia said, linking arms with Barker and setting off down the corridor.

"I thought you would be sick of hospital food by now," Barker whispered, leaning in and resting his head on hers.

"I am," Julia agreed. "But the company will make up for it."

They walked down the corridor arm in arm, and Julia thought about her happy ending. She knew nothing that ended was happy, but she was on the brink of something new, with Barker and Jessie, and that made her heart truly happy.

DOUGHNUTS AND DECEPTION

BOOK 3

CHAPTER 1

J ulia reached under her bed, her fingers closing around the baseball bat. Her gran, Dot, had given it to her three weeks ago, insisting that it wasn't safe for a single woman to be living alone, especially with the recent murders. Julia hadn't taken her seriously, but had put it under her bed all the same, just in case. As she picked up the bat, she was glad for the gift.

With the wooden bat in hand, she tiptoed towards her bedroom door. Holding her breath, she pressed her ear up against the cold oak, wanting to be sure she hadn't imagined the rustling that had woken her. The unmistakable zip of a backpack confirmed her suspicions.

She twisted the brass doorknob, wincing as the old cottage creaked around her. She didn't know what she was going to do when she came face-to-face with the mystery person digging in her kitchen, but she hoped the bat would scare them off before she had to find out if she had a good swing.

"I've called the police!" she cried out, the shake in her

voice betraying her. "I'm armed!"

The rustling stopped, and then something smashed against the tiles in her kitchen. Acting fast, she reached out and slapped for the hallway light, her fingertips narrowly missing the switch in the dark. She stepped on something fluffy, which let out an ear-piercing yowl. Jumping back, her bare heel caught the edge of her hallway rug, sending her tumbling backwards, the bat flying free in the air. She opened her eyes as gravity sent the bat soaring back towards her face. Rolling out of the way just in time, she crashed into the small table displaying the dozen roses Barker had given her. The bat clattered against the floor as she darted forward, catching the vase before it succumbed to a similar fate.

"Julia?" Jessie cried, running out of the kitchen, fully dressed and clutching a backpack. "What are you doing?"

Jessie flicked on the light Julia had been reaching for before she stepped on Mowgli, who was now cowering by the front door, sending daggers in her direction. Squinting at the light, she looked down at the vase of roses she was holding in her lap.

"I thought you were a burglar," Julia mumbled feebly, glancing awkwardly to the bat.

Jessie took the vase from Julia and placed it back where it belonged. "You keep a baseball bat under your bed? You're more gangsta than I thought, cake lady."

Julia gratefully accepted Jessie's offer of a hand. Standing on both feet, she realised she had acted thoughtlessly in her sleepy state. Her gran's fear mongering had worked.

"Are you sleepwalking again?" Julia asked as she leaned over to pick up the bat.

Jessie looked down at her clothes and then up at Julia, arching a dark brow. She was wearing her Doc Martins, baggy jeans ripped at the knees, and a heavy hoodie. They were the clothes she had worn when Julia had caught her stealing from her café two months ago, before she had offered Jessie a job and the use of her guest bedroom.

"I had a dream," Jessie said, tossing the full backpack over her shoulder. "I'll explain it over a cup of tea."

Julia followed Jessie through to the kitchen, where all the drawers and cupboards were wide open. Julia's favourite cat-shaped mug was scattered across her kitchen floor in pieces, having fallen victim to Jessie's rummaging. Julia sat at her kitchen counter, scratching her head as she let out a yawn. The cat clock, with its swinging tail and darting eyes, told her it was only five in the morning.

"I had a dream," Jessie repeated, staring out into the dark garden as she filled the kettle. "I was homeless again. It felt so real."

"It was just a dream," Julia offered, as comfortingly as she could. "You don't ever have to worry about being homeless again. I won't let that happen."

Jessie smiled over her shoulder as she set the kettle back in its stand. She plucked two individually wrapped teabags from the box in the cupboard and ripped them open with her teeth before dropping them into two mugs. While the kettle boiled, she fished the dustpan and brush from under the sink and started to clean up the shattered cat mug.

"I'll replace it," Jessie said as she swept up the pieces. "I'm sorry. I panicked. I don't want you to think I was robbing you."

Julia cast an eye over to the bag, and then to her kitchen cupboards. It appeared that most of her food had made its way into the bulging backpack.

"It's just a mug," Julia said, shrugging and ignoring the small pang in her chest as she watched Jessie toss it into the bin. "I'll get over it."

Jessie smiled again, but her young face was solemn. Julia wondered how bad the dream had been.

"I was back on the streets," Jessie continued, pouring the boiling water into the two mugs. "Back at the old Fenton Industrial Park. That's where I was most of the time."

Julia had heard of Fenton Industrial Park more than once. It was a couple of miles from Peridale, on the outskirts of Cheltenham. *The Peridale Post* had covered the devastating fire that had caused all the businesses to flee the area. What it hadn't covered was that a small community of homeless people had moved in and made the area their own soon after, but she had heard that on the Peridale grapevine.

"I know of it," Julia said with a nod as Jessie set a cup in front of her. "I can't imagine that being an easy way to live."

"It wasn't," Jessie said, sitting across from Julia, the dark circles under her eyes becoming obvious. "It was a horrible place to live, if I'm being honest, but it was home for six months. It felt more like six years. The winter seemed to go on forever, but we had each other, y'know? We were sort of a family. We watched each other's backs and protected each other. When I used to nick cakes from your café, I'd take whatever I could back and share them out."

"That was very thoughtful of you," Julia said, blowing the edge of her scalding hot tea. "You're a nice girl, Jessie."

"But I'm not, am I?" she cried, her voice suddenly

shooting up. "Because I got this cushy new life and left them all there to get on with it."

"Is that what the bag is about?"

Jessie glanced to the bag and nodded.

"I woke up in a cold sweat," she said, staring into her cup as the teabag steeped, its golden goodness swirling in small circles. "I felt so guilty. I left to find some food two months ago and never went back, not even to explain."

"Were you going back there?"

"Only to give them food," Jessie said, looking ahead at the empty cupboards. "I would have replaced it all before you woke up. I made a list."

Jessie reached into her pocket and pulled out a crumpled, messily written shopping list. Julia smiled, resting her hand on top of Jessie's.

"I don't care about the food," Julia said. "As long as you're safe, that's all I care about."

"I wouldn't trade this in for nothin'," Jessie looked around the small kitchen, as though she was taking in a grand castle. "But the others aren't so lucky, are they?"

Julia sipped her tea, the cogs in her brain churning at lightspeed. She had wanted to ask Jessie about her days of being homeless ever since first meeting her, but she hadn't wanted to appear nosy. Gossiping was the number one pastime in Peridale, and Julia hadn't wanted Jessie to think she was just another village snoop.

"I've got an idea," Julia said after taking another sip, the liquorice tickling the back of her throat. "Go back to sleep and we'll visit Fenton Industrial Park together when the sun has risen. We don't want to arrive when everyone is still asleep, do we?"

Chewing the inside of her cheek, Jessie looked at the

bag again. She seemed to want to grab it and run straight for the door, but Julia trusted her to see the sense in what she was offering.

"I guess," Jessie said, shrugging and letting out a yawn. "You don't have to come."

"I want to."

Jessie took a sip of her tea, but as usual, she didn't finish it. She slid off the stool and hovered next to Julia, looking like she wanted to say something. Instead, she wrapped her arms around Julia's chest, squeezing tightly. Closing her eyes, she rested her hands on Jessie's arms, smiling to herself.

"Go on! Back to bed!" Julia ordered, tapping Jessie's arms. "I'll wake you in a couple of hours."

Jessie let go and headed back to her bedroom. Julia waited until she heard the creaking of Jessie's metal bed-frame before she stood up. As she unloaded Jessie's bag and returned the food to her kitchen cupboards, she tried to remember her mum's old recipe for doughnuts.

CHAPTER 2

Looping around the roundabout for a second time, Julia glanced over to Jessie, who had trays of doughnuts stacked up on her knees. Fumbling with her hands on top of the plastic wrap securing the doughnuts in place, she cracked her knuckles again. She had been doing it since they had left the cottage.

"You don't have to be nervous," Julia said, finally taking the turn after driving around a third time. "I'll be by your side the entire time."

Jessie didn't seem to have heard her. She stared ahead, continuing to crack her knuckles; the sound sending a shiver down Julia's spine.

From the moment Julia had woken Jessie soon after sunrise, she had sensed the girl's fear. It didn't surprise Julia. While she had been baking over one hundred doughnuts for the homeless residents of Fenton Industrial Park, Julia had wondered if returning there was the best thing for Jessie. Despite Jessie's protests that she wasn't leaving Julia, something deep within her squirmed uncomfortably.

"We're here," Julia said, the burnt husk of the industrial park coming into view.

Jessie snapped out of her trance state and stared ahead at the blackened warehouse buildings, which looked like they could fall to the ground at any moment. Fingers tightening around the steering wheel, Julia hated the thought of this being home to anybody, let alone a teenage girl.

They pulled up outside of the industrial park, and it had a huge 'FOR SALE' sign looming next to the entrance, which in turn had a 'SALE BY AUCTION' sticker plastered across its front, with an auction date only a couple of weeks away. Through the spiked, metal fences, Julia spotted the community Jessie had spoken about, and her heart skipped a beat.

"There's so many people," Julia whispered, the words escaping her mouth before she even had a chance to think about them.

"The country's hidden problem," Jessie said with wisdom beyond her sixteen years. "We – I mean – *they* live in places like this because it's easier for people to pretend we – I mean - *they* don't exist."

Julia wanted to tell her that wasn't true, but she bit her tongue before she let a lie slip out. She thought of her own perception of homeless people before she had met Jessie. There was nobody that she knew of in Peridale who was homeless. Until she caught Jessie breaking into her café, it always felt like an issue that happened in other parts of the country. Yet here she was, staring through the gaps in the metal fence at dozens of people, less than an hour's drive from her front door. During her time living in London, there were homeless men and women on every corner asking for spare change. She would often dig a pound coin out of her purse for the most desperate looking of them, but there were so many it was impossible to help all of them. It was a problem most city folk were overly desensitised to. They blended into the pavement, huddled in doorways under rags while the rest of the world got on with their comfortable lives. Jessie was right, they were hidden, but Julia wondered if that was by choice, or because the rest of the country had stopped noticing them.

After what felt like an age of staring, Julia twisted her keys in the ignition and drove through the broken down gates. Men and women were huddled around make-shift fires in burnt out barrels, others hiding from the early morning sunlight under blankets. Heads turned towards Julia's vintage aqua blue Ford Anglia, but most didn't bat an eyelid. She drove into an empty corner and jammed the handbrake in place. She glanced at the backseat at the stacks of doughnuts. When she had left her cottage, she had been sure she had baked enough to have leftovers to sell in the café on Monday morning, but that hope quickly vanished.

Julia jumped out of her car and opened her boot. She dragged out her old folding wallpaper-pasting table and kicked it open, fastening the small hinges into place. After throwing a pale pink and blue picnic blanket over its tarnished surface, she heaved a giant Victorian silver coffee maker out of her car and placed it carefully on the rickety table. Taking the lid off the huge vat, she inhaled the still hot, rich coffee. She had been looking for an excuse to use the contraption since picking it up at a car-boot sale over a year ago.

Jessie finally got out of the car and placed the doughnuts on the table, while Julia arranged the small cardboard cups, bag of sugar cubes taken from her café, and a box of coffee whitener.

"Coffee and doughnuts!" Julia announced, cupping her hands around her mouth. "Free coffee and doughnuts to all who want them!"

All heads turned to Julia this time and a line quickly formed in front of the table. Jessie handed out the doughnuts while Julia poured coffee from a tap jutting out of an ornate lion's mouth embedded in the coffee maker. People accepted their free sweet treat and hot drink while gratefully muttering their thanks.

"Jessie?" an old worn voice called from the crowd of faces. "I thought that was you!"

A slender, elderly man hobbled forward with the assistance of a wooden walking stick that had been patched up with duct tape in more than one spot. His grey hair was long and scraggly, cheekbones high and sharp, sunken eyes, and a heavy brow casting dark shadows over his face. He looked like he had the ability to look menacing without much effort, but his ear-to-ear smile was so warm, Julia wasn't sure the man possessed a mean-spirited bone in his body.

"Tommy!" Jessie cried, matching his smile.

The old man broke through the line and embraced Jessie with one arm as he steadied himself with his stick. Jessie on the other hand gripped the man around the waist and buried her face into his mucky clothes. It brought a smile to Julia's face as she continued to serve coffee and doughnuts.

When Jessie finally let go of the man, they moved around to the front of Julia's car to talk. Julia served the rest of the people in the line as quickly as she could. When she ran out of coffee and only the crumbs of the doughnuts were left, she wiped her fingers down the front of her pale peach 1940s style dress before joining Jessie and the old man she had called Tommy.

"I've been hearing all about you," Tommy said, holding a hand out to Julia. "If I had a hat, I would take it off to you ma'dear."

Julia accepted the man's weathered hand. The strength of his grip surprised her.

"I just did what any other decent person would do," Julia said, smiling at Jessie.

"I don't think every person who calls themselves decent would take in a girl from the streets," Tommy assured her. "You really are a marvellous woman. And an incredible baker too. Jessie would bring your cakes back here when she – y'know – *borrowed* them."

"I saved you one." Julia pulled a doughnut wrapped in a paper napkin out of her dress pocket. "There's no coffee left I'm afraid."

"I never did like the stuff much," Tommy said, tipping his head to Julia as he accepted and pocketed the doughnut in one of his filthy overcoat pockets. "Not good for the heart at my age."

Julia tried to place the man's age, but she couldn't quite figure it out. His almost skeletal frame and the layer of grime covering his deeply wrinkled skin aged him, but there was a twinkle in his eyes and a youth to his smile that made her think he was younger than he appeared. She placed him in his mid-to-late sixties. Something told her he wasn't much older than her own father.

Tommy took them across the car park to a small doorway in one of the burnt out warehouses. Black smudges lined the metal door, and it didn't take much of Julia's imagination to visualise the flames licking the air as they tried to escape the grand metallic structure.

With his fumbling fingers, Tommy pulled two upturned plastic crates together and tossed a well-worn red blanket over them. He motioned for Jessie and Julia to take a seat as he opted to sit cross-legged on a folded up sleeping bag in the doorway. Julia realised she was in the man's home.

"Tommy's in charge 'round here," Jessie said. "What he says goes."

"I don't know about that, little one," Tommy laughed as he pulled the squashed up doughnut from his pocket. "People here come and go and do what they please."

Julia looked around the vast space. There were small clusters of people sipping her coffee and chatting amongst themselves. She noticed that the doorway where Tommy resided was perfectly in the centre of the units, looking out at the broken gate. Like a sheriff sitting on the porch of a small town police station in the Wild West, Julia doubted much got past this man.

"There's more people here than I imagined," Julia said, turning her attention back to Tommy as he shakily crammed the pink iced doughnut into his mouth. "I'm surprised the council isn't trying to do something to help."

"Oh, they are," Tommy mumbled through a mouthful of doughnut. "They're doing plenty to help themselves. This place has been up for sale for redevelopment since the fire. The council is doing all they can to clear us lot away from here, but there's far too many to help rehouse and the shelters are bursting to capacity. They could arrest us all for squatting, but there aren't enough cells in the county. This doughnut is delicious by the way. You really do have a talent for baking."

"Thank you," Julia said. "So you're just staying here for as long as you can?"

"And then some," Tommy said, laughing as he licked his dirty fingers. "Developers are sniffing around everyday. It's only a matter of time before one of them takes the risk and puts in an offer. They'll level this place to the ground, stick some luxury apartments on here so those who can afford it will have somewhere nice to live."

"And those who can't are just left to move on somewhere else," Jessie jumped in. "It's sick."

"It's business," Tommy said with a heavy sigh. "It's not right, but it's how the world works. I should know. I used to be one of those developers."

"You were?" Julia asked, her brows shooting up.

"Oh, yes. Don't let my exterior fool you," Tommy said, winking out of the corner of his eye as he brushed the doughnut crumbs down the front of his threadbare jumper. "Before the recession hit, I was a landlord. I had a portfolio of a dozen properties. Then the banks collapsed and people stopped wanting to rent. It started small, but I couldn't afford the mortgages and I went bankrupt pretty quickly. I lost my career, my house, my wife, and everything in between."

"That's so sad," Julia said, bowing her head.

"It is what it is." Tommy shrugged, clearly already having let go of his past life. "Life has a funny way of working out like that. It's not all bad. Folks like you are always there to provide the coffee and doughnuts to those in need. There's a nice Christian couple, Stella and Max Moon who bring their soup truck here most nights." Tommy suddenly stood up and jutted his stick out in front of him, his lips snarling. "There's one of those rotten developers now!"

Julia looked to where Tommy was pointing his stick. A handsome, clean-shaven, well-groomed man in a sharp suit walked into the industrial park, followed by a team of almost identical looking men.

"That's Carl Black," Tommy spat through gritted teeth. "He's one of the worst. Doesn't even look at us like we're people. *Get out of here! Do you hear me?*"

Carl glanced in Tommy's direction but he barely registered a reaction. Julia caught the flicker of an amused smirk, making her instantly dislike the man. He reminded her of her ex-husband.

A couple of people joined in the jeering, some of them tossing their empty coffee cups in the direction of the men. The group behind Carl flinched, but Carl marched forward to the warehouse unbothered.

"There's a sense of community here, for the most part," Tommy said proudly. "We look after our own."

"The most part?" Julia asked, glancing to Jessie.

"Well, every community has its bad eggs," Tommy said, his bulging eyes darting around the crowd. "Take alcoholic Pete, for example. He's a drunk. Spends his days begging on the streets and every penny he gets, he spends on booze."

Julia followed Tommy's eyeline. A similarly aged man was leaning half asleep against a wall, a can of beer clutched tightly in his hands.

"And then there's the deaths," Tommy added.

"Deaths?"

"Dropping like flies recently," Tommy said, his voice

lowering as he leaned in. "It's what you expect in places like this, especially in the winter. All it takes is a cold night to get those older ones on the drink and drugs, but spring is upon us and people are still dying. Not your usual type, either. We had an eighteen-year-old die last week."

"Who?" Jessie asked, suddenly sitting up straight.

"Bailey Walker," Tommy said, dropping his head. "I know you were close to him, Jessie. I'm sorry. I was the one to find him. He was still in his sleeping bag past midday, but that wasn't like him. He was usually up and spraying his paint cans 'round the back. Helped him pass the day I think. So I went over and gave him a poke with my stick, and told him to get his lazy backside up, joking of course. But he didn't move. I pulled his sleeping bag back. He was as white as a sheet, so I sent one of the younger lads running to the phone box on the corner. Ambulance pronounced him dead and carted him away."

Julia placed a hand over her mouth, which had parted while listening to the story. She looked to Jessie, who was dabbing tears from the inside of her eyes with the edge of her sleeve.

"We were in the same foster house once," Jessie said. "He got kicked out before I did. He was a good kid, he just – he just got into trouble a lot."

"What was the cause of death?" Julia asked, turning back to Tommy, who was looking sadly at Jessie.

"Inconclusive," Tommy said, his jaw gritting tightly. "They say it was a heart attack, but they don't know what caused it. At his age? Yeah, *right*. And he's not the only one. Remember the priest?"

"Father Thind?" Jessie asked, wiping away the last of her tears.

"Michael Thind." Tommy nodded. "He went two weeks after. Pete found him, dead in his sleeping bag, clutching his rosary beads. That man wouldn't have hurt a fly. And then there was Robert Culshaw, who went last week. Once again, in the sleeping bag. He used to be a banker in the city, but the recession hit him too."

Julia's mouth opened again. She looked around at the people surrounding her, wondering how many of them had lived relatively normal lives before ending up on the streets.

"Isn't somebody doing something?" Julia urged, edging closer to Tommy. "The police? They must be looking into it?"

"Three dead homeless people aren't enough to even pique the police's interests," Tommy said with a bitter laugh. "They probably think they were druggies, or drunks. Don't get me wrong, when the sun sets and we all huddle around the fires, a couple of cans of beer get passed around, but those men didn't drink any more than the rest of us. Not enough to kill them."

"And there was nothing else to connect the men?" Julia asked.

"Aside from the fact they were men, there's nothing I know of," Tommy said, shaking his head. "Michael was in his fifties and Robert was in his forties. Those two kept to themselves. Like I said, it's not uncommon for people to die 'round here, but there's usually a reason. Healthy men, homeless or not, don't just die in their sleep."

"You're right," Julia said, pulling her ingredients notepad out of her handbag along with a small metal pen. "Can you give me those names again?"

After Julia had written down the names, they walked back to her car and packed away the equipment. Jessie said goodbye to Tommy and promised to visit soon. When the man hobbled back to his doorway, they jumped into the car and slowly drove out of Fenton Industrial Park.

"Why did you write down those names?" Jessie asked, breaking the silence as they drove back to Peridale.

"I'm going to ask Barker if he knows anything," Julia said, looking straight ahead at the road as the cogs in her mind worked overtime. "There might be a perfectly reasonable explanation that the police haven't passed on."

"It is a little odd though, don't you think?" Jessie replied quietly as she chomped on her nails.

"It is more than a little odd," Julia agreed under her breath. "Very odd indeed."

CHAPTER 3

Peering over the top of her laptop, Julia looked through to the empty café. Jessie was standing behind the counter, scribbling something on a notepad, and the only customer, Julia's closest neighbour, Emily Burns, was pouring herself a second cup of tea from the pot. Julia liked the serenity of Monday mornings.

She usually used these quiet times to check her stock levels and deep clean every corner of the kitchen, but this morning she was using it to surf the web. Looking back down at her computer, she picked up where she had left off reading an article about Bailey Walker's death in the *Cheltenham Standard*. The short article, which didn't contain a picture of the young boy, treated him as nothing more than a homeless statistic, whose cause of death was '*inconclusive*' but also '*non-suspicious*'.

She flicked between the three different newspaper articles she had been reading. Robert Culshaw, the ex-banker, was referenced as having two teenage daughters, but the emphasis was strongly on his status as a homeless man. There was a picture, which was credited as being pulled from the *Gloucestershire Bank* website, showing a smartly dressed, clean-shaven man with neatly cut hair. Julia wondered if the poor man had still looked like that when he was found dead. The third article, about Michael Thind's death, was a little more colourful. As well as a picture featuring him in his dog collar and black robes, the article went into detail about how Father Thind was fired after it was discovered he had been having an affair with another local clergyman. It then went on to describe the ins and outs of his messy divorce, which somehow lead to the man ending up on the streets.

"What are you doing?" Jessie asked, her sudden appearance startling Julia so much, she slapped her laptop shut. "I thought you were cleaning."

"I am," Julia said, her cheeks burning. "I was. I was just looking at something."

Jessie folded her arms and looked down her nose at the laptop, her eyes squinting tightly. Julia knew she had been rumbled.

"Wouldn't have anything to do with what Tommy said about those deaths, would it?" Jessie asked cautiously. "Because if you're investigating, I want to help."

"I'm not investigating."

"You investigated those other deaths," Jessie said, her arms tightening across her apron. "That organ lady and her son, and your father's brother-in-law. You investigated those and cracked the cases."

"It wasn't quite like that," Julia said, shaking her head. "I just – I was *just* looking online to cross-check what Tommy told us."

"You didn't believe him?"

"Of course I did," Julia said quickly. "I just wanted to be sure."

"Well?" Jessie urged, stepping forward and placing her hands on the other side of the metal preparation table. "What did you find?"

Julia sighed and opened her laptop. She hadn't wanted Jessie to know she was looking into things because she didn't want to get her hopes up. Things did seem odd, but Julia knew even the strangest things could have the simplest explanations. Jessie hurried to her side and pulled the laptop in front of her.

"There's not a lot of information in the articles," Julia said as she looked over Jessie's shoulder. "I was trying to find a link between them, but there isn't one that I can see. Aside from them all being men, and their causes of death being '*inconclusive*'."

"What does that mean?" Jessie asked, turning to stare at Julia expectantly.

"It means they didn't find a cause of death. Sometimes when people die, the cause isn't so obvious, so they do some tests, and if they can't find a reason, they rule it as an inconclusive cause of death."

"You mean they just couldn't be bothered?" Jessie snapped, pushing the laptop across the counter and turning to face Julia.

"They only look for certain things if they're suspicious. Sometimes people do just die and nobody knows why."

"But three men?" Jessie asked, her brows dropping low over her dark eyes. "You wouldn't be saying that if three men in this village suddenly died and nobody was trying to figure out why."

Jessie pushed angrily past Julia and burst through the beads, and back into the café. Julia hurried after her, wanting to explain, even if she didn't know what she was going to say. Julia knew Jessie was right. If three seemingly healthy men had died in Peridale in a short space of time, nobody would have accepted three '*inconclusive*' causes of death.

Julia pushed through the beads at the same time Barker walked into the café, clutching a wicker hamper. Without meaning to, Julia scowled at him, angry with herself for upsetting Jessie, who was furiously wiping down an already clean table. Julia looked desperately from her lodger to the Detective Inspector she had been dating for the last couple of weeks, wondering who she should give her attention to. Before she could make up her mind, Jessie decided for her and walked back through to the kitchen, leaving them alone in the café with Emily Burns, who could clearly sense the tension.

"Is this a bad time?" Barker asked with a strained smile as he walked towards the counter.

"It's fine," Julia lied, shaking out her curls and applying a smile. "What can I get you, Barker?"

"Actually, I was wondering if I could borrow you for half an hour?" Barker looked awkwardly down to the wicker hamper, which Julia realised was a picnic basket. "I took an early lunch and I wanted to treat you to a picnic on the village green."

Julia glanced over her shoulder to Jessie, who had resumed reading over the newspaper articles on the laptop screen. Julia turned back to Barker, who was smiling expectantly at her. Could she really turn him down?

"It's not really a good time," Julia said awkwardly.

"Lots to do today."

"Oh," Barker said, frowning a little but retaining his smile. "I thought Mondays were always quiet? Unless you're expecting a sudden rush later?"

"We're not," Jessie said, suddenly appearing behind Julia. "I've got things covered here."

"Are you sure?" Julia asked, trying unsuccessfully to look into Jessie's eyes.

"Yep."

Julia reluctantly left her young lodger in charge of the café and followed Barker to the village green, which sat perfectly in the middle of Peridale. Barker laid down a red and white picnic blanket and Julia quickly sat in a position so that she could still see through her café window. Emily Burns appeared to be trying to coax some information out of Jessie, but Jessie didn't appear to be talking.

"Is something wrong?" Barker asked as he unloaded the picnic basket.

"Huh?" Julia mumbled, glancing to the food he had prepared. "I'm sorry, Barker. I'm just a little distracted."

"Well, if you can give me your attention for thirty minutes, I'll let you get back to being distracted." Barker smirked so sweetly, the butterflies in Julia's stomach danced unexpectedly, bringing her attention to the present.

"Deal," Julia said, sighing and shuffling across the blanket so that she was sitting next to Barker and couldn't look at her café. "Did you make all of this?"

"Ah," Barker said, smirking again. "Not quite. I was coming back from checking something out and passed a lovely looking sandwich shop."

"And the blanket and basket?"

"Borrowed them from the station's lost and found,"

Barker whispered. "Don't tell anyone. You'd never believe half of the stuff people hand in."

"Your secret is safe with me," Julia whispered back, her hair falling from behind her ear and over her face as she laughed gently.

Barker surprised her by reaching out and tucking the stray strand behind her ear. For a moment, the buzz of the village around them faded away as she looked into his eyes. She gulped, her throat suddenly dry. Laughing again, she turned her attention to the sandwiches as she felt her cheeks reddening.

"Bought or not, this all looks delicious," she said, her voice suddenly shaky.

Barker unwrapped tuna and cucumber, cheese and pickle, and egg and cress sandwiches, and laid them out on their foil wrappers on the blanket. Julia opted for a tuna and cucumber sandwich, not realising how hungry she was until she took her first bite. She had woken late that morning, and had had to rush through her Monday morning baking before opening the café, meaning she hadn't had time for her usual slice of toast and peppermint and liquorice tea.

Sitting under the early spring sun, with the hum of passing people and singing birds and buzzing insects, it was all so perfect, it made Julia forget about her café. When she finished her first half of her sandwich, she turned to Barker and shielded her eyes from the sun.

"This is our third date in a week," Julia said. "Anyone would think you were trying to court me, Detective Inspector."

"Wouldn't that be *quite* the scandal?" Barker joked, leaning in and lowering his voice. "You know the village has been talking about us."

"Let them," Julia whispered back. "It just shows that things have gone back to normal after these last couple of months of madness."

"Things have certainly calmed down," Barker agreed, before taking a bite of his sandwich, leaving behind the crust. "I spent my morning investigating a stolen tractor up at Peridale Farm. Yesterday, Amy Clark was convinced somebody had stolen her handbag, but she had just left it at bingo."

"Does it make you miss the city?"

Barker tossed his sandwich crust onto the foil and turned to Julia, shielding his eyes from the sun as it found its midday position in the clear blue sky.

"Not one bit," he said, smiling from ear to ear. "Besides, there are things in this village I never had in the city."

"Like?" Julia asked, her cheeks reddening again.

"Oh, you know," Barker said, shrugging softly. "Certain people."

Julia laughed and dropped her head again. When she looked up, her eyes locked with two dark circles poking out from the sitting room window of her gran's cottage.

"We're being watched," Julia said, nudging Barker with her shoulder.

Barker turned to look to where Julia was pointing. Julia realised the two dark circles belonged to a pair of binoculars being clutched by her gran. With them both looking in her direction, the lacy net curtains suddenly dropped back into their original position. The front door opened seconds later and Dot darted across the village green, her heavy binoculars bouncing under the brooch securing her blouse in place under her chin.

"Your gran scares me," Barker mumbled out of the corner of his mouth as Dot ran towards them.

"I'll tell her you said that," Julia mumbled back. "I think that's her goal."

Dot danced around a man walking his poodle, scowling down at the dog. When she finally made her way towards them, she slowed down and clutched her side, visibly out of breath.

"Afternoon, Gran," Julia called out. "Doing a spot of bird watching?"

"No," Dot said through her panting breaths. "Me and some of the girls have set up a neighbourhood watch group. Y'know, what with all of these recent murders and all."

"Nice to know my job is valued," Barker whispered under his breath.

"No *offence*, Detective Inspector," Dot said, her hearing much better than most people would think for a woman her age. "But if it wasn't for my Julia, there would still be two killers running around on the loose. Any of us could be next."

Julia held back her laughter. Her gran wasn't one to hold back, or spare on the dramatics. Barker on the other hand, was blushing and appeared lost for words. Julia knew her gran had just hit Barker where it hurt.

"What happened to your book club, Gran?" Julia asked, wanting to shift the conversation.

"Well," Dot said, taking it as an invitation to join them on the picnic blanket. "Some of the girls weren't too happy when we got to the mucky scenes in *Fifty Shades of Grey*. They didn't realise how filthy that Mr. Grey was. I quite enjoyed it myself. Are those egg and cress?"

Before either of them could respond, she reached out and plucked a sandwich from the mix. As she nibbled on the corner of the sandwich, Barker and Julia looked awkwardly at one another, neither appearing to know what to say.

"Seen anything interesting with those things?" Barker asked, a slight shake in his voice.

"The usual," Dot said. "I've been making notes. Hang on."

Dot reached into her breast pocket and pulled out a small notepad, not unlike the one Julia made her own notes in. She wondered if her gran was trying to investigate her own case so she could steal a little of the glory the rest of the village showered on Julia.

"*Eight-fifteen.* Julia and Jessie arrive at the café."

"Gran!" Julia said.

"You need protection!" Dot cried. "After what you went through when you caught Charles Wellington's killer, you need around the clock protection!"

Julia's fingers instinctively danced up to the fading scar on her forehead, which she had learned to conceal with her hair. It had only been two weeks since she had had the stitches removed, after being hit on the head with a recently boiled kettle while caught up in the middle of her father's brother-in-law's murder investigation. Her sister, Sue, was adamant Julia should talk to a surgeon to try and remove the scar, but Julia thought it added character.

"I'm fine, Gran," Julia said, trying to laugh. "Anything else?"

"*Ten-thirty-three.* A red tractor speeds through the village."

"A red tractor?" Barker jumped in. "Did you see who

was driving it?"

"Of course I did!" Dot said, turning the page. "Billy Matthews."

"I knew it!" Barker said, snapping his fingers together. "That kid has been causing me trouble for weeks."

"See!" Dot said, stabbing her finger down on the pad. "I *told* you this was useful."

"And what use could you possibly have for spying on me and Barker eating lunch on the village green?" Julia asked, tilting her head quizzically at her gran.

"Well, you know," Dot fumbled over her words, flicking through the pages. "See here. Julia and Baker are having a date on the village green. *No* axe murderers in sight."

Julia and Barker both laughed. Julia was touched that her gran cared so much, although she was sure she was just spying to see how things were going. Dot had been trying to push their relationship along faster ever since Barker arrived in the village.

"Well, I'm flattered, Gran," Julia said. "But I'm a big girl and I can look after myself. Thanks for the sandwich, Barker, but I'm going to have to get back to the café."

"And me back to the station," he said, standing up and dusting the crumbs down his trousers. "I've got to visit the Fern More estate just out of the village. Billy Mathews' mother might like to know what her son has been up to."

"That estate has caused nothing but trouble since they built it!" Dot said as she peered through her binoculars at Roxy Carter, who was leaving the graveyard with her girlfriend, Violet Mason. "I protested to it being built in – what year was it? – Eighty-two? Are these sandwiches going begging?"

Barker held his hand out for Julia as Dot wrapped up the sandwiches and piled them under her arm. Julia attempted to help her gran up off the blanket but she brushed Julia's hand away and scrambled up to her feet on her own.

"Thanks for the sandwiches, Detective Inspector," Dot said as she turned and darted away. "Saved me a job for when the girls come around later to share notes."

They both watched as Dot walked back to her cottage. The moment she was back inside, she resumed her position at the window, with her binoculars pushed through her lacy net curtains and up against the glass.

"Your gran is a character," Barker said as he packed away the blanket and basket. "One of these days we'll have an uninterrupted date."

"Oh, it's not so bad," Julia said, remembering their last date in a small country pub, which had been crashed by her sister and her husband. "If you add up all of these half-dates, we've almost had a full one somewhere along the way."

"Well, if you look at it like that," Barker said as they started to walk towards Julia's café. "I guess we have."

Outside the café, Julia peered through the window, where Jessie was serving Roxy and Violet. Jessie seemed a little happier, but her sadness was still obvious. Remembering what she had promised, Julia turned to Barker and pulled her own notepad out of her dress pocket. She flicked to a page she had specifically made for Barker and tore it out.

"Can you look into these names?" Julia asked, tucking the piece of paper into his pocket. "Three homeless men who frequented the Fenton Industrial Park have died recently, all without any real identifiable cause of death. Could you see if there's anything else out there that hasn't been passed onto the press? They were friends of Jessie's and it would mean a lot to her."

"I'll see what I can find," Barker said, tapping the pocket. "You're not – *investigating* again, are you?"

"My days of investigating are behind me," Julia said with a wink as she turned around and pulled open her café door. "Besides, my gran's got that covered now. See you later, Detective Inspector."

CHAPTER 4

With even more doughnuts and coffee, Julia and Jessie returned to Fenton Industrial Park after sunset that night. The tension from their butting of heads in the café earlier had blown over, leaving behind only a slight undercurrent.

"This is far too kind of you," Tommy said, licking his lips after finishing his doughnut. "We've never been as well fed as these last two days. They're going to start hailing you as our lord and saviour soon enough. You watch!"

After everyone was fed and Julia's equipment was locked safely in her car, they headed over to Tommy's doorway, where the two upturned baskets were still positioned from the day before.

"Julia has talked to her detective boyfriend," Jessie said quickly, nibbling on the edges of her nails. "He's going to look into it."

"Is that right?" Tommy murmured, a brow suspiciously arching.

"Well, not quite," Julia corrected Jessie, smiling

awkwardly at Tommy. "I gave him the names and I asked him to see if he could find something. Unofficially, that is."

"Sounds about right," Tommy said, shaking his head heavily. "The police don't care if we live or die."

Julia wanted to tell him that wasn't true, but she looked over her shoulder at the dozens of people crowding around various fires, wrapped up in their half a dozen layers of clothing each. Her doughnuts and coffee seemed to have brought smiles to some of the downturned faces, but it was like putting a single stitch over a bullet hole. There was a bigger issue at play here, and the police and the government weren't doing enough. Her heart ached knowing this was where Jessie had been living before she took her into her home.

"I wanted to ask you if there's anything else you knew about the men who died," Jessie said, turning her attention back to Tommy as he clutched his plastic cup of coffee for warmth, his dirty nails poking out of his fingerless gloves. "You said you found Bailey. I was just wondering if you noticed anything *suspicious*."

"Like I told you yesterday, ma'dear, I thought he was asleep and then I realised he was dead, so we called for the ambulance and the police. That's all I know."

"And the others?" Jessie asked, edging forward on her basket. "Who found them?"

"Mac found Father Thind, and alcoholic Pete found Robert," Tommy said, tossing a finger in Pete's direction as he stumbled from group to group, a can of beer firmly in his hands. "Although you won't get much from him. His mind has gone. Thinks everything is a conspiracy and aliens are coming to take him away."

"And Mac?" Julia asked.

"He's that young lad in the corner playing the guitar," Tommy said, tossing a finger across the car park. "Talented kid. American."

Julia excused herself and left Jessie with Tommy. Stuffing her fingers into the pockets of her pale pink peacoat, she approached the man as he strummed away on his guitar to an invisible audience. Leaning over his instrument, his shaggy dark hair covered his face as he played, unaware of Julia's presence. She held back and listened for a moment as his fingers delicately danced over the strings, creating a soft melody that transported her out of the urban and stark surroundings. Tommy was right, the man was talented. How could somebody with such a gift be living in such as Fenton Industrial Park?

"You play so beautifully," Julia said as she stepped forward. "Do you mind if I take a seat?"

The man looked up from under his messy hair, and his beauty caught Julia off-guard. She had been expecting somebody older and more rugged, but a soft, slightly tanned face stared up at her, his crystal blue eyes filled with as much melody as his music.

"Not at all," Mac said, the thickness of his American accent taking her by surprise. "It's always nice to have a beautiful lady to play for."

Aware that she was blushing, Julia perched herself on the edge of the upturned crate in front of Mac. He continued his playing as he looked into her eyes. The music wrapped around Julia like a warm blanket. She almost forgot why she had come to talk to the man in the first place.

"How long have you played?" Julia asked, hypnotised by the intricacy and speed of his fingers.

"For as long as I can remember," Mac said, smiling to reveal his dazzling white teeth. "It's the only thing keeping me sane."

"You could play professionally," Julia offered as Mac stopped playing and rested the guitar next to him, leaning his arm on top of the headstock.

"I did," Mac said, his smile wavering a little, but his gaze not breaking away from Julia. "The music industry is a fickle place, lady. I came over with the promise of a deal, but things don't always work out the way you plan."

"What about home?" Julia asked. "America?"

"Minnesota," he said with a nod. "There's as much for me there as here. My folks died when I was little and I was an only child. As long as I have my guitar, and people like you to appreciate my music, I'm a happy man. I have clothes on my back, and people like you who are kind enough to keep putting doughnuts in my stomach."

Julia waited for his gaze to waver, but it didn't. She actually believed that he was happy. His life was simple and his needs were as basic as a person's got, but his smile was as genuine as a man with all of the money in the world.

"Can I ask you something?" Julia asked. "Something a little *sensitive*."

"Go ahead, lady. As long as it's something I want to answer."

"It's about Robert Culshaw," Julia said, her lips trembling a little. "The banker? Tommy told me you were the one who found him when he -,"

"Was murdered?"

"So you believe it was murder?"

"Of course I do," Mac said, leaning back and looking suspiciously at Julia. "All the folks in these parts do. The man was as clean as they come. The others, I could understand, but not Robert."

"Clean?"

"Y'know," Mac said, nodding his head suggestively at Julia. "Alcohol and drugs. I'm not saying the others weren't clean. I didn't know them all that well, but Robert was a healthy man. He wouldn't just die for no damn reason."

Mac ran his hands down his face, his smile dropping for the first time. It was obvious the death of his friend had hit him hard.

"Is there anything you can tell me about the night you found him?" Julia asked softly, not wanting to upset the young musician. "Anything out of the ordinary that you noticed?"

"I was busking on the high street all afternoon. It was a Saturday, so people were generous with their tips. By the time the police moved me on, I had enough for a couple of drinks in the pub, so I took my cash and my guitar and I pitched up in a dark corner and had a couple of pints. Not many, just enough to keep me warm for the rest of the night. I stayed there until they closed because it was somewhere dry. It was raining that night, so when I got back, everybody was huddled up inside the burnt out buildings. We don't usually go in there much because it's not safe. Wind hits that place in the right direction and huge chunks of the roof cave in. I was running across the car park to the building when I saw Robert in his sleeping bag. He always slept in the same place, every night, unless it was raining. I wondered if he'd had some drinks too and he didn't realise it was raining, so I went over to wake him. His eyes and mouth were open and he was blue. I knew he was dead. I ran to the phone box on the corner and I dialled

999. I didn't notice anything else because his sleeping bag was zipped all the way up to his neck. That's the last I saw of him."

Mac suddenly broke off and looked down, his clasped hands pressed tightly against his lips. Julia reached out and rested her hand on the young man's shoulder, giving it a reassuring squeeze. He looked up and smiled appreciatively, appearing to be holding back his tears.

"Can you show me where he was sleeping when you found him?" Julia asked. "Maybe there's something the police missed."

"I thought the cops back home were a joke, but yours really do – what's the expression? *Take the biscuit*? It was just over there next to that empty gas canister."

Mac cast a finger along the metal fence to a spot only a couple of feet away. Thanking him for his help, she walked over to the red, upturned canister next to the fence. She scanned the ground, but there were no signs of anything out of the ordinary. She imagined the poor man dead in his sleeping bag and her chest tightened. Closing her eyes for a moment, she inhaled deeply before looking over her shoulder to Jessie and Tommy. They were both deep in conversation, huge smiles on their faces.

Julia looked ahead through the fence panels. An unlit path ran along the side of the industrial park, winding out of view. Pushing her hands up against the fence, she tried to see where it went. As she did, the metal slats moved under her touch. She jumped back, and frowned at the fence. She ran her fingers along the panels. All of them were securely in place, apart from two that had been unscrewed at the bottom. Parting the slats, she pushed her leg through, and then her torso. Julia wasn't a big woman, but she was fifteen to twenty pounds above average, depending on the time of year. She slipped through the opening in the fence with ease.

"Are you making a bid for freedom?" Tommy asked, startling her.

Julia slid back through the fence and crouched down to look at the missing bolts that allowed the fence panels to move. She ran her fingers along the holes, noticing how fresh the metal underneath looked. It appeared as though the bolts hadn't been missing for long.

"How long has this fence been like this?" Julia asked Tommy, who was standing behind her with Jessie.

"Is it important?" Jessie looked down her nose at Julia as she examined the ground around the fence.

"I don't know," Julia mumbled, tapping her chin. "Maybe. Maybe not."

"I couldn't tell you, truth be told," Tommy said with a frown as he leaned his entire bodyweight on his stick. "Why do you ask?"

"Where was Bailey when you found him?" Julia asked, pushing herself up from the ground and brushing the creases out of her peacoat.

"Just here," Tommy said, walking a couple of feet down the fence and tapping his stick on the ground. "He was facing into the fence. What are you thinking, Julia?"

"Nothing," Julia said, forcing forward a smile, not wanting to give Tommy false hope. "I'm just overthinking things."

"There's a soup van," Jessie said, hooking her thumb over her shoulder to a food truck that had pulled up outside of the entrance of the industrial park. "Stella and Max from the soup kitchen always bring their leftovers at this time of night and there's always plenty to go around."

"Sounds good to me," Julia said with a nod. "Lead the way."

As they joined the end of the long line for soup, Julia glanced over her shoulder at the fence, knowing it was more than possible for somebody to sneak in during the night to kill homeless people. Looking at Mac as he strummed away peacefully on his guitar, she wondered what could possibly motivate somebody to do such a terrible thing.

CHAPTER 5

Later that week, Julia found herself sitting at Barker's dining room table for a second attempt of their ruined picnic date. The bought sandwiches were gone, replaced with the rich and hearty scent of beef stew drifting through from the kitchen as Barker topped up their wine glasses.

"I see you've unpacked," Julia said, motioning through the archway to the living room, which had still been full of boxes on her last visit. "It's starting to feel a little homelier around here."

"Well, I figured if I was sticking around in the village I had to stop living out of boxes." Barker sipped his wine, his eyes twinkling in the flickering candlelight. "I'd like to think I've put my own touch on the place."

Julia looked around the cottage, which was still quite bare compared to her own. The furniture was white and sterile, more suited to a city apartment than a Cotswold cottage. That juxtaposition matched Barker's presence in the village, but both seemed to work.

Barker hurried off to the kitchen and returned with two large bowls filled to the brim with rich, bubbling beef stew. He had splashed the gravy all down the sides of the white bowl, and slapped the dish on the table without a placemat. It wasn't exactly how Julia would do things, but she appreciated the effort all the same.

"This smells delicious for a man who claimed not to be able to cook," Julia said as she leaned into the steaming bowl.

"This is one of the few things my old mum taught me," Barker said as he topped up their already full wine glasses again. "You fry some onions and garlic, toss in some bacon and beef, add the stock, a glug or three of red wine, and then you throw the whole thing in a slow cooker for the best part of a day. Idiot proof!"

Julia skimmed her spoon across the top of the stew and sampled Barker's creation. It tasted as delicious as it smelled, and the red wine definitely shone through.

"Tell me more about your mother," Julia asked as they started to tuck into their food. "You've never spoken about her before."

Barker smiled sadly down into his stew. Just from the slight crease between his brows, she could sense that Barker's mother was in the same place as her own.

"She died five years ago," Barker said, dropping his spoon and leaning across the table towards Julia. "She was a remarkable woman. She swore like a sailor but she had a heart of gold. She wasn't a woman many people would dare cross, because she would let them know about it. She raised me and my brothers singlehandedly and she never once complained."

"I'm sad I couldn't meet her. She sounds great."

"She would have loved you," Barker said with a warm smile, his eyes sparkling. "She had a sweet tooth like nobody I've ever met, so you two would have gotten on like a house on fire."

"What was her favourite cake?"

"She could never say no to a coconut cake," Barker said with a small sigh. "I haven't had one since her funeral. The whole buffet at the funeral was cakes. We knew she would have loved that."

Julia made a mental note to dig through her own mother's handwritten recipe books because she was sure she had come across a coconut cake recipe in her time. Barker was more of a double chocolate cake type of man, but she knew it would bring a smile to his face. She liked hearing about his life, even if it did make her realise how little she knew the village's new Detective Inspector.

"Are you close to your brothers?" Julia asked, already feeling full but barely making a dent in her overflowing stew.

"As close as a group of men with their own careers can be," Barker said, pausing to sip his wine. "I'm the baby of four, and I'm the only bachelor in the family, which only becomes more apparent at family parties. They've all got wives and between them they've given me nine nieces and nephews. Keeps Christmas expensive."

"Have you never thought about having kids?"

"I did," Barker said with a firm nod. "Once upon a time."

Julia sensed some sadness in his words. Were they connected to a previous relationship? She almost asked, but she bit her tongue, remembering she still hadn't told Barker that she was technically still in the middle of her divorce.

She had finally signed her papers and sent them off to her solicitor, but she was still waiting to hear if their decree absolute had been granted. Jerrad had been the one pushing the process along ever since changing the locks of their London apartment and politely informing her he was leaving her for his twenty-seven-year-old secretary, but she wouldn't put it past him to start dragging his heels in the final stages. She decided that was a can of worms better left sealed.

"What about you?" Barker asked. "Do you see kids on the horizon?"

The question caught Julia off guard. As a young woman, she had just assumed she would one day have a big family, but like Barker, it just hadn't worked out that way.

"I don't know," Julia answered honestly. "Life has a funny way of throwing things at you, don't you think? I certainly never expected to be fostering a teenager, or dating a Detective Inspector."

"What you've done with Jessie is an amazing thing," Barker said sincerely. "You should be really proud of yourself. Not many would be as understanding as you have been. How's the fostering process going?"

"Slow," Julia said, pushing her half-finished bowl away from her. "They've granted me temporary fostering rights because she's a young adult and settled, but it's a slow process. We're still waiting for anything official."

"What about when she turns eighteen?" Barker asked, copying Julia and pushing away his barely touched stew. "What are you going to do with her?"

"She's not an old couch," Julia replied coolly, arching a brow. "I'm not just going to kick her out."

"I wouldn't expect you to." Barker held up his hands

before topping up their wine again.

"I suppose I'll let Jessie decide what she wants to do. My guest bedroom isn't going anywhere, and neither is my café, so I'm here for her as long as she wants me."

"You're a good woman, Julia," Barker smiled softly over the rim of his wine glass. "If the world was filled with more Julias, it would be a better place."

"I'm nothing special," Julia mumbled, ruffling her hair as she felt her cheeks blush. "I'm just a plain old baker."

"You're anything but plain, Julia. You're so much more than that."

Julia smiled and met Barker's eyes through the candlelight. He reached out and rested his hand upon hers. It was such a simple action, but it caused such an extraordinary reaction within Julia. A rush of fire shot up her arm and spread rapidly within her body, causing the baby hairs on the back of her neck to prickle.

"Why don't we take this wine through to the living room?" Barker asked, already standing. "The couch might be a little comfier."

Julia attempted to reply, but she suddenly had a frog in her throat. She coughed and nodded, scooping up her wine glass. She followed Barker through to the dimly lit living room and they sat next to each other on the couch. He leaned forward and using a long lighter, he lit three untouched candles in a glass stand on the clutter-free coffee table.

"Quite ingenious to have a date in my cottage," Barker said, darting his brows up and down. "No worry of being interrupted."

Julia coughed again and gulped down her wine quickly. Red wine wasn't her favourite, but it had been a long and busy week and it was taking the edge off. Every time she was with Barker, she felt inexplicably nervous, something she had never felt with Jerrad. When she had explained this to Sue, her sister had been adamant those feelings were love, but Julia was sure it was too soon to feel something so strong.

"It's been a lovely evening," Julia said, perching on the edge of the couch. "You should cook more often. You're quite good at it."

"I'll take that as a compliment," Barker chuckled softly, spreading his arm across the back of the leather couch. "You'll have to teach me some of your cake recipes. Something simple to get me started."

Barker's fingers suddenly danced across the back of Julia's arms, resting on her shoulder. Her body stiffened, but she couldn't deny she liked the feeling of Barker's hands on her. Sipping her wine, she allowed herself to lean into his masculine chest.

"A Victoria sponge cake is always a good place to start," she said, the shake in her voice obvious. "Or a classic scone."

"Sounds delicious," Barker said, looking down into her eyes. "You're a kind woman, Julia. I really like you."

"I like you too, Detective Inspector."

"No," Barker said softly, shaking his head a little as he laughed. "I *really* like you."

Barker rested his glass of red wine on the square couch arm and hooked his finger under Julia's chin. They stared deeply into each other's eyes, their faces so close she could smell Barker's musky aftershave on his neck. Gulping, she blinked slowly, noticing that she was edging closer to his lips.

"I really like you too," Julia whispered, her fingers clutching the wine glass so tightly she was sure it was about to shatter.

Barker's hand slid from her chin, to the side of her face, his fingers touching the edge of her hair and his palm cupping her cheek. She closed her eyes, smiling as Barker's soft lips and stubbly chin brushed against her.

She didn't have time to savour the moment because a sudden banging at the door startled them both. Barker jumped back, knocking his red wine and drenching the front of his crisp, white shirt. Cursing out, he stood up and let the wine drip to the white fluffy rug under the glass coffee table. It almost resembled blood.

"Who's that at this time of night?" Barker mumbled angrily as he headed into the hallway, flicking wine off his hands.

Julia placed her own wine on the table and stood up, observing herself in the mirror above the fireplace. Her hair was a little ruffled, her berry-tinted lips were slightly smudged from Barker's kiss, and her eyes were a little blurry from the never-ending glass of red wine. Julia had barely finished straightening herself up before Jessie burst into the room.

"Tommy just called," Jessie said gravely, staring deep into Julia's eyes, thankfully not seeming to notice what she had just interrupted. "Somebody else has just died. We need to get there now."

"I've been drinking," Julia said reactively. "We both have."

"I'll call a taxi," Barker said, appearing behind Jessie. "Let me go and change my shirt and I'll be right back."

Barker rushed past them both and along the hallway to

his bedroom. Through a crack in the door, Julia watched as Barker pulled off his stained shirt. Shaking her head, she turned her attention back to Jessie.

"Do you know who has died?" Julia asked, resting her hand on her forehead as she attempted to steady her thoughts.

"Mac," Jessie said darkly, her bottom lip trembling. "The guitar guy."

CHAPTER 6

The taxi ride to Fenton Industrial Park was a long and uncomfortable one. Barker sat in the front seat, slapping the dashboard every time they stopped at a traffic light, demanding loudly that the taxi driver speed through them. Despite Barker flashing his badge at the driver more than once, the man barely registered any acknowledgement.

In the back seat, Julia held Jessie as she sobbed silently, dampening Julia's shoulder. She stroked the girl's back, trying her best to soothe her. The more she focussed on Jessie's tears, the easier it was to hold back her own. She had only talked to the musician at the beginning of the week. She couldn't believe such a talented young man with a staunchly positive outlook on his bleak situation was no longer among the living. She couldn't wrap her head around the injustice.

When they pulled up outside the industrial park behind two parked police cars, Barker didn't wait for the taxi to stop before he tossed the money at the driver and jumped out. Julia apologised on his behalf, but once again, the driver barely flinched.

Practically cradling Jessie, Julia helped her out of the car. Two paramedics walked by carrying a stretcher wrapped in a red blanket, so she clasped Jessie's head to her chest to shield her from seeing such a thing. Julia, on the other hand, couldn't look away. As they put the Mac's body into the back of the ambulance, a tear rolled down her cheek when she saw his dark, scruffy hair poking out.

"Jessie!" Tommy cried, hobbling out of the industrial park. "Oh, you poor thing. Come here."

Jessie let go of Julia and ran into the old man's arms. Balancing on his stick, he wrapped his free arm around her and rested his cheek on her head as he stroked the back of her hair.

"What happened, Tommy?" Julia asked, resting her hand on the old man's shoulder.

"It's the same exact thing," Tommy yelled, casting his stick towards the fence where Barker was talking to two uniformed officers. "Those pigs won't listen to me! They don't care if we live or die!"

Julia set off towards Barker, her stomach knotting when she saw Mac's guitar lying on the floor in the corner where she had listened to him playing only days ago, its neck broken, and half of its strings snapped.

"He's been dead a good twelve hours," she heard one of the officers tell Barker. "There's nothing to suggest any foul play. You know what it's like with these people."

Barker grumbled a reply but he didn't correct the officer. He walked around to the sleeping bag, pulling it open a little and peering inside.

"And this is where you found him?" Barker asked,

letting go of the sleeping bag and standing back up. "In his sleeping bag?"

"If you ask me, boss, he was a junkie like the rest of them and took it too far," the other officer said. "They're dropping like flies."

"He wasn't on drugs," Julia said, clearing her throat and stepping forward. "I spoke to him a couple of days ago and he told me he didn't touch them. He was a guitar player."

"Aren't you a little dressed up to be homeless, love?" one of the officers said, smirking as he looked her up and down.

"I'm not homeless," Julia said sternly, pursing her lips and planting her hands on her hips. "Did you know he is the fourth man to die in this exact same place in the last month?"

"I was aware of that," the older officer said, hooking his thumbs into his belt and cocking his head back. "But none of them died suspiciously as far as we're concerned."

"You're telling me there's nothing suspicious about four men dying, three of whom with inconclusive causes of death, and if I had to bet on it, a fourth one to be added to that same list?" Julia walked over to the fence and touched the moveable panels. "If you ask me, that's the most suspicious thing I think I've ever heard."

"Well, nobody asked you, love," the younger officer snickered, rolling his eyes at Barker. "Get out of here."

"Don't talk to her like that," Barker said firmly, his jaw flinching. "Julia, go and wait with Jessie."

The two officers suddenly straightened up and tossed their gazes to the ground.

"Somebody needs to take this seriously, Barker," Julia

pleaded. "This is beyond coincidence now. Three men might have been able to slide, but *four*? I'd bet my café that these men were murdered."

The older officer sighed heavily, rolling his eyes at the younger officer, his head still dropped. Julia was used to members of the police force underestimating her.

"These fence panels move," Julia said, undeterred by the officers. "I know for a fact that three of the men all died up and down this fence. My theory is that whoever is murdering these men, they're squeezing through this gap in the fence and somehow killing them while they sleep."

"And how do you suppose they're doing that?" the younger officer sneered, barely holding back his laughter. "The kiss of death? These men weren't strangled, smothered, or stabbed. There's no cause of death. And besides, that gap is tiny. Only a tiny woman or child would fit through there."

Julia grabbed hold of the young officer's arm and pulled him towards the fence. Reaching over the tall man, she pried apart the metal panels and pushed him through. The front of his uniform snagged the metal, but he fit.

"*Alright*, lady," the officer cried, pulling himself free of Julia and pushing down his jacket. "I get your point. Tell me this then, Sherlock. Why would anybody want to kill random homeless people in their sleep?"

"Because the human condition isn't predictable or logical, officer," Julia said calmly, making sure to retain the sceptic's gaze. "The question here shouldn't be why, but how. How are these poor, innocent men being murdered, and what are you doing to catch whoever it is before a fifth man is discovered?"

Both officers looked at each other, each of them

seemingly lost for words. The older officer's jaw flapped, but he didn't speak. Out of the corner of her eye, she caught Barker smirking. Before either of them answered, a call came in over the radio and they doubled back, shaking their heads as they walked away.

"You know he could have arrested you for pushing him through a fence like that?" Barker said. "Technically, you just assaulted an officer of the law."

"I know," she said, shrugging and staring firmly at the men as they walked towards the exit. "Technically, those men are idiots."

"I couldn't have protected you if they carted you off to the station," Barker whispered into her ear as they followed the officers towards the gate.

"I can look after myself, Detective Inspector," Julia said. "If the police aren't going to take this seriously, somebody has to, and if that person has to be me, so be it."

Barker shook his head and pinched between his brows. He let out a heavy sigh, but he didn't try to dissuade her. They both knew nothing he could say could make her back down.

"Do you know who found him?" Julia asked Tommy, who was sitting on the edge of the kerb with Jessie where the ambulance had been. "I'd like to speak to them."

"Cindy," Tommy said, hobbling to his feet with Jessie's help. "She's at Stella and Max's soup kitchen a couple of miles away. They were here with their food truck when she found him so they went and opened up especially for them. Most followed on, but I hung back to wait for you."

"I'll call a taxi," Julia said as she dug in her handbag for her phone. "I'll make sure to call a different one, Barker. I don't think that driver would appreciate seeing you again."

CHAPTER 7

S tella and Max Moon's soup kitchen was tucked
away on a dark backstreet, sandwiched between a
boarded up nightclub and a twenty-four hour off-
license. Just like Fenton Industrial Park, it was
tucked away on the outskirts of town, hidden from view.

"They're good people," Tommy said as they all
climbed out of the taxi. "Good Christian people."

"I didn't even know places like this existed out here,"
Barker mumbled, almost under his breath. Julia detected
the tinge of guilt in his voice.

"Most people don't," Jessie replied flatly. "That's the
problem."

Inside of the soup kitchen, an eerie silence clouded the
air. Groups of people sat around tables, some of them
whispering, some of them rolling cigarettes and drinking
from beer cans, but most were staring blankly ahead. Julia
sensed their fear and hopelessness.

"We need to help these people," Julia whispered to
Barker as they followed Tommy across the vast space. "This

can't happen again."

"Let's just see what this woman says," he whispered back, resting his hand in the small of her back. "It'll be okay."

Julia wanted to believe him, but she wasn't sure. The more time she spent in this world, the more she realised how ignored and disregarded the people living in it were. At the end of the day, she could go home to her warm cottage, take a hot bath, and sleep in a comfortable bed. She had never felt more grateful for her privilege than she had in the last week.

"Cindy?" Tommy said quietly as he approached a table where a nervous looking woman sat. "Can we sit down?"

"Free country," she said, sniffling and wiping her nose with the back of her hand. "Who are the well dressed folks?"

"These are my friends," Tommy said, smiling at Julia, who in turn smiled at Cindy. "You remember Jessie, don't you? Julia here has taken her into her home, and this is her boyfriend, Barker. He's a Detective."

"Detective Inspector," Barker corrected him. "And I'm not here on official business."

They sat at the table as Cindy tucked her scraggly blonde hair behind her ears. Julia would have guessed they were similar ages, but years on the street had taken their toll on the woman. Her eyes were sunken, her teeth were stained, and her nose was red raw.

"Tommy told me you found Mac," Julia said softly, leaning across the table to Cindy. "That must have been difficult."

"I told the police all I know," she snapped back, tucking her bony knees up into her chest and clutching them with her hands. "I don't know nuffin'. I just thought he was sleeping. I went to wake him up, to see if he had any money. He was good like that. He always gave me a couple of quid to get some cans or whatever. He'd been sleeping all day, but that's not unusual, y'know? There's not much else to do. I've never been a good sleeper myself. My mam used to say I'd wake if the wind changed direction. I put my hand on him, but he didn't move. He was stiff as a board. I pulled back his sleeping bag and I knew he was dead. Not the first body I've seen. Probably won't be the last either, if you know what I'm saying?"

"Did you see anything suspicious?" Julia asked.

"I told the police what I told them," she said again, wiping her runny nose with the back of her hand. "I said to them that I saw marks on his arm, but I told them, I said *'Mac doesn't touch the drugs'.* He wasn't like that. He was a good kid."

Julia looked down at the woman's arms as she scrambled to tuck her hair behind her ears. She noticed tiny red marks littering the inside of her forearm. She glanced to Barker and he seemed to have noticed them too, and they both appeared to think the same thing at the same time; whatever she told them couldn't be guaranteed to be entirely reliable.

"She's right," Tommy said. "Mac was clean. He was against all of that stuff."

"Are you sure you saw some marks on his arm?" Julia asked, lowering her voice and leaning in. "Absolutely sure?"

"I saw what I *saw*, lady."

Julia pulled back, glancing awkwardly at Barker, who shrugged. At that moment, Stella Moon walked over and placed a plate of pale golden toast smothered in butter on the table. Cindy dove in immediately.

"We didn't have any ingredients for soup left, so I tossed some bread in the toaster," Stella said softly, clutching the tiny silver crucifix around her neck. "How are you feeling, Cindy?"

"Sad," Cindy said as she crammed a second slice of toast into her already full mouth. "Hungry."

Stella smiled sadly at the woman before turning and heading back to the counter, where her husband, Max, was opening a new loaf of bread. Stella appeared to be in her early forties, but she dressed like a woman more like Julia's gran's age. She was wearing a pleated calf-length skirt, a lilac cardigan, and thick, clumpy shoes. Her long mousy brown hair was scraped off her make-up free face in a loose ponytail at the base of her neck. Unstylish, functional glasses balanced on the edge of her slender nose. Aside from the small crucifix on a simple chain around her neck, she wasn't wearing any jewellery.

"Somebody murdered him, if you ask me," Cindy mumbled through a mouthful of toast. "Injected something into him."

"It's the government," the man, who Tommy had referred to as '*alcoholic Pete*' said, staggering towards their table with a can of beer clutched in his hand. "They're experimenting on us. Testing a new super virus."

"Leave off, Pete," Tommy cried, rolling his eyes heavily.

"It's true!" Pete cried, slapping his hands on the table and sloshing his beer on Julia's dress. "You heard the lady. Puncture marks. Mac wasn't like that, and neither was the priest."

Julia remembered what Tommy had told her about

Pete finding Michael Thind's body. She hadn't been brave enough to approach Pete to ask him questions, but now that he was here volunteering information, drunk or not, she knew it was her chance to ask questions.

"Did you find puncture marks on Father Thind?" Julia asked.

"What's it to you?" Pete slurred, pointing in Julia's face and glancing up and down her body. "Make it worth my while?"

Barker pulled out his wallet and slapped a twenty pound note on the table and pushed it towards Pete. Pete and Cindy's eyes lit up.

"Tell the woman what you know," Barker said.

"He had three holes in his arm," Pete said sternly, tucking the note deep in his pockets. "Looked like somebody was trying to find a vein."

"And you don't think it was Michael doing that to himself?" Barker asked.

"He was a man of God!" Cindy replied. "'Course not."

"Michael was as straight edge as they came," Pete offered, leaning against the table. "Wouldn't even touch booze. I told him he was missing out, but he wouldn't listen. I told the police this but they didn't listen either."

"I'm not surprised," Tommy muttered bitterly. "Clear off, Pete."

"I'm talking to the *nice* lady," Pete cried, sloshing his can in Tommy's direction. "*Not* you, old man."

Tommy mumbled something under his breath before standing up and hobbling across the canteen to another table.

"Old fool thinks he runs things," Pete said. "He's not so squeaky clean."

"Don't you say a bad word against him!" Jessie said, jumping up.

"The prodigal daughter returns," Pete sneered. "And here I was thinking the aliens had got you too."

Jessie rolled her eyes and joined Tommy on the other table. They both glanced over their shoulder, glaring at Pete.

"Are you sure you saw puncture marks?" Julia asked, eager to get back on track.

"I'm sure," Pete said firmly. "The government injected him with something, just like the others. They're trying to wipe us out, but we won't go down without a fight."

"Why would the government want to kill homeless people?" Barker asked, clearly not taking Pete seriously.

"To get rid of us," Pete said, as though it was an obvious answer. "They've been trying to get rid of us for years. I'm going outside for a ciggie. Are you coming, Cindy?"

Cindy nodded, cramming the last slice of toast into her mouth. She untucked her knees and scurried out of her seat, following Pete towards the door. Julia turned to Barker, but it was clear they weren't on the same page.

"Please tell me you don't believe any of that, do you?" Barker asked with a heavy sigh, clearly wanting to laugh. "It's the ramblings of a drunk. Neither of them can be believed."

"What if they're on the right track?" Julia asked, lowering her voice and leaning in. "The whole bit about the government and the aliens is nonsense, but what if they're right about the injections? I spoke to Mac myself and I saw him with my own two eyes. He wasn't on drugs. What if this is the cause of death?"

"Lethal injection?" Barker asked, pursing his lips. "But why?"

"I don't know that yet, but this is the best lead we have."

"You're talking like a detective," Barker said, smirking a little.

"Somebody has to," Julia said, glancing over to Jessie. "You saw how little those officers cared. Somebody has to do something. You have to admit things don't add up."

"They don't," Baker agreed. "But there's not a lot I can do. If these deaths are being ruled as non-suspicious, it's going to be difficult for anyone to try and get somebody in the force to listen. The last thing any of them want is to admit that there might be a serial killer out there."

"We don't need the force," Julia said. "No offence."

"None taken."

"We can crack this, Barker." Julia reached out and grabbed his hands in hers. "You and me. The minute we have something concrete, you can take it to your boss and be the hero."

"It's not about that, Julia. I'm worried about you."

"I'll be fine," she said quickly, letting go of his hands.

"You always say that but you have a habit of putting yourself in danger, and it scares me."

"Don't worry about me," Julia said as she peered around the full canteen. "It's these people we need to worry about. Are you in?"

Barker exhaled heavily through his nose. He looked around the canteen, his eyes pausing on Jessie as she chatted with Tommy. He turned back to Julia and picked up her hands.

"I'll do what I can," Barker said. "Within the law."

"That's good enough for me," Julia said, concealing her smile as she stood up. "Go and make sure Jessie is okay. I'm going to talk to Sally and Max. They're at the industrial park a lot and they might have seen something."

"Why do I feel like you've just become my boss?"

"You say that like it's a bad thing," Julia whispered, winking as she turned around.

Julia left Barker and walked over to the counter where Stella and Max were buttering fresh slices of toast. They both looked up and smiled meekly at Julia as she leaned against the counter and waited for them to finish.

"You're the doughnuts and coffee lady, aren't you?" Stella asked, peering over her glasses at Julia with a soft smile. "It's nice to see another Christian woman."

"Oh, I'm not Christian," Julia corrected her. "I don't think so anyway. I believe in something, I think, I'm just not quite sure."

"God is all around," Max said, smiling in the same soft way as he buttered the final slice of toast. "There are many roads to Him. Just because you don't put the label on it, doesn't mean you don't believe."

"Maybe," Julia said. "I just wanted to say that I really admire what you both do for these people."

"We're doing what we can to make the world a better place," Stella said, putting down the butter knife and opening the door to the kitchen. "Come through."

Julia thanked her and walked into the brightly lit kitchen. It was three times bigger than her own café's kitchen, and she couldn't help but think how much easier it would be to bake in such a space, even if it was a little rundown.

"Is it just you two here?" Julia asked.

"We sometimes have volunteers helping out, but it's just us most of the time," Max said, turning and leaning against the counter. "We're a non-profit organisation. We get a little money from the government, but we stay open mostly from the donations of the kind people in the local community. Sorry, I didn't catch your name."

"Julia," she said with a kind smile. "Julia South."

"It's lovely to meet you, Julia," Stella said, holding her hand out. "If you'd ever want to, we'd love to have you volunteer here."

"I'd love to," Julia said. "I own a café over in Peridale so I could bring over some ingredients and whip something up."

"The people would really love that," Max said as he shook her hand. "I sometimes think they get tired of soup, but it's the only way we can make the most of the ingredients. Most of the stuff we get is what the greengrocers and supermarkets send on when things are ready for throwing away. We toss a lot out because it's already gone bad by the time it gets to us, but we do the best we can with the little we have."

"From what I've heard, the people really appreciate it. I actually wanted to ask you guys a question about the industrial park. You seem to be there quite a lot and I was just wondering if you'd seen anything that might be of use."

"Like what?" Stella asked, her brow furrowing slightly as she glanced at Max.

"Connected to the recent murders," Julia said.

"Murders?" Max looked to his wife, his brows furrowing. "I thought the police said there was no foul play?"

"That's what they think but I have reason to think

there's something darker going on."

"That's terrible," Stella whispered as she clutched the cross around her neck. "I'm sorry, but I don't think we can help you. We pull up outside, serve soup and leave. We only see what comes to the window of our food truck."

"I thought as much," Julia said, nodding firmly. "It was worth a shot at least."

"Are you working with the police?" Max asked.

"Not quite. They don't quite believe my theories yet so I'm trying to piece together as much as I can before it happens again."

"We'll pray for you," Stella said, clutching Max's hands. "Be safe, Julia."

Julia assured them that she would, and promised she would be back on Sunday with her ingredients to volunteer. On her way out, she spotted a framed newspaper clipping on the wall from the *Cheltenham Standard*. The headline read '*Local Heroes Help The Homeless*', along with a picture of Stella and Max with a teenage girl standing outside of the soup kitchen. After scanning the first couple of lines of the article, she realised it was their daughter. Glad that there were still good people out there in the world, she smiled to herself and rejoined Barker, Jessie and Tommy.

"How would you like a hot shower and a roof over your head tonight?" Julia asked Tommy as she sat down in between him and Barker. "It's only my old couch, but I'm sure it's comfier than your doorway."

"Bless you, Julia," Tommy said, clutching her hands appreciatively. "You're an angel."

Barker called for a taxi and they all walked outside. When they were on the kerb waiting for the taxi to take them all back to Peridale, Barker leaned in to Julia.

"I thought you could come back to mine to tuck into that trifle you brought," he said. "Finish our date."

"Another time," Julia said. "Jessie needs me right now. I give you permission to eat my portion."

Barker chuckled softly and wrapped his arm around Julia's shoulder. It felt foreign to have a man's arm around her, but she quite liked it. She grabbed Barker's hand and leaned into him. Tonight, she realised how much she appreciated him, and everything else in her life.

When the taxi pulled up, Barker climbed in the front, and Tommy and Jessie climbed into the back. Before getting into the car, Julia looked back at the soup kitchen, but movement in the shadows of the closed nightclub caught her eye. She spotted Pete and Cindy talking to a hooded man. Pete passed over the twenty-pound note Barker had given him, and the man handed over a needle.

Pausing and clinging onto the car door, Julia had to stop herself from going over to slap the needle out of their hands, but she knew she couldn't help them all. Tonight, she was helping Tommy, and that had to be enough.

CHAPTER 8

Freshly showered and shaved, Tommy sat in front of the roaring fire wearing a badly fitting fluffy pink bathrobe. It had been a Christmas present from Sue that Julia hadn't gotten around to forcing herself to wear, so she was glad she could finally find a use for it.

"I feel like a new man," Tommy said as he ran his fingers along his clean jawline. "I underestimated the power of a hot shower."

"You look so much younger," Jessie said as she sat cross-legged on the hearthrug, picking at it with her fingers. "I've never seen you without a beard."

"I don't think I've seen myself without one for years," Tommy said, leaning up and looking in the mirror above the fire again. "Quite handsome, if I do say so myself."

"Your clothes shouldn't be too long," Julia said, as she heard her two-in-one washing machine and tumble dryer click from the washing to the drying function. "Although I must say that colour does rather suit you."

"I think it does too," Tommy said, winking in Jessie's direction. "Imagine what the guys would say if they saw me now. I can't thank you enough for letting me into your home, Julia. You truly are a modern day saint."

"I'm just sorry I can't do more," Julia said, trying to smile despite not feeling very saint-like. "You're welcome to sleep on my couch for as long as you need to."

"No need," Tommy said, shaking his head and waving his hands. "One night will do me just fine. I won't impose. You've done more than enough taking this one in."

Tommy reached out and gently ruffled Jessie's hair. She smiled softly and leaned her cheek on his knee as she stared at Tommy, as though she was looking at a grandfather she adored. Julia recognised that look. It was the look of a girl who longed for a family of her own, and Tommy was as close to that as she had come.

They stayed up chatting until the fire died down and the clock had gone past one in the morning. When Julia noticed Tommy starting to yawn, she suggested they all retire for the night, something Jessie seemed reluctant to do. After Julia dug out her spare duvet from under her bed, Tommy tucked himself up in front of the flickering ambers in the grate of the fire, still snuggled up in the pink bathrobe.

"G'night, little one," he said sleepily to Jessie. "Sweet dreams."

Jessie wandered off to her bedroom, a definite sadness hanging over her. Julia went to her own bedroom and changed into the matching fluffy pink pyjamas for the first time. She looked in the mirror at the hanging sleeves and trailing legs, wondering why her sister thought she would like such things. Chuckling softly to herself, she crept out of her bedroom and along the hall towards Jessie's. Against the soft hum of the tumble dryer, Tommy could be heard softly snoring.

"Jessie?" Julia whispered through the door. "Are you still awake?"

There was a long pause. Julia could tell Jessie was thinking whether or not she should respond.

"Yeah," she replied.

"Can I come in?"

"It's your house."

Julia carefully opened the door, not wanting the creaky old hinges to wake Tommy. She winced as an ear-splitting creak echoed around the cottage.

Sitting cross-legged on top of the covers, Jessie was flicking through a cookbook, looking at the pictures but not reading any of the words. Mowgli looked up from his comfy spot at the bottom of the bed, blinked at Julia, then tucked his face back under his giant tail.

"I found him snuggled up in my laundry basket," Jessie said, reaching out to gently stroke Mowgli's head. "Thought he might be comfier on the bed."

Purring deeply, Mowgli rolled over and arched his back so Jessie could rub his belly. He only did that for people he really liked.

"He's taken quite a shine to you," Julia said, sitting on the edge of the bed to join in the stroking.

"He's cool. I always wanted a cat."

Julia smiled to herself as she stared down at Mowgli. It was just another thing she hadn't known about Jessie. Just like she had on her date with Barker, she was beginning to realise how little she knew about the people in her life. It wasn't a feeling she liked.

"*Great Cakes of the East,*" Julia read aloud from the front of the cookbook. "Another library book?"

Jessie nodded, the messy bun on the top of her head bouncing. She didn't take her attention away from Mowgli.

"Anything interesting in here?" Julia flicked through the beautifully illustrated pages.

"I don't understand most of the words," Jessie admitted. "Too complicated. I was thinking of trying something to impress you, and then you might want to put it in the café."

"You already impress me, Jessie. You've made a lot of progress with your baking."

"I'm not as good as you though."

"You will be one day," Julia assured her. "A bit more practice and you'll be even better than me."

Jessie smiled appreciatively as she took the cookbook back from Julia. She continued to flick through the pages, pouring over the photographs. It hadn't gone unnoticed by Julia that Jessie had some trouble reading recipes in the café.

"There's something I've been wanting to ask you ever since we first met," Julia started, trying her best to sound casual as she tickled under Mowgli's chin. "Considering everything that's happening right now, I don't think I'll be able to sleep another night without knowing the truth."

"The truth about what?" Jessie asked, looking suspiciously down her nose in a way only she could do.

"About your past."

Jessie immediately looked down and started fiddling with the fraying hem of her pyjama bottoms. She managed to grab a thread with her chomped-down nails and began to pull.

"What's there to know?" Jessie asked, her brows

pinching tightly as she carelessly unravelled the stitching.

"Well, I don't really know much." Julia rearranged herself so that she was sitting cross-legged, mirroring Jessie exactly. "All I really know is that your parents died when you were a baby, you grew up in foster care, and then you ran away and I found you in my café."

"Sounds like you already know everything," Jessie mumbled, snapping off the long thread and wrapping it around her index finger.

"They're just facts. You can know a recipe, but it doesn't mean you can bake a cake. I want to know more about Jessie, and how things affected her."

"Nothing's affected me."

"Why don't you start with your childhood?"

Jessie wrapped the thread tightly around the end of her finger and waited until it turned bright red before unravelling it. She exhaled deeply and looked up at Julia, her lips pursed and her eyes narrowed. She looked more uncomfortable than Julia had ever seen her.

"My mum and dad died in a car crash," Jessie said, in matter-of-fact voice. "I was in the car too, but I somehow survived. They say it was because of my car seat and that it was a miracle. Didn't feel much like a miracle to be alive. I was in the system from three months old."

"That must have been tough."

"I was a baby," Jessie said, rolling her eyes. "I don't remember any of it. My first memory was being with this really nice old couple. I thought they were my parents, until they told me they weren't, and that they were retiring from fostering. I didn't understand why they couldn't keep me. It wasn't until later I realised they could, they just didn't want to. I was the last of twenty-seven children they had fostered.

I must have been a bad baby."

"I don't think that's true," Julia said softly, resting her hand on Jessie's. "Perhaps they were just too old to look after a little girl. I don't doubt they thought they were doing what was best for you."

"Well it wasn't," Jessie snapped, pulling her hand from Julia's and tossing the thread. "I was four when I went back into care. People only want babies. I bounced from foster home to foster home but everything was only temporary. When I thought I'd found somewhere nice, I'd be turfed back into the care homes. I was always too difficult, or too loud. I never got on with the other kids."

"Is that why you ran away?"

Jessie laughed softly, shaking her head. She looked up at the dark ceiling, and then to the soft lamp on the nightstand, her gaze distant.

"The last family I got put with weren't very nice," Jessie said, still staring blankly at the light bulb. "Kelly and Tim. Along the way, I met some okay foster-parents, but these were the worst of the worst. I don't know how they got approved. It was clear they just did it for the money. Kelly was always at work and Tim was a drunk. There were five kids, two of them were theirs and the others were foster kids. He never hit his own kids. The others just took it, but I was never like that. I told my social worker, but she didn't believe me. She just thought I was being difficult, so I packed my bag, nicked his wallet, and ran."

"That must have been hard."

"Hard?" Jessie scoffed, shaking her head. "That was the easiest decision I'd ever made. The second I left, I was free of being in that messed up system. I slept rough for weeks, and then I met Tommy at the soup kitchen. He took me to

Fenton so I wasn't on my own. Took me under his wing like no other foster parent had. There wasn't anything in it for him either. He didn't need to be nice to me. I felt at home there. It wasn't easy, but we got by. It was a long winter, and the older ones were dying all the time, but Tommy looked after me. We'd helped each other, until -,"

"Until what?" Julia urged.

"Until I abandoned him," Jessie cried, her sudden loudness waking Mowgli. "I abandoned all of them because you offered me something better. What kind of person does that make me?"

"A survivor."

"But look what's happening to them now," Jessie cried so loud Mowgli jumped up and scurried for the closed door. "They're barely surviving."

"That's not your fault."

"I know," Jessie whispered, dropping her head again. "I feel so guilty because I love the life you've given me. It's the life I always dreamt of but never thought I'd have. You've given me hope, cake lady."

Jessie's words took Julia so much by surprise that she didn't have time to stop the tears gathering in the corners of her eyes. She wiped them away before grabbing both of Jessie's hands.

"You have a home here for as long as you want," Julia said, squeezing tightly. "I promise."

Jessie pulled her hands away and turned back to the lamp, tears collecting in the corners of her own eyes. She furiously wiped them away with her sleeve, her lips curling downwards.

"I've heard that before," she said bitterly. "They say they care, until they have babies of their own, and then they don't care enough to keep you around. You've got Barker."

"We're only dating," Julia said, trying her best to sound reassuring. "No matter what happens, it won't change anything."

"Everything changes," Jessie said bleakly.

"Change can be good. Look at you and me. Before I met you, I was rattling around in this cottage alone. You've given me as much as I've given you. When I wake up in the morning, just seeing you here puts a smile on my face."

"Really?"

"I wouldn't say it if I didn't mean it."

"I know," Jessie said with a nod. "You're an honest woman most of the time."

"Most of the time?"

Jessie smirked a little, wiping the last of her tears away. She looked over to Mowgli as he noisily scratched underneath the door.

"You said you and Barker were just dating, but he's clearly in love with you," Jessie said, meeting Julia's eyes properly since the first time she had sat down. "You don't see the way he looks at you when you're not looking."

Julia smiled nervously, her heart suddenly fluttering in her chest. She tried to deny it, but she didn't know what to say. Jessie was only a teenager, but she was more observant and receptive than people twice her age. She thought about the kiss they had shared earlier in the night before being interrupted by Jessie. She remembered the frustration she had felt when he had pulled away. She had wanted it to last forever.

"I should get to bed," Julia said. "Early start in the morning. Saturdays are always busy."

Jessie nodded and climbed into bed. Julia tucked her in

and kissed her on the forehead, and they both smiled at each other. She wasn't the girl's mother, but she knew she had just become the next best thing, and she liked that. Jessie had filled a void in her life she hadn't even realised she had.

"Julia, can I ask you something?" Jessie asked as Julia reached out for the doorknob. "Do you think these people are being murdered?"

Julia looked down at Mowgli, unsure if she should tell Jessie how she really felt. She didn't want to upset the girl, or give her false hope, but in the spirit of being honest with each other, she knew she couldn't lie after everything she had just shared.

"Yes, I do," Julia whispered into the dark. "I'm going to try my best to find out why."

"I know."

Leaving Jessie to go to sleep, Julia carefully opened the creaky door, making a mental note to ask Barker to take a look at the hinges. As she tiptoed back to her bedroom, she realised Barker was filling another void in her life that she didn't realise was empty. It was a void Jerrad had never been able to fill.

Julia crawled into bed and rested her head on her pillow. She closed her eyes, but she knew she wouldn't be able to sleep. Looking up at the dark beams in her ceiling, she decided to make use of her time. Grabbing her laptop, she opened it and started researching injectable poisons that could kill without leaving a trace.

CHAPTER 9

S aturdays in Julia's café were always busy and this one was no exception. While Julia and Jessie ran around the café trying to keep on top of everything, Tommy stood by the sink washing all of the dirty dishes, and doing a good job of it. When Julia promised to pay him for his time, he insisted that the unlimited supply of cakes she had given him throughout the day were more than enough payment. Julia still slipped thirty pounds into his jacket pocket as a thank you.

When the café finally closed, they ate fish and chips before driving Tommy back to Fenton. He turned down Julia's offer of another night on the couch.

Once at Fenton Industrial Park, Julia set up her table once more and served doughnuts and coffee to the grateful inhabitants, some of whom she was starting to recognise. She made a promise to herself that she would keep bringing her coffee and doughnuts as long as the people were there.

"Did you see Cindy anywhere?" Julia asked Tommy while packing up the table and equipment as the sun started to set on Fenton. "I wanted to make sure she was okay after yesterday."

"A lot of people come and go," Tommy said as he shut Julia's car boot. "You get used to people drifting in and out as they please."

Julia hummed her agreement, but Tommy's explanation didn't ease her. After seeing Pete and Cindy hand over cash in exchange for a mysterious needle the night before, she was more than a little worried about the poor woman. When she saw Pete digging around in Mac's corner, she instantly made a beeline for him, leaving Jessie with Tommy in his doorway.

"What are you doing?" Julia asked Pete as he upturned the crates, standing on Mac's broken guitar as he did so.

"What's it to you, lady?" Pete snarled over his shoulder. "I'm looking for money. Mac always had some from his busking."

"The poor man is in a morgue somewhere and you're looking for his money," Julia cried, pushing Pete out of the way to pick up the broken guitar. "Have some respect."

"A man has to eat!"

"I saw you take three doughnuts and eat them all by yourself," Julia said as she tried her best to see if the guitar could be fixed. "I saw you and Cindy last night talking to that man."

"I don't know what you're talking about, lady," Pete mumbled, rolling his eyes and pushing past Julia.

Julia sighed and placed the crates back to how they had been. Sitting in Mac's seat, she looked out at the industrial park with the guitar on her lap. Inhaling the cool night air, she scanned the sea of different faces, noticing how diverse the crowd here was. Some people smiled, some people looked like they were at the end of their tether, and some didn't look like they knew where they were. She wondered if this was why Mac sat here, so he could watch the world pass him by and turn it into beautiful music. Julia ran her fingers along the loose strings. They made a pathetic sound deep within the broken guitar. Cradling it like a baby, she carried it to her car and laid it on the backseat. She didn't know what she was going to do with it, but she knew Mac's legacy deserved better than to be trampled on while people searched for his imaginary pot of gold.

Julia had barely locked her car when a blood curdling cry pierced through the noise, forcing silence to descend on the industrial park. She turned around and saw Pete stumbling out of the burnt out shell of a building, a shaky hand over his mouth. Tommy hurried over, and Pete grabbed his shoulders as he attempted to speak. Sensing what had happened, Julia hurried over.

"She's – She's *dead*," Pete spluttered, clinging onto Tommy as he looked at the ground, looking like he was going to vomit. "Oh my God, she's dead."

"Who's dead?" A woman asked quietly. "Who is it, Pete?"

"Cindy," Julia mumbled under her breath.

"Cindy Gilbert," Pete echoed Julia.

Tommy let go of Pete and hobbled into the building, followed by a dozen others. She pushed through the crowd to be by Tommy's side as he lead on. Julia understood what she meant about the man being the leader. Tommy might feel uncomfortable with the title, but people looked to him to take charge.

As they walked towards a burnt out room, which looked as if it had once been an office, their footsteps echoing in the blackened corners, Julia gazed around the shell of the building. Huge chunks of the roof were missing, and it looked as though the rest could fall at any moment.

Tommy pulled back the door with his stick, instantly turning his head away and closing his eyes. Julia stepped around him and looked inside where Cindy was curled up like a baby on a bedding of dirty blankets. There was no way the woman was alive.

Leaving Tommy to shepherd the people out of the building, Julia stood by the door and called for the police, and then for Barker. Before they got there, she crept into the room, wary not to touch anything, but wanting to absorb as much as she could before the unfortunate woman was taken away.

Julia hadn't been there when the other bodies had been found, but she already knew this was different. Cindy's chin was glistening, as though she had been sick before dying. Her arms were littered with small puncture marks, some of them looking fresher than others. A syringe lay next to her body.

When the police arrived, Julia stepped to the side to let them do their job. She wasn't so quick to jump in this time. She joined Jessie and Tommy, who had met up with Barker.

"Has it happened again?" Barker asked quietly, pulling Jessie into Tommy's makeshift home.

"I don't think so," Julia said, careful that they weren't overheard.

"She's as dead as a door nail!" Tommy said.

"I know, but I don't think she was murdered," Julia said with a heavy sigh as she sat next to Jessie. "It's not consistent with the others."

"You're starting to sound like them," Tommy said bitterly, spitting on the ground as he watched the police officers come in and out of the building. "You saw the poor woman, Julia."

"Exactly," Julia said, leaning forward and looking Tommy in the eye. "I saw her in that building, not by the fence where the others were found. She was also a woman. If only three men had died, I might think it was more random, but four shows some kind of pattern. I think they were all killed by some kind of lethal injection, and I think Cindy was killed by injection as well, but by her own hand. I saw a needle next to her body, but no needles were found near any of the other bodies."

"That could mean anything, Julia," Jessie said, shrugging and looking to Tommy for answers.

"I saw something last night," Julia said heavily, looking up to Barker who was still standing, his hands on his hips. "When we were getting into the taxi, I saw Pete and Cindy talking to a man. They handed over money – the money you gave him, Barker – and the man handed back a needle. I think that's what killed her."

"Accidental overdose?" Barker mumbled, almost to himself.

Julia nodded, looking back to Tommy. For a moment, Tommy appeared to not be thinking at all as he stared blankly at the ground. All of a sudden, something seemed to snap in Tommy's brain and he jumped up. Leaving behind his stick, he hobbled across the car park with speed Julia had never seen in the man. He seemed to be searching for someone, and when he found that person, he sped up even more.

"You *killed* her!" Tommy cried, launching himself on

Pete and knocking them both to the ground. "You *pig*! You did this!"

"I didn't," Pete yelled as he cowered under his hands. "I didn't mean to. I just left her to sleep it off. I didn't know this would happen."

"This is my fault," Barker whispered to Julia. "I gave him the money."

"It's as much my fault then," Julia whispered back. "I saw it happening and I didn't stop it."

"It's neither of your faults," Jessie said, sandwiching herself between them. "I know these people. They would have found money somehow, Barker. Nothing you could have said would have stopped them getting a fix, Julia. I've seen this happen too many times. I think she had three kids."

"Kids?" Julia asked, her stomach knotting.

"She told me they were taken from her and that's how she ended up on the streets," Jessie said darkly. "She always said she would get clean for them one day, but she wasn't strong enough."

Julia quickly wiped away the tear that escaped, not wanting Jessie to see it. She shook her hair out and ran across towards Tommy. With the help of Barker, they pulled him off Pete. He hadn't actually hurt him; he didn't seem to have it in him. The adrenaline seemed to wear off, and he would have stumbled to the ground without Julia and Barker's support. With their help, he hobbled back to his seat and collapsed, his face dropping heavily into his hands. He started to sob the tears of an exhausted man.

Leaving Jessie to comfort him, Julia and Barker wandered towards the exit. They watched as the paramedics carried Cindy into the back of the ambulance covered by a red blanket. For the second time that week, Julia watched another soul drive away from the only home they knew.

"I've been researching," Julia said, digging into her pocket to pull out the webpage she had printed out in the early hours of the morning. "This is a list of just some of the poisons that can be injected and leave little or no trace."

Barker took the piece of paper from Julia and scanned the list. She could tell he wasn't taking it as seriously as she had hoped.

"This is the stuff of fiction, Julia."

"No it isn't," she said, snatching the paper back. "In fact, most of this can be made so easily with stuff we all have in our cupboards. Potassium chloride, for example. It's one of the things they put in lethal injections for death sentences in America. You can make it by boiling bleach into crystals in your kitchen. It kills instantly and metabolises so quickly, it's practically untraceable. I know they can only test for specific substances if they have a suspicion. If they went in thinking these things were just accidents, they weren't going to look for any of these things. Tell me that wouldn't have happened for any other person."

Barker sighed and pinched between his brows. He didn't disagree because it was obvious he knew he couldn't; he knew she could very possibly be right.

"We still have no proof," Barker said. "I checked. Bailey has been buried, Michael's family claimed him and cremated him, and so did Robert's. There's no evidence."

"And Mac?" Julia asked, pulling Barker out of the way as the police officer walked towards their cars carrying a plastic bag containing the needle. "Have they even started his autopsy yet?"

"I don't have clearance," Barker said firmly, obviously

frustrated. "This isn't my case."

"You must know somebody who can help. Somebody you can tell this to."

"They'll think I'm crazy," Barker cried, shaking his head heavily. "I have a reputation."

"And what about these people?" Julia cried back, not realising she was even shouting until she heard her voice echo back to her. "You promised you'd help me."

"I didn't promise," Barker said firmly, pointing his finger at Julia.

"I just assumed your word was as good as a promise," Julia said, already turning away from Barker. "I'm sorry I called you."

She walked back to Jessie and Tommy, her frustration and anger growing with each step. Barker didn't deserve to be on the receiving end of that, but she felt desperately useless. She had no idea who could be behind these deaths, and aside from her own theories and research, she didn't have a scrap of evidence. Barker was right. If she took what she thought she knew to the police, she would be laughed out of the station quicker than she could unfold her piece of paper.

Before Julia reached Tommy and Jessie, Tommy jumped up and clutched his stick. He walked right past Julia and headed straight for the gate.

"What are *you* doing here?" Tommy cried, his booming voice silencing the scattered mumblings. "Have you *no* respect? A woman has *just* died!"

Julia turned to see Carl Black, the developer who had been sniffing around on her first visit to the industrial park. He was accompanied by two men wearing yellow hard hats, and heavy fluorescent jackets, and all three of them stood out in their well-pressed expensive suits.

"You *do* realise *you're* trespassing, don't you?" Carl snapped back smugly, pulling back his sleeve. "As of fifteen minutes ago."

"I've already warned you," Tommy cried, pointing his stick in Carl's face and barely retaining his balance. "Get out of here and leave us alone!"

"I'm afraid I can't do that," Carl said, pushing past Tommy with the two men right behind him. "I'm the new owner of your little hovel, and I'm coming to see what I've bought, and what damage *you* people have done to it."

"Didn't you hear the man?" somebody else cried. "A woman has just died."

"One less of you to clear out," he cried back.

Carl marched forward undeterred, the smug smirk on his face not wavering. The two men behind him looked less sure, half-running, half-walking to keep up with him. She was glad when the policeman standing guard outside of the building wouldn't let Carl pass.

"That man has some cheek," Tommy said as he joined Julia by her side. "Some people have no humanity left in them."

"Our days here are numbered," a woman said as she walked past. "Where will we go?"

Julia had known this day would come eventually. A piece of land this big in such a great location wasn't going to stay vacant for much longer. She was surprised it had been up for sale for over six months. The fire had cleansed the area, giving it a purpose in housing the homeless, but the developers were about to wipe those people away in the name of progress. It didn't feel very progressive to Julia.

"What now?" Julia asked. "Where will you go?"

"We'll stay here as long as we can," Tommy said. "We're stronger together."

Julia smiled and nodded, but her disagreement was written across her face, and she knew Tommy could see it.

"You don't agree?" he asked, almost offended.

"Maybe it's better to move on?" Julia suggested quietly, watching as Carl and his developer friends walk around the perimeter of the industrial park, pointing things out and scribbling down notes. "You're being targeted here. If you left, the murders might stop."

"And go where?" Tommy snapped, looking darkly down at Julia. "The world doesn't want us. I wouldn't be surprised if Carl had paid somebody to bump us off to scare us away. It won't work! Do you hear that Carl? It hasn't worked! We're not going anywhere!"

Carl didn't pay him any attention so Tommy cursed under his breath and hobbled back to his spot in the doorway. He collapsed into his blanket and rested his head against the metal door, his thick lids clamping shut. Jessie appeared to be talking to him, but if he was listening, he wasn't responding.

"Are you pleased with yourself?" Julia demanded of Carl as she marched towards him. "Men like you make me sick."

"Men like me, sweetheart?" Carl snickered as he flicked between two pages on a clipboard. "There's nothing dirty about property."

"But there's something dirty about men like you not wanting to help people."

"I donate to charity," Carl said, laughing sourly. "These people don't need my help. They need putting down."

"They're human beings, you *horrid* man!"

"They're a drain on society!" Carl cried, pushing past Julia and continuing with his survey. One of the men smiled an awkward apology at Julia as he hurried past.

She wondered if Carl would think that way if he spent some time here and got to know the people he was judging. Julia had learned so much by being here, and she knew she would never look at the homeless the same again. They were all people with stories and pasts, just like any other person. Carl didn't look at them as being on his level because it seemed easier to disregard their humanity to make it easier to sweep them under the rug.

After collecting Jessie and getting back into her car, they drove silently back to Peridale. She pondered on what Tommy had said about Carl wanting to scare the people away so he could get on with his development. Could money really drive a man to kill in order to get what he wanted? She didn't want to think any person could resort to such drastic measures for something so trivial, but she remembered how he hadn't cared at all that somebody had just died.

"*One less of you to clear out*" she whispered Carl's words under her breath as they walked through the dark towards her cottage.

CHAPTER 10

J ulia woke bright and early on Sunday morning so she could volunteer at Stella and Max's soup kitchen. She dressed in the dark, fed Mowgli, and left a note for Jessie under a London Eye magnet on the front of the fridge.

As the sun started to rise in the distance, she drove down the winding lane into the heart of Peridale, slowing as she passed Barker's cottage. The lights were turned off and the curtains were closed. She almost pulled up and knocked on the door, despite the early morning, but she stopped herself. She didn't like how they had left things at the industrial park yesterday, and couldn't help but feel like she would handle the situation better after having had a good night's sleep.

When she was parked between her café and the post office, she let herself in via the backdoor and started to gather up the ingredients she would need to make a lot of chocolate chip cookies. She had decided on it last night after flicking through her mother's old handwritten recipe books because they were easy to make, could be easily replicated, and they always went down a treat. She had yet to meet a person who hadn't fallen in love with her rich, buttery chocolate chip cookies.

Julia poked her head through the beaded curtains and stared at her immaculate café. She loved working there, but she was glad of her one day off a week. If she was honest with herself, she would like another day off during the week so she could relax or go shopping. If she continued to train Jessie the way she was, she might be able to leave her on her own more often without the immense feeling of guilt.

She was about to leave the café when she saw a shadowy figure running across the village green through the early morning haze. Walking through her café and squinting through the glass, she saw her gran, clutching her skirt as she ran like an athlete. Pulling her keys from her pocket, she unlocked the door as her gran approached.

"Julia!" Dot cried as she breathlessly clutched her sides. "I thought you were a burglar!"

"In my own café?"

"You can never be too careful! Are you opening?"

"I'm just grabbing some things. I'm volunteering at a homeless soup kitchen and I thought I'd make some of my mum's chocolate chip cookies."

"The buttery ones?" Dot narrowed her eyes as she finally caught her breath. "Why do you want to go and do that for? Sounds like a waste of a Sunday if you ask me."

"Because these people need our help and support," Julia said firmly, expecting better of her gran. "What are you doing up so early anyway?"

"It's my turn to stake out the village green," Dot said, glancing over her shoulder at a fold-up chair in her garden.

"Me and the girls take it in shifts."

"You're taking this neighbourhood watch very seriously," Julia said through a smile. "You know you're only supposed to keep an eye out, not spy."

"We're not spying, we're staking out. Like in those American cop movies. It's very popular over there, you know."

Julia nodded, wondering where her gran was getting her information. She had expected her neighbourhood watch obsession to have died off by now, but it was taking up most of her time, so much so that she hadn't summoned Julia and Sue to her house for dinner for over a week.

"Found anything interesting yet?"

"Lots," Dot said, barely containing her grin. "Did you know Mary from the hairdressers is cheating on her husband with the butcher?"

"I didn't," Julia mumbled through half-closed lips. "But I do now. Be careful who you tell your information to. You're supposed to be helping the village, not ripping it apart."

"It's all in the name of community spirit," Dot said proudly, crossing her arms under her chest. "Amy Clark is going to take 'round a fruit basket and break the news to Mary's poor husband later today. I don't doubt he's going to be absolutely devastated, but he has a right to know."

"I didn't know you and Amy Clark were friends."

"Well, we're not really. She asked to join and I couldn't say no. What with her being an ex-bank robber and having served hard time – that's what the Americans call prison – I thought she would be a fine addition to our group."

Julia smiled, unsure of what to say. Her gran never failed to surprise her. She wondered if she had been the same way as a young woman, or if her brutal brand of honesty had come with age. If Julia had to guess, she would say her gran was born telling things like they were.

Knowing her gran was only interested in idle village gossip, Julia said her goodbyes and let her gran get back to her fold-up chair and binoculars so she could continue scribbling down the goings-on of the unsuspecting villagers.

After loading up her car, she drove to the soup kitchen, passing Fenton Industrial Park as she did, if only to make sure there wasn't another ambulance taking away another body. She wasn't sure if it was her imagination, but there seemed to be fewer people milling around than yesterday. She remembered what Tommy had said about people coming and going, but she also wondered if the recent string of deaths had succeeded in scaring people away from the now-sold land. Julia knew her theory about Carl killing off the residents of Fenton Industrial Park was a stretch, but it was all she had to work with right now.

"Julia!" Stella beamed from behind the counter as she walked in carrying her boxes of ingredients. "You came! Max, go and give her a hand."

After gratefully handing the heavy boxes over to Max, she joined Stella behind the counter, where she was chopping vegetables for the day's soup. Julia pitched up next to her and started to sift out her flour.

"Baking is a skill I always wished I had," Stella said softly when she had finished chopping the carrots. "God never blessed me in that department."

"You make lovely scones, dear," Max said, diving in to peck her on the cheek. "God blessed you in other ways."

"My scones are like rock cakes," Stella whispered to Julia when Max took the carrots away and dumped them in the giant vat simmering over a low heat. "My husband is too kind."

"Baking is like driving," Julia said as she added in the butter. "Once you learn the basics, you only really start learning for real when you've passed your test. When you have the basic knowledge of why certain things work and how ingredients come together, you'll be able to venture out and start creating your own recipes."

"It all sounds far too complicated for me," Stella said meekly, her fingers brushing over the silver cross around her neck. "I'm more suited to cutting the vegetables. Max has always been the cook."

Julia smiled and nodded. She decided against replying. She wondered if Stella knew she had put herself into an outdated stereotype of what a wife should be. It didn't seem intentional, but it upset Julia all the same. She had been the same way with Jerrad, but it was only when she realised she could fly on her own that she soared. Unlike Jerrad however, Max seemed like a lovely husband. Not wanting to judge how their dynamic worked, Julia turned her attention to sprinkling the chocolate chips into the dough.

"My mother taught me to bake," Julia said when she had achieved the perfect chip to dough ratio. "Without her, I doubt I would be able to make a simple sponge cake."

"Are you close to your mother?"

"I was," Julia said softly, smiling through her pain. "She died when I was a young girl. I still think about her everyday, but I'm not sure if much of what I remember is real, or things my imagination has created over time."

"Your mother is here with you in spirit everyday," Stella said, resting her hand on Julia's, and then immediately pulling it away. "The dead never truly leave us."

It was a theory Julia wanted so desperately to believe in. Over the years, she had felt her mother's presence, usually when she had hit rock bottom. If she felt her mother's presence when she was lying in bed at night, or doing the washing up in her café, she might have believed it was more than her own conscience creating the feelings of closeness. Somewhere in the back of her mind, she held onto the hope that she would see her mother again one day.

"Maybe you're right," Julia said as she chewed the inside of her cheek. "It's a nice idea, isn't it?"

"It's not an idea," Stella said, her pale brows tilting inwards as though it was obvious. "The Bible tells us so. When Jesus died for our sins, he returned to his disciples and walked among them in death. I believe the spirits of our departed loved ones walk alongside us, even if we cannot see them. Those we love never truly leave us."

"Stella, can you take over stirring?" Max called across the kitchen.

Stella smiled meekly at Julia before scurrying off. Julia didn't doubt Stella believed what she was saying. She wanted to believe so desperately too, but her logical brain wouldn't let her believe that her mother was walking alongside her. She glanced awkwardly over her shoulder, wondering if her mother really was there. A cold chill brushed against her neck, making her arm hairs stand on end. It wasn't until she saw Max closing the open back door she realised how silly she was being.

As she started to roll the dough into small balls, she looked over to Stella as she struggled to stir the soup with the giant wooden spoon. Julia wondered what spirit was walking alongside her. The pain hidden under Stella's conviction hadn't gone unnoticed. Reminding herself it wasn't her place to ask, she continued to roll her dough in silence.

By lunchtime, the empty canteen transformed into a hub of activity. Stella and Max's soup went down a treat, as did Julia's cookies. Some of the faces she recognised from Fenton smiled at her, but most of them were different people, only confirming to her how widespread the problem was.

"Do you have a bathroom?" Julia asked Max.

"We don't have a public one, but there's one me and Stella use in the yard."

Julia thanked him and pushed on the heavy metal door into the stone yard. The smell of rotten vegetables hit her immediately, radiating from the overflowing uncollected bin in the corner. Clutching her nose she stepped over the rubbish towards the small outhouse. She opened the door and immediately closed it again when she saw Stella.

"I'm so sorry," Julia called through the door, her cheeks flushing from embarrassment. "I should have knocked."

"It's okay," Stella mumbled back as she washed her hands.

Julia thought about what she had seen in the split second she had seen Stella. She had been sitting on the toilet, but she was hitching her blouse up, and she appeared to be injecting something into her stomach. When Stella opened the door, smiling awkwardly down at the ground, she was clutching a small needle with a blue syringe.

"I'm diabetic," Stella said before Julia asked. "Type one. I was diagnosed when I was six, so it's my version of normal."

"I really should have knocked."

"I'm not ashamed of it. It's as normal as brushing my teeth or putting on shoes. God only gives his hardest battles to his strongest soldiers."

With that, Stella hurried around Julia and back into the kitchen. When Julia was finished in the bathroom, she joined her behind the counter as Max started to clear away the bowls and plates from the tables that had already finished and left.

"I didn't think you used actual needles anymore for diabetes?" Julia asked, trying to sound casual. "I could have sworn it was those injectable pen things."

"It is usually," Stella said. "I've been a bit silly. I lost my insulin pen yesterday and I haven't had time to go to the doctors to get a replacement."

"I'd lose my head if it wasn't screwed on."

"It's not the first time either," Stella said as she filled up the sink with hot, soapy water. "I lost it on holiday in the lake district last summer. They didn't have any replacements at the pharmacy. It was a tiny village and there weren't any diabetics, so they gave me some needles and vials of insulin so I could do it the old fashioned way. We ended up cutting our trip short, so when I got back I got my replacement pen. I keep the needles here as an emergency. It's not technically allowed, but God knows I wouldn't abuse them. I would have reported the pen missing sooner, but since Fenton got so full, we've been working all hours God gives us."

"Report it, as in report it to the police?"

"There are people out there who abuse the insulin," Stella said, glancing over her shoulder and narrowing her eyes. "Why do you ask?"

"No reason," Julia said with a smile. "I'm just curious."

Stella narrowed her eyes on Julia even further but her expression didn't shift. She busied herself with wiping down the counter, and Julia almost thought her question was going to be ignored.

"So many people are scared of needles, but they have no reason to be," Stella said as she focussed on scrubbing a patch of dried on soup. "The insulin pens are a little cleaner, but I don't mind the old fashioned way. Pain is a part of living."

"I must admit, I'm not the best when I need to have an injection."

"Think about Jesus's pain hanging on the cross," Stella said firmly as she walked over to the sink to wash the cloth. "Even with nails in His hands and feet, He didn't beg for mercy like many expected Him to. He knew He was dying for our sins, and He accepted that He was going to a better place, to join His true father in Heaven."

Julia was beginning to wonder if all of their conversations were going to revolve around stories from the Bible. It reminded her of being forced to sit still in church as a little girl as the priest droned on and on in his monotonous voice about sins and scripture. She had always wondered if she had found the church experience more fun, would her faith be stronger?

"So do you keep a lot on hand for spare?" Julia asked, following Stella over to the sink, where she had already started to wash the large pile of plastic bowls and plates.

"They gave me a two weeks supply that time. It was extraordinary circumstances."

"It sounds like you have a lot left over."

"Why are you so interested?" Stella asked, stopping her

scrubbing to turn and look at Julia.

"Oh, my gran was recently diagnosed with diabetes," Julia lied quickly, hoping her cheeks wouldn't burn too brightly. "I just wanted to get to grips with it in case she needed my help."

"She'll have type two. You don't always need to inject insulin with type two," Stella said, returning to the dishes, Julia's lie seeming to wash over her. "Although now that you mention it, there were less needles than I expected this morning."

"Oh?"

"The box seems a little emptier than I remembered," Stella said. "It shouldn't be a problem."

"In the last couple of months?"

"I haven't looked at them for nearly a year because I haven't needed them," Stella said, her tone growing more and more frustrated with Julia's questioning. "Can you pass me that cloth?"

Julia decided she had pushed her luck so she started to gather up her leftover ingredients. As she did, she wondered if Stella's needles had really been misplaced, or if they had been stolen. She knew it was a long shot, but whoever was killing the homeless people could have stolen the needles from Stella's supply, a theory which didn't sit right with Julia. If it were true, it meant a homeless person was killing other homeless people, and that turned Julia's stomach.

When she had packed up her things, she decided she was going to leave Stella and Max to prepare for the evening serving. Stella seemed to be offended by Julia's questioning, so she knew it was better to retreat before the tension grew.

On her way out, she paused at the framed newspaper clipping of Stella, Max and their daughter. As she read through the article, Max joined her and started to read.

"Your daughter is very beautiful," Julia said.

"She was," Max said, sniffing as he adjusted his thick-rimmed glasses. "She died just before Christmas."

"I didn't realise," Julia mumbled, her hand drifting up to her mouth. "I'm so sorry."

"It's okay," Max said, smiling down at Julia to let her know he wasn't upset. "I'd like to say it's getting a little easier everyday, but I'd be lying. I heard you talking to Stella about your mother, so I know you understand the pain."

"Like Stella said, she's here with you."

"If you believe that," Max said, his eyes suddenly glazing over. "Death can send people closer to God in ways one never expected."

With that, he left Julia and joined his wife in the soup kitchen. She finished reading the article before heading for the door. Before she left, she looked back at Stella and Max, who were working silently in the kitchen, not speaking to each other. Their relationship suddenly made more sense to Julia. It was almost as though she could see the strain the death of their daughter had placed on them, but she could also sense how desperately they wanted to cling to each other. It seemed as though dedicating their lives to helping the homeless was a worthy distraction for both of them.

After packing her leftover ingredients and equipment in the boot of her car, she drove back to Peridale with a heavy heart and a lot on her mind.

CHAPTER 11

On Monday morning, Julia sat in her café like a customer, sipping peppermint and liquorice tea, and scribbling notes in her pad. She wrote down everything she could think of connected to the deaths, including the list of clues she had gathered, and possible motives. She flipped the page and wrote '*suspects*' at the top in big, bold lettering. After underlining it a couple of times, she realised she didn't have a single one.

"We're running low on cupcake cases," Jessie called from the kitchen. "And icing sugar."

"Hmm," Julia mumbled back as she underlined the word again before flipping to her stock check ingredients list and scribbling down '*cupcake cases*' and '*icing sugar*'. "Anything else?"

"Not that I can think of," Jessie said as she walked through the beads separating the kitchen and the café. "I wrote down a recipe from the cookbook. I didn't know if you wanted to try it or not."

Jessie unfolded a small piece of paper and tossed it to

Julia, stepping back and shrugging. Julia read over Jessie's messy handwriting, smiling as she did.

"A Chinese sticky rice cake?"

"I thought it sounded nice," Jessie said, almost apologetically. "It 'sup to you."

"It sounds great. We'll give it a shot this week."

Jessie seemed surprised and smiled awkwardly, looking down at her shoes. Julia scribbled down the ingredients before flipping back to her investigation page. She motioned for Jessie to sit across from her. Julia grabbed two giant cream and jam scones from the display case and set them on the table.

"I've been writing down everything I know about the case," Julia mumbled through a mouthful of scone as she licked cream from her lips. "It's not a lot."

"Start at the beginning," Jessie said before cramming half of the scone straight into her mouth.

Julia sipped her peppermint and liquorice tea, glancing to the door. The village green was empty, and the few villagers who were out were walking right by Julia's café. She didn't mind. She had come to look forward to her quiet Mondays and was almost disappointed when she was serving more than a couple of customers at a time.

"We have four men, all dead without a real cause of death," Julia started, dusting her icing sugar covered fingers on her dress as she licked the last of the fruity, sweet jam off her lips. "They don't seem to be connected in any way, other than that they are men, homeless and they all died in the same place. We know at least two of them had puncture marks on their arms, but we also have testimonials from people who don't believe they would voluntarily take drugs."

"Bailey wouldn't for certain," Jessie jumped in, mumbling through a full mouth and spitting crumbs as she did. "His folks died from overdoses. He told me when we were back in the system together. He hated it."

"And I spoke to Mac and he told me he didn't touch anything, and that Robert didn't either. Pete also said Father Thind wouldn't, so that's all four men."

"Why haven't the police noticed this?"

"They're not connecting the deaths," Julia said, sighing as she rubbed her brow. "You've got cream on your chin."

Jessie quickly wiped where she was pointing and licked her finger clean. She narrowed her eyes and screwed up her face as though she was thinking hard. When she was finished, she looked sceptically down her nose at Julia.

"Why wouldn't they connect them? It's obvious."

"Maybe, but Barker said they probably don't want to link the deaths because if they do, they're going to be looking for a serial killer. They probably don't want to cause a panic."

"Instead they're just letting them die one by one?"

"It seems that way," Julia said, nodding as she resumed reading her notes. "I've been researching different poisons that can kill people without leaving a trace, and the list seems endless. Most of them can be made quite easily, without many ingredients. It's rather worrying. Most of them wouldn't even show up, even if somebody went looking for them."

"And those needles that were nicked from the soup kitchen."

"That might not be connected," Julia said, tilting her head. "Although it is suspicious. It would certainly give the murderer the means to do what they're doing."

"And it would have to be someone who visited the soup kitchen," Jessie added. "Only homeless people really know about that place."

Julia flicked the page to her list of possible motives. Most of them seemed as far-fetched as the next, but they were all she could think of.

"*Motives*," Julia read aloud. "Somebody is trying to scare the homeless away from Fenton."

"So, the developer?"

"Perhaps," Julia agreed, flipping to the empty suspects page and scribbling down '*Carl Black*'. "That's one suspect."

"One is all you need."

"He certainly seemed cold-hearted enough to do something so evil." Julia circled his name several times. "Money can make people do crazy things. There are other motives though. The other idea I had is that there is somebody with a vendetta against the homeless, so they're taking it out by murdering as many as they can."

"That one wouldn't surprise me," Jessie said, rolling her eyes. "There wasn't a day that went by that I didn't meet somebody who hated me because I was homeless."

"But who?"

"The police?" Jessie offered, drumming her fingers on the table. "Those officers just want to get rid of us to save them the job. They can't rehouse us all."

Julia reluctantly wrote down '*the police*', even if she didn't believe that one. She knew it wasn't impossible, but she couldn't imagine an officer taking the law into their own hands in such a way.

"We also have another homeless person," Julia said, gauging Jessie's reaction carefully. "Perhaps there was a person who was connected to all four of the men, and had a different grievance with each of them."

"What's a grievance?"

"It's like a problem," she said. "A falling out."

Jessie looked down at her drumming fingers and screwed up her face. Julia could practically hear the cogs turning in her brain.

"I don't think so," Jessie said, shaking her head. "They're like a family."

Julia clenched her jaw as she smiled. She believed that Jessie really did believe that because it was all she had had to cling onto for so long, but Julia wasn't so sure anymore. The more time she spent with the people at Fenton, the more she realised they were normal people who didn't always get along, despite their similar situations.

"Besides, who would want to do that?" Jessie asked.

"Pete?" Julia offered. "He doesn't seem to like many people, and he knows how to use needles. He even seems to know people who could supply him with deadly concoctions."

"But murder? That seems a stretch even for him"

"Perhaps," Julia agreed, writing his name down anyway. "There are still so many people I haven't spoken to yet. The murderer could be hiding right under our noses."

Jessie flinched uncomfortably in her seat. It was almost as though they had landed on the same name at the same time, but in very different contexts.

"No!" Jessie cried, before Julia could even say anything. "Tommy wouldn't do that. Why would he?"

"I'm not saying he would," Julia said calmly, leaning forward and dropping her pen. "He's just at the scene every time, and he found Bailey."

"Exactly," Jessie said, forcing a laugh. "Why would he

draw attention to a kid he'd just murdered? They didn't always get along, but Tommy wouldn't do that."

"Tommy didn't mention they didn't get along."

"Well, it wasn't that they didn't like each other," Jessie said quickly, stumbling over her words. "Tommy just didn't like the graffiti. He didn't understand it. It was Bailey's way of expressing himself, but Tommy thought he should respect Fenton as their home while they were there. He said if we didn't respect it, people wouldn't respect us. Bailey was a good kid."

"I'm not saying he wasn't," Julia said, reaching out and grabbing Jessie's hand. "You don't have to worry. We're only throwing ideas around. Some of them will sound silly, but it allows us to rule people out. Okay?"

Jessie nodded as she ferociously chewed the inside of her lip. She pulled her hand out of Julia's and fumbled with her fingers in her lap.

"What was Tommy's relationship with the others?" Julia asked, picking up her pen and hovering over a fresh page. "Just so we can rule him out."

"He liked the priest, even if he thought his preaching was a waste of time," Jessie said as she stared blankly at the empty plate in front of her. "He used to say Michael was wasting his time reading his Bible."

"So they weren't exactly friends?"

"They're not all friends," Jessie said, frowning at Julia. "You can't like everybody."

Julia nodded, not wanting to contradict Jessie's statement that they were all a family who looked out for one another. She had members of her own family that she didn't particularly like, so she knew that didn't immediately make a man guilty.

"What about the banker? Robert?"

"I don't know. They had an argument once, but that doesn't mean anything."

"What did they argue about?"

"Robert fell asleep in Tommy's spot. He was new at Fenton, so he didn't realise not to sleep there. It was only a small thing. They were fine afterwards."

"And Mac?" Julia said, barely looking up as she scribbled all of this down. "What did he think of Mac?"

"He liked Mac," Jessie said, almost relieved. "Everybody liked Mac, even if his guitar playing kept us awake. Tommy didn't mind, too much. He told him once or twice to stop playing, but it was never anything serious."

Julia wrote down everything Jessie said, almost word for word. She wondered why Tommy hadn't told her these things before. He had acted as though he was friends with all of the victims. The more Jessie spoke, the more it sounded like he had had some kind of disagreement with each victim. As she read back her notes, she knew none of them were enough to drive a man to murder, but months had passed since Jessie had left Fenton, so plenty of murder-inducing arguments could have happened in that time.

Tommy's elderly, kind face appeared in Julia's mind and she immediately felt guilty. The man had been nothing but nice to her, and she was grateful that he had looked out for Jessie in her times of need. The guilt writhed painfully in her stomach as she added his name to her suspects list. She didn't want to believe he could be capable of such terrible things, but she didn't have enough suspects to rule anybody out.

"Tommy didn't do it," Jessie muttered. "He's good."

"I know."

"You know he didn't do it, or you know he is nice?"

Julia's smile wavered. She looked down at the freshly inked name on her suspects list and snapped the pad shut before Jessie could see.

"Both," Julia lied as she gathered the plates and hurried off to the kitchen before Jessie could further question her.

As Julia washed up the two plates as slowly as she could, she mulled over everything. She was so deep in thought, she didn't hear the bell above her café door ring out so she jumped when she turned and saw Barker poking his head through the beads.

"Is it a bad time?" Barker asked as he walked into the kitchen.

"No, you just gave me a fright," Julia said, her hand resting on her chest. "What can I do for you, Barker?"

He was in his usual work suit and camel-coloured trench coat, which told Julia he probably didn't have long. She doubted he was here to take her on another lunchtime picnic, especially after how they had left things on Saturday night. They both tried to speak at the same time, as they stepped closer to one another. Julia laughed and motioned for Barker to speak.

"I'm sorry about the other night," Barker said shyly, pushing back his trench coat and shoving his hands in his trouser pockets. "The stress of this whole thing was just getting to me. I worry about how deep you get into these things, and I reacted badly."

"I can't help it."

"I know," Barker said quickly, looking straight into her eyes. "It's what I love about you. You care about things more than other people do."

Hearing the word '*love*' did something unexpected to

Julia's heart. It suddenly started to race, causing her to feel like she was burning up. She attempted to swallow, but her mouth was as dry as an over-baked sponge cake.

"I'm sorry too," Julia said, her tongue feeling like it was swollen. "You're right about caring too much. It's all I can think about right now."

"For what it's worth, I think you're right," Barker said urgently, stepping forward and pulling something from his pocket. "I called in some favours and pushed for them to do a full toxicology report on Mac's body."

He handed the sheet to Julia and the plethora of information boggled her mind. She stared at the list of chemical symbols and combinations she didn't recognise. She shook her head and passed the sheet back to Barker.

"K," Barker whispered, pointing to the top symbol on the sheet.

"I'm a baker, not a scientist, Barker."

"K is the chemical symbol for potassium." Barker folded the paper and stuffed it back in his pocket. "They found a lot of it in his system. More than just a couple of bananas worth."

"Enough to kill a man?"

"That's where it gets complicated," Barker said, taking in a sharp intake of breath through his teeth. "Like you said, some of the lethal poisons metabolise and vanish, barely leaving a trace. This is what it left behind, but alone it's not enough to be ruled as a cause of death."

"But coupled with the needle marks and the others -,"

"There are no others, remember?" Barker interrupted, stepping closer and dropping his voice to a whisper. "The other three were all ruled as inconclusive. They were never looking for lethal poisons, or even a trace of anything. As far as they're concerned, Mac's cause of death is just as inconclusive as the others."

"Surely that's enough to suggest a pattern?"

"Only if they're being linked," Barker said, almost sounding frustrated with Julia. "Aside from their location, these men have nothing in common. They're all completely different ages, with different backgrounds. You're only linking them because you've spoken to people and painted a bigger picture."

"And the police won't because they have no reason to suspect anything?"

"Exactly," Barker said, resting his hand on Julia's shoulder. "You're right about this being discrimination. If this happened in Peridale, the frequency alone would be enough to cause suspicion."

"But because the rate of death among homeless people is higher, this is being looked at as normal."

"Unfortunately that's what's happening," Barker said, deep sadness in his voice. "I was looking into it last night and the statistics made me feel sick. Homeless people are twenty-times more likely to die just because they're homeless."

"Which means the police care twenty-times less," Julia said, pushing her fingers up into her hair. "This is so frustrating."

"Not all police," Barker reassured her. "We're on the same page now. I'm seeing this through your eyes and it's making me feel awful. I saw homeless people when I lived in the city, but I never cared. Not really. I'd give them money when I could, but I always felt so separate."

"We can help them," Julia said, grabbing both of Barker's hands. "We just have to stop this before it gets any worse."

"How do we do that?" Barker asked, clenching Julia's hands tightly. "Mac's potassium levels aren't high enough to launch an investigation. I mentioned what was happening in passing to the Chief Inspector, just to gauge his reaction."

"I'm guessing it wasn't a favourable one?"

"He laughed and told me to spend my time looking into important things," Barker said, his voice deep with regret. "We're alone."

"When has that ever stopped me, Barker?" Julia said. "We don't need resources to figure this out, we just need to talk to people and keep digging."

"But we don't have a plan," Barker said, letting go of Julia's hands and pushing them back into his pockets. "Or any leads."

"I've got some ideas," Julia said nervously. "You're probably not going to like them though."

CHAPTER 12

J ulia was running down a never-ending corridor lined with doors. She knew she was dreaming, but she clutched at the door handles anyway, sure the answer to what she was looking for was behind one of them. She ran like she had never ran in her life, daring to glance over her shoulder as the corridor melted away in a pool of fire and ash. Squinting into the dark, she saw a glimmer of light, beaming through a slit under a door at the far side of the corridor. She knew the answer to what she was looking for was behind that door. She reached out and ran, but she felt like she was walking through mud and her feet were cast in solid cement blocks. Crying out, she was surprised when no noise escaped her throat. She looked back to the door, and it was within reach. She wrapped her fingers around its metal handle. It was different from the others, more ornate and meaningful somehow. She twisted the handle, its surface hot to the touch. She didn't care, she knew when she burst open the door, everything would make sense and she wouldn't have to worry anymore. Icy hands closed around her shoulders, shaking her, dragging her away from the truth. She cried out, but this time she heard her own voice. The corridor and the door melted away and she landed with a thud in her bed, in her small cottage in Peridale.

"Julia," Jessie whispered through the dark, shaking her shoulders. "Julia! Wake up!"

Julia's eyes shot open and she looked up at Jessie. Had she overslept? She blinked into the darkness at the LED display on her alarm clock. It was a little past five, and only four hours since she had fallen asleep researching on her laptop which was still open on the other side of her bed.

"I'm awake," she whispered. "What's wrong? Did you have another nightmare?"

"I wish," Jessie said. "Tommy just called. It's happened again."

"Somebody else has died?"

"Murdered," Jessie said. "For sure this time. It's different."

Julia shook away the last of her sleep and jumped out of bed, climbing into the shape-hugging jeans and baggy jumper that she had tossed across the end of her bed. Before she could even register that she was no longer dreaming and fully awake, she was speeding along the motorway in her tiny Ford Anglia with Jessie in the passenger seat.

When she pulled up outside of Fenton Industrial Park, things immediately felt different. There were more than two police cars, as well as an ambulance, and a forensics van. Julia felt relieved that things were finally being treated differently, but that relief quickly faded when she remembered another man had died.

"Julia," Tommy called over. "Jessie. Over here."

Tommy was standing with a group of around twenty people, as close to the fence as they could get. Officers swarmed around the brightly lit scene, ducking in and out of the white and blue crime scene tape wrapped around the small area. Men in white suits were placing yellow markers on the ground and taking photographs of their findings. In the middle of all of this, a man's contorted body lay, staring lifelessly up at the sky.

"What happened?" Julia asked, shaking the last of the sleep from her mind.

"It woke us all up," a woman said, clutching her heavy coat across her chest. "I heard Jerry scream. There was a man over him, strangling him. Choking him."

"I ran over and I hit him with my stick," Tommy said faintly, barely able to hold himself up. "It was too late. The poor man was dead."

"Strangled?" Julia whispered, shaking her head. "That's not right."

"His arm was all bloody," the elderly woman said. "Like they'd tried to inject him with something, but he put up a fight. That was Jerry till the end. He was a tough old guy."

Julia looked to the scene, squinting through the people coming and going. She wasn't sure if it was her imagination, but she was sure she spotted a needle with a blue syringe next to one of the yellow markers.

"This isn't good," Julia muttered, looking helplessly to Tommy. "This is really bad. Whoever is doing this is getting desperate. They're upping the frequency, and they don't care how they're killing these men now."

"It means they're getting sloppy," Tommy said. "We all saw him."

"What did he look like?" Jessie asked, an obvious shake in her voice as she stared ahead at the scene, seemingly unable to look away.

"Well, it was dark," the woman said, frowning heavily. "And he was wearing a scarf over his face."

"He had a hood too," another woman added.

"But you're sure it was a man?" Julia asked, searching the unsure, shocked faces in the crowd.

"It was dark," the woman repeated.

"It was a man," Tommy said, nodding firmly. "He yelped like a man when I hit him with my stick. I put some force into it too. He almost fell over, but he caught himself, dove through the fence and ran. I called after him, but he was gone before I realised what was happening."

They all stood and watched silently, none of them seeming to know what to say. When forensics had photographed all they needed to, they took Jerry away on a red blanket covered stretcher. They all bowed their heads, apart from Jessie, who still couldn't seem to look away. Julia clutched her hand and they both squeezed, trying to reassure each other.

It wasn't long before the group dispersed and Julia and Jessie settled in Tommy's doorway. Perching on the edge of an upturned plastic crate, Julia shivered, wishing she had remembered to grab a jacket in her tired state. She was more than grateful when Tommy placed a blanket over hers and Jessie's shoulders.

"Where is everyone?" Jessie asked, looking around the bare car park.

"Everyone's moved on," Tommy said through gritted teeth. "Carl Black was here with his megaphone threatening police action. It scared off a lot of them. There were more here when what happened to Jerry woke us up, but that was enough to scare off the rest. We're all that's left now."

"But you've decided to stay?" Julia asked, smiling reassuringly at Tommy.

"It might not be a lot, but this place has become my home. It's all I've got. I'll stay here until the bulldozers move in, and then I'll finally move on. I have no idea where I'll go, but that's no different."

Julia regretted ever writing Tommy's name on her suspects list. If she had her notepad with her now, she would scratch his name out until she was tearing through to the sheet underneath. In the frustration of trying to place the blame on somebody, she had targeted the wrong person entirely.

"Has Pete gone?" Julia asked, looking around for the drunk.

"He hasn't shown his face since Cindy. He wouldn't dare."

"Did he know Jerry?"

"We all knew Jerry," Tommy said, arching a brow. "He was a big guy. He wasn't difficult to miss. His muscles had muscles. It would take a strong man to wrestle him to the ground and take away his last breath."

Julia mentally scratched Pete's name off her suspect's list. She had seen the drunk, with his shaking hands and wobbly walk. Even if he had managed to somehow strangle a man with his bare hands, she couldn't imagine him fleeing the scene and sprinting off into the darkness.

"At least the police are finally taking it seriously," Tommy said, nodding his head to an officer as they made their way through the small group, asking questions. "Too late for the others though. If they'd have taken this seriously from the beginning, it wouldn't have gotten this far."

Over the next couple of hours, they chatted until the sun rose, the industrial park getting quieter and quieter around them. One by one, the officers packed up and left, as did most of Fenton's residents. When the sun was fully in the sky, there were only a handful of people left, including Julia and Jessie.

"You're welcome to come to my place," Julia offered. "I don't think it's safe here."

"That's what they want," Tommy said, shaking his head. "I don't have many things, Julia, but I have my pride. If they have to take me away from here in a box, so be it."

Tommy pointed his chin to the cloudless sky and squinted into the sun, more defiant than she had ever seen the old man. Julia believed him when he said he would be here until the last minute, she just hoped it wouldn't get to that.

"We need to go," Julia said to Jessie, glancing at her watch. "The café needs opening and we both need to get changed first."

"Go," Tommy said sternly, nodding to the gates. "Don't wait around on my account. I'll be fine. I always am."

Julia and Jessie looked at each other, both seemingly as uncomfortable as the other. Neither of them wanted to tell the man he was being reckless and putting his life in danger for no reason. Despite this, Julia did understand his pride, she just thought it was misplaced. Without the people, Fenton Industrial Park was no more a home than any street corner in any city.

"He'll be okay," Julia whispered to Jessie as they walked towards her car. "He's tough."

"He's being an idiot," Jessie said, looking over her shoulder at Tommy as he curled up into his blankets.

Julia unlocked her car and opened her door. As Jessie climbed inside, she paused, resting her hands on the roof as she looked down the street. Carl Black had just pulled up in a black sports car. He jumped out, a phone crammed between his ear and shoulder. As he swaggered down the street, he clicked his key over his shoulder and the car beeped, its lights flashing.

"Another one's dead," Carl said smugly into his phone as he passed Julia, ignoring her presence entirely. "I'd be surprised if there's anybody left. Call the guys and tell them we'll be able to start demolition in a matter of days."

After quickly changing, they drove down to Julia's café, ten minutes late for opening. Dot was already standing outside, tapping her watch as Julia pulled into her parking space.

"Sorry," Julia said as she reached around her gran to unlock the door. "I couldn't get the car started."

Julia glanced to Jessie, making sure that she wasn't going to correct her. Jessie nodded her acknowledgement that it would stay a secret. The last thing she wanted was for her gran and her neighbourhood watch gang wading into things.

"I can't stop," Dot said, pulling up the seat nearest to the counter. "But I'll have a cup of tea, and any cakes if they're going begging."

Julia pulled a slice of yesterday's chocolate cake from the fridge, hoping her gran wouldn't notice it wasn't fresh. She was going to have to spend most of her morning catching up on the baking she had missed.

"Mary's husband didn't take the news very well," Dot

mumbled through a mouthful of chocolate cake.

"Huh?"

"Remember how I told you Mary was cheating on her husband with that lad from the butchers?" Dot mumbled, cramming even more cake into her mouth. "Well, as it turns out, the butcher is gay and actually Mary's cousin."

"So you're telling me your meddling almost ruined a marriage?" Julia said with a sigh as she sat across from her gran.

"How was I supposed to know?" she cried, spitting chocolate cake all over the tablecloth. "They were laughing and joking on the village green like lovers. It's an easy mistake."

"Maybe you should hang up your binoculars."

"Why? Things are finally starting to get interesting," Dot said, wiping her mouth with the back of her hand. "I think the vicar has murdered Amy Clark. She hasn't been to our meetings since last week."

"She's gone to stay with her sister in Brighton," Jessie called from behind the counter. "She told me last week."

"Oh." Dot rummaged in her small handbag and pulled out her notepad, scribbling something down and crossing out something else. "I wonder why she didn't tell me."

"Probably because she knows you don't like her," Jessie called again. "She told me you told her she wasn't a good organ player."

"I didn't say that," Dot protested. "Not exactly. I told her it wouldn't do her any harm to get possessed by the ghost of Gertrude Smith, or at least just her fingers. We all know Gertrude was the better player. The church hasn't been the same since."

"You're unbelievable, Gran," Julia said as she stood up.

"And don't pretend you go to church."

"Well, I hear things," Dot said, waving her hands. "Why read the book when you can watch the film? It cuts out all the fuss. I have eyes all over the village. What have you been up to anyway? I feel like I haven't seen you for a while."

"Not a lot," Julia said through almost gritted teeth, glancing back to Jessie who rolled her eyes. "This and that."

"How are things with you and Barker?" Dot asked as she stood up, brushing the crumbs off her pale pink blouse and readjusting the brooch that pinned the collar together under her chin. "Do I need to buy a new hat yet?"

"We're not getting married, if that's what you're saying."

"Chop chop, Julia," Dot said, tapping her watch again. "Time's ticking. You're not getting any younger."

"As you keep reminding me," Julia said, her eyes widening and her jaw gritting. "Me and Jessie will come around for dinner tonight and we can catch up."

"No can do, I'm afraid," Dot cried over her shoulder as she hurried to the door. "I'm holding an emergency neighbourhood watch meeting at my cottage to announce Amy Clark's murder. I'll have to find something else to announce before then, but I've got the whole day ahead of me, haven't I? See you later, girls."

Like a whirlwind tearing through a house, Dot hurried out of the café and across the village green to her cottage, where she immediately took up her post in her garden, peering through her rose bushes with a pair of binoculars.

"Your gran is nuts," Jessie said as she stocked the display case with yesterday's leftovers. "I like it."

Julia spent the rest of the morning baking in the kitchen while Jessie served customers out front. It wasn't like Julia to hide from the public, but she needed time to mull over her thoughts and there was no other time she mulled more than when she was baking. Whether she was cooking up a simple batch of scones, or a more complicated red velvet cake, her fingers did the work while her brain could focus on other things. Baking had saved her a fortune on therapy bills when her marriage broke down.

No matter where she tried to direct her thoughts, she kept circling around to Carl Black. Everything about him and how he acted made her think he was the man Tommy had whacked over Jerry's body. She wondered if a man would be so stupid to show up the same day as the murder, but she knew arrogant men like him didn't think anything they did was ever wrong. Jerrad hadn't seen anything wrong with his affair with his twenty-seven-year-old secretary, nor had he seen anything wrong with packing all of Julia's possessions in black bags and leaving them on the doorstep of their apartment, after changing the locks while she was at work. Men like that didn't have a compassionate bone in their bodies.

"Can I use your laptop?" Jessie asked as Julia flicked through her mother's handwritten recipe book. "The café's empty and everything is cleaned up."

"Sure," Julia said, tossing Jessie the keys to her car. "You know where it is."

Julia landed on the page she had been looking for. She ran her finger over her mother's curly, artistic handwriting. She had always wished her own was more like it, but her fingers were more suited to baking cakes than beautiful calligraphy. She read the recipe for the coconut cake aloud to herself as she gathered the ingredients. She was relieved when she found a packet of desiccated coconut in the back of her pantry.

As she measured out the ingredients, she glanced through the beads to Jessie, who was leaning against the counter and typing slowly on the keyboard. Julia imagined her tongue was poking out of her lips as she focussed carefully on the words. She tried to see what Jessie was doing but she was blocking the screen from view.

After Julia had finished the cake mix, she preheated the oven according to her mother's instructions and poured the sweet smelling mixture into a bundt pan. She always liked how the indented curvature inside of the domed pan made the cakes look. She had no idea if it would look anything like Barker's mother's favourite, but she hoped it would taste just as good, if not better. Her mother's recipe always seemed to elevate the classics, and she had spent many years wondering how her mother had gained her precision and skill when it came to writing out her recipes. Most of Julia's were in her mind, or scribbled down on scraps of paper, which were littered around her café and cottage, some pinned to notice boards, others gathered in boxes in the bottom of her wardrobe.

The timer pinged, tearing her from her thoughts. She had been trying to think of ways to convince Tommy to move on from Fenton Industrial Park. She considered offering him her couch again, perhaps insisting this time. It was a possibility that she would offend him, but she would sleep better at night knowing he wasn't going to be the murderer's next victim.

"Did you know there was another murder?" Jessie asked as she carried the laptop in, staring at the screen.

"Since we left?"

"No, before," Jessie said, placing the laptop on the table. "I just came across this article about a girl who died near the industrial park a couple of months before Bailey died. She was murdered and they arrested the guy."

"I didn't know about that," Julia mumbled, leaning into the screen and scanning over the article. "Does it say how she was killed?"

"Strangled. Sounds like a mugging gone wrong. Those used to happen a lot on those dark paths."

"Is there a picture of her?"

"No, but there's a name. Let me search it online. There might be some pictures on an old social media account."

Jessie copied and pasted the name into the search bar and hit enter. The second the page loaded and the small preview icons appeared, they both leaned back and gasped.

"I know her!" Jessie said.

"So do I," Julia said, quickly dumping the coconut icing over the cake and messily spreading it around the golden surface. "Can you look after the café? I need to speak to Barker."

"Why? What's happened?"

"I'll explain later."

Julia forced the messy cake into a box, ashamed that the icing was practically melting off the still warm cake, but also knowing she didn't have much time to convince Barker of her plan before sunset. She grabbed her jacket and her keys, and jumped into her car, securing the cake in the passenger seat with a seatbelt.

CHAPTER 13

With her cake in hand, Julia knocked loudly on Barker's door, her urgency increasing with each rap of her knuckles on the wood. She pressed her ear up against the door, but she couldn't hear movement, despite Barker's car being parked outside. Inhaling deeply, she knocked until her knuckles hurt. Barker didn't answer, so she tried the door handle. It moved and the door opened. Looking back at Barker's car, she pushed on the wood. It was an emergency, after all.

"Barker?" Julia called out, stepping tentatively down his hallway. "Are you home?"

Splashing water caught her attention so she spun around at the same time the bathroom door opened. Barker stepped forward, soaked from head to toe and covered in bubbles, a small towel fastened around his hips barely protecting his modesty. Julia quickly averted her eyes, but the definition of his surprisingly muscular physique didn't go unnoticed.

"Julia!" Barker cried, dropping his hands to his crotch

over the towel. "What are you doing in my cottage?"

"I did knock," she mumbled, turning back to the door. "I'd come back later, but it's quite urgent."

"I was listening to music," Barker said, trying to laugh through the awkwardness. "I like to listen to the radio in the bath on my days off. Helps me forget about work."

"A bubble bath, no less."

"You've got to have bubbles in a bath, Julia," Barker said playfully. "Go through to the living room and I'll throw some clothes on. What's in the tin?"

"Coconut cake," Julia mumbled as she scurried through to the living room, her eyes firmly planted on the ground. "Just be quick. Like I said, it's quite urgent."

Julia perched on the edge of Barker's squeaky leather couch and waited patiently, her fingers clasped around the edge of the cake tin. The cottage wasn't as clean as it had been on their date, but it was nowhere near as messy as it had been when he first moved to the village. She made a mental note to ask around about a cleaner for him like she had once promised him. He needed a woman's touch around the place, but Julia had enough on her plate than to be cleaning another man's cottage.

Less than a minute later, Barker walked into the living room in a pair of grey sweatpants and a tight fitting white t-shirt, a towel around his neck catching the drips from his damp hair. Now that she had seen his chiselled torso, she could see it through the t-shirt without even meaning to. Had she never noticed before because she was used to seeing Barker in shirts and suits?

"What's so urgent," Barker asked, as he perched on the edge of the couch, his fingers reaching out for the cake tin. "Did you make that for me?"

Julia slapped his hand away, put the cake tin on the cluttered coffee table, and stood up.

"There's no time for cake," Julia said, already heading for the door. "Get your shoes on. I'll explain on the way."

"On the way where?" Barker could barely contain his confused laughter. "I'm not going anywhere looking like this. These are my scruffy clothes."

"Where we're going, it doesn't matter," Julia said, waving her hand over her shoulder as she walked back to the front door. "*Shoes*, Barker! And bring your keys. We're taking your car. Mine is too recognisable."

"You're a piece of work, Julia South," Barker mumbled, and she wasn't entirely sure if she was supposed to hear him.

"I know," she replied regardless.

Five minutes later, they pulled up outside of Peridale's only charity shop, '*Second Loved*'. Whenever Julia de-cluttered her cottage, she would drive down to the charity shop with her unwanted things so Betty Hunter, the sweet owner, could sell them and raise money for various different local charities. She barely took a wage for herself, and whatever profit she made after covering the rent and the bills, she split amongst the most worthy causes in the village.

"What are we doing here?" Barker asked as he peered over his steering wheel at the small backstreet shop. "Have you dragged me away from my bubble bath to dig through a smelly old charity shop?"

"It's not smelly," Julia said as she opened the door. "And yes, that's exactly what I've done. Keep up, Detective Inspector."

Julia hurried into the shop, not turning to see that

Barker was following her. She knew he would, if only to find out what she wanted to tell him. Holding back information was something she only did when it felt necessary, and right now it felt more than necessary. If Barker knew the whole plan and her theories up front, he wouldn't go along with it, but if she at least got him halfway through the plan, he might not be so eager to back out.

"Julia," Betty said, peering over her book from behind the small counter in the corner. "What a pleasant surprise. I haven't seen you in a while."

"I don't have any donations today I'm afraid, Betty, but I have come to do some shopping." Julia pushed forward her friendliest smile, not wanting to arouse suspicion before she had even gotten started.

"I got some lovely dresses in last week from a stylish woman from the city. They'd suit you perfectly and I think they're your size. They're in the back. Let me go and grab them."

"Another time, perhaps," Julia said, just as the door opened and Barker shuffled sheepishly into the shop, looking more than a little uncomfortable. "We're looking for something very specific today. Where do you keep the clothes that nobody ever wants to buy?"

"In that fifty pence bin," Betty said, narrowing her eyes suspiciously over her glasses. "Let me know if you need any help."

Julia assured her that she would. Betty was a sweet lady who lived a simple life. She didn't frequent Julia's café because she thought the prices were too expensive, and she wasn't afraid to let Julia know that. Julia didn't take offence. Betty harked from an era where you could go to the shop with one pound in your back pocket and buy a pint of milk, a loaf of bread, and still leave with change.

"Get digging," Julia ordered, clicking at the basket. "We don't have much time."

Julia started digging in the huge basket of unwanted clothes. Most of what she was saw was garish neon prints that hadn't seen the light of day in over thirty years, but she kept digging regardless. She knew exactly what she was looking for.

"Julia, do I need to call your gran?" Barker whispered. "Have you been sleeping?"

"I'm not having a breakdown," Julia said with a sigh. "I told you I'll explain later."

"Maybe it's delayed concussion? I heard that can happen. It's wasn't that long ago that Terry Lewis hit you on the head with that kettle. Maybe you should just sit down for a second."

"Barker, I told you that I'm fine," Julia snapped under her breath, making sure that Betty couldn't overhear her.

Barker sighed and shrugged, glancing awkwardly to Betty and smiling as she sneered at him. Betty kept to herself, so Julia doubted she had seen, or even heard of the new Detective Inspector in town. She wasn't too fond of outsiders moving into Peridale.

"At least tell me what we're looking for," Barker said as he joined Julia in the digging. "I might as well play along."

"Worn, old, moth-eaten, ruined clothes," Julia said as she pulled a huge, lumpy khaki-green jumper from the mess. "Like this."

"Am I allowed to ask why?"

"It's for a disguise," Julia said carefully as she set the jumper aside and continued to dig. "We're going undercover and we're going to catch the murderer. I think I know who is behind all of this, but nobody will believe me. I'm not even sure I believe it myself, so we need to catch them in the act."

"Is there anything I can say to talk you out of this insane idea?"

"You know there isn't," Julia said, smiling behind her nerves as adrenaline pumped through her veins. "I'm doing this with or without your help, Barker, so you can either help me and take half of the glory, or you can go home and get back in your bubble bath."

Barker dug in the basket and pulled out a giant, almost destroyed woollen overcoat. He tossed it on top of the jumper and moved next to Julia, nudging her with his shoulder.

"You're going to run into that burning building no matter what I say, so I might as well run in with you."

They silently dug in the unwanted clothesbasket, their hands touching as they weaved in and out of the old garments. Julia tried to think if there was another man in the world who would go along with her without trying to rein her in. Jerrad would have made sure to squash any out-of-the-box thought before it even formed, but Barker let her mind work, regardless of where it took her. In that moment, she was glad she had Barker by her side, willingly and unquestioningly helping her.

CHAPTER 14

Julia and Barker sat in the car, tucked away in an alley across the street from Fenton Industrial Park waiting for the sun to set. By the time it had faded from the sky and they were surrounded by darkness, Julia had finished explaining her plan to Barker.

"This is mad," Barker grumbled, scratching at the thick scarf around his neck. "Are you sure there is nothing I can do to talk you out of this?"

"I'm sure," Julia said as she tucked her hair into the woolly hat on her head. "We should go. We don't want to miss him."

Julia squeezed herself out of the car and walked out onto the street. She looked down at her heavily layered outfit, hoping she had done enough to blend in, and more importantly, not be recognised. Barker joined her as he continued to scratch at the itchy scarf wrapped around his neck. He yanked his hood up and it fell over his eyes, casting a shadow across the lower half of his face. Julia copied him.

"I wouldn't recognise you," Julia said confidently.

"I wouldn't recognise you either." Barker sighed as he crammed his hands into his pocket. "I'm giving you one last chance to change your mind. What you know might be enough to take to the station and get it investigated."

Julia looked to the industrial park. There were a couple of fires burning, and it seemed that there were more people there than her last visit. She was glad. It would make it easier to go undetected. She wondered if Barker was right. It would certainly be easier to hand over what she had put together, but she also knew she was likely to be laughed out of the station. What she had didn't seem plausible, and yet she knew it had to be the only explanation.

"We should go," Julia said, dropping her head. "Try to act like you belong."

Barker audibly sighed, but he followed her all the same. They walked towards the broken gate, neither of them daring to look up. Julia crammed her hands deep into her pockets, scared that somebody might notice even the smallest detail about her. She knew she was being paranoid, but she didn't want to blow her one chance of ending what was happening.

"Where do we go?" Barker whispered as they walked into the car park and past a group of four crowding around a barrel fire.

"To the fence. That's where the others died."

As they approached the fence, Julia dared to look in Tommy's direction. He was sitting on his doorstep, thumbing through a small book under a heavy blanket. He looked up from his book but he didn't look in her direction. They had gotten away with it, for now.

Two ripped pieces of blue and white crime scene tape

still hung from the fence, fluttering in the cool night breeze. Julia brushed her fingers against the cold metal slats, relieved when they budged. She moved down slightly, not wanting to be in the exact same place Jerry had been found only days earlier. Barker pulled up two crates and they sat down across from each other next to the fence.

"What now?" Barker asked as he blew into his hands and rubbed them together.

"We wait."

"What if he doesn't try anything?"

"He will," she said with certainty. "He's getting confident he's never going to get caught. He'll be itching to kill again, if only to prove to himself he can get away with it another time."

"Are you sure you don't want to join the force?" Barker said quietly with a small laugh. "You're better than most of the people at my station."

"I'm sure," Julia said. "I don't do this because I want to, I do it because I have to."

"Part of me thinks you enjoy the thrill."

Julia opened her mouth to disagree with him, but she couldn't. A small part of her knew Barker was right. She would rather not have to keep landing in the middle of murder investigations, but there was something completely addictive about seeing things nobody else did and piecing together the puzzle. Her main purpose was to do what the police wouldn't for the sake of the dead, but she would be lying if she said the adrenaline didn't make her feel more alive than ever.

"These aren't my fights," Julia said, choosing her words carefully. "But I know if I don't do something, this will keep happening."

"I'm not so sure," Barker said as he peeked out of the side of his hood to look around the industrial park. "This is the emptiest I've seen this place."

"Some people aren't so easily scared away," Julia whispered, daring to take another peek at Tommy. "Besides, the murderer is getting desperate. If he can't find anybody here, he'll look in other places. It's not like the country is running out of the homeless. The sooner we get him off the streets, the better."

"I just hope you have this right," Barker mumbled as he leaned against the fence. "Although a part of me hopes you're barking up the wrong tree."

"Me too," Julia said with a heavy sigh. "But I don't think I am."

"After you explained who the dead girl was, I don't either."

Julia joined Barker in leaning against the fence. They both silently stared out at the people in front of them. Julia couldn't believe how different things were from her first visit. The heart and soul of the patchwork community had been torn out, and what had been left behind was sad to witness. The laughter and friendly conversation had been replaced with whispering and paranoid side glances.

"I forgot about Jessie," Julia cried, suddenly sitting up straight. "She'll be wondering where I am. I need to call her."

Julia patted down her jacket, remembering that she had left her phone in her own jacket, which was now locked up in Barker's car boot.

"Does she have her own keys?" Barker asked, patting down his own jacket. "I could run back and get my phone."

"I keep meaning to get her one cut," Julia said, already

standing up. "She doesn't even have a phone. Stay here and keep your eyes peeled."

"If she doesn't have a phone, how are you going to call her?"

"Maybe she's still at the café," Julia said, chewing the inside of her cheek. "Or at my gran's. I'm an awful guardian."

"You're far from it. My mum once forgot I was in the back seat of her car and went shopping for three hours. We all make mistakes. Go and call her. I've got things covered here."

Julia smiled her thanks and accepted Barker's car keys. Walking as quickly as she dared, she headed for the gate, keeping her chin securely pressed against her chest. When she was back out on the street, she ran across the road and towards the alley where they had parked the car. Her heart sank when she saw the dark, empty alley.

"*No!*" She cried with a strained breath. "No, no, no!"

She ran up the street, past the abandoned factories, wondering if she had been looking down the wrong dark alley. She hadn't. Turning on the spot, she pushed her fingers through the heavy hat and clutched handfuls of her curls. She felt completely hopeless. She checked the alley once more, somehow hoping the car had reappeared; it hadn't. Barker's car had been stolen.

Hurrying back, she yanked her hood over her face, her heart pounding in her chest. She looked down the street to the phone box on the corner. She tapped her pockets in vain, but her wallet was in the boot of Barker's now missing car, along with her phone, her cottage and café keys, and her clothes. Once she was back in the car park, her heart sank once more when she saw that Barker wasn't alone.

Suddenly slowing down, she approached Barker and the man who was sitting on her crate, sure that they had been rumbled. When she saw that it was Pete, her heart sank even further. Holding back, she wandered casually into the corner Mac had called home, and perched on a crate, peeping at the men under her hood.

Pete was clutching a can of beer as he leaned into Barker. She tried to focus on what they talking about, but all she could hear was faint, slurred mumbling. She looked over to Tommy, who was looking over to Pete and Barker. She wondered if the night could get any worse.

Julia sat in the corner for what felt like an age. When Pete finally stood up, tossed his empty can to the ground, and stumbled away, she slipped back in and sat next to Barker.

"I thought he'd never leave!" Barker whispered after letting out a long sigh of relief. "I don't even know what he was talking about. Something about aliens and the government. Told me to watch my back."

"Did he recognise you?"

"I don't think so. He didn't say he did. He was three sheets to the wind. Totally wasted. I doubt he even remembers meeting me."

Julia peered under her hood as Pete wandered from person to person, watched tentatively by Tommy over his book. Those who didn't completely ignore Pete pushed him away disdainfully. It seemed as though he hadn't stopped drinking, or doing a lot worse, since Cindy's death.

"Do you have any money on you?" Julia asked.

"It's in the car," Barker said after patting his pockets. "Did you manage to get in touch with Jessie?"

"No." Julia paused to think about the best way to

broach the subject. "About that. Your car is gone."

"*Gone?*" Barker quickly turned to her, frowning heavily. "What do you mean, it's gone?"

"Stolen, I suspect. I'm so sorry, Barker. This is all my fault."

"Are you sure?" Barker said, desperately looking to the gate. "Maybe you were looking in the wrong place?"

"I wish I was. I double checked. It's gone."

"They're going to kill me," Barker cried, dropping his face into his hands. "That was a company car. The boot was full of confidential files that I shouldn't have even taken out of the station. And my phone! And my cottage keys! I don't have spares."

"I think Emily Burns has a spare from when it used to be Todrick's cottage," Julia offered pathetically. "That's if you haven't changed the locks."

"I haven't," he mumbled through his fingers. "What am I going to do?"

"You can go. There's a phone box at the end of the street. 999 is free to dial."

"I can't dial 999, Julia," Barker snapped. "*I'm* the police. I'm supposed to catch people who steal cars, not let my own get stolen. My boss is going to kill me."

"You can blame it on me. I find honesty is always the best policy."

"Not in this situation," Barker said, fidgeting away from Julia. "I shouldn't even be here. *We* shouldn't even be here. What are we doing?"

"I've already told you that you can go," Julia snapped back, edging away from him and leaning forward onto her knees. "Get a taxi back to Peridale. I'm sure somebody at the station will lend you some money when you get there."

"I'm hardly going to leave you, am I?" Barker whispered, turning to her and half-smiling through his obvious anger. "It's just a car. It's insured. They'll want to know what I was doing in this part of town, but I'll think of something."

"You could tell them it was stolen from outside of the charity shop. We are in disguise after all."

"That's not a bad idea," Barker mumbled under his breath, nodding. "If they have CCTV of us driving, they're hardly going to recognise us dressed like this."

"I was kidding," Julia said, awkwardly laughing.

"I'm not. How are you going to get in touch with Jessie?"

"I don't know," Julia scratched the side of her head as she stared at the ground. "We're in a bit of a mess, aren't we?"

Barker chuckled softly as he looked up. When he looked forward, his eyes quickly widened. Julia followed his eyes to where he was looking, her own eyes widening.

"I don't think you'll have to worry about calling Jessie," Barker said, nodding to Jessie and Dot as they hurried across the car park towards Tommy. "I've always thought your gran was psychic."

"This is bad," Julia muttered, dropping her head. "How did they even get here?"

Julia looked up to see her sister and her husband, Neil, jogging to keep up with Jessie and Dot. Julia dragged her hood over her face and did the same to Barker's. They glanced at each other, half-smirking as they looked down.

"What are they doing?" Julia asked.

"Talking to Tommy."

"They're going to be so worried about me."

"Just go and talk to them."

"I can't!" Julia glanced up and watched as Tommy stumbled to his feet with Jessie's help. "This will have all been for nothing if we blow our cover."

"Like you said, they'll be worried."

"I'll explain it all later," Julia said, shrugging and biting into her lip. "They'll understand, won't they?"

"Who are you kidding?" Barker asked, glancing up and dropping his head immediately. "I've met your gran. She'll be furious you didn't ask her to join our undercover operation. I doubt she'll ever speak to you again."

Julia laughed as quietly as she could, leaning into Barker's shoulder. Taking her by surprise, he picked up her hand and looped his fingers around hers. She almost pulled back, scared it would blow their cover, until she decided it didn't matter. She told herself it would look more convincing if they were holding hands, even though she just enjoyed the feeling of his thumb stroking the back of her hand.

"I've got an idea," Julia mumbled, pulling away from Barker and standing up. "Stay here and try not to make any more friends."

"Where are you going?"

"I'll be back in a couple of minutes," Julia whispered over her shoulder. "Don't worry. I'll fix this."

Julia ran along the edge of the fence, pulled back the loose slats, and slipped through the gap with ease. Once on the other side, she paused in her tracks, staring out into the dark winding path ahead, her eyes playing tricks on her. The shadows shifted and danced, the impossible blackness bringing forward her childhood fear of the dark. Just like the monster under her bed, she knew it was her imagination taunting her. Monsters didn't hide in the shadows never to be seen, they walked among the living, and she knew the monster she was searching for wouldn't come out until he was sure he wasn't going to be caught.

Julia walked around the edge of the industrial park and lingered by the broken gate. Staring ahead at the road, she didn't dare move or lift her head until she heard her gran's loud and distinctive voice.

"She's *dead*!" Dot cried. "I just *know* it! I have a *fifth* sense, you know."

"It's a *sixth* sense, gran," Sue replied. "And I've already told you, knowing Julia she's probably off somewhere getting herself into trouble, thinking she's doing the world a favour."

"Well if she's not dead yet, she *will* be by sunrise!" Dot snapped back. "You mark my words, young lady. Your sister is up to no good. She can't just keep her nose out of other people's business."

"Bit rich, coming from you," Sue mumbled back.

Julia looked up from her hood as the voices moved closer. She watched as Sue and Neil walked back towards her car, followed by Dot and Jessie. As loudly as she dared, she coughed deep within her throat, hoping it was enough to catch Jessie's attention. It wasn't. Watching them walk back to the car, she looked around desperately, landing on an empty beer can. Wrinkling her nose, she picked up the can, closed one eye and threw it at Jessie. She clasped her hand over her mouth when it bounced off Jessie's head.

Clutching her hair, Jessie spun around, ready for a fight. Julia waved her over, her finger pressed hard against her lips. Jessie glanced over her shoulder at the others, before running quickly towards Julia.

"What the *hell* are you doing?" Jessie cried as Julia yanked her into the shadows. "Have you completely lost the plot? What are you wearing?"

"It's a long story," Julia said, pulling back her hood a little and grabbing Jessie's shoulders, looking over to the car. "I need you to tell them I called you and that I'm out for dinner with Barker, but you have to wait until you're back in Peridale."

"You're hardly dressed for dinner," Jessie snapped, looking down her nose. "You stink, you do know that, right?"

"I know. It's stuff I grabbed from the charity shop."

"You look homeless."

"That's the point, Jessie," Julia said, sighing and rolling her eyes. "Just do what I say? Please? I'll explain it all tomorrow."

"Tomorrow?" Jessie's eyes suddenly widening as she seemed to figure out what was happening. "You're trying to catch him, aren't you?"

"No."

"You're lying," Jessie muttered through tight lips. "I can always tell when you're lying. Your cheeks always go red. It's the same look you give me whenever you try one of my cakes."

"It's not," Julia lied again. "Please, just go back to the car and do what I asked."

Julia looked over Jessie's shoulder to the car, but like Barker's, it was nowhere to be seen. In the distance, she saw Neil's car drive around the roundabout and take the turning back to Peridale.

"Looks like you're stuck with me," Jessie whispered smugly. "Your gran is so busy planning your funeral she didn't even notice I wasn't there."

"They'll come back looking for you," Julia said desperately, her cheeks burning hotter than ever. "Just go and wait over there."

"They won't find me when they get here." Jessie pulled her hair back and fastened it in the small of her neck with the hair tie she always had wrapped around her wrist. When she was done, she pulled her black hood down to her eyes and zipped the front up to her chin. "You're not the only person who can go in disguise."

"You can't be here," Julia whispered, looking up and down the street for a sign of a way out. "He's not going to approach if he sees you."

"You told me you didn't know if I was a boy or girl when we first met." Jessie hunched her shoulders, looked down and crammed her hands in her baggy jeans' pockets. "Remember? I can handle myself, Julia."

Julia saw more of herself in Jessie than she liked to admit in that moment. She wondered if this was what Barker felt like every time Julia refused to back down from one of her ideas. Knowing there was nothing she could say to her young lodger to change her mind, Julia reluctantly turned on her heels and walked back around to the narrow path leading back to the gap in the fence.

"There's somebody there," Jessie whispered, putting her arm in front of Julia. "Up ahead."

"My eyes did the same thing to me."

"No, seriously." Jessie yanked Julia into the trees and dragged her down behind a bush. "You need to get your eyes tested, old lady."

"Less of the old."

Julia peered over the bush, quickly darting down again

when she saw the figure Jessie had seen. Wearing a dark trench coat, he pressed his nose up against the fence, only metres away from Barker.

"Let's get him," Jessie whispered, ready to spring up at any moment. "You hold him down, and I'll sock him on the nose."

Julia had to practically wrestle Jessie to the ground to stop her from springing up and launching herself at the man. Resting her hand over Jessie's mouth, Julia peered over the bush once more, and watched as the man disappeared back the way he came.

"Get off me," Jessie said as she yanked Julia's hand away. "You just let him get away."

"It might not have even been him."

"Who even is *he,* anyway?" Jessie asked, standing up and brushing the leaves and dirt from her jeans. "How am I supposed to know who to attack if you don't tell me?"

"You're not going to attack anyone, do you hear me?" Julia said, wincing as Jessie helped her up from the ground, the creak in her knees reminding her she was more than double Jessie's age. "You're going to sit quietly, and not ask too many questions, okay?"

"Sure," Jessie scoffed. "You're funny when you want to be."

They walked back to the fence and Julia held out the slats for Jessie to climb through. Keeping her head low and her hands in her pockets, she walked along to Barker and sat down. As Julia pushed herself through the gap, she looked around to make sure they hadn't been seen, and it didn't seem like they had.

"This was your plan?" Barker snapped as he pulled Jessie in. "Are you crazy, Julia?"

"I have ears," Jessie replied, leaning into Barker and scowling. "I'm not a kid. I'm seventeen next month."

"You're a kid in the eyes of the law."

"The law can kiss my -,"

"I didn't have a choice," Julia jumped in, apologising with her eyes to Barker. "They drove off without her. They'll probably come back to look for her when they realise."

"Too bad I'm staying here," Jessie said, rubbing her hands in front of her mouth. "It's just like old times. Shall we start a fire?"

"I have a terrible feeling about this," Barker said, sighing and shaking his head. "I'm going to wake up in my bubble bath and this will all have been a bad dream."

"You have bubble baths?" Jessie mocked, snickering under her breath. "Who's the little girl now?"

Julia stopped herself from laughing, instead smiling under her hood at Barker. Exhaling and frowning, he leaned against the fence, crossed his arms and closed his eyes. The people were showing no signs of going to sleep anytime soon. It was going to be a long night.

CHAPTER 15

J ulia's eyes shot open. She knew she had been asleep for more than a couple of seconds. Blinking into the darkness, she pulled her coat tighter around her body. It hadn't been so cold when she had closed her eyes. Sitting up straight, she let out a long yawn, noticing how eerily quiet things were. The fires had died down and everybody had bedded down for the night. Barker's snoring next to her told her she wasn't the only one who had allowed herself to rest her eyes.

When her pupils adjusted to the blackness, she looked ahead and noticed a slim figure moving away from her in the darkness. Remembering Jessie, Julia jumped up.

"Jessie," Julia whispered into the dark. "Where are you going?"

"I saw something near the gate," she whispered back over her shoulder. "Don't worry, I've been keeping watch since you fell asleep."

Guilt surged through Julia as she fast-walked to catch up with Jessie. How long had she been asleep? Just from the temperature, it already felt like the early hours of the morning.

"What did you see?"

"I thought I saw a man walking past."

"Thought?"

"It's dark," Jessie whispered before letting out a long yawn. "It's been a long night."

Julia's guilt increased. How could she have put them all at danger by being so stupid? She glanced back at Barker as he slept peacefully by the fence. Why did she have to drag other people into her mess? She wished she had done it alone, with a flask of strong, hot coffee.

They reached the street and the warm safety of the streetlights. The road was completely silent in either direction, the only movement coming from the soft shadows of clouds rolling past the pale yellow, almost-full moon.

"There's nobody here," Julia whispered, moving in closer to Jessie. "Let's get back to Barker."

"I saw a man," Jessie said, ignoring Julia and walking down the street. "It could be *him.*"

"It was probably just a trick of the light," Julia whispered, jogging to keep up with Jessie. "Let's just get back to Barker."

Jessie suddenly ground to a halt, putting her arm out to stop Julia. She turned around, her expression angry and firm. Julia's heart sank. She knew what was coming next.

"You left Barker, a man, alone next to the fence where men are being murdered?"

Julia's heart sank to the pit of her stomach. She didn't realise she was running until she felt the wind rip back her hood, tear off her hat, and unleash her curls. Almost in a daze, she could feel Jessie directly behind her as she rounded the corner back into the industrial park.

When Julia saw a shadowy figure climbing through the fence, her heart sank even further, but when she saw a second figure climbing through, her heart practically stopped. She wanted to scream out for Barker, but her vocal cords were paralysed.

"There's two of them?" Jessie cried, hot on Julia's heels.

"I – I didn't know," Julia said, unsure if her words were vocal or just in her mind. "I didn't know."

When the bigger of the dark figures grabbed Barker, Julia let out an ear-piercing screech, but she didn't hear it. Her legs ran faster than they had in her life, outrunning the girl half her age. Barker's eyes shot open, but before he could scream out, the figure's hand wrapped around his mouth. The second, smaller figure pulled a needle out of their pocket, their hands obviously shaking.

"Do it!" the bigger figure, a man, cried. "Do it *now*!"

"*Stella*!" Julia cried, grinding to a halt metres from the fence, her palms darting up in front of her. "Drop the needle, Stella!"

Julia's use of the smaller figure's name had been a guess, but when the woman turned and looked at Julia, fear alive in the whites of her eyes through the balaclava, Julia knew her guess had been correct.

"I have to do this," Stella mumbled, her hands shaking so out of control it looked like she had just been dunked in a cold bath. "It's God's will."

"Is this woman for real?" Jessie cried.

Julia edged closer, her hands outstretched and her face kind. The man yanked back his balaclava. Julia wasn't surprised to see Max.

"Stella, don't listen to her," Max growled, his teeth bared like a dog ready to attack. "You know God spoke to me. Spoke to *us*!"

Stella nodded, fumbling with the plastic end of the needle. She yanked it off and dropped it to the ground, some of the poisonous solution falling from the metal tip. Julia saw it drip to the ground as though in slow motion.

"God spoke to us," Stella said, echoing her husband. "He wants us to make the world a better place."

"By murdering innocent people?"

"God was vengeful, Julia." Stella turned to Julia and pulled back her balaclava, a deranged, sweet smile consuming her pale, slender face. "When God spoke to Noah and told him to build the ark, he told him to save the animals, not the people. The people needed to be taught a lesson. They *needed* to die."

"What is this woman on?" Jessie cried. "Somebody call the police!"

Barker started to scream behind the gloved hand, his eyes wide and staring at Julia. She felt as though she was looking into the eyes of a dead man. She held back her tears, knowing she had to remain strong. She had to fix her mess.

"I know what happened to your daughter," Julia said, taking another baby step forward. "Bethany. I know she was murdered by a homeless man, right there on that path. I know she was walking him back from the soup kitchen, and that he attacked her. I can't imagine what that feels like, but this isn't the answer."

"You're right," Max spat, his nose so wrinkled and tight, he no longer resembled a human. "You can't know what that feels like. None of you can. We did nothing but *help* these disgusting people, and that's how they repay us? By taking our daughter?"

The crack in Max's voice broke Julia's heart. For a moment, she saw the eyes of a grieving father, not a murderer.

"Just because the awful, evil man who took your Bethany was homeless, it doesn't mean you need to punish every homeless person."

"We're making the world a better place," Stella repeated. "They're a disease."

"I know you don't believe that," Julia whispered, stepping closer, her palms spread wide. "You put your love into your soup to help these people. You care about these people."

"God -," Stella started, her voice trailing off as her bottom lip wobbled uncontrollably.

"God wouldn't ask you to kill," Julia said, smiling through her own pain. "Would he, Stella? Remember what you told me about the dead? They never really leave us. What would Bethany say if she saw you like this? You said she walks beside you. If that's true, she's here right now, seeing you do this."

Stella looked desperately from Julia to Max, searching for answers from the devil and angel on her shoulders. Max tightened his grip on Barker, his arm secure around his throat. Beads of sweat trickled down Barker's bright red face, his eyes darting from Julia to the shocked crowd that she could feel gathering behind her.

"Max?" Stella pleaded. "What does God say?"

"I think Max lost his faith when you lost Bethany," Julia whispered, stepping within reaching distance of the needle. "Isn't that right, Max? You can't speak to God any more than I can."

"I'm tired of this," Max cried, his grip tightening so firm around Barker's neck that the Detective Inspector's eyes started to flutter. "Give me the needle, Stella."

Out of the corner of her eye, Julia spotted movement. She didn't turn to look but she could sense a slow, lumbering figure edging closer to Max. She wanted to cry out, to stop them doing anything stupid, but she couldn't take her eyes away from Barker's fluttering lids.

"Stella," Julia choked, unable to hold back the tears anyway. "You loved your daughter, didn't you?"

"Of course she did!" Max barked. "We both did!"

"Well, I love this man," Julia stepped forward, not caring if Stella lashed out with the needle. "Don't take him from me before I've even had a chance to get to know his middle name, or his favourite colour. Please, Stella. I'm not a mother, but you know I understand loss. Remember when I told you about my mother? I understand your anger. I *understand* your desperation to believe you're doing the right thing, but you're not. This is your first time even holding a needle at somebody, isn't it? All the other times Max was on his own, wasn't he?"

Stella nodded, tears streaming down her face as she stared down at the needle.

"I didn't understand when he told me what he had done, but when he told me it was an order from God, I knew we had to finish his mission."

"There's no mission," Julia mumbled through her tears. "Please stop this."

The lumbering movement came into Julia's full view, and she involuntarily turned her head. So did Max, but not quick enough to duck out of the way of the solid gas canister heading for his skull. With a solid thud, Max let go of Barker, swayed on the spot for a moment, and collapsed into a groaning heap.

"Enough talking," Tommy cried, dropping the gas canister and stumbling into the fence, his legs giving out without the aid of his stick. "Hold him down, boys."

Three men rushed forward, all of them jumping on Max like a pack of starving dogs on a sliver of meat. She expected them to hit the unconscious man. She wouldn't stop them if they did. To her surprise, they just pinned him to the ground.

"I'm sorry," Stella whispered, her eyes as wide as the moon in the sky as she lifted the needle up. "Bethany, Mummy is coming."

Julia heard her own cries echo around the industrial park. She dove forwards, her hand clutching Stella's wrist. The frail woman didn't fight. She relaxed her hand and dropped the needle to the ground. In that moment, every muscle in Stella's body seemed to vanish and she crumbled like her husband had. Julia caught her, and they both fell to the ground. As Stella sobbed, Julia wrapped her arms around the poor woman's shoulders and pulled her in, as though she was her mother. She felt every ounce of her grief, every drop of her pain, every tear she had shed for her daughter. That agony consumed Julia. She didn't try to hold back her own sobs.

Through her tears, she opened her eyes to see Barker clutching onto the fence, gasping for air. She knew some of her tears were for him. Her declaration of love echoed around in her mind and she sobbed even harder, the fresh tears from a place of relief and elation, rather than pain.

Police sirens echoed in the distance, letting her know it

was all over. She released her grip on Stella and let Jessie help her up off the ground.

"I thought she was going to kill you," Jessie whispered through her tears as she buried her face into Julia's heavy overcoat. "You're so stupid."

"I know," Julia said, gripping Jessie's head tight to her chest. "I'm so sorry."

As uniformed officers stormed the scene, Julia caught Barker's eyes. Through his pain, he smiled at her. Rubbing his neck, he staggered forward, wrapping his arm around the both of them. He pressed his lips against Julia's head, his palm gripping the back of her head so tightly she couldn't help but feel safe. None of them let go until officers pried them apart, demanding statements from all of them.

CHAPTER 16

J ulia had never been in her café at sunrise, but as she hugged a mug of peppermint and liquorice tea behind the counter, she began to wonder why she wasn't there every morning to witness the vibrant orange sky illuminating the grass.

"*Julia*!" Dot cried as she stormed through the cafe full of everybody who had been at Fenton when Max and Stella had been arrested. "Oh, Julia! I thought you were dead!"

Julia set her mug on the counter and let her gran hug her tightly, until she practically couldn't breathe. When she finally managed to pull her away, guilt flooded her when it became obvious her gran hadn't slept.

"What on *Earth* is going on?" Dot cried. "Who are all these people? Where's Jessie?"

"I'm here," Jessie stood up from the table she had been sharing with Tommy, pulling her hood down. "Come with me, I'll explain everything."

Jessie looped her arm through Dot's and practically dragged her through to the kitchen as she stared around the full café, her mouth opening and closing, the questions appearing to flood her brain faster than her mouth could process them. Julia mouthed her thanks to Jessie, who winked in return.

"I've said it before, and I'll say it again, you're an extraordinary woman, Julia," Tommy said, motioning to the seat across from him. "Not many would do what you did tonight."

"I'm a stupid woman," she said as she sat down, glad to be off her feet. "I almost got Barker killed."

"If you hadn't been there, it would have been one of us."

There was a chorus of mumbled agreement through the mouthful of free cake and coffee.

"I'm just glad it's all over," Julia said, letting out a sigh of relief.

"When I said not many would do what you did, I wasn't just talking about trying to catch that evil man," Tommy said thoughtfully as he leaned back in his chair. "A lesser person would have let Stella Moon take her own life."

"It wasn't even a decision," Julia said over the second chorus of mumbled agreement. "She's already been through enough."

"And that's what makes you so great," Tommy said. "You did them all proud. Bailey, Michael, Robert, Mac, Jerry – you did those men proud tonight."

A round of applause ran through the café, and Julia smiled as gratefully as she could, even if she didn't feel very worthy of the applause.

"How did you figure it out?" A woman asked through a mouthful of Victoria sponge cake.

"I didn't really," Julia said with a sigh, her eyebrows

drifting up her forehead. "I owe that to Jessie. She was looking online, trying to find some help for you guys, *you* especially, Tommy. She did a search for Fenton, and she came across the article about Bethany Moon's murder just before Christmas."

"That was all a terrible business," Tommy said regretfully, bowing his head. "She was a lovely girl. Frank Benton was a monster. He wasn't one of us. He might have been homeless, but he wasn't welcome at Fenton. We all knew what he was capable of. There were rumours. I wish I could have done something to protect that poor girl. Maybe none of this would have happened if I was firmer on him."

"This isn't your fault, Tommy," a man said, leaning over and slapping him on the shoulder. "You've always tried your best for us. You were right there till the end."

It suddenly struck Julia that none of them could really go back to Fenton Industrial Park, tonight, or ever. Now that Carl Black owned it, it wouldn't be long before work started on his luxury apartments, and a new community of people moved in. Julia scrambled her brain for a way she could help, but like Tommy had already told her, she couldn't help them all.

"Frank Benton took that poor girl's life, and they didn't even throw the book at him," Tommy said, his voice dropping to barely above a whisper. "I was there in court the day they sentenced him. They gave him life, but life doesn't mean life anymore, does it? He could be out in fifteen years with good behaviour."

"That man doesn't know how to behave," another man jumped in. "He stole my only pair of shoes, y'know."

"Took my jacket," somebody else added.

"He took a girl's life," Tommy reminded them. "I'm

not surprised her father was driven to the brink of insanity."

"Using God as an excuse!" The man jumped in again. "That's the real crime here."

"Max Moon lost his faith," Julia said, looking up at the ceiling, wondering if she had gained some in her experience tonight. "He killed those men not in the name of God, but in cold-blooded revenge. I suppose he killed Bailey to try and fix the pain, and when it didn't work, he kept doing it."

"And what about the wife? She was in on it too."

"I believe her when she said she didn't know," Julia said firmly, shifting in her seat. "I volunteered at their soup kitchen not long ago, and I know she didn't know then. I'm certain of it. She's diabetic, and she told me a box of her needles had gone missing. I knew it was connected, I just didn't expect that it was her husband who had taken them."

"What did they even inject?"

"Potassium Chloride," Julia said. "Or at least that's what I think. High levels of potassium were found in Mac's body. We'll never know with the others, but I'm confident it was the same throughout. Of course, he strangled Jerry to death with his bare hands because Jerry wasn't such an easy target."

"How could a man like that even know how to get something so lethal?" Tommy whispered, leaning across the table.

"It's all out there on the internet," Julia said. "One quick search and you've got a recipe for murder. All you really need to do is boil down some household bleach and you're already halfway there. I wouldn't be surprised if he was cooking it up in the soup kitchen in the dead of night while Stella slept."

"Frank Benton was a monster, but Max is just as bad,"

Tommy said, stamping his finger on the table. "Grief isn't an excuse for murdering five men!"

"I agree," Julia said with a nod. "But it does explain it, at least. There's never an excuse for murder."

"I wouldn't mind getting my hand's around Max's throat!" The same man jumped in. "An eye for an eye, I say."

Julia's café door opened, and Barker walked in, dark bruises on his throat. She immediately jumped up, leaving the conversation before it turned nasty. She hurried over to Barker, desperate to know what his examination had discovered.

"Light bruising and swelling," he croaked, rubbing at his purple throat. "It will heal itself, but I will be talking like I've got a frog in my throat for the next couple of weeks."

"That's perfectly fine with me," Julia whispered as she pulled him into a hug. "You're okay. That's the main thing. Did you manage to find out what's happening to Max and Stella?"

"They've been taken to Hesters Way station in Cheltenham for questioning. It's out of our hands now," Barker said as he pulled away from the hug. "I do have some good news though. They found my car abandoned on a country lane, all smashed up, but they recovered what was in the boot."

"Small victories," Julia whispered with a wink. "Sit down, I'll make you a nice hot cup of honey and lemon tea for your throat."

Barker sat across from Tommy, and Tommy immediately shook Barker's hand. Julia peered through the beads and chuckled when she saw her gran gasping in horror as Jessie explained everything that had happened, her hands telling most of the story. When she wrapped her hands around Dot's throat, Julia knew she was probably embellishing a little. She didn't doubt Jessie's version of events would be around the village by midday. Julia wouldn't be around to find out. For the first time since opening her café, she was putting a '*CLOSED*' sign in the window, and her and Jessie were going to catch up on some much needed sleep, if their minds would allow.

"I'm disbanding my neighbourhood watch!" Dot exclaimed as they thrust through the beads. "I'm clearly not up to it!"

"This didn't even happen in the village," Julia reassured her jokingly. "I'm not sure your binoculars would stretch all the way to Fenton."

"Even so, I should have spotted the signs that you were up to something," Dot said regretfully before kissing Julia on the cheek. "I better go and call Sue to let her know you're okay. She'll be worried sick sitting by the phone."

"Apologise from me, okay?" Julia asked. "Tell her I'll call her later."

Dot nodded and waved her hand as she walked through the café, eyeing the heavily dressed men and women with suspicion as she went.

One by one, the last remaining residents of Fenton Industrial Park went their separate ways, some of them leaving together, some leaving alone, but all of them making sure to thank Julia before they went on their way. She wanted to ask each of them where they planned to go, but she stopped herself, knowing she wouldn't like the answers. There was one person she could help today though, and she wasn't going to take no for an answer.

"Tommy, you're coming to mine," Julia ordered as she grabbed her jacket. "After a nice long sleep, and a relaxing bath, we're going to figure something out for you."

Tommy stood up, laughing and shaking his head as he rested his weight on his stick. He walked over to the door, and Julia almost thought he was going to leave, but he opened the door and waited for them. With Barker and Jessie by her side, they walked out into the fresh morning air. She looked up at the pale sky, more grateful than ever for breathing the fresh air of a new day.

"Are you going to join us, Barker?" Julia asked as they walked towards his cottage.

"I think I'll resume my bubble bath," Barker said as he unhooked his gate. "I suspect I'll have to run a fresh one, but I'd like to finish my soak and pretend all of this never happened. Well, maybe most of it at least."

He winked at her before turning and heading towards his cottage. She knew exactly what part he was talking about, and it caused a smile to spread across her face.

"You so love him," Jessie whispered, jabbing her in the ribs as they walked up to their cottage. "I told you he had the hots for you."

Smiling up at the sky, Julia didn't even bother denying it. She had meant it when she said she loved Barker. She didn't know how or why, she just knew she did, and it had never felt so good to admit it to herself, possibly for the first real time in her whole life.

CHAPTER 17

When Julia returned from the shops late in the afternoon, Jessie was still fast asleep in bed. Julia's own sleep had been cut short when Mowgli had pawed at her face, so she had decided to make use of the day after a prolonged soaked in the bath with a cup of peppermint and liquorice tea.

"Afternoon," Tommy said as Julia dumped the shopping bags on the counter. "I hope you don't mind, but I used your house phone."

"Not at all," Julia said as she shrugged her coat off, walking through to the hallway to hang it on the hat stand by the door.

"She's been out like a light all morning," Tommy said with a gentle smile. "You can almost pretend she's a normal kid when she's asleep. I didn't sleep much myself. How can you after what happened?"

"Who did you call?"

"I decided to swallow my pride and call my brother," Tommy said, his fingers nervously drumming on the countertop. "I haven't spoken to him in fifteen years, but he still had the same number. It's the only one I know by memory. We talked a lot of things out, and I'm sure we're going to talk even more over a couple beers, but he said I can go and stay with him and his family up in Manchester until I get back on my feet."

"That's amazing news."

"Seeing you and Jessie together reminded me what family meant," Tommy smiled tightly as he glanced up at the ceiling. "I've been hiding from mine for too long. It's time I faced my mistakes and got my life sorted out. I have you to thank for all of this, and before you tell me it's what anyone else would have done, it's not. Not at all, Julia South. They don't make them like you anymore."

Julia didn't argue. Tommy's words touched her, so all she could do was smile her thanks before filling the kettle to make him a coffee. As long as he was her guest, she would continue to look after him.

"I'll cover your train fare," Julia said as she poured fresh milk into the coffee. "I won't take no for an answer."

"I hadn't even thought about that," Tommy chuckled. "I suppose I'll have to join the rest of the world and start worrying about money. I'll pay you back when I'm sorted out. My brother thinks he can get me a cleaning job at the place he works at. Part time, but I'm not far off retirement as it is."

"I won't accept a penny from you," Julia said as she set the coffee in front of him. "Have you eaten?"

"You're going to make somebody a great mum one day," Tommy said with a soft smile. "Well, I suppose you already have actually."

At that moment, Jessie staggered through from her

bedroom, her long, dark hair matted at the side and her eyes still half-closed.

"What time is it?" She croaked.

"Just gone four."

"I slept like a log," Jessie muttered through a yawn.

"Us too," Tommy said, sending a wink in Julia's direction.

Jessie climbed onto a stool next to Tommy, her hands instantly diving in for his coffee. He let her take it, so Julia refilled the kettle and made him a second cup.

"I got you a present in town," Julia said as she fished through the bags. "I know it's not your birthday until next month, but this is separate."

Julia placed the mobile phone box, which had been gift wrapped in red paper with a white bow, in front of Jessie. She rubbed her eyes, and frowned up at Julia, staring down her nose in the way only Jessie did.

"What is it?"

"Open it and find out," Julia whispered, leaning against the counter. "It's a token of my appreciation for you staying awake all night and keeping watch over us."

Jessie forced out a yawn as she ripped back the packaging. Her eyes widened when she saw the shiny, white mobile phone box.

"The man said it was the latest model," Julia said, unsure of what Jessie's reaction was. "He said all the kids have this one."

Jessie looked up at Julia, and then down to the box, and then to Tommy. Julia wasn't sure if the stunned silence was a good one, or a bad one.

"I've never had my own phone before," Jessie mumbled as she opened the box.

On top of the phone was the metal key Julia had had cut from the spare she kept under the plant pot next to the front door.

"I thought it was about time you had your own key," Julia said, her voice shaking with nerves. "Since this is your home now too."

Jessie picked up the key and clenched it in her fist. She looked up at Julia, and it become obvious she was holding back tears. They smiled at each other, and Julia let her know it was okay not to thank her verbally with a little wink.

"You'll be able to call me on that gadget," Tommy said, pointing to the phone in the box. "I'm moving up to Manchester to stay with my brother for a little while."

"Your brother?" Jessie dropped the key onto the counter and turned to Tommy. "Manchester? You can't!"

"I can, and I am," Tommy said, resting his hand on Jessie's shoulder. "You've coped without me all of these months, and rightly so. Julia is your family now, and you couldn't ask for a better mother."

Julia rested her hand on her chest, determined not to let another tear leave her eyes today. She had cried enough over the past twelve hours to last her a lifetime.

"I'll miss you," Jessie whispered, dropping her hair over her face.

"I'm only a train ride away," Tommy replied, tucking her hair behind her ear. "When I've got my own little place and I'm all settled, you can come and visit me. Promise?"

Jessie nodded, but she didn't look up. Julia could tell she was silently crying under her hair. As tough as Jessie wanted to act in front of other people, when it came to her family, she was still a vulnerable girl, and they were both the only family she had. Julia made a mental note to hold Tommy to that promise. She didn't doubt for a second that he wouldn't try his best to keep it.

After they finished their coffees, there was a knock at the door. Julia left Jessie and Tommy chatting in the kitchen and she hopped over Mowgli and into the hallway. Through the frosted glass panel, she made out the outline of Barker. Smiling like an excited schoolgirl, she pulled open the door.

"Afternoon, madam," Barker said, both of his hands behind his back. "I have a special delivery for a Julia South."

Barker pulled a bunch of two-dozen white roses from behind his back, and peered over the top, his eyes glittering at Julia.

"Who are they from?" she asked playfully, a grin spreading from ear to ear as she accepted the bouquet.

"A very charming and handsome man," Barker said as he stepped into the cottage. "But he wasn't available to deliver them, so you're stuck with me instead. I have something else for you too."

Barker pulled a plastic bag from behind his back and Julia let out a huge sigh of relief when she saw her clothes, her purse, her phone, and her keys. She had been embarrassed asking Sue to drive her to the shops, and to pay for everything, but she was relieved to know she could pay her straight back.

Julia took the flowers through to the kitchen and put them in a vase of water. Jessie and Tommy both smirked, glancing knowingly at each other. Barker hung back and tossed the bag onto the couch as Mowgli circled his feet.

"Can we go somewhere and talk?" Barker asked.

"*'Talk',*" Jessie mocked under her breath.

Julia pursed her lips at her, before turning to Barker and noticing the sudden seriousness of his expression. She put the flowers on the counter, blocking Jessie's face, and walked through to her bedroom, motioning for Barker to follow.

"Is this about Max and Stella?" Julia asked quietly as she closed her bedroom door. "Sit down."

Barker perched on the edge of her bed, exhaled heavily and looked up at the low-hanging beams in the ceiling, the seriousness of the bruises on his throat all the more obvious.

"Sort of," he said as she sat next to him, glad she had made her bed that morning. "Max is singing like a canary, telling them everything. He's still going with the God line, but they know it's a load of codswallop. Stella only really knows Max's version of things, so I think they're leaning towards her being more of an accessory, or at least attempted murder, but that depends on the judge she gets. We all heard and saw her, and the main thing is, she stopped, so I think a jury will look favourably on her. Max, on the other hand, he'll never breathe the air as a free man again. I'll make sure of that."

"I hope somebody takes over the soup kitchen," Julia whispered, staring at the rug against her dark floorboards. "It would be a shame if the good they did do stopped now."

"I love that your mind goes straight there," Barker said softly, nudging her gently with his shoulder. "I'm sure somebody will."

"At least it's all over."

"Yeah," Barker mumbled uncertainly.

"You don't sound so sure?"

"There was something else."

"What?" Julia edged forward and turned to him, her

brows pinching together as she attempted to read the dark expression taking over his face. "What's happened?"

"This isn't your fault," Barker said, grabbing both of her hands tightly in his. "I want you to know that."

"What's not my fault?" Julia said, trying to sound firm, but her voice shaking.

Barker inhaled deeply, glanced up to the ceiling, and then down to her, a forced smile pushing the corners of his lips up.

"I'm under investigation at work," Barker said, dropping his head to the floor. "For operating outside of the official borders and for putting civilians in danger. I couldn't deny any of it after my statement and my involvement."

"Investigation?" Julia replied, shaking her head. "What does that mean?"

"It means they're going to look into my conduct," Barker said, his voice darkening. "They're going to try and see how well I do my job, and if I deserve to keep it. I've been suspended without pay until they make a decision."

Julia pulled her hands away from Barker's and jumped up. She immediately started to pace her bedroom, her hands disappearing up through her hair. How could she have been so blinded by her own need to discover the truth? Had it been worth destroying Barker's career?

"Are they going to fire you?"

"Not necessarily." Barker jumped up and grabbed Julia's shoulders, forcing her still. "You did the right thing. *We* did the right thing. You were right about them never believing you. After Jerry, they had been questioning Carl Black and they were close to charging him because he didn't have an alibi. He might not be a very nice man, but he's not being charged for a murder he didn't commit because of you."

"But this has ruined your life." Julia sighed heavily, leaning into Barker's hand as he rested his palm on her cheek.

"Far from it," Barker whispered, pulling her in closer. "Even the darkest clouds have silver linings. You said a lot of things when you were trying to get Stella not to kill me. I wouldn't blame you if you stretched the truth to get through to her."

"I meant every word," Julia said automatically without taking a second to think about it; she didn't need to.

Barker pulled her in and he softly brushed his lips up against hers. All of the stress, and the trouble her meddling had caused melted away. She was old enough to know happy endings didn't exist, but she felt as close to happy as a person could be in that moment, and that was enough for her. They pulled away, their eyes slowly opening and their smiles spreading.

"I love you too," Barker said, cupping both of her cheeks in his hands. "And since you asked, my favourite colour is green, like your eyes, and my middle name is Fergus. Don't ask. My mother was Irish."

"But you love your job too," Julia mumbled, her stomach knotting out of control as her heart thumped wildly in her chest.

"It's just a job," Barker said, shrugging and letting go of Julia's face. "Some things are more important."

Hand in hand, they walked through to the kitchen. Julia didn't care about Jessie's sideways glances, or even what the village would say. They could talk all they wanted because she had realised what, and who was most important to her. Tommy had been right about family being important, but she knew he hadn't just been talking about the family people are born with, but the family people choose. The people at Fenton Industrial Park had been a family, Jessie and Tommy were family, and Julia felt like she had just added three new people to hers.

Inhaling the floral scent of the white roses, she squeezed Barker's hand and smiled at Jessie through the petals as she hugged Mowgli, knowing she was more than ready for whatever life threw at them next.

If you enjoyed *this box set*, why not sign up to Agatha Frost's **free** newsletter at **AgathaFrost.com** to hear about brand new releases!

OUT NOW! Julia and friends are back for another Peridale Café Mystery case in *Chocolate Cake and Chaos*! Order on **AMAZON**.

92784086R00285

Made in the USA
Lexington, KY
08 July 2018